bring you BACK

AVA HUNTER

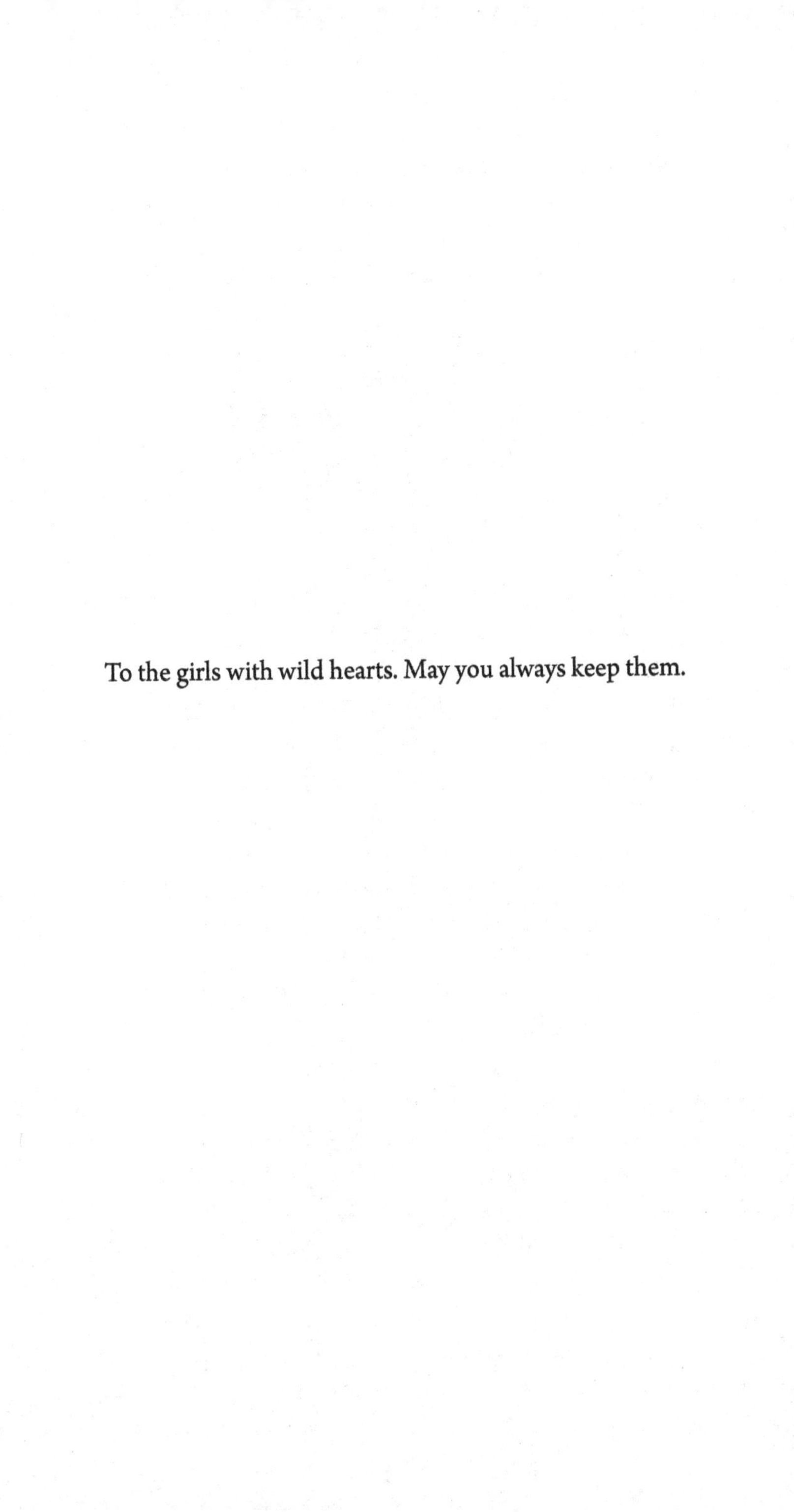

To the girls with wild hearts. May you always keep them.

chapter ONE

THIS ISN'T JACE TAYLOR'S GODDAMN DAY. OR NIGHT. In fact, the last eight months haven't been his goddamn life.

He's tried to hide the mess he's in. Tried to fix it. Now there isn't anything to do but own it and try to make sense of the last twenty-four hours. Because he's got to figure out what in the hell to do next.

His mantra.

Figure it out. Fix it. Always fix it. Get it the fuck together.

Sweat beading his brow, Jace groans, dragging his sorry ass up the staircase of the rustic apartment overlooking the river. It's late, nearing midnight, the humid July night reminding him of all the better things he could be doing right now if he were a better man. Like relaxing in his own bed, a stiff drink in his hand, his wife curled tight in his arms. Instead, all he's got is a black eye, a headache, and the coldest shoulder Emmy Lou's ever given him.

He pauses on the dark stairwell, clenching his teeth at the radiating pain pulsing through every inch of his body. Hissing a breath, he tucks his right hand against his ribs. Then, stomach knotting, he raises a fist—his good fist—and knocks.

He fucked up royally. He can't go home. He's got nowhere to go. Nowhere except—

The door swings open.

Seth Kincaid, fiddle player of the Brothers Kincaid, stands blinking in the doorway of his apartment, his sandy-blond hair standing on end.

"Damn, man," Seth says, his voice rumbling out in his signature baritone drawl. "We waited for you after practice. Luke damn near drank up all of Tootsie's. Think he's still on a high from signin' that contract."

Luke should be on a high. Earlier today, the Brothers Kincaid closed a deal that landed them a residency in Vegas next January. Big-deal star status. Two months. Quarter million dollars a show. And Jace should have been right there beside his best friend celebrating, only he wasn't because he was too busy getting his ass beat in the parking garage at Six String.

Seth cocks his head, squinting in the dim light. "Where you been?"

"I've been screwin' up." Without waiting for an invitation, Jace pushes his way past Seth and steps inside the apartment. "Can I get some water?" he rasps, licking dry lips.

"Sure, you can get some water, but what—"

The sunny grin drops off Seth's face.

In the light of the apartment, Seth's blue eyes widen as his gaze takes full stock of Jace. "Holy fuck." He draws back, horrified. "You got a damn hole in your mouth, man."

Wincing, Jace sits on a leather stool. He swears at the blood dripping onto the white countertop and sticks a tongue through his busted lip. Then he unveils his hand. Bloodied, knuckles busted, crumpled like a piece of paper.

Seth swears and rips a hand through his hair, standing it on end. "Shit. It's broken."

Jace waves him off, flexing each swollen finger one by one. They all work. "It ain't broken. It's busted as shit, but it ain't broken." He tries to grin, but the motion feels numb, feels exactly the way Jace does right now.

There's a flurry of commotion as Seth, bypassing a vase of tulips and a thick stack of wedding magazines, grabs a rag from the sink, wets it, and tosses it to Jace. Jace catches it without looking up, in sync now as much as they are when they're onstage.

As Seth steps around the counter to hand Jace an ice pack,

there's a harsh suck of air. They both turn to see Lacey coming around the corner.

Seth swears.

Lacey freezes in her tracks, drawing her short black robe tight around her. Her big green eyes are as wide as saucers as she stares at Jace.

Jace stiffens. *Shit.*

Lacey tilts her head, her long blond hair falling over one slender shoulder. She takes a step toward him, her pretty brow a frown. "Jace, what happened?"

"I'm fine, honey," he says good-naturedly, not wanting to scare her. That's when he glances around the apartment, feeling his asshole status skyrocketing. Music blasts from the back bedroom. Two glasses of wine sit forgotten on the counter. Lacey's high heels strewn across the living room.

Jace internally groans. He's a shithead, coming here unannounced, interrupting their night.

Curious, confused, Lacey drifts toward Jace, but Seth's quick. He intercepts, scooping her up protectively in his arms, like he doesn't want whatever is touching Jace around his girl.

"Emmy Lou's got a mean right hook," Seth jokes, but Jace can see Lacey doesn't buy it.

"He's bleeding all over the counter, Seth." She peers at Jace. "Should I call Sal?"

"Nah." Jace lifts a hand. "It's just a bar fight."

She arches a brow. *Bullshit,* her stubborn gaze says.

Seth leans in close, touching Lacey's cheek. "I got this, princess."

Lacey gives Seth a doubtful look but kisses him, then disappears into the back bedroom.

When he's sure Lacey's out of earshot, Seth turns to Jace. "What the hell happened?" The kid's voice, more serious than Jace has ever heard it, has him grimacing. "I've seen a bar fight. This ain't a bar fight."

Jace buries his face in his battered hand, wondering where to fucking start.

Maybe he starts at the beginning.

Maybe he goes back three years ago, when he made the worst mistake he could fucking make.

He started gambling. At first, it was a release. A therapy of sorts. Luke was off his rocker with the loss of Sal, who was presumed dead in a plane crash. That left Jace and Seth to try and pick up the pieces of their best friend and brother. They were both exhausted, mentally frayed, but still, they swapped shifts taking care of Luke.

Needing some way to cope, an outlet to burn off stress, instead of going home to his wife, Jace went down to Broadway. He met some guys in a bar, and soon drinks and pool turned into rolling dice in some shady honky-tonk backroom. He welcomed the distraction, the mindless entertainment, knowing the next day he'd be back at Luke's, trying to get the guy to eat something or to stop him from chain-smoking himself to death. It was supposed to be a short-lived thing.

But it wasn't. Because five months after Sal was gone, Luke picked up a gun and tried to end things. It took Jace down. He couldn't handle the gun, always a gun ingrained in his memory. Couldn't handle losing his best friend, his only family like that.

Not after his mother had done the same damn thing.

After that, gambling wasn't just an escape, it was a refuge. The thought of winning money, of placing bets was all he needed to feel better, to take his mind off Luke, off his own exhaustion and stress, and his worried wife at home. He kept going back. Playing cards. Poker. Blackjack. Betting on horse racing. He borrowed money, too much money from the wrong kind of people. He got in too deep and then he sank.

He gambled away his and Emmy Lou's savings. Put their farm in jeopardy. The truth came out when Luke returned to the

Brothers Kincaid and Jace was forced to admit he was broke. The gigs they took allowed Jace to get the money to pay off his loan.

Thank God for his best friend. Thank God for his brother.

But the beginning doesn't matter. Because Seth knows all that. He and Luke both do. It took a drunken night last summer, but Jace spilled it all. It felt goddamn great to confess. To finally unbury that dark part of his life.

What they don't know about is the last seven months. The cherry on the sundae of the shitshow that is Jace's life.

He thought he had put it behind him, thought the past was over, that he and Emmy Lou could finally fix their broken marriage, but last Christmas his rambling and gambling came back to bite him in the ass.

He started getting calls from an unknown number. Threats. Warnings that he owed money. At first, Jace thought it was the *Nashville Star* fucking with him. That they had discovered what he had done and were trying to get him to admit to something. It would be just like them to play dirty. They had been crucifying the Brothers Kincaid after Luke wouldn't play by their rules, wouldn't give them the juicy scoop on Sal coming back, the first look at his son.

But the phone calls hounded him for months, had Jace slipping out of events, of dinners, of bed late at night to handle it. Trying to dig himself out, trying to keep it from Luke and Emmy Lou. The *Nashville Star*, snapping their photos, spun it as an affair, when really, Jace was telling the guy on the other end of the line to fuck off because he had paid his debt. He was done. He was out.

But he wasn't.

Tonight, he learned just how in he still is.

"You been gamblin' again?"

Seth's deep rumble of a voice has Jace blinking himself back to the present.

Lifting his head, Jace forces himself to take the brunt of Seth's steely gaze. Hell, he deserves it. How did it fucking get to this point? Him and Seth Kincaid in opposite roles for once.

In that second, Jace feels like a damn hypocrite. He always gave Seth shit for the way he acted and now look at the guy. The kid's engaged, happier, more damn in love than Jace's ever seen him. Seth's grown up a lot from that wild and reckless kid who made bad decisions in the past. Hell, when they both started out in the band, they hated each other's guts. They only stopped their bickering long enough to play a set. Both of them vying for Luke's friendship. What Jace never told Seth was that Seth didn't have to work for it. He and Luke were blood. Jace was just the neighbor. Some scrawny kid who couldn't wait to get the hell out of the life he was living.

"No." Defensiveness raises his hackles, but as much as it irritates him, Seth has a right to be worried. He fucked up once. Jace sighs and scrubs a hand down his face. "I paid off that loan. All of it. I haven't gambled since I fucked up in the first place."

"Then what happened?"

"There was someone else."

"What kind of someone else?"

"A loan shark." Seth hitches a breath. Jace goes on. "The bookie, the guy I placed the bets with—Snake—"

"His name was Snake?" Seth's grinning.

Jace needles his brow. "Don't fuckin' start, man." An inhale, then he restarts. "The guy I paid off three years ago left town with the money I paid him. Money that wasn't his. He owed a cut to his partner, McCade. McCade was in the goddamn slammer—he's out now."

Seth lifts a brow, his gaze on Jace's black eye. "And he did that."

"In the parking garage after practice."

Seth swears.

"I told him to fuck off. I paid the loan. But apparently"—Jace gestures at his lip and Seth winces in sympathy—"that was a bad idea. And now I'm fucked because he got fucked." Jace shakes his head, helpless fury storming over him. "I didn't know this was comin', Seth. I thought I was paid up and done."

Even now, even to Jace, the excuses seem lame. He always

prided himself on responsibility. He kept Seth and Luke in line. Paid every bill on time. Wore his seat belt so he didn't die like his father. You couldn't find a speck of dirt on him. Until now.

Christ, how is this his life? He's a country singer. A bassist with a low-key life. He's steady. Responsible. He lives reckless one time and look where it gets him.

Fucked.

Jace slowly shakes his head. "I got twenty-four hours to get him his money."

"Lord. Luke's gonna take you to school," Seth breathes.

Jace winces. Understatement of the century. His best friend is absolutely gonna lose his shit.

"You know who this McCade is?" Seth asks, running a hand through his hair.

"I ain't sure." Jace touches his cut lip, feeling the lacerated skin courtesy of McCade. "Some mean son of a bitch."

"You think we should get the cops involved?"

Jace stiffens. "No goddamn way." He'll take a fist to the face a thousand times over before he lets his fuckup overshadow what the Brothers Kincaid have worked so hard for. "No one can know," he tells Seth, pinning him with a look that means business. "Especially the *Star*."

Seth looks worried. "So, you got the money?"

Jace nods slow. "I got it."

"Okay. Good." Seth looks doubtful but relieved. "And then what?"

"He'll find me tomorrow."

"Where?"

"I don't know." Jace presses the heels of his palms in his eyes. "I don't fuckin' know."

What he does know is he's lucky. Lucky that last year he made fifteen million. Lucky that the Brothers Kincaid hit the top of the charts year after year. Lucky that he learned his lesson and saved up every last cent he could over the last three years. Thanks to his gigs, to the success of the Brothers Kincaid, Jace managed to replenish their drained account.

Even paying off McCade won't be enough to drain his and Emmy Lou's nest egg.

Nausea churns within him.

Emmy Lou.

He can't tell her he fucked up again.

He'll handle it. He'll fix it.

Like he did the first time?

Shaking off the nagging doubt, Jace looks at Seth. "Can I stay here tonight?"

Seth exhales. "Yeah. Sure. Couch is all yours."

Jace pushes off the counter. Seth follows at a slow lope. "What about Em?"

Jace sinks onto the couch, ready to forget, ready to sleep off the shitshow of the day. "I'll text her," he says and pulls out his phone like the sight of it will convince Seth everything's okay between him and a wife whose heart he hasn't been able to reach for years.

Seth lifts a brow but says nothing. But Jace knows what he's thinking.

Emmy Lou is already convinced he's stepping out on her thanks to those *Nashville Star* articles. Staying out all night ain't gonna do him any favors.

Jace cups the back of his neck and squeezes. "I'm sorry, comin' here when you got Lacey. I just . . ." He sighs. "Couldn't go to Luke."

Seth snorts. "What, you think I got lower standards than my brother?"

He winces, the truth to Seth's words stinging. "Sorry, man, I—"

"Nah, it's okay." Seth flashes him a crooked grin and tosses him a pillow from the corner chair. "I get it." His face turns thoughtful. "We've all been there, Jace. Just get out from under it."

With that, Seth heads out, flipping off the lights and disappearing down the hall.

Jace wipes a tired hand over his face, tilts his head back against the couch cushions and closes his eyes. Fatigue weighs him down. His jaw aches. The phone feels like a ticking time bomb in his hand. He has to text Emmy Lou. But text her what? The hell if he knows. He promised to always be honest with Emmy Lou. And here he is breaking that promise.

Again. He's a damn liar.

And lying ain't in Jace's blood.

Especially not when, after months of dating, of soft kisses and long talks into the night, Emmy Lou explained that trust was it for her. Her dealbreaker. *I need to trust you, Jace. My heart can't handle lies.*

She never explained why it was important to her, even after ten years of marriage, even after Jace had tried to dig around and find out why her pretty eyes would dim when she talked about her past, but Jace fulfilled that promise. He knew he could give it to her. He was the type of man his father never was. Honest, dependable, steadfast. He vowed to always do right by Emmy Lou, to never hurt his wife.

But he did.

He broke her trust.

He fucked up. He failed her.

Jace squeezes his eyes shut and tries to picture Emmy Lou's sweet smile. Emmy Lou's lips on his after he asked her to be his wife. Her whispered yes in his ear. The way she chewed on his bottom lip and then swallowed his heart like the best kind of hunger.

But who is he kidding? She hasn't smiled at him like that in months.

The tiny bit of tentative trust he's managed to build back up with Emmy Lou—it'll all be down the drain if she finds out about this. That is, if he doesn't fix this. Which he will.

Tomorrow.

He'll fix everything tomorrow.

chapter TWO

ALL EMMY LOU NEEDS ARE WIDE-OPEN SPACES.
Not secrets.
Not lies.

And most certainly not a trifling man who didn't come home last night.

Thankfully, she's out here in the crisp air, on her favorite horse, absorbing every single moment of the glittering morning. It's enough to make her forget Jace.

Almost.

Emmy Lou clicks her tongue and kicks her heels. Beneath her, Lolli, a dappled mare, gives a snort. Reins held loosely in her left hand, Emmy Lou steers Lolli down the snaky dirt road back to the pasture. They pass the meadow of tall grass and turn onto a steep path lined with tall evergreens. As Emmy Lou rounds the bend, her heart launches itself high, the way it always does when she sees what's down in the valley. Her farm. The wrought-iron sign that reads Montgomery Stables and Rehab Center.

As if picking up on Emmy Lou's mood, Lolli nickers impatiently but continues her steady trot. Emmy Lou laughs.

"Oh, Lord," she drawls, her Georgia accent coming out full throttle, the way it always does on one of her country rides. "You can go faster than that. If you got it, you gotta flaunt it, sugar."

Lolli's nostrils flare.

Emmy Lou lets out a whoop. The noise spurs the pony. The earth thunders beneath her as Lolli takes off in a gallop for the pasture.

The ground tilts as they rush across green grass, Lolli moving faster and faster in a race against the wind. Emmy Lou laughs in delight at Lolli's excitement to get back to the farm. She remembers how skittish Lolli used to be when she and Jace picked her up five years ago. The poor thing had been through the wringer. Chained to a tree next to a dilapidated trailer out in the boonies, one ankle broken, surrounded by junkyard dogs and not a lick of love.

Lolli's come so far. She's a different horse.

All thanks to the farm.

Located on an adjacent piece of property a mile from the main house, Montgomery Stables and Rehab Center is Emmy Lou's pride and joy. A fifty-acre sanctuary that holds ten horses at a time and is fully staffed. She and Jace started this center a year after they were married. At first, it wasn't much, just a place to take in abused or unwanted horses, but as Jace and the Brothers Kincaid got bigger and bigger, so did the center. Emmy Lou put whatever money she could into the place, used all of her knowledge, her connections from her family's lucrative horse breeding business down in Georgia, to make it a success.

For Emmy Lou, riding, her farm, these horses are her sanctuary. Her sanity. Her salvation. Because in another life they were broken, but they survived.

Just like her.

Seeing the pasture, Lolli slows to a walk. Emmy Lou dismounts next to the gate and scours the empty driveway in front of the pillared Greek Revival–style mansion. As her eyes rove, she scowls at the debris piled up alongside the barn. She's been after Jace for months to clear it. But he hasn't because she's not a priority. The band is. Himself.

At the thought of her husband, she pulls her cell phone from her back pocket and rereads the two a.m. text he sent last night.

Late night at Tootsie's with the guys. Gonna crash at Seth's. See you tomorrow.

Love you.

To Emmy Lou, the *love you*'s an afterthought.

Everything about their marriage the last three years has been an afterthought.

She bites her lip.

Maybe all those *Nashville Star* articles have merit. He's stepping out on her. Jace swore up and down they had no truth, but there's no reason for the distance. For staying out all night.

He's hiding something again. She knows it.

Heart pounding, she closes her eyes and wishes herself back. Back to when they were newly married. Hell, back to a few years ago. Once upon a time, wherever she was, was where Jace wanted to be. He'd come home after a show, but the night wouldn't stop. Instead, they'd start. In every room in the house, Jace's big, broad hands slipping up her dress, tracing the hem of her silk panties and whispering that she was his favorite flavor.

And now, now, there's an ocean between them a mile wide. One she wouldn't even know how to swim if she tried.

A gentle nudge on her shoulder gets her attention. "Okay, okay," she says, rubbing Lolli's nose. She keeps her voice light, not wanting the horse to pick up on her sour mood. "Carrots, soon. I promise."

The crunch of gravel has her turning. A black Land Rover pulls into the circular driveway. Emmy Lou frees Lolli from her saddle and bridle, then turns her out into the pasture to graze, before rushing across the yard to the dark-haired woman hopping out of the vehicle.

"Oh, Sal, sugar," Emmy Lou trills. "Let me help you."

Sal, a diaper bag hanging off one shoulder, leans out of the back seat, her seven-month-old son, Cash, cradled in her arms. Sal smiles, the sunlight catching the emerald green of her eyes. "You want to carry a butterball of a baby?"

"I would love to." Emmy Lou reaches for Cash, nestling the baby in the crook of her arm. Cash is itty-bitty just like Sal with pink cherub cheeks and dark wispy hair. Just as precious to her and Jace as one of their own.

Emmy Lou dips her head, inhaling his sweet scent. "Oh my, seein' this darlin' angel again lifts my spirits." Cash screams with delight, his chubby little fists gripping the ends of her icy blond waves.

Sal laughs. "I'd say he's definitely happy to see you too."

Emmy Lou adjusts the baby, giving a start as proper southern manners kick in. "Oh Lord, I must look a mess. Dressed in ridin' clothes, plum covered in dust."

"And I'm covered in baby spit." Sal bumps shoulders with Emmy Lou. "We're a perfect pair."

Inside the house, Emmy Lou fusses, settling Sal and Cash in the parlor. She cracks the screen door to let in a gentle breeze. Bustling around the kitchen, she's hit with a feeling of contentment as she takes in her warm home. Her light lavender world. Spacious rooms filled with natural light. Lilacs in mason jars. A vintage quilt from her mother's collection hangs on the wall behind the couch. Her rodeo crowns and trophies shine bright in an ivory china cabinet.

Soon, out come sweet tea, champagne and orange juice. Emmy Lou sits beside Sal on the couch. "I'm thinkin' we could use a mimosa."

Sal's green eyes glow. "I think I could use two."

Emmy Lou smiles warmly, grateful to catch up with her friend. Grateful their friendship is back to where it started when they first met, over twelve years ago on a disastrous double date where all four of them ended up pushing Luke's busted truck out of the mud when it got stuck after a long day of fishing.

But just like the truck, their friendship stuck. Now, even with Sal's memory loss, it's still as strong as ever.

If only she could say the same about her marriage.

Emmy Lou taps a light pink nail against the side of her champagne glass and smiles down at Cash, the newest and cutest addition to their country music family. The baby's rolling around on a fuzzy blanket, his happy coos filling the air.

Lifting her eyes to Sal, she says, "Where do we start? I feel like we're long-lost friends these days."

Sal sends her a smile. "I know. With Cash and the tour, it's—well, it's a lot."

A small pang of wistfulness spears her at the mention of the tour.

As always, she sat it out. The lone straggler. Even Lacey had gone with Seth for the monthlong tour. It wasn't for everybody. Living cramped on a bus. Jace understood her real reasons for always skipping out on tour. He never pressed her to come.

It's not that she doesn't want to go. She loves the shows and the awards, being with her family and friends. It's just that she can't.

She can't do small spaces.

The first time she set foot on the tour bus, a narrow tomb of metal enclosed on all sides, her entire body cringed. It was too close to that night.

Too trapped.

"You didn't miss much," Sal adds kindly, seeing Emmy Lou's silence. "The bulk of my days was spent trying to keep Cash from killing himself."

When Sal dips down to tickle the babbling baby, Emmy Lou thinks of her and Jace. Of trying to get pregnant before he came clean about his gambling. About how she called off their plans to expand their family. About how she still hasn't forgiven him.

Emmy Lou shakes herself out of the suffocating memories as Sal continues. "Cash is trying to crawl, so naturally, Luke's already barricading the house. Which, I have to say, a baby gate would have come in handy last night."

"For Cash?"

"No, for Luke." Sal laughs, sweeping a lock of dark hair away from her face. "I swear, he came home so drunk last night he still had a buzz this morning."

"Oh, I know," Emmy Lou says, mustering up some good humor. She may be irked at Jace, but she's still so damn happy for their boys and their big news. "They must've had a grand ol' time celebratin' that big contract business, especially since Jace was sleepin' it off at Seth's."

Sal, reaching for a flute of champagne, freezes.

Emmy Lou frowns, caught off guard by her friend's strange reaction. "Sugar, what is it?"

Sal shifts in her seat, hesitates. "Oh, it's, it's nothing."

"Sal, you look like you ate a lemon. That ain't nothin'."

Sal's mouth opens. Closes. When Emmy Lou narrows her eyes and fixes her with a look, Sal sighs. "Jace wasn't there last night, Em." This time it's Emmy's turn to freeze. Sal's eyes are all apologies. "Jace didn't show. Griff was there, and Seth, but Luke was wondering all night where he got to."

For once, Emmy Lou's tongue lies speechless.

Then, down goes a flute of champagne in one fell swoop. Trying to numb the pain. Trying to keep it together. It's what her mama always said. She's a Montgomery and Montgomerys don't cry. They storm around the house fixing things. And yelling. A lot of yelling.

Sal's biting her lip. "Em?"

She feels her bubbly facade slipping. She can't hang on much longer. Then—

A jumpstart, a flare of anger.

She hisses, driving a small fist into her palm. "I am gonna kill that damn man. He's steppin' out on me. I know it." She shakes her head, her icy blond bob swaying in her periphery. "All those articles in the *Star*, they're true. They're gospel."

"No, Em." Sal scoots close, wrapping her hand around Emmy Lou's. "Jace wouldn't do that. He loves you." Sal's tone is genuine. Strong.

Emmy Lou leans in like she can absorb some of Sal's good faith. Her trust in their relationship.

But she can't. Ever since Jace broke hers.

Broke *them.*

Emmy Lou looks down at her hands, too ashamed to meet

her friend's eyes, but needing to confess. Needing a lifeline. "He didn't come home last night, Sal." She forces back tears. "For the last three years, we ain't been the same."

"Because of the gambling?" Sal asks, her face sympathetic.

Emmy nods and lifts her head. "I thought we were doin' okay. We worked so dang hard these last few years. And then Christmas last year, it was good. Real good between us. I thought we were gonna make it. But now . . . he's distant again, and . . . and we ain't been happy for the last six months," Emmy Lou chokes out in one long blurt of a ramble. Though she knows she's letting down her prim and proper guard, confiding to Sal is a relief. She hasn't had this in a long time. Someone there. Someone listening.

"Oh, Em," Sal says softly, her own eyes wet. No doubt remembering what it was like to be on the opposite end of awful rumors, especially those involving cheating. "This is the *Star*. It's what they do. Cause trouble."

Pain splinters through Emmy Lou's heart. "But what if the trouble's true?"

Silence falls, the only sound Cash's light cooing. Emmy Lou squeezes her teary eyes together. Resentment, devastation burning a hole through her heart.

Sometimes she can't believe it's gotten this bad. Sometimes it still seems like a dream, that day three years ago when Jace came to her and confessed that he had gambled away their savings. That they could lose their farm, their sanctuary for hurt horses. It hit Emmy Lou hard. Those horses had nowhere to go and Jace putting everything she loved in jeopardy, including their marriage, her trust—she never forgave him.

She was so angry, she put the kibosh on everything. Jace kissing her. Touching her. Starting a family. Eventually all the anger, the jabs, the resentment, the minutes of separate lives, they all stacked on top of each other like river pebbles until they toppled.

She could have dealt with Jace's betrayal if he had just talked to her in the first place. If he had opened up and explained why he'd lied, why he'd hidden it from her. But he didn't. Because of that, their marriage never fully recovered. For the past three years, all it's been doing is hanging on by one guitar string, ready to fall apart with the strum of an off-key song.

Envy, petty envy hits Emmy Lou as she stares back at Sal, at a woman who has a fairy-tale marriage, a man who's so in love with her, every song he sings screams her name. She doesn't have that with Jace. Not anymore. And especially not now, not when he's been lying to her about Lord knows what.

She and Jace—they used to be so good together. Living, loving their lives. Emmy Lou working at the horse sanctuary, Jace killing it as bassist for the Brothers Kincaid. Always walking the red carpet together.

Nothing could stop them.

Maybe that's why it hurts so damn bad. Maybe that's why she feels like such a fool for believing they could work it out.

She thought that after last Christmas, they'd be okay. That blissful time they spent in the Smoky Mountains, the way she and Jace finally made love—tentative and fumbling, but hopeful and with enough promise that their marriage could survive. Only it all fell apart when they returned to Nashville. The *Star* started publishing those awful cheating articles and Jace was buried in the band, or his phone. Always turning away from her when she came down the hall. Coming to bed late at night. Leaving early in the morning.

Jace promised over and over he wouldn't let her down. He wouldn't lie again.

But where was he last night?

Sal squeezes her hand.

"I'm sorry," Emmy Lou whispers, feeling her skin come apart at the seams.

"Don't apologize," Sal says. "We'll figure this out, okay?"

Not wanting Sal to witness her tearful meltdown, Emmy Lou ducks her head. Her friend's sad eyes are too much to bear.

Emmy Lou twists the large diamond on her finger. "I love Jace, I do. I just don't know if it's—"

Sal's sharp gasp of air cuts off Emmy Lou's next words.

Emmy Lou follows her gaze to the front door, blanching at what she sees.

A man stands in the foyer, dressed in a black suit. The imprint of a holstered gun at his hip. A sharp jawline and even sharper eyes. He points a finger at Sal and then swivels it to Emmy Lou.

"Mrs. Taylor, am I right?" The floorboards creak as he steps into the sitting room.

Emmy Lou's hands rise to her heart. "Who are you?" she asks, studying the man. Panic claws its way into her throat. "What are you doin' in my house?"

"Name's McCade. May or may not be a friend of your husband's. You'll have to ask him."

Emmy Lou glances at Sal, a sinking feeling in her stomach. *Lord Jesus, what kind of mess did Jace get himself into now?*

When she turns her attention back to McCade, every part of her body, some deep voice inside of her, the voice she should have listened to long ago, says, despite the smile, the charm, this man is dangerous. Her eyes dart around the room. The path to the front door is blocked, the only thing around the horses, the still silence of the late morning.

McCade approaches and the room gets smaller. Emmy Lou can feel the space around her shrinking, the way it always does when she's cornered or enclosed. It has her nervous. Shaking. Still, Emmy Lou balls her small hands into fists of power.

"My husband ain't here." She forces the words out. Forces bravado. Beside her, Sal is tense, barely breathing. "If you need him, you can wait for him. Outside."

"I don't need him. Not yet." Though McCade keeps a light-hearted demeanor, his words burn with a threat.

Slowly, his eyes rove around the house. Around her and Sal.

The look on his face sends a shiver down Emmy Lou's spine. The champagne sloshes in her stomach, acrid bile rising in her throat.

Cash begins to mewl, as if picking up on his mother's mood.

McCade grins and takes a step onto the rug. He stops in front of Cash, his foot dangerously close to the baby's hand.

Sal rockets to standing. "Don't you touch my son," she hisses, positioning her body between Cash and the man. Sal's shaking, terrified. The woman's been through hell and back, and still, she'll fight.

Emmy Lou follows suit, standing beside Sal. A look passes between the women. An assurance they're in it together. They're family. They protect each other.

In that second, Emmy Lou rallies memories of her brothers. All five of them, how they picked on her, fought with her, taught her to fight, only to cackle in wild glee as she finally got that right hook down and kicked all their asses.

Crossing her arms, Emmy Lou draws herself up to her full height, which isn't very much. Between her and Sal, they barely have four feet on the man. But they've got Cash, and damn if that's not enough to go woman-wild and feral.

"Mister, if you ain't outta my house in two damn minutes," Emmy Lou says, steel in her voice, her heart a coiled rattlesnake ready to strike, "I am callin' the cops."

McCade chuckles and holds up his hands. "No harm, ladies. At least not right now. I'm just here to take inventory." He looks at Sal, sucks his lip. "Now you're Sal Kincaid. And you have a sister, right? A Lacey Sutton? Works in Germantown?"

Sal pales.

"Out," Emmy Lou demands, despite her sinking stomach. She flings an arm toward the door. "I ain't tellin' you again. Right the hell now."

McCade lets out a light laugh, and after evaluating her for one long second, he gives a nod. "I'll be seein' you, ma'am."

As McCade disappears out the front door, Sal lets out a sob and collapses to the ground. Shoulders shaking, she cradles Cash to her chest like she'll never let him loose.

Emmy Lou stares for a long second and then she lets herself explode. A female bomb of fire.

She runs.

She runs after the man as if he has all the answers, as if she could kill him, as if her fear is already buried and forgotten, six feet under just like when she left Wildheart.

Because Emmy Lou isn't done. If Jace won't give her answers, she'll get them herself.

Rage licking through her, she slams out the screen door and onto the porch.

"Wait," Emmy Lou demands, and McCade turns around to face her. "Tell me what you want with my husband."

chapter
THREE

J ACE CRACKS HIS EYES OPEN, GROANING AS A BLAST OF sunlight fries his retinas. He lies there on Seth's leather couch, taking in the quiet stillness of the morning. Shuffled footsteps. Soft whispers. Lacey and Seth doing their damnedest to let him sleep in.

After the night he had, he'd like nothing better. But he can't. He's got shit to do today. Hit up the bank. Pay off McCade. Then go home to Emmy Lou and fess up. Take responsibility for this mess he's made and only hope she forgives him.

They've worked it out before. They can work it out again.

Swinging his legs off the edge of the couch, Jace sits up. Every muscle screams its protest. His body aches like he got run down by a damn freight train. After checking his phone—five missed calls from Emmy Lou—he groans and scrubs his face in his hands.

When he looks back up, he grins. Lacey, dressed for work in an electric-blue pantsuit, is trying to tiptoe quietly through the kitchen.

"It's your house, honey," he says. "You ain't gotta be quiet."

Her pretty face pulls into a wince. "Oh, Jace." She reaches into her purse and digs around, then crosses the room to sit beside him. With a gentle touch, she examines his black eye, then plops a silver tube into his hand.

He looks down, perplexed.

"I think Sandstorm is your color." She tilts her head, her green eyes narrowed. "Fix your face, Jace. Otherwise, Emmy Lou's going to give you matching eyes."

"Yeah." He grunts, feeling undeserving of Lacey's kindness. "I know."

A *tsk* from across the room. Seth swaggers in, coffee cup held in his hand. "One night sleepin' over and she's already got you wearin' makeup."

Lacey scoffs. "Shove it, Seth."

Seth hands Jace the cup of coffee. "Can you believe I've been engaged to this absolute ray of sunshine for only three months?"

Jace chuckles.

A roll of her green eyes. Lacey stands and palms the front of Seth's chest. "You'll pay for that comment at the wedding. A tux, Seth. White. With tails."

Seth's deep laugh rolls out. He sweeps Lacey into his arms. "Princess, you just tell me the date and the time."

An adoring smile graces Lacey's face and she leans into Seth for a kiss.

Jace tries to ignore the pang of envy that hits him square in the gut. Tries not to notice the way they grip each other, pull each other into them like they're each other's last breath.

Christ. When was the last time he touched Emmy Lou like that? When was the last time she let him?

Seth and Lacey—they're just getting started while his own relationship with Emmy Lou is crashing and burning. And Jace wonders when trying to fix it turned into sticking it out, and sticking it out turned into shutting down.

"See you after work," Lacey murmurs against Seth's lips. "I love you."

"Love you," Seth says, his expression hangdog with want as he watches Lacey head out the door.

Once again, Jace can't stop the comparison. These days, Emmy Lou's I-love-yous and soft touches are scarce. Coexisting is the name of the game. Bickering over idiot things like who unloaded the dishwasher last. Snapping at each other in the car, then putting on smiles in front of their friends. Barely talking. Their at-times-separate lives became all-the-time.

He wants nothing more than to rekindle that flame with Emmy Lou. The first, the only woman he's ever loved. But goddamn, he doesn't even know where to start.

The couch jostles, and Jace blinks away his cloudy thoughts to see Seth sitting beside him. "Well?" his friend says, arching a brow.

"I'm gonna get the damn money and pay the guy. I'm puttin' this shit to bed today," Jace says with more determination than he feels.

Seth nods slow. "You need help?"

The offer's a kick to his heart. Seth's sticking by him despite the mess he's in means the world. But getting Seth mixed up in this ain't an option. It's dangerous, and the last thing he wants is this touching anyone he cares about.

Jace blows out a breath. "Nah. You've done enough. This is my dirty work. I'll take care of it."

Seth's blue eyes take him in. "I gotta run and meet Greyson, but go get a shower. You smell like shit."

Jace raises his coffee cup. "Thanks."

Seth smiles. "You got it."

Jace sits there, hearing the front door close, numbness, stillness creeping in. He needs to rally, to move, to clean himself up.

He can't go home to Emmy Lou looking like shit. She'll be pissed enough as it is. Jace staying away all night won't prove the point that he wants to get back to them.

That slice of time they had late last year in the Smokies before he got involved in all this mess was the closest to heaven he's been in a long time. It showed him they could revive their relationship if they wanted to. If he worked hard. Instead, he was so distracted by this whole damn mess with McCade, he let his marriage slip.

He forgot about them.

About Emmy Lou.

Well, no fucking more.

After today, he'll make it up to her.

After today, everything changes.

Jace parks his truck in the circular driveway of his house, then reaches behind him for the cooler in the back seat. Fifty grand stacked inside like bricks. A Yeti's never been so damn expensive.

After he left Seth's, he stopped by the bank and took out the money he needed from his safe deposit box. Then he texted McCade that he was ready to pay him. He doesn't want to wait on this guy. He's dangerous as hell and Jace wants him as far away from his family as he can get.

"Fuck," Jace swears. He sits there in the cab of his truck, sweating in the bright noon sun.

It feels like a bad dream he can't wake up from. But it ain't a dream. It's his life and he's got to face it. Especially Emmy Lou.

He gets out of the truck, climbs the porch stairs and slips into the farmhouse. He sets the cooler in the foyer. "Em?" he calls out, glancing around. The sitting room is a mess, even by Emmy Lou's standards. Champagne flutes, warm orange juice, a left-behind bottle telling him Sal and Cash have been over. "Honey?"

After evaluating the lower level, Jace limps up the stairs. Bypassing the guest room where he's been staying, he heads to the master bedroom suite.

Emmy Lou's head snaps up when he walks in. She's at the dresser, clouds of chiffon hair scarves in her hands. "Well, look who finally decided to come home."

He winces at the fierceness of her Georgia drawl. The magenta flush on her cheeks tells him she's pissed as hell. "Em, it's not what you think."

She fixes him in her burning brown-eyed gaze. "Oh, I know it ain't. It's worse than all those *Nashville Star* articles sayin' you're out tomcattin' around." Her voice drops to a hush. "You owe money, Jace. You owe more money?"

His heart plummets to his boots.

Fuck. How the hell did she find out?

He licks his lips. "I was gonna tell you—"

"No, you weren't." She shakes her head, moving fast around the room, her hands opening drawers at the top of her dresser, taking out lacy underwear, rose-gold jewelry. "You never tell me anything. Always clammin' up, stickin' your head in the damn sand. I had to hear it from that man, that man who—"

"Whoa, what?"

Jace strides forward, all the breath stunned from his body. He grabs her hands, stilling her. This time really seeing her. Her icy blond bob is disheveled, her eyes red-rimmed like she's been crying. "What happened today, Em?"

Christ. If it's what he thinks it is, he'll never forgive himself.

She juts her chin, defiant. "That's why I've been callin' you. That man came by. McCade. He came to our *house*. While Sal and her baby were here."

Jesus. He's going to fucking puke.

McCade promised he'd leave them alone. Promised he wouldn't touch Emmy Lou. *Motherfucker.*

Jace grips his wife tight. Rage pounds inside of him. "Are you okay? Did he hurt you?"

Emmy Lou shakes her head, her eyes sparking with anger. "No, I ain't okay. He cornered me. He threatened Sal. He threatened Lacey. Sal left in tears, Jace."

Jace closes his eyes for a brief moment, trying to keep it together.

He can't imagine what that did to Emmy Lou. Ever since she was locked in a horse trailer after a rodeo show, she's had a fear of tight spaces. A fact he's known since he first met her. It's why she's never on the bus. Why he mucks the stalls dotting the backyard of their farm.

It must have scared her shitless. He knows it did.

A gale force of guilt nearly knocks him over. Demons from his past.

This is all his fault. He should have been here today. He should have protected her.

A sharp gasp from Emmy Lou has him opening his eyes to see her reaching for his face. She palms his scruffy cheek. More contact than he's had in a month. She touches his puffy eye gently, taking in his disheveled hair and busted lip.

"Oh Lord, Jace, did he do that? You look beat halfway to dead." She takes a step back and covers her mouth. "You're gonna end up gettin' buried in the Cumberland."

"Emmy—"

But she doesn't hear him. Biting her lip, Emmy Lou paces around the room, wringing her small hands. Her mind on a tilt-a-whirl to the worst. "He said if you don't pay, he's comin' back." Her eyes flash wide, worried. "He's gonna break our legs, Jace. Hurt our friends."

"No," Jace says quickly. "No one's gettin' hurt." He exhales. "I got the money, Em."

She stops pacing. "You do?"

"I do."

"How? What money?"

This time it's Jace's turn to pace. "I've been savin' for the last three years. There's a stash in the bank no one knows about. We got that big payday comin' from the Vegas deal. We'll be okay, Em. I swear, honey, I got it handled."

A vow he made three years ago after he nearly lost them everything. As a kid, he grew up knowing the importance of a dollar. Any little bit of money he and his mama had, his father squandered it on booze. Letting his wife down again wasn't an option, so he started saving. It was his fault—it was his responsibility to fix it.

Emmy Lou's eyes cloud with relief. Then anger. "A stash, huh?" She stares, defeated. Forlorn. "No one knows, not even me."

His words parroted back at him have his gut twisting.

Fuck.

All this time he thought he was protecting her, but all he did was lie to her.

Again.

Shaking, Emmy Lou crosses her arms against her chest. "Not even your wife, Jace."

He sees the betrayal on her face. The last straw of it all.

Taking a deep breath, Jace steps forward, hands out, aching to take her in his arms. "Em, honey, I'll make this right."

A thrash of her blond head. "You won't have to."

He frowns. "What're you talkin' about?"

That's when he notices the suitcase on the bed. The lavender nightgown in Emmy Lou's hand. Christ. This entire time he's been talking, she's been packing. How long did it take him to realize? He's been blind as a goddamn bat. A fucking metaphor for their entire marriage.

"I'm glad you got the money, Jace," Emmy Lou says tiredly, stepping forward to grab a pile of clothes on the end of the bed. She drops them in the suitcase. "Now I don't have to worry 'bout you no more."

"'No more'?" He feels coldcocked by confusion, panic. He runs a hand through his hair, gripping the back of his neck. "Em, listen—"

"I meant what I said, Jace. No more secrets." Swiftly, she grabs up a seersucker blouse, a pair of black leggings. She crams the clothing into the suitcase, almost violently, and then zips it. "We're just wastin' time stayin' together."

He staggers back, all the blood leaving his face. It feels as if the room's been drained of air. He can't breathe, can't think.

Emmy Lou's leaving him.

He knew their marriage was shaky, but slowly, he thought they were getting there. That he could explain and fix everything, but now . . .

Now he just blew it all up.

Now his wife's saying words he never imagined.

"No, honey," he says, crossing the room. Desperately, he tries to take her in his arms, tries to anchor her to him. "You're my wife. Nothin' will ever come before you."

"It already has." Her voice drops to a whisper. Tears well up in her eyes. "You pick everything before me. The music. The money. The lies."

He can't deny it. Can't even refute it. She's right. So damn right it makes him sick inside.

"Em . . . I'm sorry. I'm so goddamn sorry." His fingers curl around hers, his mouth lowering to her cheek. He inhales her scent, wild, fragrant like honey and clover. Emmy Lou whimpers. She leans into him. Soft, warm, full of curves.

Jace closes his eyes. The feel of her against him is more than he can take.

"I'll make it up to you. I'll make it right."

For a second, he thinks she'll stay. For a second, he thinks she'll be the grace he doesn't deserve.

But then Emmy Lou rips out of his arms, turning his blood to ice.

"No more chances," she hisses. "No more lies." Her eyes flash wild and teary. "I want a divorce."

His world spins. He blinks at her.

"I'm goin' home and I'm stayin.'" She grabs her bag off the bed and wrenches away from him. "It's been a long time comin', Jace Taylor."

The words are a stinging slap. All he can do is stand there and watch her walk away. His balls clench at the hard slam of the front door, and then he sinks to the edge of the bed, numb, frozen. His vision blurs, and he wipes at his eyes as if clearing them will make sense of it all. But it won't.

Because Emmy Lou's gone.

Gone.

He doesn't know how long he sits there. Only that the darkening sky and the sharp ringing sound of a phone cut the silence of Jace's daze.

He answers without glancing at the screen. Maybe it's the firing squad come to put him out of his misery.

Worse. It's Luke.

chapter FOUR

P URE FURY PROPELS EMMY LOU DOWN I-24 TOWARDS HER hometown of Wildheart, Georgia.

Using her knee to steer, she tosses her wedding ring, a big, sparkly knockout diamond, into the glove box.

There. That oughta show Jace, show her heart that she's serious.

Emmy Lou punches the gas, hard, like she can stamp down any flicker of love she's ever held for Jace and drive straight into the sun. The Nashville skyline disappears in her rearview mirror. A brief pang of regret hits her at leaving Lolli.

Twice in her life she's left her horse.

And now a husband.

Well, she ain't stopping. More importantly, she ain't staying stupid any longer.

A smart woman knows when to get out. Knows when she's beat.

Knuckles white, she grips the wheel in a stranglehold as three years of resentment hit her like a Mack truck. Bubbling up, spilling over from the molten core of her heart.

She can't stay with someone who's untrustworthy. Never again. Jace and his lies, his pitiful excuses, can pound sand. She's done watching their marriage crumble. True, she had a hand in the crumbling of their marriage. It was their never-ending cycle. She pushed for an explanation, Jace shut down. He reached for her hand, she iced him out. Put the kibosh on starting a family. Punished him because he hadn't been honest with her. She knows it ain't the right way to be, but it's the only thing she could do for her own self-preservation. She held a grudge to protect her heart.

A growl of frustration tears from her lips.

If he had just talked to her in the first place. If he had opened up and told her the truth, the *why* of what he did. All she wants to know is: what made him cross that line?

Well, it's too late now. She's done pushing. Done caring.

Today, Emmy Lou reached her last give-a-damn.

Being trapped by that man McCade, all it did was explode her back to the past. To her deal breaker. To Slayton.

She gave him her heart, her trust, and he . . . he—

She shakes off the thought and instead concentrates on Wildheart. Her hometown.

Emmy Lou whispers a quick thank-you to the good Lord above that she's able to go home to her family's horse farm in Georgia. That Slayton finally left her alone and went off to college. It's the only way she could come back to Wildheart without breaking into a million pieces.

Her gut twists at the thought of facing her family, especially Mama Belle. The majority of the Montgomery clan will be home for the summer season. And even though coming clean about her troubles with Jace doesn't align with her closely guarded gates, she needs this. A return to her wild roots. The rodeo. Her brothers. She misses them. Grady especially.

Still, there's a melancholy sadness to coming home.

She's admitting defeat. She's running. Back to the one place she ran from so many years before.

And Jace will let her run. She saw the light die in his eyes when she told him she wanted a divorce. They were harsh words, but she thought, foolishly, maybe, they could get him to talk.

Instead, he let her go.

Because that was Jace. Calm, cool, collected. All the damn time. It's what she loved about him way back when. Never impatient or annoyed. The brooding to her bubbly. The harnessing calm to her huffy diva. The patience to her short fuse. Always kind, maybe too kind, but she knew a kind man in this world was something to hold on to. But today . . .

Tears fill her eyes.

He just let her walk off. He let her go.

She wipes her eyes and cranks up the radio.

No. She ain't doing that. Turning into some weepy, nostalgic, fragile flower. Her daddy taught her better than that. *Chin up, Em Bug*, he'd always say, and that's what she plans to do.

Get over it quick.

Besides, why is she crying over a man who doesn't give a hang about her? She was right to leave him. She deserves better.

Jace is stuffy and serious and never has any fun. He doesn't dance. And he sure as hell ain't romantic anymore. These days, the closest Jace gets to romance is gas station flowers. He ain't that same sweet boy she met at the stables who stole her heart so long ago. The one who brought her colorful wildflowers from a field. Who pressed the silky petals to her cheeks, matching the colors to her lips before kissing them so hard they bruised, kissed her like nothing else mattered, like everything would always be perfect between them.

Still, despite the doubt and despair, she can't help but think back to only hours ago. Jace apologizing, taking her in his arms, the hard press of his muscled body, his heartbeat, against hers. The tender way he held her like he actually gave a damn about her in the last three years.

Her attention taken by a familiar voice on the radio, Emmy Lou scowls at the song that's just come on like it's personally set out to drive the stake back in her heart.

"What's the point of this ol' life if we don't do it together? Because, girl, I'm needin' you, needin' you, needin' you now, needin' you now and forever . . ."

The song Seth wrote for Lacey, a gorgeous ballad assuring her of his love for her, blasts from the speakers.

Another thing she's never gotten from Jace. Fool man never even wrote her a song.

"Damn you, Jace," she spits out. Channeling a southern woman's rage, she grits her jaw and snaps off the radio.

She pushes Jace, Jace and his handsome, busted face, out of her mind. He's got it handled, or so he claims. He doesn't need her. He did this to himself. Singing her all the lies in the songbook.

Her gaze going to the window, Emmy Lou sets her jaw and makes up her mind.

She's moving on.

Without Jace Taylor.

Wild Antler Farm looms like an incoming fist. Heart in his throat, Jace steers his truck down the winding road, the setting sun at his back, and pauses at the security gates to punch his code into the keypad. The gates were installed months ago. Ever since Sal had Cash, the *Nashville Star* has been gunning for a photo of the baby. Needless to say, Luke went to whatever lengths necessary to protect Sal and his son.

Jace parks in the dirt driveway and hops out of his truck. Dread fills his stomach. He climbs the porch stairs and hesitates at the front door. Normally, he doesn't knock. Tonight, something tells him he'd better.

After a few long minutes, the door swings open. Seth stares at him, a muscle twitching in his jaw.

The dark look on Seth's face says it all. He's heard about the threat to Lacey.

"Hey, man," Jace says.

Seth takes a step back to let him in. Down the hall, a rustle of movement. Lacey, arms wrapped tight around herself, hovers on the threshold of the living room. She gives Jace a wan smile. Seth looks from Lacey and then back to Jace, his expression stiff.

"Luke's upstairs," Seth grits out. Though his eyes hold sympathy for Jace, they also hold anger, and more importantly, they hold Lacey, and that's a contest that Jace will never win.

Jace put all of them in danger today. Their wives. Their families. How Seth's not kicking his ass here and now is a miracle.

Upstairs, Jace pauses outside the nursery. Luke's singing "Ramblin' Man" in a low drawl to Cash. Inhaling a breath, Jace gives a light, determined rap on the door frame.

Luke turns, his dark eyes sweeping over Jace's cut lip, his black eye. Cash, cradled in Luke's arms, coos, a smile lighting up his face. The baby looks like Luke. Long limbs, dark hair, but tiny like Sal.

"Hey, kiddo," Jace says to Cash, stepping inside the room. "Looks like I made it in time for the nightly burp."

Luke chuckles. Winston, their scruffy terrier, on the rug beside Cash's crib, lets out a low woof.

Jace lifts his eyes to his best friend and clears his throat. "Listen—"

The softness on Luke's face flickers, then hardens. "Not here." He places Cash gently in the crib. "Outside."

Jace nods. The knot in his stomach grows larger as he follows Luke down the stairs and out onto the back porch overlooking the river. The sky's ablush with sunset, the full moon visible in the early-evening sky. For a few long seconds, they stand there, silent, waiting, and then Jace, whisking his hands together, says, "Luke, I'm so damn sorry about today. I never—"

"My wife was there," Luke says suddenly, his no-bullshit voice cutting clean through the dusky night. "My son."

Jace winces. It's Luke's biggest fear. Losing Sal. Their baby. Christ, if anything happened to that kid because of him . . .

Luke's face is fierce. "You know I had to go pick Sal up on the side of the road? That's how damn shook up she was. Just holdin' Cash and cryin' her heart out. So shaky she couldn't make it back home."

"Fuck." Guilt tearing through him, Jace drops his head, smears his face in his hands.

Of goddamn course, Sal would be freaked out. Some guy cornering her after her nightmare with Roy, her kidnapping last year, threatening Sal and Luke's only son, the baby they worked so hard to have after Sal's miscarriage, would devastate her.

Jace swears, reeling. "Is she okay?"

"She's restin'." Luke sighs and shakes his head. "I should be spendin' the day with my family, man. Not dealin' with this shit." Luke's soft admonition guts Jace.

How many times can he fuck up? Luke and Sal are his and Emmy Lou's best friends. His only family. To let them down, especially after everything Luke's done for him, kills him.

"I love you, Jace, you're like my goddamn brother." Luke's voice breaks, but he recovers, pinning his gaze to Jace. "But if this touches my family, if it touches Sal or Lacey or Seth or my son . . ."

Jace hears what Luke's saying.

If he loses Sal to this, loses anyone in his family, Luke will never forgive him. So Jace had better fix it. Fast.

"It's handled, Luke. Tonight, it's over." His gut dips. He said that the last time and look where it got him.

Luke leans back against the railing and scrubs a lean hand through his hair. "Seth told me what's goin' on. You shoulda talked to me. You didn't have to do it alone."

Jace squeezes his eyes shut.

That's what he always does. Do it alone. Because he's Jace-idiot-Taylor. Always serious. Level-headed. A solver. An attitude he adapted for self-preservation. You play by the rules. You make it. You survive.

"It won't touch the band," Jace mumbles.

A long pause.

Then: "I don't care about the band. I care about my family. About you." Luke's voice is softer now. Sad. And that cuts Jace worse than his anger.

"I let you down," Jace says.

"You did." Luke stares out across the field to the river, his jaw tight. Then he nods. "But we're straight."

The message is clear: Luke's done. The lecture over.

Jace's chest compresses. The need to talk, to confess that his entire world's falling apart, wrenches at him. "*I ain't straight.*" He lets out a breath that rocks his body. "Emmy Lou left me."

A hiss from the dark reveals Seth stepping out onto the porch, a bottle of whiskey in his hands.

"I'd need a night away from you too," he drawls, but his eyes hold understanding, pity. He passes Jace the bottle. "She'll be back." Seth cackles, claiming a spot next to Luke. "Em runs hot. Remember that time she left you at the gas station in Reno because you didn't notice her damn shoes?"

At the memory of his wife, his feisty Georgia girl, hot tears bead Jace's eyes. The memory sticks out in his mind clear as day. Jace failed to notice the new boots Emmy Lou had bought. She had been so damn excited, so pleased she had finally found the perfect boots for one of the Brothers Kincaid's first shows, and all he could do was sit down to write a song with Luke.

Still as fucking clueless now as he was back then.

Jace takes a long swig of whiskey, his nerves shot. "You don't understand. She left. For good. She packed her bags. She wants a divorce."

Seth gapes at him. "You ain't serious?"

Jace grips the neck of the bottle. "I sure fuckin' am."

It feels surreal. Telling his best friend that his wife, the love of his life, has walked out on him. His world as he knows it is off its damn rocker and he doesn't have a clue how to right it.

For so long, he and Luke had been on the same path. Go to Nashville, chase girls, get famous. Sing their songs. Sleep beside their wives every night. Have babies. Sounded like a damn good life. Only Jace's plans took a sharp right off a steep cliff after he lied to Emmy Lou, and he hasn't been able to climb up since.

Luke blinks, his brow furrowing when he realizes it's serious. He gives Seth an *oh shit* look that has Jace drinking more.

"You and Em . . . ," Luke says slowly. "You had your issues, sure, but were always good together."

Jace doesn't know how to tell them. About the cold dark nights of his and Emmy Lou's marriage. Coming together only to fall apart all over again. Separate beds. How they put on a show at every barbeque, every Sunday Supper, every red carpet, not wanting their friends to know the depths of their troubles.

"We ain't like you and Sal," Jace says bitterly. "Not no more. Not for a long damn time."

Luke winces, pained, and Jace knows Luke's going back to his own marriage troubles. Back to when he nearly lost Sal to secrets and lies. All he had done to protect her; it had almost cost him his marriage.

Jace supposes he's welcomed to the fucking club.

Another drink. The bottle halfway empty. Jace's vision blurs. Luke says something in a low voice to Seth as Jace braces a steadying hand against the porch railing.

"It's my fault," Jace mumbles, guilt sinking him like an anchor. "I shoulda played it straight with Emmy Lou."

It's Seth who asks the million-dollar question. "Why didn't you just tell her, man?"

So many reasons. None of them right. Because he was embarrassed. Because he wanted to protect her. Because he didn't want to ruin the tentative steps he and Emmy Lou were slowly taking back to each other.

"Because I was supposed to handle it," he says. "And I didn't."

Darker now, his thoughts, mixing with the whiskey, the noise of the past, his mother's sweet, steadfast voice in his ears.

You protect the ones you love, Jace. You do anything.

Jace's eyes simmer and he rakes a hand through his hair. "I'm as bad as my father. I lied. I put her in danger. I didn't protect her."

"Jace." Luke's voice is grim. His best friend can read him. Knows where his mind has gone. "Don't go there."

But as Jace looks down at his busted fist, he can't help but go back to the past.

Back to when he broke the rules once.

Back to when it should have been him his dad hit, not his mom.

Back to when he vowed always to play by the rules, to do the right thing, so the people he loved wouldn't get hurt.

But they did get hurt. Emmy Lou and his mom both got hurt.

Seth's deep voice rumbles. "You still love Em?"

Jace nods, numb.

"Then what're you gonna do about it?"

"What do you mean?"

Seth rolls his eyes, his expression half-amused, half-annoyed. "For bein' such a smart guy, you're pretty damn stupid." He grips Jace's shoulder. "Go find her and go fuckin' get her."

Jace shakes his head, lost in his own self-pity. "She hates me. I don't blame her. I messed everything up. She doesn't understand . . ."

"Jace." Luke's look is pointed. "If she needs to understand, you tell her about me."

It's permission. A reminder to Jace that Emmy Lou still doesn't know about what Luke tried to do nearly three years ago. The catalyst that set everything in motion. Not an excuse, but a reason.

"If you got a chance to get her back, take it," Luke says, his voice thick with emotion.

Jace closes his eyes. He ain't seeing clear. His entire world's spinning out of control and the only thing helping him stand straight is the liquor. The night suddenly feels too heavy, too damn desolate for words.

"I don't know. I don't know, man . . ." Jace takes a swig of whiskey, stumbles across the porch.

Seth and Luke meet each other's gaze, their expressions worried.

Jace leaves Luke and Seth.

He keeps the whiskey.

Back at his house, Jace staggers across the driveway. Instead of going inside, where all that waits for him is an empty house, he takes the whiskey and he takes his pain and heads for the pasture.

Fumbling, he checks his phone for a text from Emmy Lou.

A text from McCade. But there's nothing. Only the longest night of his goddamn life stretching in front of him.

"Shit," he swears as he crashes into a pile of something sharp and hard.

Dumbly, he stares at the lumber piled up alongside the barn. Emmy Lou had been on his ass for the last six weeks to clean it up. And what did he do? He forgot. Because he put the band first. Because he's a fucking idiot.

In the light of the full moon, his eyes scour the farm, the stables, the overgrown weeds and empty troughs, and he realizes how much he stopped helping her.

How much they've grown apart over the last three years.

Because he stopped doing the little things that mattered. When she passed on a tour because of her fear of small spaces, he stopped asking if she wanted to fly. Hell, he stopped wanting her to. Two weeks on the road without Emmy Lou meant peace, meant he didn't have to hear her voice in his ear reminding him of his mistake. She had a right to be angry, to be hurt, but after three years, her resentment never ebbed, which pissed Jace off because she wouldn't give him the chance to make it up to her. So they pulled and pulled away, like a taffy stretched too thin until it snapped. *They* snapped.

They stopped talking.

They stopped touching.

Which is where this all started.

Which is why Emmy Lou's gone.

A sudden sense of loss overwhelms him as he stares out over the pasture, at his farm. The farm he and Emmy Lou bought and built together.

His heart clenches.

And then he screams.

"*Fuck!*"

His strangled voice rings out over the pasture, the horses nickering at the sound. Emmy Lou's paint, Lolli, comes trotting over to see what his deal is. Jace drains the bottle of whiskey and gets a tight grip on its neck. He steps close to the fence, itching to smash the bottle against the hard wood, to shatter it into a million pieces, but he can't even do that for fear of hurting the horses.

He's such goddamn Boy Scout.

Jace breathes hard. Drops the bottle to the ground.

This is where all his Sunday school bullshit has got him. For his entire life, he's followed the rules. He never smoked. Kept to the speed limit. Always read the fine print on the contract. Never started a fight unless it was to back up Luke or Seth. And the one time he steps a toe out of line because he needed a place to lay his grief, one small rebellion so as not to lose his damn mind because his best friend lost his, it cost him everything.

It cost him his wife.

Lolli's there. The dappled mare nuzzles his hand, her dark brown eyes an echo of his sadness. Jace steps closer and strokes her long ear, memories stirring inside of him.

Suddenly, it's twelve years ago, and he's back in Montgomery Stables, a poor country boy trying to make it in Nashville, mucking stalls during the day so the Brothers Kincaid could play nights in dingy dive bars with chicken wire barricades. And then he met Emmy Lou. He worked right up alongside her for two straight months before he realized he was working *for* her. Never mind that her family was one of the biggest horse breeders in the south, that she was miles out of his league, because the minute he laid eyes on that girl, he loved her.

She was a sassy Georgia peach with a fire in her big brown eyes that drove him crazy. Tight blue jeans. An angel smile. She was unlike anyone he ever met. She was the opposite of him in every way and he craved that difference, that kind of happiness in his life. Bubbly to his mellow. She was a talker. She could talk his ear off about any damn thing and he loved that.

It was their summer. Falling in love. Their connection, their chemistry, raw and pure, bubbled up on its own like some clear mountain stream. He remembers it all. Stealing away from farm chores to get to first, then second base in the stables. How, every morning, he brought her a wildflower from the field. Emmy Lou's bright smile as she tucked it above her ear. Watching every guy working on that farm dream about holding Emmy Lou, but he was the lucky son of a bitch with her in his arms. Nearly missing practice because he couldn't tear his eyes, his lips, away from her. But best of all, there were the horses. She was twice the rider he was, and they bonded over their love for the animals. Rodeos, late-afternoon rides, were their love language.

Christ. How he wishes he could go back to the man he was before. Before he lost them their savings, before he put her horse farm in danger, before he lied to her, before he became a pathetic excuse of a husband.

"Emmy," he whispers into the night, hot tears beading his eyes.

A soft chuckle from the shadows.

Lolli backs away, nostrils flaring. Jace, picking up on the horse's distress, turns.

A figure emerges. A shadow of a man. McCade. He holds the cooler in his hand, raising it up as he approaches Jace. "Mr. Taylor. Nice doing business with you. I trust that your wife told you I stopped by."

Red.

All he sees is red.

Jace explodes in rage. He rushes the man, grabs up a fistful of shirt and slams him back against the barn. "You motherfucker," he snarls.

Kill the guy.

That's the first thought in his brain. Let that dark, dangerous, desperate place sweep him up like it did his father. Why should he give a shit anymore? Why bother playing by the rules? He lost everything. Go to jail, get his reputation skewered by the *Star*, his life doesn't fucking matter without Emmy Lou.

Jace gives McCade a shake. "You came to my house. Threatened my *wife*?"

McCade stares at him, almost drolly, then says, "She's real pretty, your wife. Feisty too, that Emmy Lou."

Jace tightens his grip, thanking God Emmy Lou's out of town. Safe from the madness and the danger that is his life.

"Don't you fuckin' talk about her. Don't you goddamn say her name."

McCade chuckles. "I want to inspire confidence, Mr. Taylor. I have my money. And we, my friend, have no more beef. At least until next time."

Jace releases McCade and steps back, his body shuddering out a disgusted laugh. "There ain't gonna be a next time."

McCade adjusts his collar, the cuffs of his suit jacket. "Let this be a lesson, Mr. Taylor. There are always dangerous men out there who want to hurt the ones you love. 'Next time' could be anyone. Be careful."

A threat. A warning. A promise, Jace doesn't know.

What he does know is he wants this over with. He wants this done.

Now.

Fists clenching, Jace draws himself up, his heartbeat thrumming in his ears. "Don't come back here. And stay the fuck away from my wife."

McCade doesn't answer. He turns to walk toward the outline of a big black Cadillac. Then he stops. He looks back at Jace. "I'm pleased to see it, Mr. Taylor. Fire. Fight. It's what you've been missing."

Jace stands there, chest heaving, watching as McCade disappears. The soundtrack of the night swirls around him. The sound of a car engine. The crunch of gravel and dirt. The chirp of crickets and the soft whinny of the horses. It should be a weight released, but it isn't. Because Emmy Lou's still gone.

Emmy Lou.

He closes his eyes, his brain snagging on all his past mistakes. All the should-haves in his life.

He should have stayed home that night, stayed with his mother.

He never should have picked up those cards.

But most importantly, he should have fought for Emmy Lou today, before she got in that car and drove away.

Too late. It's all too late.

But it's not.

Jace opens his eyes.

Luke's words, McCade's, ring out in his head.

If you got a chance to get her back, take it.

Fight.

He has one last chance to do what he's gotta do.

Fight for Emmy Lou.

Bring her home, and bring her back to him.

"I THINK SHE'S DEAD."

"Dead? I think she's drunk."

"Hell nah. She ain't none of those. She's hidin' out. That's what I'd do."

Emmy Lou's eyes flash open as if remembering where she is and what she's doing and how it doesn't involve Jace Taylor. Then she groans at the trio of familiar voices jabbering bright overhead. Curling tighter into a ball of mortification, she buries her face deeper into the pillow. It's too early to face the breakup music.

Or her brothers.

The bed jostles. A finger wraps around a strand of her hair and uses it to tickle her cheek. A poke of another finger into her armpit. She resists the urge to giggle.

Then there's the click of a tongue. A smug drawl of a voice. "Think she turned tail and ran?"

That's it. She ain't letting these knuckleheads talk trash about things they know nothing about one second longer.

Lifting her head, Emmy Lou rips off her almond-colored silk eye mask and blinks as the stern faces of her brothers come into focus. Charlie, lounging up against the headboard, heads the pack. Wyatt and Grady are sprawled out at the foot of the bed.

She narrows her eyes at her third-oldest brother. "I wasn't aware I'd be wakin' up with judgment, Charlie."

Charlie levels a wry brow. "You came back to Wildheart. You're askin' for judgment."

She reaches up to tug at his wiry beard. "Lord, when are

you gonna trim up this mess of a beard, Charlie? You look like a prospector."

He scowls. "Stop fussin', Em."

Wyatt's somber gaze studies the shadows under her eyes. "You look like shit, Em."

She feels like shit. Her sleep was all kinds of fitful. She tossed and turned, waking numerous times, second-guessing her decision to leave Jace.

"Well, *I'm* glad you came back." Grady, the youngest, stares down at her, his expressive brown eyes jovial. "I need someone to cook me breakfast."

She swipes at him like a fly. "Smart-ass." All her brothers love to fight, grumble, and annoy her endlessly.

Grady snickers.

She looks at her brothers. They're missing two. "Where's Ford? Davis?"

"Davis is stuck in Bozeman. Got roped into helpin' at the livestock show," Wyatt says. "Ford's at the ranch. Both fillies are pregnant and he ain't gonna leave 'em."

Emmy Lou pooh-poohs. As cowboys running a ranch in Montana, it's rare that all five of her brothers come home at one time. Still, Davis and Ford, the twins, can do no wrong. Big, gruff golden boys who Mama Belle lets get away with anything. Then there came Charlie, Wyatt, Emmy Lou, and last, Grady.

She leans over, sweeping her cell phone off the nightstand and into her hand. It's eleven a.m. She has a dozen text messages. Sal. Lacey. Alabama. Luke. Even Seth's sent her a popular meme of a weepy-faced James Van Der Beek.

But none from Jace. It figures. Because that's Jace. Predictable, reliable Jace. He never fights. Especially not for her.

The thought should fell her.

Instead, it jump-starts her, lights her up inside like a thousand screaming fireworks.

Taking a deep breath, she extracts herself from the primrose comforter, from the jumble of brothers, climbing over long limbs and earning grumbles of disgruntlement. She makes her way to the cherrywood vanity, spying the quarter-full bottle of Boone's Farm she had picked up at a gas station last night and promptly started chugging the minute she walked through the door.

She squints at the bottle. Huh. She remembers it being fuller than that.

She scrapes her tongue against the roof of her mouth. Yep. She definitely drank it.

"Hell, Emmy Lou." Charlie wears his serious older brother face, the one he tacks on when he needs to get answers. His cornflower-blue eyes pin her down. "You wanna tell us what happened?"

Emmy Lou turns to stare at her gruff big brother, her entire body tensing up at his question.

No one knows. Yesterday as she was flying down the highway, she had sent Grady a cryptic text that said, *I'm coming home. Alone.* And that was it. All she had the bandwidth for at the time. But now. Now's the time to explain.

Inhaling a breath, Emmy Lou squares her shoulders. "I left Jace."

Charlie rockets up. His fists clenched. "He hit you. That son of a bitch."

Emmy Lou rolls her eyes at his dramatics. Trust Charlie to immediately think the worst. While Davis is the firstborn, Charlie always takes up the slack by playing the protective-older-brother card when he isn't around.

A prop of her hands on her hips. An exasperated raise of her brows. "No, he did not hit me, Charlie."

Wyatt's brows sweep together. "Did he cheat, Em? Are those articles true?"

Grady holds up a hand. "Hold your horses and let her explain."

Emmy Lou smiles, floating Grady a look of thanks. Out of all her brothers, even though she'd take it to her grave before admitting it aloud, Grady's her sibling soul mate. Only a year apart, she and Grady were always paired up. He's the sweetest of her bunch of grumbling brothers—she's only seen Grady mad once.

And that was her fault.

All her fault.

She looks around the room, her brave front faltering. Her brothers, perched on the bed, wait for her to explain. But how? How does she explain this?

She shakes her head. "No, it's nothin' like that."

Charlie frowns, not letting it go. "Then what is it?"

A flare of frustration goes through her.

Damn Charlie. She can't even have one day alone to settle in before she's got her family on her back. Still, despite her grousing, she loves it. Loves her big, wild, crazy family. A house overflowing with love and so many dang people they could fill an ark. She and Jace wanted that.

Her smile falters.

Once upon a time.

Heart stalling out, she pushes herself away from the vanity, grabs her velvet robe from the chair and strides for the door. "Y'all are infuriatin'. I ain't givin' you a lick of information until I get some caffeine."

A Q&A ambush from her brothers is not on the agenda this morning.

Her head held high, Emmy Lou exits the room and walks fast down the stairs. She can hear her brothers scrambling up, swearing, quick on her heels.

She sweeps down the stairs and into the hallway, taking a minute to appreciate her surroundings before having to get into the shit with her brothers. The Happy Hideaway—what she and Jace nicknamed their home—was always a nice reprieve from Nashville and the chaos of the *Star*, the music, the fans. They had purchased the two-and-a-half-acre farm and built their house with the Brothers Kincaid's first big paycheck. They were married here. Spent holidays here. With 360-degree views of the horse pasture and valley, the sprawling five-bedroom farmhouse backs up to the stables and her parents' Colonial Revival manor up on the hilltop.

The Happy Hideaway still looks the same as when she last left it. Quaint, cozy and country, not like their modern Nashville home. With buttery leather couches in the living room, a towering fireplace, and dark hardwood floors that creak and groan with every footstep, it's her own little slice of country paradise.

In the kitchen, Emmy Lou opens the windows, dumps coffee in the pot, pulls out every baking supply in the pantry. She ain't staying in bed to mope. What she does plan to do is make a big bowl of angry muffins with a side of forget-about-him champagne. She thanks the Lord that last night she was in her right mind enough to stop at a grocery store and stock the fridge. She's determined to keep busy, determined not to think about Jace, not once. All she wants to do today is ride her horses and bake away her troubles. It's what she does best when she's at her worst. She cooks a feast.

She freezes at the fridge, mid-grab on the bottle of champagne. On the front of the fridge is a whiteboard with a long-ago note from Jace. His letters slanted. Serious.

I love you, Em. Em, my gem.

Swallowing hard, she raises a hand to wipe away the evidence, to not be swayed by his words—only Grady's voice stops her.

"You ain't really leavin' Jace," Grady ventures. "Are you?"

Emmy Lou, pulled from her daydream daze, turns to see all three of her brothers on barstools at the massive marble counter.

She sighs and sets down the champagne. She can't duck and dodge any longer. She came back to Wildheart—she owes them an explanation.

"Well?" Charlie's nostrils flare like a bull's. He's impatient. That's Charlie. Tall, solidly built, stubborn and stern. That's all her brothers. Dusty, disheveled daredevils. They have to be if they're gonna rope those horses right.

She bites her lip. Grady and Jace are close. She doesn't know how he'll take the news.

"I did. I asked for a divorce," she says, jutting her chin defiantly, and Grady winces.

Wyatt snickers, stretching his lean body over the counter to uncork the champagne. "At least you don't gotta worry about Mama being brokenhearted."

Charlie crosses his arms, biceps bulging, a rare smile tugging at the ends of his bearded lips.

Emmy Lou scowls at the two of them, even though Wyatt is right. Mama Belle and Jace are like oil and water. Lord, just the thought has her itching.

Emmy Lou wags a prim finger between Charlie and Wyatt. "Y'all can be nice and listen to my story, or y'all can go back to Montana and shovel cow turds."

Her retort is met with rueful grins. With light brown hair and steel-blue eyes, Wyatt and Charlie look more like twins than the twins do.

She pinches the bridge of her nose. "Oh Lord, I don't even know where to start with y'all. It's a long, long, long story."

"Take a breath," Grady says, knowing her nerves. He meets her eyes. "You got this."

With Grady's words backing her, she rallies strength.

She begins.

As she mixes up muffins, her brothers listen as she tells them about the last three years. The dark parts of her marriage she hid because she was embarrassed. Jace's gambling. Their money troubles. The near-loss of their farm. The man that came to the house yesterday. McCade and his threats.

When she's finished, she's pulling a tray of steaming blueberry muffins from the oven, fully aware her brothers are staring at her with stunned expressions.

Wyatt exhales at her long-winded explanation. "Shit, Em. Did you stretch before you said all that?"

Emmy Lou sticks out her tongue.

"That's it," she says, taking a prim sip of her champagne. "That's all I got."

"That's it?" Charlie's blue eyes flash with anger. "Some man came to your house yesterday and threatened you." He draws himself up, his jaw flexing. "I need to know. Are you in trouble, Emmy Lou?"

"I ain't sure. Jace said he handled it." She looks down at the tray of muffins, willing herself to keep it together. "But that's what he said last time."

"Well, we'll make sure it's handled." Charlie stands, the stool scooting out, and Wyatt follows suit, his fists clenched. While Charlie leads the charge, Wyatt's always ready to take it in a reckless, wild direction.

Emmy Lou frowns. "I busted my ass to make you breakfast and you're leavin'?"

"We're gonna find your husband," Wyatt says, his eyebrows rising dangerously, as Charlie finishes his beer in one long slug. "And have a talk."

Have a talk is her brothers' code for *Jace is a dead man.*

She props her hands on her hips. "Y'all ain't seriously drivin' to Nashville right now."

The only response she gets is the slam of the front door.

Grady, wearing a T-shirt that says Armadillo by Morning, looks at Emmy Lou. "Don't worry. They'll get as far as Main Street before they find a bar."

"Wild cowboys." Emmy Lou *tsks* at the sound of a pickup truck backfiring. "The both of them." She looks Grady over. "What about you? How's Layla?"

Grady scowls at the mention of his girlfriend. "Halfway back to Macon."

"What happened?"

"Nuh-uh. We ain't talkin 'bout me. We're talkin' 'bout you." His expression turns soft and he runs a hand through his shaggy mop of dark blond hair. "Are you really sure you wanna divorce Jace, Em? Shoot me straight, because damn, I gotta know if I punch him in the face the next time I see him or not."

Sadness balloons in Emmy Lou. At least someone in the

family cares. Every holiday, Grady and Jace were inseparable. She knows Jace considers them all his family. Grady's like his kid brother. Then, as quick as it comes, she stomps away the thought. She refuses to feel bad for Jace Taylor. Not when he got himself into this mess in the first place.

"I don't know," she admits.

She had said the words in anger. She was at her breaking point with Jace. But is that what she really wants? An end to their forever?

"It doesn't matter," she whispers. "He let me go." Out of everything that's happened it's those words that have tears welling up in her eyes. "He doesn't care."

Grady winces.

"Oh, Grady." Covering her mouth, she turns away from him, embarrassed by how bad she let their marriage get. She wipes her face and sniffles. Lord, even her tears are angry.

"Y'all and Jace are like pizza," Grady goes on. "Sometimes it gets burned or it's soggy, but at the end of the day, pizza's always good. Even bad pizza is good."

She turns back to him. "We're pizza that's sat out for three long years, Grady."

"Then why did you stay?" Her brother stares at her, curious, waiting on an answer.

"Because . . . because it got better sometimes. We fought but . . ."

She trails off at the lie that's so easily dropped from her lips. She and Jace didn't fight for each other. They didn't work together to fix it. Or try therapy. They retreated. Jace to his music, Emmy Lou to her horses. The only thing they shared was a house. But not a heart.

Not the one thing that mattered.

"Do you still love him?" Grady asks, his tone soft, like he's trying to corral a frightened calf.

Emmy Lou stays quiet. Grady's question sends a flood of despair straight through her.

She does. Against every angry bone in her body, she still loves Jace. But she doesn't know if that's enough. He broke her trust for the second time.

Her heart can't take anymore.

When Grady raises his eyebrows at her silence, she shakes her head. "All I know is I'm hopin' whatever happens between us doesn't mess with your contract."

An aspiring singer/songwriter, Grady's leaving Wildheart at the end of the summer for Nashville. With the Brothers Kincaid's connections, Luke helped Grady get signed to a small label with one of the strictest contracts around, thanks to the issues they had with Griff Greyson. No fighting, no drugs, no overnight guests on tour.

Only now . . . with her and Jace . . .

Emmy Lou lowers her lashes. "I hope you still have that shot."

"I will," Grady says with youthful confidence. He grins. "Don't look so sad, Em. Luke's a good guy. 'Sides, with or without him or Jace, I'll be okay."

"You tell Daddy?"

"Sure did. Gave him my notice last week."

"How'd he take it?"

"He thinks Nashville is perfect for me. Hell-raisin', fightin', that's where I belong."

Grady drops his eyes. Though his shrug, his tone is easy, and though a hell-raiser, some rowdy Griff Greyson doppelgänger, is the last thing Grady is, Emmy Lou sees it's all an act. He's hurt.

It's so unfair. Their father, Boone, never forgave Grady for getting in trouble with the cops at sixteen.

Just another bad memory Wildheart carries.

"Don't listen to Daddy," Emmy Lou says. She reaches over the island to squeeze his hand, hoping to boost his spirits. "I'm so proud of you, Grady."

He grins. "Speakin' of summer, what're you gonna do back here in Wildheart?"

She bites her lip, another plan she hasn't thought through.

Still, she tucks away the negativity. Conjures a cheer, an optimism she doesn't feel.

She gives a flippant toss of her hair. "Ain't sure yet."

To punctuate her statement, she swigs straight from the bottle of champagne. Grady arches a brow and laughs. "Damn, tiger."

She drinks fast, feeling the sharp sting of bubbles on her tongue. "I'm livin', Grady. I am finally livin'."

He arches an amused brow. "Oh, you are?"

"I'm tired of Jace's routine," Emmy Lou drawls, sidling around the kitchen. She dances a knife into the sink. Tosses her apron across the counter, trying to play it cool, instead of act like the heartbroken end-of-her-rope woman she is. "He's ho-hum. I am gonna change my world. And not just change it. Blow it up."

Grady gives her a skeptical look. "How you gonna do that?"

"I don't know. Maybe I'll color my hair or somethin'."

"Sounds borin'." He grins. "I have a better idea."

"What?"

Emmy Lou follows his finger as he points at the front door. She gasps. Through the thin glass, she sees the silhouette of a beehive ready to blow up her day.

"Mama Belle." She whips her head to Grady. "How's she know already?" She fumble-grabs the bottle of champagne by its neck and stuffs it under the sink. Drinking in the morning. Mama'll have her hide.

Grady downs his, choking on the fizz of the bubbles. "Shit, you already know Mama was the first one sendin' that news down the AP wire."

"Damn it." Emmy Lou edges close to Grady like together they can fend off Mama Belle. She can't bear the thought of Mama's tears, her dramatic proclamation that once again her only daughter's a disappointment to her, to Wildheart.

Grady reaches across the counter, steals a muffin and takes a step for the back door.

She stares, flabbergasted. "The hell you're leavin'."

Emmy Lou grabs his wrist, anchoring him to the spot. But

Grady's stronger, taller, and he walks the distance to the back door, easily dragging her across the slick floor as she pulls at his arm.

"No, don't—" Emmy Lou says, then yelps as Grady smoothly untangles himself from her.

A wiggle of his eyebrows. "Good luck, Em."

And then he's biting into the muffin, ducking out the back door, leaving Emmy Lou alone in the kitchen.

"You little weasel," Emmy Lou hisses. "You are a shit, Grady Montgomery," she mutters, rushing around the kitchen, shoving dishes in the sink and flicking off the oven. "Leavin' me alone to deal with Mama Belle all by my lonesome. Well, I tell you what, the next time you need a helpin' hand, see how far I go to shove my boot up your ass."

She dips to fix her face in the toaster and winces.

The woman staring back at her from the greasy reflection wears tangled hair, smudged makeup, sad mascara streaks that could be read like tea leaves. A far cry from Wildheart's rodeo queen. Mama Belle's only daughter. Emmy Lou tries for a smile, only to have it miss her eyes.

Then she inhales deep and sends up a quick prayer to Jesus.

Lord help her.

Jace downshifts his pickup truck, easing off the gas as he enters Wildheart proper. Outside the window: the familiar scenery of a town he's come to love as his own. The graffiti-tagged water tower stands like a tall rusted sentry in the distance. Rolling green horse pastures with white fences. The lone diner. The town's welcome sign, proclaiming GOOD FOLK LIVE HERE, hangs by a single metal chain, never fixed after the tornado passed through four years ago.

Christ, was that the last time he and Emmy Lou were back here? Together? Happy?

Everywhere Jace looks there's a reminder of his wife. Hell,

the Montgomerys are like the royal family in the state of Georgia and their small town. He can't go a mile without seeing a sign for Montgomery Farm and Stables. The premier farm for training, breeding and raising horses for rodeos and racetracks. Emmy Lou, Wildheart's rodeo queen, was treated like royalty every time she came home.

Jace takes a right at the stop sign and scrubs a hand over his face. He knows Emmy Lou will be surprised to see him, and why wouldn't she? He let her leave without going after her, without a phone call or even a text.

She's come to expect that from him.

Silence.

His own damn fault.

It shames him to admit he hadn't realized how bad things had gotten between them. No matter how fractured their marriage, she was still it for him. But he sat it out. He became complacent and quiet. He was worrying about what she'd think of him if he told her the truth, instead of being honest and worrying about her. Then, like the slow reveal, the pullback of the curtain in the shitshow that was his marriage, it took Emmy Lou packing up and walking out to see the hallelujah-light.

Sure, they bickered, nagged, but he hadn't realized Emmy was fed up. That she already had one foot out the door.

Her leaving was a wakeup call. That he's got to do better. That he took her love, her trust for granted.

That he has to fight for her.

This morning, he got his shit squared in Nashville. Hired someone to watch the farm and the horses and then made one of the hardest decisions of his life. He took a temporary hiatus from the Brothers Kincaid. Luke's blessing is ringing in his ears: "Go get your wife, man."

Jace lets out a long breath and grips the wheel tight. Damn if that ain't what he's gonna do. He put Nashville in his rearview and lit out of there. He had his fucking pity party, his mental break, his midlife crisis, whatever the fuck he wants to call it. Now, for once in his life, he's making a gamble he can't lose.

He knows it's too little too late. All he can do is try and hope like hell she'll give him a second chance.

Because wherever Emmy Lou is, he wants to be there, with her. He hasn't liked being without her these last few hours. Not knowing what she's doing, if she's safe, if she's crying or celebrating since she walked away. All he knows is that he can't lose her.

He won't. He ain't a good person, but he's got one good thing in his life. His Em.

Now he's coming to Wildheart without a plan. All he's bringing with him is a broken marriage, a busted face and one single goal: bring Emmy Lou home. Yet, as much as he wants to, he just can't bundle Emmy Lou up over his shoulder caveman-style and take her back to Nashville. She'd slap the shit out of him. He's gotta talk to her. Grovel. Stick it out no matter what. Their marriage won't miraculously be fixed by him showing up. He has to put the work in. Taking it calm and quiet didn't work the first time. He disappeared into himself. Took Emmy Lou for granted and left her to the wayside. Now, he's gotta be present. Be focused on her.

No matter how embarrassing, how painful, he deserves this.

He has to face her.

Face her family.

Shit.

His stomach twists at the thought of looking Boone, Emmy Lou's father, in the eye and knowing he broke his promise never to hurt his daughter. This time, this homecoming, he ain't in for handshakes and hugs from Emmy Lou's parents and her army of brothers. He's in for a load of earsplitting grief and tough words.

Because he let Boone down. He let them all down.

The only family he had.

Something he always craved in life.

Dread curls his fist over the steering wheel. His dark past fencing him in.

His alcoholic father, always swinging a fist. His mama, broken, battered, always protecting Jace. Which meant Jace grew up to be the one who took the reins, who protected his mama when she couldn't protect herself. It was how he stayed sane as a kid. Jace became everything his father wasn't. Methodical. Calm. Responsible. Never fucking up.

Until that night.

That damn night.

The closest thing he had to a family when he was a kid was the Kincaids. More nights than not, he was over there for a porch song and a home-cooked meal. Seth and Luke, the two of them will never know just how damn much the name of their band means to Jace. In that band, he always had a family.

And then there was Emmy Lou. Ever the constant soundtrack to his life. His girl. His wife. His family. A family *he* made. Emmy Lou agreeing to marry him was one of the best days of his life. Emmy Lou taking the Taylor name, vowing to spend the rest of her life with him—it was a damn honor.

Her father, Boone, treated him like another son, shook hands with him like he meant something. Grady confides in him. Davis is easy to shoot the shit with. Wyatt always good for a game of pool. He can hold his own with Charlie and go hunting with Ford.

Jace slows on Main Street, stuck behind a tractor.

The only one in the family who disliked Jace was Mama Belle. He didn't have a dollar to his name when he married Emmy Lou, and even now, even at the height of his career in the Brothers Kincaid, Mama Belle still turns up her nose. Despite that, Jace can survive Mama Belle's barbs and arrows.

What he can't survive is Emmy Lou calling it quits. For good.

Failing at his marriage, breaking his promise to Emmy Lou to love her forever, it ain't in his cards. Those vows meant something damn serious to him, and though he knows he hasn't treated his marriage like he should, no fucking way is he letting go of the woman he loves.

Losing Emmy Lou—he'd be an absolute goner.

His attention is diverted from the road to a giant billboard above Boone Montgomery Rodeo Arena. The big block letters screaming that the town's annual rodeo is happening at the end of the summer. Labor Day weekend. THE EVENT OF THE YEAR. Sponsored by Yeti and Montgomery Farm and Stables.

Warfare fills his heart, his fists, at the memory of the Yeti cooler. The cash. McCade. His threat to Emmy Lou.

He's well aware he keeps checking his rearview mirror for that black Cadillac, keeps replaying McCade's last words. Was there another threat there, lingering somewhere below the dark surface?

"Next time" could be anyone. Be careful.

Jace rubs his temple. Fuck. Getting beat to hell scrambled his brain.

He reminds himself it's over.

Like last time? a paranoid voice inside asks.

Or is that a lie too?

He shakes his head and mutters, "Pull it the fuck together."

Starting with Emmy Lou.

He wants to be the king of Emmy Lou's heart like he used to be. The man who put that smile on her gorgeous face, who dimpled her cheek. Who took up space in her bed at night, the good kind of space filled with her soft sighs and sweet moans. But most of all, he wants to be good to her, be there for her.

When he shows up to ask her to come home, will she go back with him? Will she turn away and kick him out? Or worse, what if—the terrifying thought strikes Jace straight in the heart—what if she doesn't love him?

Jace winces. He wouldn't blame her if she didn't.

Christ, he never even wrote her a song. He was always too damn chickenshit to put his heart on the page. Luke was the lovesick bastard of the band. Seth, some wild party child until he met Lacey, and then there was no calling him back. And Jace . . . he was just Jace. Trusty, dependable Jace. Backup on bass. Backup in a bar. Back on his bullshit.

Emmy Lou, she deserved a song. He should have given her that. Given her so much more these last few years.

If he had . . . would she be gone right now? Would their marriage be hanging on by its last thread? Would they have that baby they were hoping for?

Jace swears, chasing away the what-ifs. It doesn't do any good to look back and try to piece together where it went wrong. The way they got here is gone, and now, he's gotta move forward and fight for Emmy Lou. Be the man she needs. Show her the fire she's been missing. Kiss her goodnight and good morning every damn day. Tell her he loves her, that he can't live, can't fucking breathe without her.

As Jace passes Tiny's Tavern, one of five bars in town, something else snags his focus.

"Shit," he mutters. All the air rushes out of his lungs as he spies the familiar truck. Montana plates. Browning Buck bumper stickers.

Charlie's truck.

Steeling himself, Jace punches the gas, resisting the urge to duck behind the steering wheel.

Emmy Lou.

Just the thought of her name returns his focus.

He's gonna write her a song.

If her brothers don't kill him first.

chapter
SIX

EMMY LOU STEPS OUT ONTO THE FRONT PORCH AND into dewy morning air. The sun's already hot, a humid heat brewing. The fragrant scent of magnolia blossoms. The faraway whinny of the horses.

In front of her stand Mama Belle and her father, Boone. Mama is sleek and polished in leather ankle booties, trendy jeans and soft powdery blue eyeshadow.

Emmy Lou plasters on an Elle Woods smile. "Mama, hi, I was just about to—"

Instead of getting hit with a stern scowl, she's rocked by a blast of a smile. "Oh, my sweet darlin' girl." Mama Belle throws her arms around Emmy Lou's neck, drowning her in the scent of luxurious perfume. "It's so good to have you home, sugar."

As Emmy Lou untangles from Mama Belle's arms, she frowns. Mama's nicer than normal. Uncaring about Emmy Lou's impoverished state of dress—no makeup, tattered pajamas, bare feet and bedhead.

Emmy Lou gives her mama a smile and then her eyes sweep to the first man she's ever loved. "Hey, Daddy."

Boone Montgomery's brown eyes light with pride. "Em Bug," he drawls, sweeping her up in a crushing hug.

Emmy Lou pulls back and stares up at him, stunned by how much he's aged since she's last seen him. Boone, a big bear of a man, is thinner than she remembered. Gaunt cheeks, hunched shoulders. She's hit with a pang of regret she's stayed away as long as she has.

Boone ruffles her hair. "You sure look good on the farm, kiddo."

"Thanks, Daddy."

Wrapping an arm around her, Boone gestures out across the farm. "Still as pretty as you remember?"

Emmy Lou leans into him. "More beautiful than ever."

Her eyes follow her father's. The bright, brilliant green of the land unfolding in front of the farmhouse, the glittering pond, the white-fenced pasture and paddocks, the Colonial Revival manor up on the hill where she grew up. No matter how old she gets, she'll always be in awe of the place where she was born and raised. Boone built Montgomery Farm and Stables himself. At first, it was only a two-room stable, and then it blew up into a booming horse business that serves Georgia and the southern states.

That's when her eyes light on the For Sale sign. With a little sigh, she tips her head to her daddy's shoulder. "I still can't believe you're sellin' it."

Montgomery Farm and Stables has been on the market for the last year, but Boone's been selective about the right buyer.

"Sure wish my girl could keep it."

"I wish it too, Daddy."

Mama Belle purses her lips. "A woman runnin' a farm? That's unbecomin', Emmy Lou."

Before she can politely disagree with her mama, Emmy Lou notices Boone making a tight fist. "Your hand hurting you, Daddy?"

Boone smiles, massaging his palm. "Nothin' a little Vicks can't soothe."

A flare of concern kicks up in Emmy Lou. "Mama, you know about this?"

"This man is just fine," Mama Belle's sleek drawl cuts in. "Now you're hoggin' her, Boone."

Boone chuckles. Her father's even-keeled when it comes to Mama Belle's theatrics. "I'm gonna let you women talk." His eyes take Emmy Lou in. "You stayin' here for a spell, Em Bug?"

She meets his keen gaze. "Yes, Daddy."

"I'll have Gentleman sent over."

"Thank you." Her heart warms at the offer. Gentleman's her first horse, her rodeo horse she left when she went to Nashville.

Boone rests a hand on his broad belly and looks at Belle. "An hour sound okay to you, Mama?"

"Yes, my darlin'," Mama Belle says, turning her cheek to Boone's chaste kiss. Emmy Lou hides a smile. There's no denying her parents' relationship is old-school. Southern. Chivalrous.

As Boone strides toward the Mercedes, Mama Belle drops into a porch chair, fanning herself with a well-manicured hand. "Oh, my word. I wish Hester were here to bring us some sweet tea."

Emmy Lou moves for the screen door. "You want some, Mama? I can—"

Mama Belle huffs dramatically but snatches Emmy's wrist. "No, darlin'. Sit and talk with me."

Emmy Lou sits, biting her lip. There's no telling if she's in for an ass-chewing or what. Whenever she comes back to Wildheart, she always tries to reconcile the Emmy Lou she is now to the one she used to be in her mama's presence. Prim. Proper. The perfect southern daughter who keeps her mouth shut and says *yes, ma'am*.

Mama Belle's frosty pink lips purse. "Now, you know I hate gossip of any kind . . ."

Emmy Lou keeps a straight face like the saint she is. Lord, if that's not the lie of the century. The woman could go toe-to-toe with the *Nashville Star*. In Wildheart, gossip is Mama's morning fuel, one of her daily ten commandments. Be sunny, smile, keep big hair and an even bigger mouth.

Emmy Lou was raised on small-town gossip. A bad habit she's been trying to shake ever since she left Wildheart. It did come in handy at times. Dealing with the *Star*, being able to shake off bad press like it was nothing. Talking too much like she always does, filling the space around her. She always thought if she was talking, no one was talking about her.

"I heard about you and Jace." Mama Belle lands her sentence and stares at Emmy Lou, her expression unreadable. "You left him."

She swallows. "I did."

A beat. And then Mama Belle lets out a crow of a whoop. She reaches over, her hand squeezing Emmy Lou's. "He didn't give you trouble, did he?"

"No, Mama. He didn't fight me."

Fight for me.

Mama Belle raises prayer palms to the sky. "Praise the Lord."

A numb feeling settles over Emmy Lou. She'd take Mama's disappointment any day over her ghoulish glee that they've broken up. All at once it makes sense, the reason for her mama's friendly, uncritical demeanor. It's because she's happy, so damn happy that Emmy Lou and Jace have separated.

You'd think Jace being successful, being one of the biggest country acts around, would change her mother's mind, but Mama Belle refuses to be swayed. Mama never liked the fact that Jace was a poor boy from the backwoods of Tennessee, that he wasn't born into family money and privilege and power, when the real truth was that Mama Belle didn't like Jace because he plain wasn't Slayton.

Which is why Emmy Lou loved him.

"What is important is that you're takin' a stand. That you came home to Wildheart. To your family." Mama Belle opens her Louis Vuitton and starts digging around. "I was on the phone all mornin' tellin' Ellen Sue you were back in town."

Emmy Lou sags in her chair. "Oh, Mama, why?" Any hopes of lying low are dashed.

Mama Belle looks at her like she has a rusted screw in her head. "Why, for the rodeo, darlin'." When Emmy Lou opens her mouth to protest, Mama Belle says, "You didn't think I'd let you sit here and mope all summer? Not when it's shapin' up perfectly. My daughter home, me and your daddy's anniversary party. And the divorce. We'll deal with it. Somehow. I want you to know I forgive you."

Her eyes widen. "Divorce?"

"Of course you're gettin' a divorce." Mama Belle laughs, her snow-blond beehive bobbing. "I always knew you'd see my light one of these days."

Out of Mama Belle's purse comes a thick stack of cream papers. "Now the good Lord willin' and the creek don't rise, he won't fight you. You don't have kids and God knows you don't need *his* money." Mama Belle spits it like poison. "You're a Montgomery, and we always get what we want and we get it fast. In Tennessee, the soonest you can get a divorce is sixty days after you file. However, I know a judge in Nashville who owes me a few favors."

Emmy Lou's head spins. "Mama, I—"

"Now I want this to be as easy on you as possible, sugar, so I took the liberty of fillin' out everything," Mama Belle says, placing the thick stack of papers in Emmy Lou's lap. "They're notarized and ready to go. All the heavy liftin' done. Minus the signatures, of course."

Emmy Lou's jaw drops in disbelief. Small-town southern favors are costly, and she wonders what kind of secrets Mama Belle has to move these kinds of mountains.

She stares down at the papers on her lap like they're a landmine ready to detonate. The words *Marital Dissolution Agreement* glare up at her.

Divorce.

She said it in anger. A word flung at Jace in the heat of the moment. To shake some fire into him, some fight.

But to actually do it . . . to lose friends, to divide up their farm, to break her own heart, can she? Is she strong enough? Is that what she wants?

Mama Belle's cackle sideswipes her attention. "We can sign 'em today and get a courier up to Nashville tomorrow."

Emmy Lou watches as Mama Belle unveils a pen. She takes a deep breath, fighting to control her emotions, to plaster a smile back on her face. Admitting what she'd never admit to Jace. "Mama, I ain't sure I want this at all. At least not yet."

Mama Belle arches a sharp brow, her patient tone replaced by one of annoyance. "Of course you're sure. You don't leave your husband if you ain't sure." Mama Belle waves a hand as Emmy Lou tries to hand her back the papers. "Fine, if you need to pretend to need some time, you take that time, darlin'. Just don't take too long, you hear? I need some grandbabies before I meet my maker." Before Emmy Lou can reply, Mama Belle claps her hands together. "Now let's talk about you. My perfect little rodeo queen comin' home to roost."

Emmy Lou's cheeks flush from the one source of constant praise from her mother. For as long as she can remember, she's always loved horses, always wanted to ride full-out like her rodeo brothers. But Mama Belle, Miss Fayette County 1979, forbade rough-and-tumble contact, forbade her only daughter from a sport meant for the boys, so Emmy Lou settled for the in-between. She entered the rodeo queen pageant, where there were no dangerous moves, only prancing and preening and perfecting speeches in the ring. As a child, she loved it, but over time she grew bored with perfect riding patterns and interviews about horsemanship. She wanted to compete like her brothers. She wanted to go fast and race against a timer. Get dirty and run wild and never worry about being perfect.

But it pleased Mama Belle. Pageant princess or rodeo queen, as long as Emmy Lou was waving and smiling and wearing her crown, Mama Belle didn't care what she did.

And oh boy, does Emmy Lou have crowns. Dozens of them. Age six, she took the title of Little Wrangler Princess. Age fifteen, she was crowned queen at the National High School Finals. Age seventeen, she was crowned Miss Rodeo Georgia. She became the face of Wildheart. A source of tourism, fanfare and pride. Hell, Jace wasn't the only one who signed autographs.

As queen, her win should have opened up so many opportunities in her world. She could have competed at the Miss Rodeo USA pageant, then gone on to judge or host events in cities across the country. It was her job. To represent the association, her state of Georgia, and introduce others to the sport of rodeo and her own fierce love of horses. Instead, she avoided anything and everything to do with it.

Instead, she ran.

She put her secrets behind her and ran all the way to Nashville, and a year later, she met Jace. Fell in love. Got married.

Got divorced . . .

"The rodeo is in six weeks and I want you to have a part, Emmaline."

Emmy Lou drags herself out of the daze of morose memories. She turns her attention back to her mother. As chair of the rodeo, it makes sense Mama Belle would want to use her to boost ticket sales.

"Sure, Mama." She licks dry lips. "Whatever you want. I can tear tickets or—"

"Nonsense. I want you to ride, darlin.'"

"Ride?"

"You know what I mean. I want you to smile and look pretty and wave. Not ride-ride, Emmaline. My goodness."

Her nerves flare violently, and her hands tremble. "Mama, I haven't been in the arena since—"

"Since the night you broke up with Slayton? Yes, I remember." Mama Belle presses a hand to her heart, pained. "That is a sore subject, Emmy Lou, and I do not thank you for the reminder."

"Yes, Mama."

Emmy Lou closes her eyes, wanting to stop the conversation before it happens. Wanting to keep the past, her ex-boyfriend, at bay. But Mama Belle leans forward, her gaze burning a hole in Emmy Lou. The conversation is always a point of contention, always one of Mama's favorite bones to pick. To gnaw on over and over again.

"You know I still don't understand what happened. You and Slayton were like two peas in a pod." Mama Belle *tsks*. "Our families were best friends. The Holts still say it's a big family shame y'all broke up."

"Yes, Mama."

"He's a good man, Emmy Lou. A successful man, too. Even with his divorce last year, he's still a mighty fine catch . . ."

Mama Belle goes off on her tear, and Emmy Lou tunes out. She keeps her eyes on the old oak tree she and Jace were married under, keeps her mouth shut. Even though she wants to scream. Even though she remembers everything.

In that moment, memories fade in and out like bright bursts of television static. Slayton. Best friends first, then her boyfriend all through high school. They were inseparable. Homecoming king and queen. Football player. Cheerleader. They both planned to go to the University of Georgia, had their life planned out: a porch swing, two dogs and a couple of kids. She and Slayton were the teenage dream, and she bet it all on him.

Her heart. Her future.

And then she ran. It was the only thing she knew how to do. She survived the past. She *made* herself survive.

But now, miles from Nashville, Jace in her taillights, the past descending like a dark cloud, she's not so sure. She doesn't know what she was thinking coming back here. All her secrets, secrets she's kept from Jace, from her own family, claw at the surface of the clean slate she's tried to keep.

"That poor man's stayed away from Wildheart all these years," Mama Belle continues, in a heartsick syrupy tone, taking Emmy Lou's attention. "He's heartbroken, Emmy Lou. Just heartbroken. What you did to him . . ."

Emmy Lou bristles. What *she* did to *him*?

How about what he did to her? What about the night of the rodeo, the night she won the crown, the night she never knew would be her last night in the ring? What about when she moved to Nashville? All those letters he wrote her, long missives, apologies in one breath, threats in the other, proclaiming that Emmy Lou was still his. That he'd find her one day. That he'd make her pay for leaving him.

"You should have been the Holts' daughter-in-law, not that mousy woman he married from the city . . ."

Emmy Lou screws her eyes shut. Her mother's words are like machine-gun fire, shooting up her heart, her soul. She knows. She knows. She knows everyone was so damn heartbroken they broke up. She was to blame. It was her fault. She ruined everything.

"We just loved y'all together, Emmy Lou—"

"Mama."

"Slayton's divorced. You're divorced. The proper thing to do—"

"Mama, stop!" she snaps, her voice echoing in the high beams of the porch.

Her mother frowns at the overly loud breach of etiquette. "Emmaline Louise, what on earth has got you in a tiff?"

"Nothin'." She swallows, plastering on a sunshine smile. "I'll do the rodeo. Okay? Just stop talkin' about Slayton. Please, Mama."

Her mother stares unflinchingly at her. "And then you'll lose the dead weight, won't you, Emmy Lou?" She looks down pointedly at the divorce papers still sitting on Emmy Lou's lap. She hands over a pen. "Just sign 'em, sugar. See how you feel."

Numbly, Emmy Lou takes the pen. It feels like a lead weight between her fingers. But it's nothing compared to how she feels—her day, her emotions firebombed by her mother.

All she wants is to get Slayton out of her head. His voice. His face. His hands. All over her.

All she wants is Mama Belle to let it go, to drop the subject of Slayton, of a past she thought she had outrun.

Anything to get Mama Belle gone.

So she does. She signs them.

An hour of tedious conversation later, Emmy Lou trudges inside the house and into the kitchen. The smell of burnt coffee chokes the air. The afternoon sun sifts through the window blinds.

Batter-covered bowls and empty beer cans scattered across the countertop.

With a sigh, Emmy Lou evaluates the mess and tilts her head back to stare at the ceiling. She's spent from her conversation with Mama Belle. Her mind, her emotions, feel put through a meat grinder. Hell, what did she just agree to? Planning the rodeo? Parading around like a pageant princess? Dredging up bad memories she'd rather keep in a lockbox?

And worse—she signed divorce papers?

Lord almighty, she's losing her damn mind.

Mama Belle took the papers with her, claiming she'd hold on to them until Emmy Lou was ready. But will she ever be ready? Talking about divorce is one thing, but to actually go through with it, to have that power to end things . . .

It scares her.

At least her mama's off her back. Happy that she's ending things with Jace. But the thought doesn't soothe her. In fact, it makes Emmy Lou feel worse.

It makes her feel guilty.

It makes her feel like she's betrayed Jace somehow.

For as long as she's been married to Jace, it's been the bane of her existence.

Never being able to strike the right balance between defending Jace and making Mama Belle happy. She'll never get it right. Being a loyal wife or a good southern daughter. Usually she ends up failing at both.

She scowls at her fool emotions. Why is she getting sentimental over Jace? Mama Belle's right. She should divorce him. All he's ever done is lie to her.

She makes her way across the kitchen, heading to the refrigerator for a glass of sweet tea. Herky-jerky thoughts swirl around in her mind as she stares into the void of fluorescent light.

Foolishly, she thought coming back to Wildheart would have all her answers. If nothing else, have her seeing her life clearly. But what even was her life? A cold bed with Jace? Cooking food he doesn't eat? An empty house when he was on tour? Never being asked to go along with him? At least not for the last three years.

Steeling her resolve, Emmy Lou pours herself a glass of tea. She's doing the right thing by leaving Jace. She is. It's not running away. It's . . . it's finding herself. She's a woman who has needs, who lost herself a long time ago, and neither Jace nor anyone else can help her find it.

A squeaky floorboard behind her.

She shuts the fridge and turns.

Standing in the living room in jeans and a black T-shirt, looking for all the world like some heartbroken, shamefaced cowboy, is Jace, a canvas duffel bag in his hands.

She blinks in surprise. The sight doesn't compute.

Jace in Wildheart.

He followed her. To their house. The thought has fangs, has fluttery feelings, but she shakes her head violently to get rid of them.

Strike that. *Her house.*

"Em." Jace's husky voice washes over her like a calming breeze.

Her toes curl.

Then her spine stiffens and she refocuses on the man in front of her.

She props a hand on her hip, a jolt of irritation zipping through her. "What on God's green earth are you doin' here?"

He takes a step forward into the kitchen. Face contrite, he removes his cowboy hat to drag a hand through his rusty-brown hair. "I came to talk to you, Em. I came to bring you home."

"Apparently you had mud in your ears because I don't want to fix a thing." She takes a big gulp of sweet tea, sets the glass on the counter so she doesn't hurl it at him. "I am happy here and I am stayin'. So leave. Now."

"No."

Emmy Lou goes hot. Then cold. Jace's voice is so sure, so strong, it's as if it'd take a bulldozer to move him out.

"I know you're pissed at me, but—"

"Oh, I am beyond pissed."

"I ain't leavin', honey. That's how we got into this mess in the first place." He sets his bag down. "It's my fault, I'll admit it, but we ain't endin' like this."

She moves around the kitchen counter, keeping a safe distance between them, her hackles rising. "Do I need to call my brothers and have them move your ass out? Or better yet, call Sheriff Porter and have you arrested for trespassin'?"

Jace crosses his arms. A smile tugs at his lips, one that used to drive her crazy; now all it does is piss her off. "I don't know, Emmy Lou." He takes a step into the kitchen and shrugs. "Could be trouble gettin' the cops involved. *Star* might find out and then how would it look for the Brothers Kincaid?"

Her jaw drops at his bluff. At how damn right he is. She narrows her eyes. "That is a damn dirty card, Jace Taylor."

Jace stares her down, no shame in his game. "We own the house, Em. It's ours. And I ain't leavin.'"

Emmy Lou tries to ignore the faint flutter of her heart. The way her brain turns off completely. It's the most fight she's seen in Jace in ages.

"Fine." Anger simmering, she tosses her hair. Getting the cops down here, the press, Jace ain't worth the trouble. "You can stay. In the basement."

His mouth forms a tight line at the demand. But he doesn't argue. "Works for me."

"And I ain't cookin' for you."

His throat bobs. "I'll cook for myself."

She snorts. "Please. You couldn't find a kernel of corn in a cob."

Jace pushes himself forward, his hazel eyes pinned to her. Locked.

Emmy Lou's heart leaps into her throat. She's not ready for this. She should hurl a glass, a muffin, a shoe. Oh Lord, where's that champagne bottle? Anything to avoid close confines with Jace Taylor, to keep that gulf of distance. Because Jace closing in on her, getting too close to her body, those deep hazel eyes on her, has her wanting to forget what an ass he's been the last few years and forgive.

She can't back down. She's still so damn mad at him. But one fact she can't ignore—he's here.

For her.

As Jace gets closer, her gaze slides to his hands. Big broad hands that plucked a bass string better than anyone, that plucked her and made her hum better than anyone. Hands that brought her wildflowers when they first met. Hands that roped their horses, once upon a time roped her.

Hands that brace the counter to steady himself.

Jace halts in his tracks. His expression flattens. "Where's your ring?"

"I took it off," she says evenly.

"Christ." He stares down at her bare ring finger, then lifts devastated eyes to her face. "Tell me you ain't filed already."

Her stomach twists, thinking of the divorce papers Mama Belle packed away. "What if I have?" She tips up her chin, trying to ignore the lick of guilt rushing down her spine.

"It's been one goddamn day, Emmy Lou." His voice comes choked. His handsome face drawn in anger, in confusion.

"I'm takin' responsibility for us. That's somethin' you should appreciate."

He winces.

"Get it through your thick, stubborn head. I don't want you, Jace. Not anymore."

He draws himself up and Emmy Lou takes a step backward at the raw anger flashing in his eyes. "I'm stayin' for the summer. Six weeks. Give me that. And after . . ." He swallows. "After that, if you still don't want to make it work, if you don't love me," he says, and all the air leaves her, "then tell me. Better yet . . ." A muscle clenches in his square jaw. "Serve me papers and I'll sign 'em. No questions asked. Until then I ain't goin' anywhere without you."

Her stomach bottoms out and she stamps her foot,

desperation working its way through her. She hates that she's stuck here with Jace. Hates the small thread of a thrill that goes through her at his words. Hates herself for hoping.

Ninety percent of her heart and soul is certain a divorce is the answer. Jace staying—it's pointless.

What're they going to do? Kiss and make up?

It's too late.

It is.

And yet . . . there's still ten percent of her that holds out hope. A slim possibility they could make it work. A loss she doesn't know if she wants yet.

One thing's for sure—he's gotta work for it. If he thinks he can just waltz back into her life, he's got another thing coming.

Emmy Lou sniffs. "Fine. Six weeks. No promises." She crosses her arms. "But I'm doin' what I want, Jace. Since you did for so many years."

He flinches.

Quiet enters his eyes. A quietness she's familiar with. A shutting down.

He turns away from her, toward the basement.

The summer, she thinks resolutely.

She'll give him the summer.

One last chance.

SEVEN

J ACE TRUDGES UP THE STAIRS, A PITIFUL BAG OF GROCERIES in his arms. After being banished by Emmy Lou to the basement, he spent the afternoon at the local convenience store stocking up on prime bachelor food like Dinty Moore Stew, Spam, and sixers of PBR. Now, he's headed to the kitchen, tortured by the delicious smells that waft down the hall.

He's unsure how he'll be received. Hell, Emmy Lou said she wasn't going to cook for him, but she said nothing about him using the kitchen. He can't stay in the basement forever, can he?

Yes, he thinks. *To Emmy Lou, the answer is probably yes.*

His wife's made it clear she doesn't want to tolerate six minutes alone with him, let alone six weeks. Still, he's ain't backing down. He's gonna take it all. Every uncomfortable thing she wants to dish out.

Like sleeping in the basement.

She gave him the summer. A slim possibility, but still, it's enough for Jace. A small glimmer of hope that he can make this right. That he can convince Emmy Lou to change her mind about the divorce and give him one more shot.

As he passes through the house, his eyes rove the Happy Hideaway. Creaky hardwood floors. The spiral staircase. Down the length of narrow hallway, wedding photos. The piano, his banjo, an old bass sit in the living room, the instruments covered in dust.

Too long since he's been back here.

Jace takes a bracing breath and enters the kitchen. Instantly, he's hit by the warm aromatic scents of herbs and spices.

Emmy Lou's at the island grating a brick of cheddar cheese into a casserole dish. A glass of white wine to her left. A knife to her right. She doesn't look up when he enters, telling him she's lost in thought.

Or more apt, in Emmy Lou's case, working off some nervous energy. Her stress relief—baking.

Not that he'd ever complain.

His wife's a fantastic southern cook. As a kid, he never had a full supper table. Early on in his career, busking with the Brothers Kincaid meant greasy takeout, bags of chips for lunch, ramen for dinner. He loved coming home after a long day and having a home-cooked meal, a conversation with his wife. Emmy Lou's place isn't in the kitchen, hell no, and he'd be more than happy to slap together a sandwich, but she cooks because she loves to do it. It's how she showed she cared, how she showed him that she loved him.

Just another damn thing he took for granted.

Emmy Lou's brown eyes lift his way, her pretty face adopting a lemon-sour pucker when she realizes he's staring.

Great. This should be fun. Jace eyes the knife. Or dangerous.

"Sorry," he mumbles, shifting the bag in his arm. "I just need to stick some things in the fridge."

Emmy Lou stares daggers at him. And why wouldn't she? All he's done is fuck up her life. Disappoint her. Now he's here, in her space. But she says nothing, instead turning her gaze to the window. The early-evening sun is a bright blaze through the sheer curtains, the entire kitchen sticky with humidity even with the loud blast of the air conditioner.

He pauses at the island, dropping bananas in the fruit bowl. Unable to help it, he glances at her bare ring finger. The atom bomb that nearly lit his heart on fire. Christ. Seeing all the what-ifs in the divorce playbook—it stung like hell.

With everything in him, it's not what he wants.

Sure, he didn't expect Emmy Lou to roll out the welcome

mat, but he thought he'd at least have a chance to talk to her before she made any decisions. But no. That woman's pissed as hell.

Beautiful, too.

He can't help but notice how goddamn good she looks, standing at the counter looking like forbidden fruit. Her tight blue jeans and little white tank top cling to her hourglass figure. Her icy white-blond hair is disheveled in an adorably bedhead type of way. There's a light dusting of dirt across her cheek. Earlier today, Jace watched as she spent the entire afternoon readying the farm for the horses.

He stares at her lips. Her pink cupid's bow pulled into a pretty pout.

"Stop."

He blinks himself out of his horndog daze. "Stop what?"

"Lookin' at me like"—she swirls a hand around him, makes a face—"that."

He heads for the fridge, grimacing, aching for a blast of cold air to cool himself off. He adjusts the stiff crotch of his jeans. The last thing he needs is Emmy Lou seeing him sporting an erection the size of Texas.

When he gets to the fridge, he stops and stares at the whiteboard. At a message he wrote an eternity ago. *I love you, Em. Em, my gem.*

He can still see Emmy Lou, four years ago, dancing around barefoot in her cutoff jeans to some off-key song Jace was strumming on his banjo. It was them and the music and a couple of beers. How she crawled up on the kitchen island, crawled onto his lap, the look on her face full of wild freedom, desire, before she opened her mouth to him, opened her heart, and said *let's make a baby, let's make a family, let's make love, Jace.*

He glances back at Emmy Lou, taps the whiteboard. "I still remember this night."

An exasperated huff. "Jace. We ain't doin' this."

Jace swallows hard, trying to keep his voice calm. "Why not?"

Her gaze darts away. "Because."

Fight with me, he thinks, wanting her to show anger like she first did when he got them into this mess. In hindsight, that should have been his warning. Emmy Lou losing her fiery streak, her need to talk, giving up the fight was the nail in the coffin that was their marriage. And he's a fool for not seeing it until now.

He puts the six-pack of beer in the fridge and approaches the island. Braces his hands on the lip. "I ain't leavin, honey. I ain't leavin' till we talk."

"Oh, now you wanna talk?"

A flare of hope. "I sure damn do."

"Guess you're gonna be talkin' to the wall, then, because I wasted my last give-a-damn years ago, Jace."

"That's bullshit."

She makes a sound of contempt. "You gambled away our savings. You lied to me. Over and over again. I didn't do those things, Jace. You did."

Her accusation has his neck going hot, a flare of bitterness welling up at the past getting dragged up again. But it's her right. It's the hurt he's earned.

"I deserve that. I do. You're right," he says, pushing away his old instinct to shut down. He's going to call her bluff and not walk away. Never again. "I did that. All of it. But I fixed it. I paid it off."

"You shouldn't have been gambling in the first place," she snaps.

He stiffens at that.

The look on her face is confusion. Pain. And he knows why. Because in three long years he's never told her the whole damn story about why he gambled. He wasn't an addict; it wasn't a one-night thing that got out of control.

It was to cope.

It was because Emmy Lou was mourning the loss of Sal, trying to keep it together herself, baking enough casseroles to feed an army. He didn't want to burden her with his bullshit.

It was because of Luke. Because his best friend had tried to—

He was too late for his mother. He was almost too late for his friend.

Jace fights the memory. Luke, drinking a whole bottle of whiskey and barring the bedroom door. The rack of the shotgun. Jace and Seth bulldozing into the room in the nick of time. Seth, tackling Luke to wrench the shotgun away from him. Luke crying, crying for hours over Sal, until he finally sobered up and pulled it together.

The worst night of Jace's life.

But now. Now he's got Luke's blessing. If telling Emmy Lou will help her understand, he'll damn well do it.

"We almost lost everything, Jace."

"Yes, I know," he says, ripping a frustrated hand through his hair. "You know how I know, it's because you never stop remindin' me. Maybe that's why we can never get on with our life, because all you're doin' is livin' in the past."

Her eyes flash fire. "Oh, you're blamin' me for this?"

No. Yes.

Fuck.

This isn't what he wants to be doing. Arguing right now. What he wants is to grip Emmy Lou by the shoulders, look her in the eyes and kiss her. Hard. Desperate. Because that's what he is. A desperate man, working on a woman who means to kill him.

"I haven't forgiven you," she flings. "I need an explanation, Jace. Why you lied to me."

He snorts, resentment rising at the sting of his failure. "Hell, I'd give you one if I could get a word in edgewise. All you seem to do these days is nail me to the goddamn cross."

"You son of a bitch."

Nostrils flaring, Emmy Lou grabs the brick of cheddar cheese and flings it at him.

He ducks. It hits the wall behind him in a bright orange spatter. He straightens up, glancing over his shoulder at the mess, and then looks back at her. He grins. "You missed."

"Damn you, Jace Taylor." Emmy Lou grabs up a banana and

raises her arm, preparing to hurl it at him, but before she can, the front door crashes open.

Emmy Lou yelps at the thunderous sound, her brown eyes wide with fear.

Instinctively, Jace lunges forward, yanking her into his arms to block her with his body. His mind automatically goes to the worst. To McCade. The threat to his wife.

But it's not McCade.

It's Emmy Lou's brothers.

Charlie, Wyatt, and Grady stand tall and murderous in the living room.

Emmy Lou twists in Jace's arms. She's pressed tight against him, her small frame braced by his chest. One of his hands cups the back of her blond head like he can shield her. Every atom in his body fires at the feel of her. His girl's all warm curves and soft sweetness. The nearness of Emmy Lou has him damn near on his knees.

As if sensing his thoughts, Emmy Lou gives Jace a shove and disentangles from him. Then she narrows her eyes at her brothers. "What are y'all doin' blowin' in here like GI Joes? Y'all scared the tar outta me."

All three pairs of narrowed eyes laser in on Jace. Charlie advances, his features, his fists drawn tight. "You got some goddamn nerve showin' up here and upsettin' our sister."

Jace lifts a calm hand, unfazed. "Good to see you too, Charlie."

"Hey, man," Grady drawls, thumbs hooked in his belt loops. He gives Jace a sympathetic smile. "Emmy Lou put you through the wringer yet?"

Jace forces a shrug, trying not to let on he's damn near shitting his pants. He should have known he wouldn't make it a day without getting past her brothers. "Too soon to tell."

Wyatt's eyes move from Jace to Emmy Lou. "You okay?"

Emmy Lou smiles at her older brother real sweet. "Why, Wyatt, I am just fine." Jace sees an unsaid dialogue pass between her and Wyatt.

Kill him?

Not yet.

Then Wyatt's stomping toward Jace, his cowboy boots rattling the floorboards. His lips curled up into a smile. But there's no warmth in it. He jerks his chin at Jace as Charlie jerks open the front door. "Let's take a ride."

Fifteen minutes later, Jace is at Tiny's Tavern. Although Jace wasn't too sure he'd survive the trip to the bar. Charlie grunted at Jace as he slipped into the passenger-side seat, but aside from that no words were spoken. One of the scariest drives of his goddamn life. Part of him expected Emmy Lou's brothers to drive him out to the countryside and bury his ass in a cornfield.

Here, now, in the neon glow of the tavern, at least there are witnesses.

Charlie, Wyatt and Grady belly up to the bar. Human rifles ready for execution.

"Tequila," Wyatt tells the bartender. "Bottom shelf. Keep 'em comin'." He looks at Jace. "You're gonna drink when we tell you to drink. You're buyin' too."

Grady slides him a shot and Jace downs the white-gold liquid, breathing through the sting.

"Emmy Lou told us what happened," Charlie says sharply, his arms crossed. "What you did."

Jace smears a hand down his face.

Fuck.

He's the worst kind of man. A shithead, a coward, the biggest asshole on earth for putting his mistakes on Emmy Lou to explain. He should have been the one to do that.

"Well?" Charlie growls, his eyes boring accusing holes in Jace. "Is she wrong?"

"No," he says and meets Charlie's gaze dead-on. Years of trying to handle it himself, of covering it up so he can fix it, won't work with these guys. Part of fixing his fuckups includes being honest. Tonight, he starts.

"She's right. I was wrong. About everything. The gamblin', the lyin'. I never meant for it to get this out of hand."

Grady's quiet voice cuts in. "My sister is hurtin', man."

"I know," Jace says, taking another shot.

Charlie, stone-faced, serious, asks, "How'd this happen, Jace?"

Jace shrugs. "I'm good at rollin' dice."

Wyatt scowls at his answer. "You got some balls, Taylor."

Jace lifts his palms, exposing his chest. "If you want to hit me, free shot."

"Nah, man," Grady says, leaning over the bar to grab up a beer. "We ain't gonna hit you."

"I will." Charlie steps forward, flashing a fist so fast Jace can't even flinch. The hard punch connects with his stomach.

"Fuck," Jace wheezes and doubles over. He grimaces, squeezing his eyes shut, breathing through the pain of having his liver personally pulverized by Charlie.

"We're cool." Wyatt lifts a hand to the bar even though no one's made a move to come forward to help.

"You're fuckin' lucky Davis ain't here," Charlie snarls.

Jace grits his teeth. He knows he is. The one person who wouldn't wait for an explanation, who would kill him dead on sight, is Davis. Ford would just sit back and tell him how to cut up the body.

"Take it easy," Grady interjects, and Charlie raises an eyebrow at his youngest brother's defense of Jace. "He looks like he's been put through the wringer already." He circles a finger around Jace's fading black-and-blue eye. "Those guys who want your money do that?"

"Yeah." Jace straightens up, a hand on his ribs. "But we're square because they already got my goddamn money. Twice."

"Drink." Wyatt gestures to a shot, and Jace does.

"Is she safe, Jace?" comes Charlie's deadly quiet voice. His eyes close. A flash of fury. "I swear if somethin' happens to our sister because you—"

"She's safe," Jace reassures. "I swear it."

The most important promise he's ever made. Over his dead fucking body will he let anyone harm Emmy Lou. Thinking about what could have happened to her back in Nashville, McCade coming to the house, the fucker threatening his wife, it's enough to make him lose his sanity.

Charlie's fierce gaze evaluates him, then he nods, his tense posture relaxing. "As long as she's safe, we ain't got problems."

Wyatt snorts. "Yeah, now Em and Jace got the problems." He points to a shot that's suddenly appeared. "Drink."

Jace does, wiping his mouth on his arm.

Christ. How many is it now? It's gotta be his fourth shot of the night.

But this is what he gets. He's gonna take every last ounce of harassment and disappointment and anger Emmy Lou's brothers can dish out. He'll take it all. Stand tall. Go toe-to-toe to show them that he's serious.

"I ain't lettin' her go," Jace says wearily. "I made all the mistakes in the goddamn book." He smears his face in his hands, the truth flowing easy thanks to the alcohol. "But it ain't endin' like this. I'm stayin' for the summer. I got six weeks to convince her to come home."

Grady arches a brow. "Sounds like you're in for a whole lot of grovelin.'"

"He should be on his knees beggin' for forgiveness," Charlie snaps at Grady.

Jace nods. "You're right. Anything I gotta do, I'll do it. Make a fool of myself, bust my ass on the farm, write her a love song, I'm gonna do it all."

Grady gives him a look. "You ain't gotta share your every thought, man."

Charlie finishes his beer and evaluates Jace. "Well, we ain't gonna stop you."

"Yeah. We'll just kill you if you fuck it up." Wyatt leaps off the barstool, clapping him on the shoulder. "I like you as a brother-in-law, Jace. You piss off Mama Belle. Drink."

Jace laughs, swallows another shot, and the tension suddenly lightens around them.

Wyatt shifts, a shudder rolling through his body. "C'mon." He motions to Charlie. "All this relationship talk is givin' me hives. Let's go shoot some pool."

Jace settles on his stool, watching as Charlie and Wyatt head to the back of the bar. Grady sits beside him. Peers at him closely. "What are the odds this works? You and Emmy shackin' up, when it looks like she wants to take a fryin' pan to your face?" He shakes his head. "She's talkin' divorce, Jace."

"It's gonna work out," Jace says tiredly. "I ain't proud of how I acted, but I ain't givin' up. I ain't losin' her." He shrugs and gives Grady a cocky grin. "It's a flawless plan. Winnin' Emmy Lou back."

"Right." Grady rolls his eyes. "Nothin' could go wrong with you livin' at the house for six damn weeks except she realizes she's really fuckin' sick of you. Drink."

Jace chuckles despite his situation. While he likes all of Emmy Lou's brothers, Grady is more like a best friend than a brother-in-law.

They sit there in silence amid the chaos of the bar, beer glasses clinking, pool balls rattling in pockets.

Finally, it's Grady who breaks the silence.

"Six weeks is a long time to be away from the Brothers Kincaid. Might get rusty."

Jace grins, seeing what Grady's after. The kid's a fool for the music. The first time Grady met Luke, Jace thought the kid would stroke right out. Now, he's trying to get his own star off the ground, with a little help from the Brothers Kincaid. It's not a handout or riding coattails—the kid can sing, and he's willing to work hard for it, fight his way up in the industry, a fact Luke and Jace appreciate.

Jace lifts a brow. "What're you thinkin'?"

"We could play here." Grady's eyes move to a small stage in the corner of the bar. "Got live music every night."

"I'd be down with that." He nods at Grady. "You ready for Nashville?"

"End of summer. I'm hopin' everything still works out with CMI."

Another pang of worry. Another life he could have ruined with his damn mistakes.

"You set it up," Jace says. It's the least he can do for the kid. "I'll play."

Grady grins, his brown eyes lighting up. "Cool. Drink."

"Everything's gonna work out," Jace says, leaning back on his stool and letting the alcohol work its magic. Letting confidence take over doubt. "You'll see."

"I know it." Grady's brow wrinkles. "Just . . . do me a favor, will ya?"

"Name it."

"Don't hurt my sister, Jace."

"I won't."

His stomach twists. Alcohol or Charlie's slug in the gut.

But he doesn't think it's either of those.

It's guilt.

Goddamn guilt. Hell, he doesn't know how to feel anything else anymore.

All he knows is that this summer is the scariest gamble he's ever made. Because he's got everything to lose.

Including Emmy Lou.

For the third time tonight, Emmy Lou crosses her bedroom floor and goes to the window. She's looking for Jace, for her brothers. It's nearly eleven. They've been gone hours, the sun long since set, the moon high in the pitch-black sky. Not that she's worried about them. Or about Jace.

She couldn't care less what they do to him.

She smiles slightly, remembering the look on Jace's face. The cool panic that set in as her brothers stormed through the front door like a trio of heathens hellbent on personally destroying her husband.

They wouldn't hurt him. Would they?

She swallows the lump in her throat, shakes off the thought, and pulls her lavender robe tighter around her.

So what? Jace deserves it. Not a body-in-a-shallow-grave type of way, but more of a leave-him-high-and-dry-on-the-side-of-the-road kind of thing.

Breathing. That's all she asks.

That's when she spies it. Headlights coming down the snaky trail of road. The orange pickup stops at the gates, pauses, and then resumes its course for the house.

Emmy Lou leaves the bedroom and descends the stairs.

She's entering the living room right when the front door blasts open. Bright, bursting laughter fills the house. Grady, already inside, floats her an apologetic smile. "We kinda got carried away."

Emmy Lou narrows her eyes.

"What are you talk—"

Her eyes flash wide as Wyatt and Charlie, wearing shit-eating grins, fill the doorway of the front door. Their tall frames swaying, buckled down from holding Jace up.

Jace grins at her as he stumbles in. His russet hair stands on end, his hazel eyes bright and unfocused. "Hey, Emmy Lou, howdy do?"

Emmy Lou gasps and steps forward. "Oh my word." She scowls at Wyatt, no doubt the one who got Jace into this mess. "What did y'all do to my husband?"

"Ex-husband," Grady adds with a smirk and Emmy Lou deepens her scowl.

Charlie grunts brusquely. "Ain't our fault he can't hold his liquor."

"You lie, man, you lie," Jace drawls, waving Charlie off.

"It most definitely is your fault," Emmy Lou hisses, her gaze flitting between Jace and Charlie. "You got him drunk."

"I don't know what you're talkin' about." Wyatt's expression is angelic. "Jace volunteered his liver to us tonight."

She sniffs, wrinkling her nose. "Good Lord, Wyatt, you drink up all of the tavern?"

Wyatt flashes a goofy smile. "Just about."

"Where do you want him?" Grady asks.

"Basement." Emmy Lou eyes Jace warily. He sways on his feet, propped up against her older brothers. "Before he barfs."

Wyatt scoffs. "We're sure as shit not carrying his dead-ass weight down there."

Charlie ambles forward, an arm around Jace. "He's your problem now."

Emmy Lou gapes at them. Her lot of fool-headed brothers. She'd like to wring their necks. "Y'all are unbelievable."

Grady steps around her, a grin on his face. "Hey, ol' Wyatt wanted to leave him in the river. You're lucky I brought him back."

Then with a smooth flourish, Charlie and Wyatt haul Jace under the arms to dump him on the sofa. Jace laughs and then groans, rolling over into the pillows like a hound dog readying himself to get comfortable.

Wyatt flips a wave, locks his steel-blue eyes on hers. "See ya tomorrow, Em." Then he and Charlie barrel out the front door, slapping shoulders, guffawing.

Grady, pushing off the wall for the door, nods at Jace. "You okay with him here?"

She eyes Jace warily. "I might wake up and choose violence tomorrow mornin', but tonight, I will play nice."

A honk from outside.

"Remember this," Emmy Lou warns, sticking a finger in Grady's face. "When y'all are married, I am gonna pay you back so damn hard you'll be eatin' crow till the end of your days."

Grady sidesteps her, laughing. "Married? Never heard of it."

And then he's gone. The door shut. Jace and Emmy Lou left alone.

She whirls around, taking in the slumped-over man with his head in his hands. She stalks toward him, touching his shoulder, pressing him roughly onto the couch. "Go to bed, Jace."

He makes a grab for her, fumbles, but catches her wrist. He lifts his face, his gaze drifting up her body with a heated intensity. "Em."

Her spine stiffens. Her body painfully aware of the sensation of his skin on hers. Pressed together. Hot. It's too much.

"Good night." She gives her arm a rough wrench and turns away from him.

A groan from Jace.

She stops in the hallway, listening. Another groan. One of drunken agony.

Emmy Lou stands there cursing her brothers, cursing Jace. Bastards. All of them. Dumping some drunk-ass man on her doorstep. But not just any drunk-ass man. Her husband.

Ex-husband.

Almost ex-husband.

She lets out a growl and storms for the stairs. No. Absolutely not. She ain't takin' care of Jace Taylor. Who cares that he sounds as miserable as a dying dog? That he could upchuck the entire contents of his stomach and sleep in the sick.

Another groan from downstairs. A thump.

She freezes on the sixth step. Her nails grip the banister so tight they could be claws, they could shred wood. Her heart twinges. Twists.

"Ugh," she groans, hating herself. She turns and descends quickly, unable to stop that ingrained urge to take care of him.

Stupid. She is a stupid, stupid sucker of a woman.

In the kitchen, she steals a cup from the cupboard and fills it with water.

One drink. Get him hydrated up and then she's gone.

In the living room, Jace sits, his face in his hands, shoulders slouched. He breathes heavily.

"Jace," Emmy Lou says softly, sitting beside him. "Drink this."

He raises his face, looking up at her with hangdog hazel eyes. He takes the glass, chugs down the water and then exhales. "Thanks." He flops back against the couch. Her gaze dips, suddenly lighting on the way his T-shirt rides up, exposing tan skin, lean, flat stomach.

A flutter sparks through Emmy Lou, and she glances away, fighting composure. Fighting good memories of her and Jace, once upon a time, napping after a show in Kalispell, waking to his heated kisses, his mouth on hers, eating her up like his last meal.

Jace digs around in his shirt pocket. Then, oblivious to her stare, he unearths a fry. He offers it to her sheepishly. "We stopped at McDonald's. You want it?"

Emmy Lou bites her lip, smothering a laugh.

"No, but thanks."

She rolls her lips together, evaluating his disheveled look. So different from the Jace Taylor she knows. Always so put together. Always so strong and emotionless. But here, tonight, he's vulnerable, silly. A lock of russet hair drops across his brow and Emmy Lou's hit by an irresistible urge to wipe it away.

His eyes clear and he tosses the fry on the coffee table. "Remind me to never go out drinkin' with your brothers again."

She purses her lips. "I'm honestly shocked they didn't kill you."

Jace hiccups. Or maybe it's a chuckle. "Me too." He tries to sit up straight, but all he accomplishes is falling back into the couch cushions. "But nah. They wouldn't do that. They're family. The only family I got."

A fist of pain burns in her chest at the rawness of his words. Family means the world to Jace. He has Luke and Seth, but no living parents, no blood.

"You got a lot of family," she says softly. "What about the Brothers Kincaid?"

"I ain't goin' back to the Brothers Kincaid," he says, and her heart instantly jolts. "Not until I have you."

The comment upends her anger. Her heart. He loves playing in the band, with his brothers. For him to give that up . . .

She shakes her head, leaning over him. She grips his broad shoulder, trying to straighten him out on the couch. "Jace, you're talkin' foolish. Luke and Seth need you."

"Nah. They don't. I'm just backup."

She winces.

She hates that he feels that way. Knows he's always been content to stay in the background. But Emmy Lou never thought that. She always believed Jace was like the very instrument he played—the bass. Essential, holding together the harmony in its own subtle way. You missed it if it wasn't there. That's what Jace was. Important. Crucial. She always saw that. And Luke and Seth did too.

"I fucked up, honey." Jace rolls his head across the back of the couch to look at her. "Your family, mine, they all fuckin' hate me. I did it to myself."

She hesitates. Pats his hand. "No one hates you, Jace." Giving in, she finally swipes the bothersome lock of hair from his brow. "You're drunk. Get some sleep. You'll see clear in the mornin'."

He looks up at her with those bright golden-green hazel eyes and her heart stutters.

"I see clear now."

He reaches up to cup her face, his tan fingers fanning out over her cheek, into her hair. He stares at her, the last three years of drought between them etched all over his face.

"Em," he whispers. "Em, Em, my gem."

Emmy Lou's mouth goes dry at Jace's age-old term of endearment. He always said she was the most precious thing he had ever found in his life. The words like some fiery missile launching straight for her heart. She needs to move, needs to get the hell away from Jace. Because all he's doing is making her see her husband. The Jace from before. Romantic. Always there. Impossible not to love.

"Stop callin' me that."

She tries to shift away, but his arm snakes around her waist, pinning her to him. He presses himself up on the couch, his body so close it's burning a bright hole of desire straight through her.

She frowns harder, forcing herself to dial up her anger, to remember every reason she's pissed off at Jace in the first place. Only she can't.

Because her husband's looking at her in a way she hasn't seen in years. How long has it been since Jace held her like this? How long has it been since she's let him?

Jace's hands slide lower. They cinch her waist, and a soft whimper parts her lips. She arches helplessly in his grasp, shocked to find that shameless lust she's always had for Jace coursing through her. The only man she's ever been with. A man who holds her so tight he could snap her in half with just one kiss.

A man who could break her heart all over again.

"You're so beautiful, Emmy Lou." He dips his brow to hers. "So damn beautiful." His husky voice, his words ruffle her hair.

She lowers her face, pulsing down below.

There's the gentlest graze of his lips on hers and then, then—

The tequila on his breath calls her back.

Reminds her of all the awful decisions she can make in one weak moment.

Emmy Lou braces a hand against his broad chest and pulls sharply away. "We can't."

Jace closes his eyes. "Em—"

With a sigh, she moves to sit on the other end of the couch so she doesn't touch him again.

"It's too late, Jace."

His expression flattens, hope fading from his eyes. "It ain't too late."

He reaches for her, still always reaching for her.

Emmy Lou stands, and Jace drops his hand.

"It is," she says fiercely, trying to ignore the way her body's revved and ready to go. What she does do is dig her nails into the palms of her hands so all she feels is pain. So all she can focus on is chasing away the raw need to go back to him, to lie in his arms and forgive him his everything. Their past. Their mistakes. Their anger.

She crosses her arms primly. "Go to sleep, Jace."

The look on his face could detonate her heart. "Emmy," he says in a strangled tone.

But she doesn't wait around to hear what he says next. She whirls on her heel and walks fast down the hall, the mad pump of her heart like a mocking sound, a reminder of what Jace Taylor's always been able to do to her.

Absolutely wreck her.

J ACE CRACKS AN EYE TO THE SOUND OF BIRDSONG, THE warmth of the sun, and then he throws an arm over his face. "Fuck."

The groan out of his mouth is guttural. Last night was extreme. Even for him. His head throbs with the force of a thousand hammers. His mouth feels like he drank up a sand dune. Christ, he hasn't been this drunk since he and Emmy Lou—

He freezes. His eyes shoot open as the memory of last night coldcocks him across the face.

He put the moves on Emmy Lou last night. He was drunk, desperate, and being around her was like cocaine. A compulsion, a habit. Like the ghosts of past Jace and Emmy Lou were there last night, hovering between them, waiting for them to come alive. He can still feel the graze of her silky lips against his. The delicate arc of her body, curving into him, her honeyed scent filling the air around him.

Devastating him.

It was enough to have Jace believing, for one long second, that they could get back to them.

Grunting, Jace sits up. He swings his legs off the couch and smears his face in his hands, willing his ever-stiffening dick to cool it.

What the hell was he doing going in hard-on blazing? Did he really think one night of drunken moves would have Emmy Lou running right back into his arms? Hell, she should have booted him out on his ass. Made him sleep on the front porch like a damn dog.

The truth is, he wasn't thinking. All he wanted to do last night was get back to him and Emmy Lou. But he didn't get far before Emmy Lou cringed, her body rejecting him like a bad kidney.

She'd made the right call. Stopping things before they got started.

Still. He rips a hand through his disheveled hair.

Fuck.

He wanted her. So damn bad.

Christ, he'd never thought he'd be pining this hard for his wife when he's goddamn married to her.

One thing he can't deny, their heat is still there. Blazing between them. He felt it last night, felt the tremble of Emmy Lou's body as he held her. A tremble that told him it's not over. She wanted him as much as he did.

Was he wrong?

Lifting his head from his hand, Jace roves his eyes around the living room. No sign of Emmy Lou.

He needs to fix this the way he always has. The right way. The responsible way. The hold-your-horses way. Get a grip on his emotions and keep them under control. Because as eager as he is to get his wife back, if he doesn't move slow, if he doesn't keep his cool, all he's gonna be is back in Nashville, alone, nursing a bottle of Jim Beam, and the memory of everything he lost.

His eyes drift to the window. To the ancient gnarled oak tree. To this day when he sees that tree, he thinks of his wedding day. Luke and Seth and Sal, young, just kids, laughing on the front lawn. He can still hear Emmy Lou whispering against his lips, "I don't care what my mama thinks. Now marry me, Jace Taylor."

And he did.

They said *I do.*

They meant it.

He still does.

"'Bout time you're up."

The flat voice drifts through his memories, and Jace turns around.

Emmy Lou's breezing through the room divider, already dressed for the day in jeans, heeled boots, and tight white T-shirt. Any ounce of sweetness he was granted last night disappeared like sugar in the lemonade.

"Hey," he says, but Emmy Lou ignores him. She heads to the window, ripping open the curtains.

He winces at the blast of bright sunlight.

She turns around, smirking at Jace's discomfort. "Serves you right for goin' out and drinkin' all night."

"Your brothers got me drunk," he says miserably.

She snorts. "Blamin' others for your problems. Same ol' Jace, ain't it?"

Damn. She's got him there.

Jace pulls himself off the couch, ready to apologize, to tell her last night was a mistake, *his* mistake, when there's a banging on the front door.

Jace winces. Even his teeth ache. "Christ, can you get that?"

Emmy Lou hits him with a ferocious glare. "Get it yourself."

It's torture dragging himself to the front door, but he manages.

He blinks. Standing outside is a FedEx delivery driver with a vase of flowers in his hands. Behind him on a small loading container—more flowers.

The driver snaps his gum. "Jace Taylor?"

Jace pinches the bridge of his nose. "That's me."

"Got a flower delivery you ordered. For a, uh, Emmy Lou Taylor."

Jace stares, trying to remember, and then grimaces at the assault of mortifying memory. Last night, speeding down the backroads with Emmy Lou's brothers, drunkenly dialing up a flower delivery service and ordering fifty bouquets of purple roses.

Fuck. Instead of drunk-dialing and ordering pizzas, he ordered flowers. Lots and lots of fucking flowers.

"Sign here."

"What—" The forms are shoved into his hands and then the flowers are bustled in bouquet after bouquet. Emmy Lou stands with her arms crossed, a deep frown on her pretty brow, and watches stone-faced as the living room is filled with a fragrant scent. Vases of purple roses on the desk. The piano. The side table. Under the coffee table.

Ten minutes later, the front door slams, the delivery guy gone.

Emmy Lou looks at Jace with an expression of annoyance. "I don't suppose you ordered these for yourself."

"No," he says, rubbing the back of his throbbing head. He plucks a long-stemmed rose from a vase and offers it to her. "These are for you."

"Huh." She tilts her head, evaluating the flower held out to her. "They look expensive. Did you and your stash pay for 'em?"

He stares, frustrated at the dig about money. It's too early—he's too hungover to fight like this. Not to mention the way Emmy Lou's looking right now. Class A top-level beautiful. His hot, gorgeous wife who he's not allowed to touch.

Damn alcohol. Damn Wyatt. Damn his dumbass self.

The glare she flings his way says flowers ain't the way to her heart, not by a long shot.

"I don't want these, Jace. Feed 'em to the horses for all I care."

Then, without another word, Emmy Lou simply turns away from him.

"Hey, where you goin'?" It's compulsion to take a step forward, to follow her, to wonder about her day. He doesn't know why. It's not like he can keep her here. Not like she owes him anything.

Her right eyebrow arches in a you-got-some-damn-nerve look. But she sighs and says, "While you're workin' off your hangover, I'm goin' ridin'."

She tosses her hair, her eyes glittery with something he can't make out. Nerves? Excitement?

"Mama asked, so . . ." A little shrug. "I'm ridin' in the rodeo."

He blinks, taking her in. Her outfit. Her posture full of sass and confidence. "Whoa, really?"

Emmy Lou often talked about her rodeo queen days, and while he's seen her in photos, all dressed up in sashes and tiaras, waving proud like some regal beauty, he's never seen her in action in the arena. Though it was her life for a long time in Wildheart, she kept the rodeo quiet, kept it close to her, without a reason as to why she gave it up.

"Yes, really." Her mouth pulls up into a wry grin. "If you want to make yourself useful, you can clean the stables. Who knows, might be good for sweatin' it out." A flick of her hand, her hair, and then she's out the door.

He hears what she's saying. Clear as day.

Shovel shit, Jace.

Summer in Georgia. It's enough to make Emmy Lou want to scream.

Same goes for Jace.

Stupid man, thinking he can charm his way back into her heart with flowers. Not that they weren't beautiful. She wants more than empty promises, money, grand gestures. She wants Jace. The man she married. The boy with wildflowers.

Emmy Lou lifts a hand to Wyatt, who stands with his own horse, and with Gentleman, a chestnut-colored quarter horse, in the pasture. Her brother already has her horse saddled.

Crossing over the gravel drive, Emmy Lou pretends not to see the horse trailer hooked up to Wyatt's pickup truck. A memory of the past, unwanted, dips its way into her mind.

Slayton, the voice whispers in her ear, but she grits her teeth. Shakes it off.

Gentleman paws the earth, nostrils flaring as he sees her approach.

Bypassing Wyatt, Emmy Lou goes straight to Gentleman.

"Oh, you sweet, beautiful boy," she croons, resting a hand on the horse's silky nose. Gentleman dips his head, until they're brow to brow. "I haven't seen you in so long. I'm sorry I've been a bad horse mama."

"How about a 'hey' for your big brother," Wyatt drawls, looking offended.

"You don't get a hey," Emmy Lou says, still caressing Gentleman. One man who doesn't aggravate her. "Not after what y'all did last night."

A snort. "He hurtin'?"

"Big-time."

Reaching out, Emmy Lou puts her left foot into the stirrup, grips the saddle horn and pulls herself up, swinging her right leg over Gentleman's back. She settles on him like they haven't been apart for years. Wyatt blinks up at her, the brim of his cowboy hat shielding his blue eyes from the sun. "Mama Belle says you're ridin' in the rodeo."

"Guess so. Gonna look pretty and wave."

Wyatt smiles crookedly and mounts his own horse. "You sound thrilled."

She shrugs and urges Gentlemen into a slow lope around the pasture. Wyatt and his horse keep pace beside her. "I mean, it's a favor to Mama. Somethin' to do this summer besides—"

"Besides play house with Jace?"

"I ain't doin' that, Wyatt." She scowls. "Wish he'd stop bein' so damn stubborn and go back to Nashville."

"You wanna know what the only true way to get rid of him is?"

"What?"

"You gotta push him off a mountain."

She laughs but rolls her eyes.

Wyatt watches for a few long minutes, then asks, "So what are you gonna do, then?"

Emmy Lou bristles. All these damn men having designs on her time.

The truth is, she doesn't know. Though she loves her little

town, it's a town of six thousand. No good shopping. No friends. Gossip reigns supreme. The doctor doubles as a vet, makes house calls. At least her finances, her career would be fine if she and Jace divorced.

But what about her heart?

"I ain't sure," she muses. "Take care of the farm. The horses."

"Sounds rivetin.'" Wyatt's quiet, and then, "But is that you, Em? You like the spotlight. Walkin' the red carpet with Jace. Goin' to shows."

She makes a sound of annoyance. "Lord, Wyatt, I'm a country girl. Whether it's farmin' or bein' fancy, I can do Wildheart just as well as Nashville."

Wyatt makes a nod of agreement, his face thoughtful. "I always thought it would be you, you know?"

"Be me what?"

"Buyin' the farm from Daddy."

Regret sparks through Emmy Lou.

She thought it would be her too.

She always planned to come back to Wildheart after that summer in Nashville, after Slayton had left, but then her life changed. She met Jace. She fell in love. She went to college. Now, with all her brothers on the ranch in Montana and Grady off to Nashville, that leaves Montgomery Farm and Stables up for grabs.

She wanted to make an offer when it first went up for sale, but then came her and Jace's money problems and she thought it best to hold off. And now, with her and Jace self-destructing, there never seems to be a right time to make the farm hers.

The clatter of the screen door brings her back from her thoughts. Jace, dressed in jeans and a white T-shirt, is hauling a bucket and trudging in the direction of the horse stalls.

"Sounds like you're goin' back to your roots."

She glances sharply at Wyatt, his words playing around in her mind. "What'd you say?"

"Get back to your roots," he says with a grin. "Wild child Emmy Lou."

She smiles, an idea coming to her. A plan.

Unstick herself.

Back to her roots.

Back to herself. Hell, she was the rodeo queen of Wildheart. If she's got it, why not flaunt it? Why not do what she always wanted to do when she lived here? Why not amp it up to a million?

She pulls back on the reins, bringing Gentleman to a stop. "Will you teach me to ride?" she asks Wyatt. A two-time world champion saddle bronc rider and rodeo trainer, Wyatt's the perfect person to teach her.

Her brother stops his own horse, his dark brows pinched together. "You know how to ride."

"Not like that. Prim and proper's borin'. I wanna ride like you and Charlie do." She wiggles her eyebrows. "Spice up my act instead of just sittin' pretty and wavin.'"

The thought excites her, has her heart swelling in her chest. She likes the thought of doing something so unlike herself.

She wants to do something she's never done before. Show Wildheart she's more than just the pretty daughter of Boone Montgomery. She ain't no housewife. No debutante doll. She wants to feel wild, reckless, alive.

The way Jace used to make her feel.

Wyatt, considering her request, nods. A devilish grin spreads across his face. "Hell yeah, I'll teach you to ride."

"You can't tell Mama."

"Fuck no. You think I want my ass in a sling?"

"Teach me somethin' dangerous."

"Danger, huh?"

She grins. "Teach me to barrel race."

She remembers trying it as a girl, wild hair flying behind her, her and Wyatt using trash cans as their targets, and right before she could mount Gentleman, right before she could take that cloverleaf pattern, being caught by Boone. Being sat down and forbidden by Mama Belle. Because she was a lady, because she was a Montgomery and she wasn't a cowboy. She wasn't wild.

Wyatt cackles. His eyes are impressed—thrilled. "Hell, who are you, Emmy Lou?"

"I am a free woman," she says with a casual toss of her hair.

Words she tries—and fails—to believe.

Anticipation coiling her stomach, Emmy Lou gives a nod and trots Gentleman around the pasture. "Let's go, then."

"If you're gonna do some danger, Em, it ain't gonna be on Gentleman." Wyatt chuckles as he and his horse circle around her. "Not on him." He points toward the horse trailer, where a big dark eye stares back at them. "On him."

chapter NINE

"**H**E DON'T LIKE ME," EMMY LOU SAYS, LOOKING doubtfully up at the steel-black stallion named Outlaw who's currently snorting and pawing in the pasture. A fitting name since he scares her and thrills her at the same time.

"He don't like anyone. That's why he's in the rodeo. So he can take out his aggression in the ring." Wyatt wipes his brow. He and Emmy Lou are sweating their asses off. They've spent the last half hour trying to get the stubborn horse saddled up. "I was plannin' to take him to Mama and Daddy's, but he's yours now."

She stares, intimidated. This isn't any old racehorse; Outlaw's a beast.

"You need someone hotheaded. Like you." Wyatt nudges Emmy Lou with his shoulder. Behind them, Gentleman watches with a saint's patience. "Well, go on. Get on 'im."

"Just like that?"

"Just like that."

"Why him again?" She swears if this is payback for tattling on him for kissing Stacey Houston in fifth grade, she'll wring his fool neck.

"Gentleman's an old softie," Wyatt says and Emmy Lou gasps in indignation. "You need a fast horse with drive. Outlaw is it. He can turn on a dime and you should see him explode out of the turns."

"Fine."

Doubtfully, she approaches the skittish horse. "Easy, boy," she says, her voice low and even. Any normal person would turn tail and run, but Emmy Lou has experience. In her years of working at the horse rehab center, she's worked with hundreds of timid horses.

"Watch out," Wyatt warns as she ventures closer. His brows bunch. "He's a kicker."

"He ain't a kicker, he's just scared," Emmy drawls. "Ain't you?"

Coming to stand on Outlaw's side, she slowly reaches out to pet his neck. Nostrils flaring, he snorts and she steps back, waiting for him to settle, clocking his emotions. The horse needs space so he feels less trapped. Something she knows all about.

Too enclosed and you panic.

You run.

"You have personal space issues too, don't you?" She smiles up at him, unoffended by Outlaw's standoffishness. She and this horse have a connection. She can feel it. Even if he is currently giving her the stink eye.

Gradually, she's able to inch closer. She picks up the reins and leads Outlaw around the pasture in a square pattern. A walk designed to put them both in an equal position of power. If she can show Outlaw they're equal, that she won't push him, she's got a chance to earn his trust.

She needs his trust. She has to make this horse her partner or it won't work.

Wyatt, settled on a fence post, shouts, "Keep a tight hold on the reins."

Emmy Lou does. Feeling eyes on her, she glances over her shoulder to see Jace watching her. He stands near the barn, a bag of feed in his hands, a baseball cap tugged low over his eyes.

Tension. Yeah, she knows all about tension.

She knows all about wanting to kiss a man and kill him at the same time.

Her stomach rolls thinking about last night. How close she and Jace came to locking lips. How Jace had her soft and helpless against his muscled body. The husky begging tone in his voice that told her how bad he wanted her. The way he called her *Em, Em, my gem.*

Stop.

Stop thinking about Jace.

So instead, she focuses on the horse and their walk. The soft quiet of Outlaw's hooves whisking over the green grass, the flick of his jet-black tail, the easy thump of her own heart, calm like it always is when she's around her horses.

"Good," Wyatt calls out after ten minutes have gone by. "Now go for a mount."

A hot wind wraps around her, smothering and humid. She hesitates, trying to read Outlaw's emotions. If the last exercise was enough to build trust between the two of them or if he's gonna toss her flat on her ass.

"Hustle," Wyatt says, snapping her back to reality. His rodeo voice is in effect. Stern. Curt. The boot camp tone he uses to train the talented young bronc riders who come to the ranch for lessons. "We ain't got all goddamn day, Emmy Lou."

Emmy grits her teeth and rolls her eyes. The only one bossier than she is is Wyatt in the ring.

Reaching up, Emmy Lou grabs the saddle horn. As she's preparing to swing her leg over the top of the horse, Outlaw rears up, whinnying, front legs thrashing the air, his dark eyes wild.

"Shit!" Wyatt swears, racing toward Emmy Lou, his arms raised, his face alarmed.

It's the last thing she sees before she loses her grip and hits the ground with a thunderous crack.

The humid afternoon air hangs thick with silence. Jace races across the field, his heart in his throat at the image of Emmy Lou crumpled motionless in the pasture.

Goddamn it.

Goddamn him.

He should have seen it coming from a mile away. The horse was antsy, wild-eyed, could crush Emmy Lou with one powerful kick. She had no business being on its back. Hell, Wyatt had no business letting her.

When Jace reaches Emmy Lou, she's coughing, pushing herself up on her palms. He drops to his knees beside her, relieved to see she's conscious. He palms her shoulder, wanting to get a better look. But she waves him off, shaking her head, her contorted expression telling him that only the air's been knocked out of her.

Outlaw, who's moved away from Emmy Lou, now munches clover in the pasture.

From the sidelines, Wyatt barks, "C'mon, get up, Em."

A hot flare of anger zips through Jace. Every muscle in his body tenses at Wyatt's cavalier attitude. Before he can stop himself, he's standing, moving for Wyatt. "What's your fuckin' problem?"

Wyatt's eyes widen at Jace's tone, then narrow. "What the hell are you talkin' about?"

"You're actin' like a goddamn maniac," Jace thunders, getting in Wyatt's face. He's heard about the guy's reputation as a rough and tough rodeo trainer, but not like this. "It's your sister," he snaps, gesturing at Emmy Lou, who's standing, her arms wrapped around herself like she can stop her insides from shaking. "Not some cowboy in the ring who can take a fall like a pro."

The hard expression on Wyatt's face clears out, like he was a thousand miles away and only now dropping back to earth. "Fuck." He exhales, looks at Emmy Lou, his blue eyes pleading. "Em, I'm sorry. I wasn't thinkin'. Are you okay?"

"I'm fine, Wyatt," she says, dusting off her hands on the thighs of her jeans. Though her face is untroubled, her voice comes out wobbly. "Got the wind knocked out of me is all."

Jace eyes her warily, clocking her for injuries. Sure, Emmy Lou's tough. But she's also tiny. She hits the ground harder than most, especially her rough-and-tumble brothers. Not to mention, she's stubborn. She's hurt, she'll hide it.

"Yeah, well, it could have been a lot worse," Jace snaps.

"Where's your helmet? What were you thinkin' gettin' on a horse like that?"

He can't help the flare of concern, of worry. He's been to enough rodeos to know what she's working on. Dangerous stunts that could get a cowboy hurt, even killed.

Emmy Lou bristles. "This ain't your business, Jace. So mind it and stop carin.'"

He stares, hurt. "I care about you, Emmy Lou. I'll always care."

"Well, don't." She runs a shaky hand through her sweaty blond hair. "You just worry about your midlife crisis and I'll worry about mine."

Jace sucks in a breath, irritation sideswiping his worry. Suddenly he's sick of it. Sick of them never talking. Of Emmy Lou putting him through the wringer, getting to have her say when he can't even get in a few words in edgewise.

He rounds on her. "Oh, okay, we're gonna go there?"

For a minute her big brown doe eyes widen in surprise. Then she scowls. "I ain't doin' this, Jace."

Wyatt whistles. Sensing a big blowout, he edges out of the way. "Listen, I'm gonna go, Em. We'll pick it up tomorrow."

They don't hear him.

Emmy Lou turns on her heel, away from Jace.

"Oh, we're doin' it," Jace says, following her. He watches as she grabs Gentleman's reins and leads him to the barrel for a drink of water. "Big surprise," he drawls, not bothering to hide his sarcasm. "I'm tryin' to talk to you and you're goin' to the horses instead." He snorts. "You love those goddamn horses more than me."

She wheels on him. Her pretty face contorts. "Don't blame the horses. You loved them too. You're just angrier than a hornet because they give me more attention than you any ol' day of the week."

His throat goes tight thinking of the few drunken nights he and Emmy Lou had late last year. But nothing passionate. Nothing like how they used to be. Crazy about each other.

"You wouldn't let me," he says. "For the last year it's been like sleepin' next to an iceberg."

She gasps. "Rude. You're a rude pig of a man."

Red-faced and shaking, Emmy Lou leads Gentleman into the stable, where she takes off his saddle and bridle. Into a stall he goes for feeding. When she goes to shut the door, she can't do it, her hands are shaking so bad.

Unable to help it, he takes a step forward. "Here, let me."

"Go away, Jace," she mutters as she wedges her body in front of him to get the lock bolted.

Jace sighs heavily. "Goddamnit, Em. You're so damn stubborn."

She hits him with a murderous glare. "I told you, I don't want your help. I don't want anything from you. This is all your fault."

Resentment boils. The cool calm he's tried so hard to keep cracks. "Hell no. You ain't allowed to give me all the blame in this."

"Oh, no?" Her eyes daggers, Emmy Lou draws herself to full height. All five foot three of her.

"If I remember right, you had just as much fault as me in our marriage fallin' apart."

Emmy Lou makes a sound that comes out as an indignant squeak. "You're outta your mind. You're the one who started this. You broke my trust, you nearly gambled away our farm. We were fine before you made all your mess, Jace."

"You wanna talk about trust," he snaps, bitter memories welling in him. "How about the fact that you never even told me you went back on birth control?"

Emmy Lou pales. Her mouth forms a tight line at the reminder. "Can you blame me?" she hisses. "Havin' a baby with you—"

He winces.

Emmy Lou snaps her mouth shut.

The memory stings.

He and Emmy Lou—they had been trying to have a baby when Jace came clean to her about the money he lost. That's when they forgot about the baby and started fighting instead. Jace was blindsided when he found out she started taking birth control without talking to him about it.

Just another nail in the coffin of their marriage.

Silence around them, the only sound Gentleman chomping on his feed.

Instead of apologizing, Emmy Lou whirls around. She pushes out of the barn and storms up the steps and into the house.

Jace hitches his thumbs in his belt loops, exhales a hard breath and follows. No way. She ain't walking away again.

When he slams into the kitchen, Emmy Lou has a cutting board and a bag of carrots. Treats for Gentleman.

He opens his mouth, determined to try again, when she says, "Vacation. Christmas. Last year." She picks up a knife. "You weren't there. You were on the phone all the time. Hidin' it."

"I was tryin' to handle it."

"You should have told me." Violently, she chops a carrot in half. "I would've been there. I could've helped you."

"Like you were there after I told you the first time?" he says, and Emmy Lou freezes. "I made a mistake, Em, but the minute I made that mistake, your walls went up. You didn't trust me. You lived next to me like a ghost, never seein' me, always cookin' or with the horses, but never with *me*, not when I needed you. All you did was run and pretend everything was okay when it got tough for us."

The words come out bitter, too bitter. It's wrong to bring up the past, but it's the truth. Jace still feels the sting from her absence. He broke her trust, he never gave her an explanation for his gambling, he knows that, but Emmy Lou turning away, shutting down on him, shutting *him* down over and over again . . . it hurt.

Her nostrils flare. "I wasn't there because you shut down."

"Because you iced me out of everything. Our bed. Makin' a baby. Goin' on the road with the band. No goddamn wonder I shut down. I don't talk because, hell, Emmy Lou, you make it goddamn hard. You make it a fuckin' chore to be honest."

Emmy Lou sucks in a harsh breath mid-chop. Her big brown eyes are wide, like a wounded animal's. Like Jace just poured all kinds of salt into their wounds. "So is that what I am?" she asks, a hitch in her voice. "A chore?"

Jace swears, angry at himself for letting their fight get this dirty.

He's so damn sick of this. Fighting for the sake of fighting because they're both too damn angry to do anything else. This is what gets them into trouble. Why they can never ever fucking fix it.

"No. You ain't a chore." He steps forward, past the island, giving Emmy Lou space so he doesn't box her in. "Honey, I'm sorry. I shouldn't have said that. Where we are now is my fault, and mine alone. But you gotta give me a chance to fix it." He tears a hand through his hair and stares at her, tortured. "I don't want to be without you, Em."

"We already are without each other, Jace." She gives a shake of her blond head and stabs a carrot. Eyes on him, she chops. "I gave you a million second chances and I don't know why you think six weeks is gonna fix all this worry and storm between us when—shit!"

The clatter of the knife on the cutting board. Emmy Lou holds her thumb to her heart, her pretty face a wince.

Jace grabs up a dishtowel and quickly crosses her way. "Let me see it," he says, cupping her hand in his. Pulling her close, he inspects the cut. Though it's shallow, blood spills over into his palm. Gently, he wraps the towel around her hand. "You okay?"

Emmy Lou looks up at him, a softness crossing her face. Then, she rips her hand out of his grip and turns away to the sink. She breathes hard, head bowed, refusing to look at him.

Jace waits for the argument to crank back up. For her to sling verbal arrows. Instead, still not looking at him, softly, so softly he strains to hear, she says, "This is why it doesn't work, Jace. Because we fight. And we get nowhere. And I'm tired of fightin.'"

When she looks up at him, Jace is taken aback to see tears in her eyes.

"Em . . ." Heart clenching, he takes a step toward her, hand outstretched. All he wants to do is touch her, hold her, take away that sad look on her face.

"I love you," Jace says, pain in his voice. He closes his eyes. Opens them. "Tell me. Tell me you don't love me."

"I never fell out of love, Jace." Her voice shakes. "I fell out of trust."

His heart squeezes at the aching truth of her words. "Then this ain't no lost cause." He grabs her hand. "This is us."

"Jace . . ." Shaking her head, Emmy Lou tears her hand from his and backs up, bracing herself against the counter. "Let's just you keep to your side of the house and I'll keep to mine." Her tone is resigned; the hunch of her shoulders tells him she's done.

Jace frowns and blows out a leaden breath. "I don't want it like that."

"I do." She hugs her bandaged hand to her heart. "Okay?"

Jace remains silent, until finally, Emmy Lou takes her carrots and walks out. A moment later, the front door slams.

A sick feeling settles in Jace's stomach. Already, he's seeing the future with his wife go up in a cloud of country dust.

He's so damn afraid that when this summer is over, he and Emmy Lou will be further apart than they've ever been.

chapter
TEN

TEN DAYS PASS.

Ten days of Emmy Lou and Jace living separate lives.

The schedule she's posted on the fridge has them using the kitchen at different hours. Most nights, she'll hear Jace creeping like a mouse back to the basement. Despite seeing each other around the farm, there's been no more conversation, no more knock-down, drag-out fights.

At least not like the last one.

Since then, she's buried herself in work around the farm.

Ten days of topping off hay boxes, watering, grooming and feeding the horses. Farm chores that leave her entire body tan and aching. Most days, she's in the pasture with Wyatt, dedicated to her horse and her training.

She's pushing it trying to ace barrel racing in less than five weeks, but she ain't a novice rider. It's a thrill of a challenge, made even tougher by Outlaw. Damn horse hasn't taken a liking to her yet. Keeps trying to buck her every chance he gets, which means the majority of her training has been spent trying to make friends with Outlaw.

Lord, how is she ever gonna do this?

The truth is, she has to. She's determined not to run away when problems are tough. Not anymore.

Emmy Lou shakes her head ruefully at Gentleman as he willingly trots across the pasture toward her. Behind him, Outlaw stands stubborn and skittish, content to be by his lonesome.

She laughs as Gentleman noses her pockets for treats. "Practice first, then food," she says, swinging herself up on his back.

Her eyes drop to the ground. She frowns.

In the long tall grass, a cigarette butt.

"What on earth . . . ," she murmurs.

A snort from Gentleman tells her to pick up the pace and ride.

She squeezes her legs, leading the horse into a lively trot. Raising her eyes, Emmy Lou scours the sky above. A strong breeze has kicked up. Dark black clouds roll in over the brilliant green hills.

As her gaze roves across the farm, it lights on Jace. He's coming around the corner of the barn, bare-chested, red-faced from the afternoon sun above. Sweat runs down him in streams, over his forehead, his biceps. She stares. Then frowns. Has he always been this muscled and stocky? This perfectly chiseled? This *fierce*?

A little laugh rolls out of her. It's a ridiculous notion. Jace working on their farm ain't nothing new.

But you haven't seen him like this, a voice says. *Hot and take charge and here for you.*

Emmy Lou growls. But the voice is right. After their big blowout, she expected him to shut down, to walk out and go back to Nashville. But he didn't. He's been here.

He stayed.

Truth is, she wouldn't have blamed him if he left.

Ever since their fight, her mind's been going round and round about what she said. She's not proud of how she acted, and knowing that she betrayed his trust as much as he did hers left her guts churning. She lobbed around words, pieces of the past, like they were grenades of pain. She wanted to hurt Jace because he had hurt her. It was cruel to say she didn't want a baby with him, to remind Jace of what they both had lost.

Hope. Love. The future.

Like always, their fight dredged up everything but resolved nothing.

Jace calling her out on her trust issues had uprooted her past and set her mind whirling to a dark place. Because she had no defense. He was right. She does run and pretend everything's okay when times get tough. It's how she was raised. Hell, she's been doing it ever since Wildheart, since Slayton. She knows if she'd only tell Jace the truth, he'd understand, but it feels too much like digging up a body, and she wants that body to stay buried.

Six feet deep.

Even so, she can't shake the memory of Jace asking if she still loves him.

That haunted look on his face that told her if she said no, it'd destroy him.

She couldn't say no. But she couldn't say yes either.

Giving him that . . . it takes a kind of trust she isn't ready for.

It's then that Gentleman comes to a standstill next to the pasture fence, sending Emmy Lou lurching forward. "Whoa," she says, unbalanced, gripping the reins to stay on. She pats his neck, then dismounts. She looks up into Gentleman's dark eyes. "What on earth's goin' on with you?"

"He's rusty."

Her hackles prickle at the pointed critique of her horse. She turns to see Jace standing there, a bag of feed in his hand.

"He ain't rusty," she says, scowling. "It's the weather." She points at a big dark storm cloud looming on the horizon. "He's nervous."

Jace raises a doubtful brow. "Well, weather or not, you gotta get back on that bronco if you're plannin' to do tricks the right way."

"I'm tryin'."

"You're scared."

"I'm never scared." Emmy Lou sniffs. "I don't know why you're hasslin' me, Jace, you don't know nothin' about ridin' in a rodeo."

"Maybe not," Jace replies easily. "But I know a rodeo. I know horses."

She stares, grudgingly giving it to him. Jace is no slouch at riding horses. He was brought up on a farm like Emmy Lou. In fact, back before the Brothers Kincaid made it big, her and Jace's hobby was traveling around, chasing the rodeo. Jace's love of horses is what drew her to him in the first place. Working at the stables in Nashville, she saw firsthand how kind and gentle he was with the hurt horses.

The way he was with her.

Gentleman nickers, trotting closer to Jace.

Traitor, Emmy Lou thinks, tugging at the reins.

But it's too late. Gentleman's pressing close to Jace and Jace reaches out with a broad hand to scratch the horse's nose.

"So how come you're doin' this?" he asks, feeding Gentleman a hunk of apple.

She sticks out her chin. "Mama Belle asked me. As a favor. Play pretty in the ring. But—"

"But you got somethin' else up your sleeve."

"Yeah," she says tartly. "I do."

He says nothing, instead only staring at her, his hazel eyes clouding with something she can't puzzle out. "It's a tight timeline. Can you do it?"

Emmy Lou's stomach goes fluttery and she shifts her gaze to Outlaw. Jace is right. She's got to get on that damn horse and if she can't . . .

"You should ride him in the field."

Emmy Lou blinks. "What?"

"Outlaw," Jace says, lifting a finger. "The next time you try for a mount, take him out into the field behind the house. You had him cornered last time. Blocked in on all sides by Wyatt's trailer and the fence." Jace jostles the bag of feed against his side, his expression thoughtful. "He don't like bein' cornered. He's just like you."

Emmy Lou stares at him, wanting anger to fill her up, only to be met with thankfulness. A quiet marveling that Jace knows her so well. She saw that same skittish fear in Outlaw but never expected anyone else would. Not to mention, she never thought about taking him out to show him greener pastures, a slice of living without confines. Something bigger than a rodeo ring. It's what she's doing here in Wildheart. Trying to find her way out in the big old universe.

Emmy Lou shrugs her shoulders. "Fine." She ain't giving Jace credit. Not by a country mile. "Maybe I will."

"If you need help . . ." His gaze meets hers, warm and hopeful. "You let me know."

"I . . ." Emmy Lou's voice is mush in her mouth, his offer knocking her off-balance.

Before she can make some semblance of a reply, the slam of a car door has both her and Jace turning.

"Shit," Jace swears, his expression suddenly darkening.

Emmy Lou lets out a yelp.

Parked in the long gravel drive is a jet-black Mercedes, and stepping out of it are Mama Belle and Boone. Boone, stone-faced, wears crisp blue jeans and a blazer. Belle's dressed in her Sunday best, frills and lace, and carries a large bag beneath her arm.

"Oh Lord, Jace," Emmy says, her nerves lit.

Today is not the day for Mama Belle and her daddy to have a run-in with her husband. She's not sure how he'll be received, not sure if they even knew he was here, especially since she threatened death upon her brothers if they so much as breathed a word that Jace was staying on the farm.

She steps toward Jace, gripping his arm as he shrugs on the blue jean shirt tucked in the back pocket of his jeans. "Not a word to Mama about me doin' tricks. You hear?"

Jace's eyes meet hers, understanding there. "I got you, Em."

Emmy Lou tries to ignore the shiver that goes down her spine at the sound of his husky voice, the strength of his reassurance. She inhales a bracing breath and draws back her shoulders.

Here comes Mama Belle.

Jace stiffens as Mama Belle and Boone stride their way. He saw the heated look Mama Belle shot Emmy Lou as she exited the car, no doubt readying for a verbal smackdown.

He chances a quick glance at his wife. Her face is panicked, her hands twisted together so tight the knuckles are white. Hell, he's damn near there himself, the tight knot of tension in his back growing bigger by the second.

Facing down Boone Montgomery is something he dreads. Not because a dressing-down is in order, but because Boone's the closest thing to a father figure he's ever had, and disappointing him cuts deep.

Not to mention, the interruption couldn't have come at a worse time. After a week of silence, of cold shoulders, of patching drywall in the basement, this is the most he and Emmy Lou have talked in days. He saw what it meant to her, being up there on Gentleman. She was having fun. She was happy.

He hasn't seen that side of his wife in a long time.

Emmy Lou steps close to him, digging her fingers into the meat of his shoulder. She's biting her lip, a nervous, adorable habit he's always loved.

"Did you tell them I was here?" Jace asks quick under his breath.

"No. Although I'm sure they've heard all about it from my loudmouth brothers." Emmy Lou runs her fingers through the wavy ends of her hair, trying to make herself look presentable for Mama Belle. "Let me handle it."

Jace hides a smile as he watches Emmy Lou plaster a sunshine-and-honey smile on her face. That's his southern belle right there. Gearing up for formalities.

"Mama," Emmy Lou drawls, extending an arm toward her mother. "What a surprise."

"Apparently, we're all full of surprises, aren't we, Emmaline?" Though Mama Belle's narrowed eyes light on Jace, they leave him just as quick, without a word of hello or an acknowledgment.

Emmy Lou flushes.

Mama Belle jostles a large bag. "I'm here for rodeo duties. I need a sign-off on these little ol' posters, darlin.'"

With a flourish, Mama Belle unveils a large poster featuring Emmy Lou's smiling face, a glittery tiara photoshopped on top of her head. WILDHEART'S RODEO QUEEN IS BACK is emblazoned across the photo in dramatic gold script.

Emmy Lou gasps and covers her eyes. "Oh, Mama, you didn't."

Jace stares at Emmy Lou's gorgeous face, pride swelling in him. He can't help himself; he reaches out to finger a glossy poster edge. "Hell, they look good, Em."

Slowly, she turns, floating him a stunned stay-out-of-this look.

Mama Belle rips the posters away from Jace.

"Can you blame me, sugar?" Mama Belle reaches out to fuss with Emmy Lou's sweaty locks. "It's time to let the town know. Our star girl is back in town. For good."

Jace ignores the pointed jab, even though he's pretty damn sure what Mama Belle is trying to tell him. Emmy Lou and him are done.

Hell no. He ain't letting her think that for a damn second.

"Hello, ma'am," Jace says, refusing to let Mama Belle ignore him.

"Jace," she sniffs, her posture as stiff as her snow-blond beehive.

"Oh, Mama, be nice." Emmy Lou's biting her lip, the tension in the air painful.

Though Mama Belle treated Jace lower than dog shit, Jace never gave a damn about that. He took her barbs on the chin, in good humor. What he gave a damn about was Emmy Lou. The sweetest girl in the world, trying so hard to play peacemaker between Mama Belle and Jace.

"Jace," a booming voice comes from behind Mama Belle.

His stomach bottoms out as Boone approaches. The man looks as tough and as rigid as he did the night Jace asked him for Emmy Lou's hand. Beside him, Emmy Lou stiffens, looking like she'll leap between them if it comes to blows.

Boone lasers his gaze on Jace and sticks out his hand. "Hello, son. It's good to see you."

Son.

The word fills Jace with relief.

Boone still calling him that is a sign he hasn't completely fucked everything up between them.

A sign Mama Belle doesn't like. The woman lets out an exasperated huff and rolls her eyes to the storming sky.

"Hello, sir. How've you been?"

As he shakes Boone's hand, it pains Jace to see how much the man has aged. Deep lines are etched across his face, his tall frame hunched a bit more every year. But he still has that stubborn fire in his eyes that will never let anyone tell him to call it quits—just like his daughter.

"Mighty busy. Mama's plannin' our anniversary party." Boone drops his voice to a conspiratorial whisper. "Don't think I'll make it out alive."

Emmy Lou giggles.

"How long has it been?" Jace asks.

"Forty years next month."

His chest tightens. This is the last place Jace wants to be. Making small talk about Boone and Belle's marriage when his own has crashed and burned.

Emmy Lou shifts her stance, her eyes suddenly dull like she's had the exact same thought. "That's amazin', Daddy."

Boone booms a laugh, his broad chest straining against the pearl-button snaps of his shirt. "Feels like an eternity."

"I heard that." Mama Belle scowls, swatting at him. "While we're on the subject of the party, Emmaline, I expect you to be there with bells on. Black tie. Ball gown. You how our family does it."

"Yes, Mama. Yes, Mama, I do."

"It will be nothin' short of spectacular. A live band. Every well-to-do family in Georgia. Caviar flown in from Russia. Not that cheap kind Colleen Thorpe served at her birthday last year, bless her heart . . ."

Jace fights to keep a straight face as Emmy Lou's laughing eyes meet his, and for just a moment, there's a snap of connection. An unconscious simpatico—they know each other better than any-one. That familiar in-cahoots feeling that hits them every holi-day, every family visit for the last ten years. Chuckling at Mama Belle's prissy antics, stealing kisses or tequila shots in the hallway before dinner, giving bolstering pep talks before one of Mama Belle's fancy dinners.

Mid-diatribe, Mama Belle freezes. Then she frowns, looking back and forth between the two of them. Not liking what she sees, she steps up as if to pull Emmy Lou aside, but she's interrupted by the chime of her cell phone. Irritation comes off her in waves as she moves away to take the call. Like if she leaves Emmy Lou and Jace alone for one minute they'll fall right back into each other's arms.

Boone wraps an arm around Emmy Lou and dips his head conspiratorially. "Never mind Mama. She's not really used to vis-its that aren't all about herself."

Emmy Lou giggles. "Daddy, you're trouble."

"What about you two?" Boone's solemn eyes tick between Emmy Lou and Jace. "How y'all gettin' on?"

A loaded question. Boone's solemn eyes say he's content to stay out of it, but if he needs to, he'll get in the thick of it.

"We're fine, Daddy." Emmy Lou crosses her arms. "I'm trainin' with Wyatt for the rodeo. And Jace . . ." She bites her lip. "Jace is . . ."

"A good man to have around," Boone finishes.

Emmy Lou's lips flatten, and Jace can't help but grin. He doesn't deserve Boone's grace, but it's still good to know that at least someone in Emmy Lou's family ain't gonna shove him in front of a tractor.

Above them, a storm cloud rumbles, threatening to unleash havoc then and there. The branches of the old oak tree rustle as the wind kicks up.

Boone looks at Jace, looks skyward. "Storm's comin'."

"Yes, sir."

"Could be a bad one." Boone sucks his lip, considering. "Now if I were you, and don't let me tell you what to do, son, but I'd think of settin' up some sandbags on that bank there." Boone points to the pond, which is set back twenty feet from the house. "Could flood."

"I reckon you're right." Jace crosses his arms. "Horses might do better in the stable so they don't get spooked."

"Mighty good idea . . ."

And just like that the two men lapse into a tedious conversation about last summer's tropical storm that has Emmy Lou's eyes glazing over in boredom until a shrill screech brings the conversation to a halt.

All three of them glance over to see Mama Belle clutching the phone to her ear, saying, "No, this can't be. Lord Jesus, it absolutely cannot."

Emmy Lou takes a step forward, her brow furrowed. "Mama?"

Eyes wild, Mama Belle hangs up and turns to her audience, her gaze on Boone. "Hollis Grainger canceled on us!"

Jace arches an eyebrow at the familiar name. Hollis Granger is a rough-and-tumble country singer who came up fast in Nashville on one eye roll–worthy hit song about roping women just like he roped his horses.

"He can't do that," Emmy Lou huffs, hands fisted at her hips. "Can he?"

"They said somethin' about needin' time off to take care of personal issues."

Jace snorts. Probably more like rehab, but he'd never say that to Mama Belle.

"Oh Lord, Boone, what're we gonna do?" Mama Belle moans. "How on earth can we get someone else on this short of notice? It's Labor Day weekend." She presses a hand to her brow. "I can just hear Ellen Sue tellin' everyone in town about how the Montgomerys can't get their act together. We'll be laughingstocks!"

Boone's weathered face is creased. "Now, I ain't too sure about that, Mama. But it hurts us. That's for sure. Sponsors won't be too happy. If they pull out . . . we lose the money we invested. And with the farm up for sale . . ."

A pang of worry hits Jace. He can tell by the tight tone in the old man's voice that this matters. It matters a whole damn lot. Probably more than he's letting on to his wife and daughter.

"Oh, Daddy," Emmy says, clutching her father's arm, her pretty face pained.

Jace knows the annual rodeo is the main source of income, of jobs for Wildheart. If the acts fall through, if the sponsors bail, that doesn't look good for the town or the Montgomerys. And that's when it hits him. Jace can help them out.

For once, he can fucking fix something.

"Excuse me, sir," Jace says, meeting Boone's eyes. "I ain't sure if you'll be receptive, but if you're in a tight spot, the Brothers Kincaid would be happy to step in."

Emmy Lou's eyes widen at Jace's offer.

Boone chews on it for a second and then slowly nods. "That sure would get us out of a pickle." He turns to his wife. "Mama, what do you think?"

Mama Belle's mouth twists up. She hates the idea. Still, she needs it. Mouth pursed, she fixes those steely eyes on Jace. "Jace."

"Yes, ma'am?"

"Will Luke Kincaid be there?"

Jace sure as hell hopes so. He's committing the band without talking to them, but it's something he has to do. It's the right risk to take.

"Yes, ma'am."

"Well, in that case it'll do." Her smile is brittle. "We need a family man around."

The light dig pits his stomach.

Mama Belle pats her beehive and looks at Emmy Lou. "Next Tuesday, then. Be at the arena for rehearsal." She turns a scornful eye Jace's way. "I guess you'll be there too."

Boone shakes Jace's hand. "You're good people, Jace. We

might not be family for much longer, but the fact that you're willing to help us out says a lot."

Jace's heart twists at the words. "You're welcome, sir. Happy to help."

Boone wraps an arm around Mama Belle. "C'mon, Mama, let's git and leave these kids be."

"How on earth does somethin' like this happen? You know I still remember when the Judds played back in ninety-one..." Mama Belle waxes reminiscent as Boone leads her to the car.

Jace and Emmy Lou stand there, watching as they disappear down the long drive. A clap of thunder has Emmy Lou jumping. Then she wheels around, eyes blazing. "You better not let my daddy down, Jace."

Her hard glare has his stomach bottoming out.

As Emmy Lou storms off toward the house, Jace tilts his face to the ever-darkening sky and sighs. What in the hell did he get himself into now?

chapter

ELEVEN

EMMY LOU STANDS IN THE KITCHEN, READY TO RUSTLE up dinner. Outside, the rain's coming down in sheets. She had gotten the horses situated safe in the stables while Jace sandbagged the pond right before the sky opened up and the clouds let loose. Even though it's barely seven o'clock, it's dark as ink. Tornado warnings play on the small radio by the bread box. Thunder rumbles. The old house creaks from the force of the wind.

Emmy Lou goes to the fridge and opens it, blankly staring into the fluorescent light. Though the fridge is stocked with food, she can't find a damn thing to eat. She's irked by the weather. Irked by Jace. Stepping in to help like some big hero of the day. Not only are they living in the same house, now they're working together on the rodeo. She wrinkles her nose at Jace's sad package of bologna. And what was he doing playing nice with Mama? Sounding so gentlemanly, so cowboy he might as well have been tipping a hat.

Emmy growls in frustration and grabs a bowl of eggs. She shuts the fridge and drifts to the counter. She'll bake. Frustration cookies. Work off some of this restless energy that's building.

As angry as she is about Jace, she can't deny that he got her family out of a tight place by offering up the Brothers Kincaid to play at the rodeo. Today, he helped her out. Helped her family. Without being asked. That was a glimpse of the Jace she knows. Always willing to lend a hand, so damn loyal it steals your breath.

Emmy Lou, cracking an egg, catches sight of Jace in the hall. She hears his low, rough voice chatting up Luke. He's pacing, which means he's nervous. Which means he's trying to fix something. A small smile curves her lips. That's Jace. Always a fixer. Jaw clenched, his attention focused and laser-sharp.

He glances up, his gaze softly brushing hers, and then he's turning away, moving toward the back living room.

"Stop," Emmy Lou mutters to herself, hating the warmth that's sparked through her. "You're divorcin' the man, not daydreamin' about him."

Is she, though?

Uncertainty swirls over her like a fog. A week ago, she was so damn angry, and she still is, but . . .

She shakes her head, chasing away her indecision. It's been three years of bad. They can't come back from this, from what's been broken.

Not anymore.

She tosses the eggshells into the trash. At the sink, she washes away sticky egg white. As the water runs warm over her hands, she peers out the window streaked with rain.

What Emmy Lou sees has her heart dropping into her toes.

The door to the barn is open. Outlaw and Gentleman are bolting sideways into the front yard.

Her mind spins. How'd those fool horses get out? She locked the stable door. She's positive.

Without thinking, Emmy Lou breaks into a run, rushing out the front door and down the porch stairs into the blackened night. Humidity, ozone choke her throat. Bullets of rain pelt her as she desperately scours the yard for the horses. She curses herself for not shutting them in better. They're terrified, spooked, and if they run into traffic, get impaled by debris . . .

Safe. Safe. She's gotta get these horses safe.

"Gentleman," she shouts, frantic.

Emmy Lou starts across the yard. Her eyes narrow, adjust to the night's dimness. The gnarled oak tree she and Jace were married under looks like a monster, its limbs unnaturally twisted, giant branches trembling. Water pools on the ground, soaking the soles of her thin tennis shoes. It's like the sky's suddenly turned into a faucet, the downpour of wind and rain deafening.

She's nearly to the pond when she hears a snort. She whips her head to the right. Gentleman thunders past her, eyes wild. She starts, reaching for him, but thunder claps across the sky, spooking Gentleman and sending him racing.

Fear tightens her gut.

Before she can go after him, a terrible wind batters Emmy Lou, knocking her off her feet. She screams, but it's lost in the howl of the night. For a few long seconds, she lies there in the mud on sopping wet earth, blinking away blackness, fighting the roar in her ears.

And then she sees them.

Footprints, illuminated in a bright bolt of lightning, sunk deep into the muddy ground. Making a path from the road to the stables.

A whinny from Outlaw jerks her back to the present. He's standing near the pasture gate. Unsettled by a thunder clap, he stamps his hooves, his eyes rolling wildly.

In an instant, Emmy Lou's on her feet, slipping over the mud and rushing for him.

She's gonna save that damn horse.

Even if it's the death of her.

Jace presses the phone tight against his ear, trying to hear over the din of the storm outside. The rain sounds as if it's kicking and screaming to get inside to take shelter of its own. He's just explained the situation with Boone and the rodeo to Luke, and now he waits on word from his best friend.

"I know it's a hassle," Jace says, pacing in the living room. Over the line he hears a baby crying, Cash, and then Sal's murmured whisper. "Goin' from a Vegas residency to playin' in Wildheart..."

Luke's quiet for a long second, then he says, "Nah, man. We

ain't never too big for somethin' like that. If your family's in trouble, we'll be there."

Jace exhales in relief, scrubbing a hand over the grit on his jaw.

"Thanks. I appreciate you doin' this. God knows you don't owe me shit."

"I got a personal investment in you and Emmy Lou." Luke laughs. "Y'all are my best friends. I ain't got no problem helpin' you out, Jace. Scorin' you points with Em won't hurt either."

Jace grins at the shared connection he and Luke have. Both of them meeting Sal and Emmy Lou around the same time. He swears he doesn't know how they got the band off the ground, both of them tripping over their own feet to get those girls.

A clap of thunder has Jace swearing. He's itching to get out there and check out the farm. The horses are probably spooked as hell.

"Shit." Luke chuckles over the phone. "I can hear that over here."

"Damn near biblical out there." Jace raises his eyes to the ceiling. The old floors creak as the house shakes from the wind.

"Speakin' of Emmy Lou," Luke says, "any chance of workin' things out?"

"I got no damn idea." Jace shuffles down the hall, pausing once to check in the kitchen. It's a disaster, eggs and dishtowels strewn haphazardly, only Emmy Lou's nowhere to be seen. "She hates my guts. But she gave me the summer. I'm just tryin' to hold on to that."

One more shot. It's been the steady refrain in the back of his mind this last week. It ain't a lot, but it's a glimmer of hope that Emmy Lou's left the door open a crack for him. But it's still not a sure thing. Until his wife's back in Nashville, his ring on her hand, divorce off the table, Jace ain't breathing easy.

"You're workin' together now." Luke's voice holds hope. "Might be like old times at the stables."

"Maybe," Jace murmurs, peering out the front window to check how his sandbags are holding up. He squints into the dark night and takes in the rising pond, the debris whipping across the yard. The large oak tree looks ready to crack in half. Then, with horror, he realizes what he sees.

Emmy Lou. She's racing across the yard, a rein in her hand, her feet slip-sliding in the shifting mud.

What in the hell is she doing out there? The whole world's coming down around them and she's right in the middle of it.

Terror grabs Jace by the throat. "Fuck. I gotta go, Luke."

Fast as he can, he grabs a flashlight from the junk drawer, whips open the front door and shoots out of the house.

Immediately he's drenched and pummeled by the roar of the wind.

"Emmy Lou!"

He breaks into a run across the gravel driveway, sprinting past the pond to the large live oak near the pasture. Emmy Lou stands in the downpour, her T-shirt plastered to her chest, trying to calm Outlaw.

"What the hell are you doin'?" Jace shouts, braking hard as he makes it to her. He grabs Emmy Lou and pulls her into him, like he can shield her from the wind and the rain. "You oughta be in the damn house!"

She twists in his arms, her voice coming out as a wobbly shout. "I got Gentleman in the stable, but Outlaw's stuck. He's tangled."

Jace swings the flashlight down to see that one of the horse's hind legs is stuck in the bars of the metal fence. There's a slight bend, a gap, where Outlaw must have kicked it before getting stuck.

"I can't leave him out here, Jace." Even amid the roaring wind, he can hear the shaky snap of fear in her voice. Outlaw's working himself into a panic that's breaking Emmy Lou's heart.

A clap of thunder has Outlaw lunging forward frantically, damn near tearing his leg off in the process.

Jace swears.

Emmy Lou moves closer to the horse, slipping the rein

around Outlaw's neck to control him and keep him from thrashing. She whispers, shushing him, stroking him gently on his withers, and for a second, all Jace can do is stare. He's never seen anyone calm a horse like that. Pride and awe and worry swell in him. It's just like Emmy Lou to take care of a frightened horse even when she's in danger.

Thunder and lightning crack the sky, snapping him into action.

He can't wait any longer. He has to get the horse to safety and then Emmy Lou. His wife being out here, getting hurt, ain't an option.

"Take this," Jace says, handing Emmy Lou the flashlight. His eyes meet hers and she nods. "Keep him calm."

Jace kneels in the squelching mud, positioning himself next to the gate. Squinting through the lashing rain, he manages to grab Outlaw's trapped hoof through the gap in the bars. His biceps bulging, Jace strains. He doesn't know how he does it, but he does. Using every last ounce of muscle, of grit, of blood and bone, he lifts Outlaw's hoof high. Higher. Somehow, despite his hands being slick with mud and rain, Jace keeps a tight grip as the horse continues to struggle. He knows he's hurting him, but he has to get him out of there.

Finally, Jace maneuvers the leg to the bent gap in the bars. He looks up at Emmy Lou, shouts, "Make him move!"

She nods, and then with a gentle tug on the reins, she pulls Outlaw forward. The horse lunges, and at the exact same time, Jace forces the hoof back through the bars.

Outlaw's free.

They both jump when lightning cracks the sky. Close, too close, is the smell of smoke. The power to the house goes dark.

"It's gettin' close," Jace yells. "Get inside, Emmy."

"He'll never go with you," she shouts through the wind.

He hesitates. She's right. That horse will never trust him without Emmy Lou there.

Together they struggle through the wind and rain, gently

leading Outlaw forward. The barn in their sights, Jace keeps a tight grasp on Emmy Lou's wrist as they cross the driveway and pass the old oak tree and its shaking branches.

It feels like an eternity, it seems impossible, but finally, they do it. They get Outlaw in the barn, where Gentleman waits, calm and munching on feed. Emmy Lou kneels. Jace follows. Without speaking, they work together in the dim barn light to check over Outlaw's leg. It's not broken, only slightly swollen, a feat Jace considers a miracle from on high. Once they wrap Outlaw's leg, they add more straw to the floor of his stall to make him comfortable if he lies down.

When they're finished, Jace looks to Emmy Lou. "Let's get back to the house."

She nods.

Back outside, it takes the two of them to shut the sliding barn door. Emmy Lou looks unsteady on her feet as she latches it, her petite frame no match for the whipping wind. Jace shouts something to her over the din and she shakes her head. He tugs her toward him, pulling her into his arms, his mind on one end goal: get Emmy Lou safe.

"You okay?" He looks down at her and she shivers against him. Damn. She needs to be inside. Cold. Too cold.

"I'm okay." There, in the hazy light, her eyes search his, and for just a moment, something passes between them.

"C'mon," he says, forcing himself to tear his eyes away from hers. He grabs her hand and begins to lead them back to the house. Battered by a wall of wind, Jace keeps his face down but plows ahead, determined to get Emmy Lou to safety. He feels like he's drowning, so drenched by rain it's become harder to see, harder to keep a hold on Emmy Lou.

They're almost there, the house so close he can see it, when a hurricane-force wind tears them apart.

"No!" Jace shouts, whipping around. He watches in horror as the wind tosses Emmy Lou into the trunk of the old oak tree.

She lies there for a long second, dazed, but then pulls herself unsteadily to her feet.

Jace is halfway to her.

Then he hears it.

A thunderous cracking sound.

Emmy Lou freezes. She looks up. Above her, the old oak tree, the one they were married under, the one where they carved a heart around their names, is coming down. Straight toward Emmy Lou. Jace sees her mouth move in a desperate scream, her face pale and terrified.

"Emmy Lou!" The ragged shout tears through his throat and vibrates through his chest.

His core.

His heart.

And then he does the only thing he can think of to do. Protect Emmy Lou. Protect his wife.

He lunges toward her. Using all of his strength, he drives his body at Emmy Lou and shoulders her out of the way of the incoming tree.

She hits the ground with a cry.

That's when the tree comes crashing between them, knocking the two of them back and into blackness.

EMMY LOU SHRIEKS AS THE TREE CRASHES BETWEEN HER and Jace. The sound loud and deafening, the impact tosses her to the ground like a rag doll. For a second, everything goes black, goes to pinpricks and then she's up and scrambling, trying to work her way around the branches, over the trunk.

"Jace!" Her scream is hoarse, and she breaks off, her words choking into a sob as she searches the ground.

Emmy Lou feels faint.

Oh God, if she finds him lifeless, unmoving . . .

No. She shakes off the dark thought and pulls herself together. *No.*

She scrabbles on the ground, in the mud and debris, stumbling over the thick tree limb and unearthed roots. She nearly face-plants but picks herself back up. She can't see anything around the spindly branches. By now, she's running on sheer adrenaline, the wind and rain barely noticeable.

"Jace! Jace!"

She barely recognizes her own voice. It's raw with fear. A shriek from another dimension.

That's when she hears it. A low chuckle mixed with a groan. Across the yard, knocked clean back maybe twenty yards or so, is Jace.

He's pulling himself up into a sitting position, a dazed look on his face.

"Oh my God!"

Emmy Lou rushes to Jace and collapses beside him. She dives

into his chest, pressing herself against the hard pump of his heart-beat. Savoring it. With shaking hands, she clutches at him, touching him everywhere, feeling for injuries, feeling *him*, because he isn't hurt or dead, he is here.

"Oh Lord, Jace, are you alright? Are you hurt?"

Her focus zeroes in on his face. Aside from a small gash on his forehead where blood seeps, she can see he's okay, he's really okay.

"Em, honey, I'm fine," Jace says, his voice tight. His face twisted in a grimace, he pats his ribs and extracts his legs from the dark tangle of branches. "Nothin's broken. Goddamn." He sounds mystified. Then his eyes seek out the dark sky, the fallen tree. "Dodged a bullet."

He stands and pulls her up with him. And then he laughs. A great husky laugh.

Emmy Lou stares at Jace, stunned by his cavalier attitude. All at once, a rush of emotions swirl around her, like razors beneath under her skin, a hungry need to peel everything back to the bone.

Her temper flares, a strange combination of relief and helpless rage. "I'm so glad you can laugh about it," she snaps right before bursting into tears.

"Hey." Jace's handsome face sobers in concern. He reaches for her. "Why you cryin', Em?"

She hits him in the chest, heat rushing across her face. She hits him again. She tries for a third shot but Jace grips her wrists. He yanks her close, pinning her to him. His hazel eyes—furious, amused—stare her down.

"You gonna keep hittin' me or talk to me?" he growls.

"You asshole," she hisses and jerks in his hard grasp. But Jace won't budge. He maneuvers her closer and when she looks up at him, she sees the hard set of his chiseled jaw. Her heart stutters. It's a look that tells her she ain't getting away this time and that she better start talking.

"Tell me why you're cryin'," he says in a softer tone, his eyes still on hers.

"Because you're an idiot. Because you could've died." She

swipes tears and rain from her eyes and stares at Jace, wanting to burn him up with her fury. Not only is she angry at him, she's angry at herself for caring. For realizing too many truths all at once. Jace nearly took a tree to the face for her. Worse, he would have given his life for her.

She can't lose him.

Because the thought of a life without Jace is impossible.

All the words she's wanted to say rush up like a wave. "Because I was scared, Jace. I was worried, and I don't want to be worried. Because I am still so damn mad at you, but I also care about you. I still do and I hate it."

A trembling sob rushes out of her. Like something feral and raw and uncontained.

Jace shakes his head; his brows knit. "Em . . ."

"I can't love you anymore," she blurts.

His face goes slack. "Don't say that."

"I can't because it hurts too much."

She shakes Jace off, wrenching away from his grasp. Whirling around, she moves fast across the yard, ready to get away from her feelings, even though she knows she's running away, running again, her most miserable trait.

She's on the front porch, sheltered from the rain beneath the eave, when Jace's voice stops her. "Em, goddamn it, talk to me."

"Go away," she says, turning around to face him.

Jace stands inches from her, his shirt plastered to his muscled chest, his expression one of pain and disbelief.

"I ain't doin' this with you, Jace. Not again. We just fight. All we do is—"

She never gets to finish her sentence because Jace strides forward, grasps her wet face in his big hands, and kisses her.

Just like that. Like he owns her.

His kiss is deep and hard and damn near violent. Tongue, teeth, lips knock. Emmy Lou fights the kiss, grasping at his shoulders and shoving him back.

They stare at each other, panting.

She wipes her lips. The nerve of him. Kissing her like it's a first date. It's improper and rude and so damn perfect she wants to scream her head off. She bares her teeth. "How dare you."

"I'm going to kiss you again," Jace drawls, his hazel eyes wild. Intense. "And kiss you goddamn good and then you stop me."

The rough promise in his voice sends an anticipatory shudder through Emmy Lou.

Her stomach clenches as Jace advances. *More like prowl*, she thinks and then she shivers because he hasn't looked at her like this in a long time. Raw. Yearning. Straight up slavering.

Emmy Lou shifts, her body simmering with impatience. His kiss has her ignoring everything. Reason. Sanity. The wind whipping her hair, the cold settling into her bones. There's only Jace in front of her. His eyes, the tense posture of his body a warning that if she doesn't say no, say stop, he's gonna give it to her. And give it to her good.

Emmy Lou bites her lip and balls her fists.

Then, before she can say a word, Jace's mouth is on hers again. Hungry and searching and hot. She moans as Jace hauls her to his chest. His kiss is like that first-time knock-you-to-your-knees kiss. Breathtaking. Heart-stopping. Maddening.

The screen door rockets open. Jace picks Emmy Lou up in his arms and carries her inside, their lips still locked.

Inside, the house is dark and humid. The air electric.

Emmy Lou gasps between kisses, getting air, then goes back to Jace. She—they—haven't done this—no-holds-barred passion—in so long, she almost can't remember how it goes. The steps to be loved, to show love. But her body, her heartbeat down below remembers. It tells her exactly what she wants, what she needs.

Jace breaks the kiss and sets her on the couch. He kneels between her legs, reaching up to brush a wet strand of hair from her face. "We ain't fightin', Em. Not tonight."

She stares into Jace's hazel eyes, her defenses down. Adrenaline from earlier has her shaking, has her wanting to hold on to that I'm-alive feeling. She should say no. But she can't. She aches from head to toe, and the only thing that can make her feel better is Jace.

They reach for each other at the same time. Fumbling, frantic. Their kisses border on senseless. Desperate. Off go her shoes. Emmy Lou arches her back as Jace works her soaked jeans off over her hips. But he paces himself, licking the rivulets of rain up her calf to her naked thigh, his massive hands gripping her hips tight. Then, Jace slowly peels off her wet top, her bra, to leave her in only her panties. Her nipples pucker at the cool air.

Jace stares and Emmy Lou blushes, suddenly cognizant of how long it's been since he's seen her like this. Naked and open and all his.

"Jesus," he breathes, staring. "You're so damn—"

She cuts him off with a kiss. She doesn't want sweet words, words that threaten to break down all her defenses. But she still can't help that tendril of worry curling around her mind. If they do this . . . what does it mean?

Emmy Lou shakes off the thought. To hell with her pride, with her worry, she can deal with it all tomorrow. Right now, for one night only, it's just sex.

With her husband.

Who she may or may not be divorcing.

"You're freezin'," Jace murmurs, reaching for a quilt.

"Body heat solves everything," she whispers against his lips.

Emmy Lou twists her hands in his shirt, grappling for a feel of him, for a glimpse of Jace's toned body. As she shucks the shirt away with carefree abandon, it's like the old Emmy Lou's come to life inside of her. One that remembers the good times with Jace, the way he made her body sing, the way she lost herself with him, and the way he always found her and brought her back to him.

Jace groans and cups her face in his hands. "I want you, Em. So damn bad, honey. I can't fuckin' stand it." An erection strains against the crotch of his pants.

The desire in his voice has Emmy Lou shivering, his words

unbearably hot because she can hear the need, the absolute shameful want in them, the power she has over him.

He's a man on fire and the one burning him is her.

Brave, emboldened, she scoots into him, pressing her sex up against his sculpted stomach.

His eyes go dark at the feel of her. Sticky. Warm. He drops his fingers to the edge of her panties, slipping into the soft folds of silk, into Emmy Lou. Toying, teasing, they dip in and out of her before moving over to slowly caress her clit.

"Oh . . ." Emmy Lou's eyes flutter. Her head tips back and her body arches. Jace grins in approval, slowly letting her melt back against the couch cushion as his graceful fingers work her over below.

It's so damn hot. She's first. She matters. Not to mention, she can't believe they're doing this here in their living room. Her brothers could walk in. Anyone could see them, and the gossip in Wildheart would reign supreme. Still, it feels so illicit and tawdry and so damn freeing she's about to lose her mind. They haven't done something like this since they were kids kissing in the stables.

A strangled moan pours from Jace's lips. "I'm gonna go slow, Em. I have to."

Her eyes shutter. She knows what he means. It's been so long. She wants to savor it as much as he does.

A warm hand slides up her stomach, her sternum, to cup her breast.

Emmy Lou whimpers in appreciation. She can feel every inch of Jace in his hands. Knuckles lashed by scars. Knicks and cuts from barbed wire, rope, and rock. Calloused fingers from plucking his big bass. Sexy hands. Strong hands. Hands that are swift and searching and massive.

Her mind lights on minutes earlier—Jace, sexy, strong, tearing apart the gate with his bare hands to free Outlaw—and a needy desperation rushes through her.

"Touch me, Jace," she whispers. "Harder. Right . . . oh . . ."

Her words trail off as Jace sweeps his thumb over her nipple like the sweetest kiss, while down below, he slides two fingers inside her.

Emmy Lou gasps as a delicious warmth spreads between her thighs. Her nails dig into his broad shoulders, breaking bare skin. "Oh God, Jace."

The two intertwined sensations, Jace's massive hand cupping her breast, his clever fingers sweeping over her clit—it's sensory overload.

"I know," he says, his voice feral and over the edge. "Fuck. I know, Em."

She lets out a little cry as he tears off her underwear, tossing them into the dark shadows behind him. Her gaze meets his, his eyes watching her, his fingers fully controlling her now, waiting patiently for her to come, giving her what he knows she loves in bed and then some.

He's never touched her like this before.

Haunted. Tortured. Trembling.

Another graze of his thumb.

And then Emmy Lou lets go. She gives in.

Her cry is breathless, a belly-deep burst of an explosion. A complete surrender as she lets the orgasm swallow her up just like Jace's hands have done.

She lies there, trembling, until finally, her body is limp and content and sated.

"Em?"

Dazed, she sits up, blinking at Jace who's kneeling in front of her. "You good?"

She sighs. "I am very good, Jace Taylor."

"Tell me the night's not over," he breathes, his muscular arms bracing the couch to cage her. His jaw flexes, fierce want breaking in his eyes. "Tell me we ain't done, honey."

Her eyes flutter as she takes in her husband. One of the steadiest men she knows, looking at her like she's his undoing. Like if she says no, she'll shatter him. Absolutely kill him dead.

But the truth is, she doesn't want to say no.

She wants more.

She wants Jace.

Unable to take it any longer, a wild squeal tearing from her throat, she launches herself at him. They both fall backward onto the rug, Emmy Lou ready and willing to lose herself in the arms of her husband.

One night, she thinks. Their last night.

She swears it.

Jace watches as Emmy Lou slides on top of his lap, her brown eyes dusky with desire. He can barely believe this damn night. A night that's been all kinds of crazy. Worrying about Emmy Lou, trying to get them out of that storm, and now, now she's straddling him like he's a bronco.

He doesn't know if this is the right thing to do. Winning his wife back, the way to Emmy Lou's heart ain't gonna be through her legs, but it's too damn late to call it off. Because his wife's on top of him, her small body clamped around him, her hourglass curves trim and lush, and he's losing his goddamn mind.

It's been so long since he's seen her naked, seen her like this. Open and needy and so damn beautiful—every ounce of self-control in him has been replaced with a rock-hard dick and savage impatience. He's got his wife on top of him and he's gotta have her.

Now.

They'd be crazy to stop this fire between them. There ain't nothing like what he's got with Emmy Lou. When it comes to his wife, his willpower breaks a thousand times over.

His hands tremble as he grips her hips, loving the way his fingers sink into the creamy flesh of her skin. Making gorgeous dimples, holding her in place.

At her harsh inhale of breath, Jace glances up to make sure he hasn't hurt her. She's smiling, her lips curved, her back arched like some breathtaking sight of woman. Erotic and primal.

Emmy Lou dips down into him, her breasts plumping against his chest. Jace curves his arms around her waist and kisses her. "Fuck," he breathes against her lips. "Are we doin' this, Em?"

She kisses him back, then straightens up. "Oh, we're doin' it," she drawls. Her small hands palm his broad chest. "Because I am naked, Jace. And I ain't goin' anywhere."

Jace grins. "That's what I like to hear."

He leans up, trapping her in his arms, against him. Emmy Lou cries out in delight and then, in one swift motion, he flips them over. He hisses his approval at what he sees: Emmy Lou laid out beautifully on the living room rug.

"Goddamn," he says.

With heavy-lidded eyes, she slowly raises her gaze to his.

Taking a deep breath, he grasps her wrists and raises her arms over her head. Emmy Lou arches her back, excitement shining in her eyes, expectantly, knowing what he's about to do. He leans down, licking the plump swells of her breast, her nipples, bringing them to hard points.

Sitting back, he parts her legs, staring at the blond curls. Her body radiates heat. Lust. He touches her down below, groaning at what he finds. Slick trails of wetness stain the inside of her thighs. "Fuck," Jace breathes.

It's been too long. So damn long for either of them.

Emmy Lou closes her eyes. "I can't wait, Jace."

Her breath's a pant. A desperate plea.

He devours her words, devours the response of her body, the way she's hotter than a pistol, the arch of her spine, the jut of her hips. The sight of her body writhing for a taste of him almost sends him over the edge.

Impatient, a roar rips out of him. Off go his boots. Then his jeans. As fast and as impatient as a horny teenager.

As he hovers over Emmy Lou, her gaze moves to his groin, her hands too. She palms his cock. Jace closes his eyes at the feel of Emmy Lou's hands on him. A shudder rolls through him as she strokes.

Finally, it's too much. He doesn't want to rush it, but he can't wait any longer. His eyes snap open. Roughly, he reaches down to spread her legs. Emmy Lou's shocked but pleased whimper has him grinning.

He loves that she wants this as much as he does. One of the best parts of their marriage was the sex. Emmy Lou always gave off a prim air, but in their bedroom, she came alive. Unabashedly brazen. For him and only him.

His girl. His queen.

Groaning, Jace grips her hips and slips into her.

A gasp comes from them both. One of wonder, of pleasure. It's been so long, he's forgotten how good, how soft she feels.

Yet he'd wait again for this moment. A million years if he had to.

Emmy Lou lets out an agonized cry and grips his shoulders with her nails. "Oh, Jace," she says on a moan. She rocks and writhes beneath him. The viselike clench, the hold she has on him, has his own determination to last crumbling.

Her heat. Her smell. Her heart.

Forever's not enough with Emmy Lou.

His brain overheats and he sinks in deep, burying himself inside of her. Emmy Lou sighs and opens her sweet mouth, surrendering to Jace's kiss.

Like always, they fit together. Perfectly.

All the years, the anger, the pain, disappear. They mean nothing. Here, tonight, they start over. His love for Emmy Lou is feral and on fire and hell if he's giving that up.

A savage cry escaping him, he thrusts forward. He hammers into her over and over, his hips pumping, and Emmy Lou clenches tight around him. She bucks beneath him, wild, sucking him in, her juices bathing his cock in molten heat.

Jace throws his head back and thrusts forward one last time. He shudders as he erupts, leaning down to bury his face in the curve of Emmy Lou's neck. Her arms, soft as silk, wind their way around his back, and he can feel the tiny rhythmic jerks of her slim frame as she comes with him.

For a long minute, they lie there on the ground, blissful, collapsed and sweating.

Then, hating to move but not wanting to hurt her, Jace carefully lifts up to gauge his wife's reaction. He scours her face, searching for regret, but finds none. Only those dark doe-brown eyes and cheeks tinged with a gorgeous honey-peach flush.

"Em, you okay?"

She lets out a soft giggle that has his heart lurching. That's when he sees chill bumps all over Emmy Lou. He rolls off her to grab a quilt from the couch. "You cold?" he asks, draping the quilt over her body.

"Mmm," she says, curling her small frame into him. She nuzzles his neck sleepily, her soft blond curls obscuring her face. "Not anymore."

Elbow on the ground, he props his head on his fist. Then, hooking one arm behind her head, he pulls her into him. She's exhausted and freezing and all he wants to do is keep her close and warm.

Emmy Lou makes a sleepy little noise. Her eyes are closed, her long lashes dark against her cheek. "Thank you."

Jace dips his head to hear her better. "For what, honey?"

"For helpin' with Outlaw. For takin' care of me tonight."

The words sock him in the chest. He leans back to take her in. Moonlight frames her face, her beauty lighting up the dark house. Sudden emotion overwhelms him. She could have been hurt tonight.

Christ. He could have lost her.

"I'll always take care of you," Jace says, his throat working out its kinks as he smooths damp air away from her forehead. "No matter what."

So much more he could say. Tell her about Luke, about his mother, about how damn much he loves her, only, when he looks down, she's asleep.

Jace chuckles, lowering himself beside her on the hard floor. His back's going to pay for it in the morning, but sleeping beside his wife is worth it.

Everything—this terrifying, endless night—has been worth it.

That's when he catches their reflection in the dim reflection of the television. Emmy Lou holding him, him holding her.

Something they haven't done in a damn long time.

THIRTEEN

THE NEXT MORNING, EMMY LOU WAKES ON A SOFT surface, swaddled in blankets. She sits up, groggy, and takes in her surroundings. She's on the couch, curled cozy as a cat. Soft sunlight streams through the gauzy curtains. She clutches at her shoulder. It's bare. She's naked beneath the blankets, wearing them like some kind of tattered dress. She frowns, wondering. She feels worn out, achy, and warm down below.

Like she slept so damn deep, buried in dreams, in memories, in muscled arms—

A little yelp slips from her lips.

The bleary cogs in her brain finally jumpstart.

Jace.

Oh Lord.

Oh, Holy Lord in heaven.

Inhaling all her breath, she closes her eyes, raises a pillow to her face and screams. Her heart pounds hard in her chest, beating out a tune called *idiot, idiot, idiot girl, you're a damn idiot.*

When she raises her face, she sees Jace stacked her panties and bra in a neat little pile on top of the coffee table. Somehow it makes her feel worse.

What on earth was she thinking doing what she did with Jace? Not like it wasn't good. It was. It was hot and passionate and everything they had been missing from their marriage for a long damn time. Her mind orbits back to last night, the memory of Jace knocking her out of the way of the tree, taking her face in his hands and kissing her without permission, how damn sexy it all was, how strong he was helping her, protecting her.

She peers around the living room. At the flash of Jace, outside, passing by the window, Emmy Lou sinks down into the couch, wanting it to suck her into another dimension. He's whistling a cheery tune, a bucket of feed in his hands. But he doesn't see her and moseys on across the gravel drive.

With Jace out of sight, she jolts up and the blanket tumbles from her lap. Glancing down, she flushes at the bruises on her thighs. Evidence of last night. Jace's tight grip.

He could have held her all night. Fucked her all night. At the thought, her nipples pinch in response.

This is awful. She's awful. She feels all kinds of vulnerable, of messed up inside, and the only one she can blame is herself. She didn't mean to kiss Jace like that. It's been too many lonely days on the farm, watching Jace taunt her with his ridiculous body.

That's it.

She'll chalk up her lapse in judgment to the storm. Adrenaline. Jace's near-tree-crushing. Wildheart.

Her hometown's pulling at her carefully sewn-together seams, unearthing memories, secrets she thought she had buried. Threatening to uproot them just like that damn oak tree.

This wasn't part of her plan. She was supposed to come to Wildheart to get away from Jace, not closer to him. Not hop in bed with him like some silly oxytocin-riddled woman. But now some part of her wants to take those six weeks seriously, to say to Jace, *Let's try again, let's kiss like crazy and make a ton of babies, and ride our horses into the sunset, you'll be the cowboy who gets the girl at the end of the song, because I'm it.*

I'm your girl.

She still wants to be his girl.

Because last night she saw her husband. The man she loved. The man who always came through for her. Who never let her down or lied to her. Who worked beside her, easily, effortlessly, reading her mind, just as well as his hands read her body.

But it's a fantasy, a wish that can't be trusted, because Jace can't be trusted. Because he'll mess it up again. And she'll run. She can't keep doing this her entire life, trust that things with Jace are okay, are safe, only to have it all blow up in her face.

Again and again and again.

When she spies a small vase of wildflowers on the coffee table, she groans and smears her face in her hands.

Lord, one night together, and he's already bringing her flowers.

A smile softens her lips. She likes these flowers, though. They're the right kind of flowers.

Growling, Emmy Lou shakes her head, shakes off her romantic nature.

She's getting as bad as Jace.

He wants something she can't give. At least not yet. As good as last night was, she isn't ready to forgive him, to call off the divorce, to go back to Nashville.

One night isn't enough to erase the lies. Her broken trust.

Just because they slept together doesn't mean they're getting back together.

It absolutely does not.

Inhaling a stoic breath, Emmy Lou slides to the edge of the couch and stands.

She has to tell him last night meant nothing.

And she has to believe it.

Jace shakes his head when he comes around the side of the barn. The morning brings with it bright sunshine as if Mother Nature herself is personally trying to make up for last night's storm.

While the old house weathered the wind and rain like a champ, outside is a different story. Pieces of the oak tree are strewn in dark heaps across the front yard. The gravel drive is thrashed and the pasture needs a good picking up. Rubble and wreckage scattered everywhere. It'll be a project to get the farm in order.

But he doesn't care about any of it, because all that matters is that Emmy Lou's safe.

He closes his eyes, the memory of the tree lingering in his mind. Thank Christ, she wasn't hurt. He wouldn't survive it.

As much as it pained him to leave Emmy Lou's side this morning, he wanted to get a head start on the day and take care of the farm. He doesn't want his wife to worry about a damn thing. That's his job. No more will he let their farm go to shit. Telling her he plans to change won't help him—he intends to show her.

Jace rakes the ground, trapping trash and debris.

A giant grin sideswipes his face. He feels like every bit of a lovesick son of a bitch.

He hasn't had hope like this for years.

Last night, his patience, his do-the-right-thing ways, were shattered. He and Emmy Lou came together in ways they hadn't for years. It was a damn gift from the universe. Taking her to bed, waking up with her this morning, Emmy Lou pressed against his side so tight, she was like a tattoo against his body.

He can only hope this means he's one step closer to bringing her back to Nashville. The way she felt last night, like some angel he doesn't deserve, has him wanting to be the best man for her for the rest of her life.

Starting with getting this damn farm in order.

Jace frowns when his rake hits something. He glances down.

A beer bottle lies strewn among leaves and hay. He nudges it with the teeth of the rake, turning it over to get a better look. Peroni. His frown deepens. *Fancy beer for Wildheart,* he thinks.

At the slam of the screen door, Jace glances up. Emmy Lou's descending the porch steps. Her blond hair mussed, she wears tan boots and a lavender sundress that hugs her supple curves. He can't keep his eyes off her.

"Hey, good mornin'," he says, setting the rake up against the side of the barn.

"Mornin'." She shields her eyes against the bright sunlight, her mouth turning down into an unhappy pout. "Lord, Jace, you let me sleep the day away."

"Ain't nothin' to worry about. I got everything handled, Em."

She blinks. "You do?"

"Sure do. Doc Harper will be here at noon to check over Outlaw, but he seems to be doin' alright."

She nods, her eyes brushing to the pasture where Outlaw and Gentleman graze easy like last night never happened. "Thank you," she says, tucking a wavy lock of hair behind her ear and looking at Jace. "I don't know how those horses got out last night. I swear I locked that damn door."

He shakes his head at the guilt lashing her voice. "Don't do that, honey," he says, taking a step toward her. "It ain't your fault."

He leans in to kiss her. It's automatic, the need to comfort her, only Emmy Lou sucks in a harsh breath and takes a step back.

"Jace." She's biting her lip.

Fuck.

His stomach flips over.

He wasn't looking for an easy fix, but after last night, Emmy Lou freezing him out is like salt in the wound.

"Last night," she begins, before he can. "We shouldn't have done that."

He stiffens. "Em . . ."

"*I* shouldn't have done that." She lowers her eyes. "It doesn't mean anything. It was just something stupid and impulsive and it'll never happen again. Okay?" Her voice holds a sharp let's-change-the-subject tone.

Jace wants to argue with her, wants to tell her last night wouldn't have been that good if it didn't mean something, but he doesn't. If he pushes, he gets nowhere. Instead, all he says is, "Okay."

"We still have the rodeo," Emmy Lou hedges, giving him a small smile like it's his consolation prize. "We can work together on that at least."

"Yeah," he says around the rock in his throat. "By the way, Luke's in."

Her small smile turns to a beam. "Look at you. Jace Taylor comin' in to save the day."

He laughs. "Now I ain't so sure about that."

"Well, I am." Her eyes drop, landing on the beer bottle. She looks up, quirking a teasing brow. "You ain't been out here day-drinkin', have you?"

"Nah. Wind must have blown it in. I got better taste than that."

She stares at him, like their easy banter has unsettled her, and then tips up her chin. "I want to go check on Outlaw. Unless . . ." Her brown-eyed gaze scours the farm.

"Nah," he says, hating the awkwardness between them. He lifts the rake. "You go on. I got it here."

As Emmy Lou strolls away, Jace grits his jaw and picks up the rake. He's defeated, but he ain't giving up or giving in. If it takes the next twenty years, he'll stick it out. Why? Because three bad years ain't worth throwing away what he and Emmy Lou have together.

She's got every right to doubt him. She expects him to lie again, to break her trust. Because she still doesn't know the real reason . . .

Jace sighs, dreading it, but knowing he has no choice. For so long, he worked hard to shake the ghosts of his past, not wanting any of his dark shit to touch Emmy Lou. No way did he want his girl knowing about the hellhole he grew up in. Worse, he didn't want Emmy Lou thinking he was like his father.

But now, he has to tell her the truth and nothing but. Even if this summer ends with him packing his bags and tucking tail back to Nashville, Emmy Lou has to know he never meant to be reckless with her heart, or their love. He never meant to put her in danger.

An image of his mother's face flashes in his mind.

The truth about his family. The truth about Luke.

His gaze drops to the beer bottle.

Jace shifts, uneasy, as a shiver of foreboding spreads inside him like wildfire.

"Next time" could be anyone. Be careful.

D AY SEVENTEEN HAS JACE AT BOONE MONTGOMERY Rodeo Arena. He walks the perimeter and evaluates the stage setup. The view's strange. He hasn't played with the Brothers Kincaid in over two weeks. He's a shithead for putting his band through this—postponing gigs and dragging them out here—but it's the way it has to be. He's here for Emmy Lou. He's put the music before his wife too many times now, and it ain't happening again.

"What do you think?" Grady asks, nodding at the stage. He's been asked to give the tour in place of Mama Belle. "Still look the same as you remember?"

"Sure does." Jace glances up and around at the impressive covered arena. Big cities ain't got nothing on Wildheart and their rodeo arena. Cowboys and city folk come from all over the world just to see one of Wildheart's world-famous rodeos. The boast-worthy arena plays host to seven hundred seats, a performance stage, concessions, and executive suites.

Jace pauses near a stall and gives Grady a wry look. "Sure you don't want it?"

"Hell no. Not me." Grady shakes his head. "Daddy's tryin' to sell it with the farm. To who, I ain't sure."

A flash of guilt hits Grady's face so quick Jace almost misses it. Jace knows Boone always had high hopes of passing down the stables, the arena, to one of his children.

Grady lets out a breath. "Me, I'm goin' to Nashville end of the summer."

Jace eyes him. The kid wants it bad. He just hopes Grady knows what he's in for. Nashville's a good town, but it can also eat you alive. It's hard work, and scraping at the bottom of the barrel to survive the music industry isn't what he wants for Emmy Lou's youngest brother.

"Speakin' of Nashville," Grady drawls, "how'd Mama take you volunteerin' to play? She bust a gasket?"

Jace chuckles. "Somethin' like that."

His eyes move across the dirt to land on Mama Belle. The woman holds court at a long table with Boone and a few other women wearing Kentucky Derby–style hats. Plush loveseats and lounges. Catered deli trays. Buckets of champagne. Mama Belle's attempt to impress.

"And Emmy Lou? What's she think?"

"She thinks I better not fuck it up."

Automatically, his gaze seeks out his wife. She left the house early this morning, avoiding any talk of sharing a ride. Emmy Lou's surrounded by a circle of Mama Belle's friends, wearing a smile, tight blue jeans and a glittery sash and tiara. With big loose curls in her hair, Emmy Lou looks so damn pretty all Jace can do is stare.

His hands itch, not to play bass but to touch Emmy Lou.

He twists the wedding band on his finger.

It's been a week since he and Emmy . . . what's the word for it? Fucked? Made love?

Christ. His own damn wife and he doesn't even know what they did or where they stand. All he knows is that night was like injecting Emmy Lou into his bloodstream. And while she's been avoiding him like the plague, he's been thinking. Too damn much, in fact. His brain running a mile a minute with thoughts about Emmy Lou and all he can do is scribble them down on the small notepad he keeps in his back pocket. He feels like some dopey lovesick kid, crushing over Emmy Lou. How the hell does Luke do it? Write all those songs about Sal without losing his damn mind?

"Emmy Lou seem okay about today?"

Caught off guard by the question, Jace turns. Grady's face is screwed up in an expression he can't place. "Ain't like I saw her enough to ask, but yeah, she seemed ready."

Grady stares at Jace a long second and then nods. "Good."

"Remind me who we're meetin' again?" Jace asks. He raises his phone, snapping a photo of the stage to send to Luke. By now they're pros at this business, and playing in a small town is a cakewalk. Still, it's in Jace's planning nature to be prepared. And that means scope out the stage and get all the details.

Grady slaps his hands on the thighs of his jeans. "Erica. The arena manager. She's gonna walk you through the logistics of the night."

As they cross the dusty arena, Jace's ears prick on a familiar sound. A car engine. Distracted, he takes a step toward the sliding barn doors. They're open to a slit, but enough that he can see a black sedan slowly rolling into the gravel alleyway behind the arena.

His mouth goes dry.

"Jace? You comin'?"

Jace blinks himself back to the present. He and Grady have come to a stop right in front of Mama Belle's table. The women are quiet, eager smiles on their faces. Sharks out for blood.

Jace fights a smile of his own at the pained look on Emmy Lou's face. Knowing Emmy Lou, it's killing her to be in the middle of Mama Belle's clucking hen club. No doubt gossip central. Though Emmy Lou always bemoaned her own gossipy nature, Jace never saw her like that. What he saw was the real Emmy Lou. A woman who could rope a horse in six-inch heels and then take on the red carpet. A woman who knew how to work a crowd, to control the press, so Jace and their friends didn't get attacked by the *Nashville Star*. A woman who loved to talk, who loved the limelight and was one hell of a fierce defender.

One of the women, turning a wry eye to Mama Belle, pipes up, "Why, Belle, ain't you plannin' to introduce us?"

Emmy Lou, a sparkly crown in her hands, rises from her chair. Her eyes are wide. "This is . . ."

"Jace," Mama Belle finishes. "He plays bass for the Brothers Kincaid. They're playin' the rodeo next month. Luke Kincaid was kind enough to fill in for Hollis Grainger."

A murmur of appreciation ripples through the women. Emmy Lou flushes and looks down at the crown in her hands.

His stomach curdles, the words stinging him more than he wants to admit.

Hell, everything stings right now. The way Grady's staring at him with sympathetic eyes. The way Mama Belle introduced him like he was goddamn backup. The furtive glances and hushed whispers. Emmy Lou's eyes on her hands like she's gone mute. This ain't Nashville, it ain't the *Star*, but still, he knows the gossip's spread like wildfire thanks to Mama Belle. These women, they ain't talkin' about him being Emmy Lou's husband, lead bass player of the Brothers Kincaid, one of the hottest country acts around.

They're talking divorce.

To all of Wildheart, he's just a guy who lost his wife, his money, and is out of the Montgomerys' good graces. The honor of being Emmy Lou's husband ain't his anymore. And Mama Belle is sure as shit seeing to that.

A hand on his shoulder. Grady, trying to steer him away from the unwanted attention. "C'mon. Erica's here. You got four weeks to get this shit right."

Jace's stomach twists. *Four weeks.*

Time's ticking down like bomb.

Small-town gossip. The rumble of whispers and conversation claw at her eardrums. Spiking her anxiety and setting her teeth on edge.

Still, Emmy Lou stands patiently as Mama Belle trots her out in front of her friends. It's been a day of *Yes, Mama* and *No, Mama* and *You don't say, Mama*. A day of smiling pretty like a good southern girl and gabbing with all of Mama Belle's high society friends who are clearly using the excuse of the rodeo as a chance to get together and sling gossip.

Truth be told, she'd rather be anywhere but here.

She glances over her shoulder, her eyes seeking out Grady, but instead, they find Jace. She bites her lip, her stomach instantly bottoming out. It was cruel what Mama Belle had done. Dismissing Jace like he was no one.

He looked so hurt. He didn't deserve that. She should have said something, stood up for Jace somehow. But she didn't, did she?

Mama Belle, dressed in her best bedazzled jean-and-vest combo, primly sips her champagne. Her left hand, bedecked in sparkling rings, lifts into the air. "Now, as I was sayin' . . ." Everyone in Mama Belle's circle leans forward expectantly, absolutely famished for some good gossip. Satisfied she has their attention, Mama Belle continues. "Emmy Lou is plannin' on movin' home soon. My darlin' girl, my sweet rodeo queen, back in Wildheart. Ellen Sue, I'm sorry you never knew what it was like to have a daughter win a crown."

Emmy Lou groans at the dig. "Mama," she chides, sitting back in her chair, "that ain't nice."

Ellen Sue's daughter, Tara, had been her best friend in grade school and lost at the competition a dozen times before joining the 4-H club.

But Ellen Sue takes the barb on the chin. "Oh, you're so right, Belle. I'll have to relay that message to Tara when she's home from yachting in Europe."

Emmy Lou coughs to hide a laugh. Point one for Ellen Sue.

With a huff, Mama Belle adjusts the crown on Emmy Lou's head. "Well, if that isn't my cue to give my big speech." She stands and looks down at Emmy Lou. "You're up after me. I want you wearin' this crown the entire time, Emmaline, we don't need no dusty cowboy hat. I want you shinin' brighter than the sun, you hear me?"

"Yes, Mama."

Emmy Lou watches as Mama Belle takes the stage, making a big to-do about the importance of Wildheart's rodeo, how happy everyone is to be part of it, and the new act that's replacing Hollis Grainger.

Ellen Sue scoots her chair closer. "You and Jace. Is it true?"

Emmy Lou inclines her head, eyes on Mama Belle. "Is what true?"

A hushed whisper. "The divorce."

Emmy Lou's stomach rolls like a tumbleweed. This time, she looks at Ellen Sue. "I don't—we're still figurin' it out."

"Don't fret, dear. There's no scandal in it anymore. It's common now." Ellen Sue pats her hand, genuine sympathy in her eyes. "Tara got a divorce last year, and it's no lie the splittin' up of assets and dividin' of friends was a real chore, but she survived. And sure enough, you will too."

Emmy Lou stiffens in her seat, trying to rein in her heart. She doesn't want to divide up the house or her friends. She wants to be back in Nashville having lunch with Sal and Lacey, picking out her next dress for the red carpet.

Before she can respond, Ellen Sue tuts. "Take it from me. Sometimes bein' with no one is better than bein' with the wrong one."

"But Jace isn't—" Emmy Lou's next words, instinctual, cut off.

Ellen Sue stares. "What?"

She had been about to say Jace isn't the wrong one.

He's always been the right man for her.

Ellen Sue hisses a breath. "Oh, I better hush. Your mama's givin' me that look."

"Alright, now," Mama Belle says into the mic, her voice a shrill echo in the near-empty arena. "This is where I'd introduce you. Emmaline? Emmy Lou?"

Shaken out of her daze, Emmy Lou grabs her notecards and inhales a long, deep breath. A reminder to herself that she's not that seventeen-year-old girl anymore. She's not running away. She is just getting started.

She makes her way to the stage, taking her daddy's hand as he helps her climb the stairs.

The claps die off as she settles behind the podium. Emmy Lou smiles bright as she channels enthusiasm and sunshine and perfection. Everything Mama Belle wants.

"Welcome to the Wildheart County Rodeo. I suppose I oughta say somethin' about how great my daddy is." A stern *ahem* comes from stage right. Emmy Lou laughs. "And my mama too. They're the very best. And the two of them, the Montgomerys, they've been the drivin' force of Wildheart. Keepin' the rodeo alive, and keepin' jobs in our town."

Her heart thumps hard as she stares out across the arena.

She can do this.

She's a Montgomery and Montgomerys don't get nerves. They stand tall and smile and never let anyone see them break.

She clears her throat, her head, and holds tight to the podium to come back down to earth.

"The last time I was in this arena, not in the stands, was near on thirteen years ago. Ancient status." She smiles as a titter of laughter sweeps through the small crowd. "That night I collected my crown. I was so honored to be Wildheart's rodeo queen. It's a moment that will stick with me forever. And though it's been—"

She breaks off at the sound of a clanging screech. Twisting in her seat, Mama Belle scowls at the interruption. A horse trailer's being backed into the dusty arena.

All Emmy Lou can do is stare at the horse trailer, the cool confidence she had channeled minutes earlier faltering. Sideswiped.

Memories crowd her brain. Demons. Demons she tried to forget, tried to run away from. But she can't run anymore. Because they've finally found her and are ready to drag her back down to face them.

C'mon, Slayton whispered, the night of the rodeo, after the crowd had cleared out, after she had won her last crown. *Let's celebrate.* He tugged her toward the horse trailer.

She followed, giggling, feeling like the luckiest girl in the world. Feeling so in love nothing else mattered but her and Slayton.

He pulled her inside the horse trailer, close, quiet confines. His breath was ragged as they kissed in a corner. The smell of hay and sweat around them. When his hands moved to her breasts, up the hem of her shirt, Emmy Lou whispered, *No, no, no, not yet.* She was a virgin. She wanted to wait until they were married. Their first time wasn't meant for some dirty horse trailer. But with her protest, his face changed. Man to monster, wild eyes, someone she had never seen before. He drew himself up; the entire trailer seemed to fill with his body.

You can't say no. You're mine, he swore in her ear, his words burning against her neck. He pressed himself close, pressed her back against cold, sharp metal. Emmy Lou felt like she was drowning beneath him as his heavy body covered hers. She squeezed her eyes shut. All she wanted to do was evaporate into the night. All she could feel was Slayton and his giant hands all over her. Tearing at her clothes, ripping her blouse, her precious, beautiful jeweled blouse her daddy had bought her for the occasion, off her shoulders. She heard the zip of his jeans, the jingle of his belt, and went somewhere far inside herself. It was only when she heard Gentleman's panicked whinny that she woke up. It snapped her alive. He saved her. She turned into a wildcat. She fought back, kicking and scratching, finally getting a hold of a rein hanging on a hook. She hit Slayton, lashed him across the cheek, drawing blood. Enraged, he hauled back and slapped her. But his anger, his lapse was enough, and she broke free and ran.

Running, running, she was running half-naked back to her house until she was stopped by Grady in the parlor.

Her younger brother, Grady, sweet Grady, by then two feet taller than her, took her into his arms. *What's wrong, Emmy Lou? What is it?* He shook her. Hard. She could barely get it out, admit what Slayton had tried to do. When she did, Grady's face changed too. Enraged. Unseeing. He blasted out of the house, determined to kill Slayton. Two hours later, the town sheriff brought Grady home busted up. Boone blamed him for making trouble, for Emmy Lou's breakup with Slayton.

Slayton.

He was the reason for everything.

Why she gave up her dream of the rodeo. Why she hates tight, enclosed spaces. Why she can't tour with Jace.

It's why she talks so damn much. So she can fill that futile and helpless space in her head. She learned fast that if she talked, if she buried her nose in someone else's problems, she could quiet that voice inside her head, the memories of that night, rattling around like a lost marble, always ready to wreak havoc on her waking thoughts. Her mouth runs so her mind can't.

Slayton.

He's the reason she never understood. How she could love someone for that long and never know them. How she could *trust* them.

It's why she fell in love with Jace. Why she never told him about Slayton.

Slayton had wrecked her world back in Wildheart. She vowed he wouldn't ruin it in Nashville. Spook her away from this new boy that she loved. She wouldn't make her trauma part of her present. But to do that, she had to bury it deep. Hide it from Jace.

From everyone.

For years, she thought she had successfully put the past behind her. That she'd survived it. But now . . .

Now . . .

"Miss Emmy Lou?"

Her audience, Mama Belle, her daddy, are all peering up at her with curious eyes. A few whispers flitter through the silence. Grady stares at her, his brow wrinkled in worry. Jace watches intently, his head tilted at her lapse in concentration.

Emmy Lou exhales, coming back to herself. She presses her palms down on the podium, the cool wood, and splays out her fingers. Her hands tremble like leaves.

"Sorry." She shakes her head and gives a weak laugh. The words on the card blur together. "Seems like I lost my place."

Taking another deep breath, she closes her eyes and focuses on all the things she loves. The smell of the horses, the dust of the arena, the groan of the bleachers, the rough scrape of cowboy boots, dirty and nicked, well loved and worn, but when she opens her eyes, she sees him.

Slayton.

He's standing at the back of the arena, arms crossed, his gaze lasered on her.

An icy chill sweeps over her bones.

No. It can't be.

Emmy Lou blinks, shaking her head to process the shadowy image, but before she can, the man, the shadow, is gone.

It's too much.

The familiar feeling of claustrophobia grows around her, like a rolling wave, drowning her in memories, in her own grief and shame.

Emmy Lou goes cold, then hot.

She grips the podium, but she can't hang on.

Lord, Jesus, she's going to face-plant in front of her mother and half of the Wildheart gossips.

Her eyes flutter.

But before her knees can buckle, a firm body braces hers. Solid weight at her back, a soothing hand on her shoulder blades, the other on the curve of her hip. A husky voice in her ear, "I've got you, Em."

"Jace," she whispers, turning her face into him to rest her cheek against his collarbone. His body feels like a brick wall, tense, on alert as he cups her against him. For a brief second, she allows herself a sniff of his masculine scent. Leather and hay and sunshine. She closes her eyes at the comforting sensation. The smell of happy memory, of Jace, there's nothing better.

"Can you walk?"

"Yes."

She tries to take a step to prove she can, but she goes limp, slumping in Jace's arms.

The world around her spins into blackness.

Jace catches her, sweeping her into his arms and carrying her down the stage.

Her face buried in the curve of Jace's shoulder, Emmy Lou keeps her arms locked tight around his neck. All she wants to do is shut out the looks of concern. She can already hear muffled whispers, the worried boom of her father's voice, Mama Belle's shrill assurances that everything's okay. She doesn't want any of that. All she wants is Jace.

Slowly, she's eased out of the warmth of Jace's body and down into a chair, her brain fog dissipating. Jace crouches in front of her. Keeping his gaze on her face, he barks an order for a bottle of water. Grady, who's barreling toward them, pivots and sprints off to the nearest cooler.

Jace cups the side of her clammy cheek. "Honey, you okay?"

She takes a shaky breath. Her heart pummels against her chest like it needs an escape. "I think so."

"*Think-so* won't cut it, Em." His deep hazel eyes dance with worry. "I'll drive you to a doctor in Macon." He moves to rise.

She grabs his arm and stills him. "No."

Reluctantly, Jace lowers himself back down, beside her. "Convince me, then."

Her cheeks flush, her lips tremble to get it all out, but she forces a pretty smile. The last thing she wants is attention on this, on her. "I've been runnin' wild all day. I didn't eat breakfast," she lies, her tongue numb in her mouth. "With all that champagne ..."

Jace frowns, his rusty brows drawn together like he doesn't buy it. "You're white as a ghost." He reaches up, smoothing a hand over her hair, her damp brow. His touch anything but uncertain, his hand lingers by her face like it could stay there forever.

"I feel like a ghost," she murmurs and Jace's brow creases even deeper. "I'm talkin' stupid," she says, trying to regroup, to keep her cool, to sit up straighter in the chair. "I don't know what I'm sayin'. I just need a minute."

Jace chuckles, a husky sound that stirs her stomach. "I need a minute too." He brushes a finger across the arc of her cheekbone. "You scared the hell out of me."

She lowers her lashes, the concern in his voice overpowering. "Jace, I—"

"Emmy Lou, darlin'!"

Her mother's voice cuts in, sharp and shrill.

Emmy Lou winces. Jace stands, keeping a hand on her shoulder.

Striding forward, Mama Belle elbows Jace aside and steps between them, breaking their connection. Behind Mama Belle, the crowd of ladies, her father and Grady hover.

"You locked your knees, darlin'." A huff of a laugh. "Silly girl," she drawls to the crowd more than to Emmy Lou. "You'd think she'd learn after all this time."

Boone grunts in worry.

Emmy Lou twists her hands together and looks up at her mother. Trying to play the perfect part even though she's exhausted. "I'm okay, Mama. I just need to sit here a second."

Mama Belle leans in, her voice a low tone of warning. "We can't have another incident like this, Emmaline. It doesn't look good."

"Emmy Lou don't look good," Jace says softly, and Emmy Lou gives him a wan smile.

Mama Belle's face turns red, but she ignores the comment. "Poor girl," she croons. "You need some love and care, is all. We'll get you to the house and—"

"I'll take her home," Jace says, his voice one of cool authority. "I'll take care of her."

Mama Belle's lips pucker, unused to Jace standing up and taking charge. Stiffening, Mama Belle turns to rebut, but it's Boone who says, "If that's what Emmy Lou wants, we'd sure appreciate that, Jace." He puts a hand on Mama Belle's shoulder, silencing her objections.

Emmy Lou nods. "I do."

Jace steps up and Emmy Lou lets him pull her to her feet. He wraps an arm around her waist, bracing her against him like he knows just how shaky she is inside and out. Emmy Lou leans into him, the solid sureness of his body, the unwavering strength in his eyes, giving her what she needs to get through this. A safe space.

Before she knows it, Grady's by her side, the two men steering her out of the arena and toward the truck.

Emmy Lou squeezes her eyes shut. *It's okay*, she thinks. *You're okay.*

But she's not.

She never was.

J ACE FILLS A GLASS OF WATER UNDER THE TAP AND THEN shuts it off. He takes a quick walk through the house, locking the front door but leaving a window open. The sun is still high in the sky despite it being seven o'clock. Summer hours. They let you get the work done long into the night.

He walks down the hall and up the stairs to Emmy Lou's bedroom. After the scene at the arena, she had been dead-on-her-feet exhausted. Not to mention distracted as all hell. In the car ride on the way home, she had lain limply against the seat, pale, not speaking, almost as if she was in another world completely. It worried him. Together, he and Grady managed to coax her into getting some rest.

He doesn't buy her excuse about drinking too much. He barely saw her touch the champagne Mama Belle poured out. Her eyes were far off. Far away from him. Like they were when he first met her.

Jace always thought there was something about Wildheart that made Emmy Lou a paler version of herself. He chalked it up to Mama Belle. A stressed-out Emmy Lou always fretting about coming home and playing the perfect part for her mama, playing the peacemaker between her and Jace, but now he ain't so sure.

Because today, she was as skittish as a jumpy horse. His Emmy Lou doesn't get nervous in front of a crowd. He knows his wife. She can handle the *Star*, a magazine interview, a red carpet with the calm coolness of a pro.

Something spooked her up on that stage.

Hell, she spooked *him*. He's never getting over that heart-stopping scene. Turning to see Emmy Lou, pale and unsteady, swaying on her feet, about to go down. He never ran so damn fast. He thanks Christ he caught her, can still feel the violent tremble of her small frame against his.

On the second-floor landing, Jace takes a right off the stairs. When he reaches the bedroom, he pauses. Inside, he can hear the low tones of Grady's drawl mixed with his sister's. Through the shut door, their voices drift straight to him.

"You feel okay now, don't you?"

"I'm fine, Grady. Stop bein' an ol' nag," Emmy Lou insists. Jace smiles, picturing his wife sitting up in bed, a stubborn frown on her pretty face. "I'm not sick. It was just all of today. It was overwhelmin.'"

"Tell Mama you ain't doin' the rodeo."

An aghast gasp. "I can't do that."

"You damn near fainted. You faint on a horse next time . . ." Grady trails off, letting the terrifying scenario linger.

Then, Emmy Lou's voice, smaller, quieter. "I thought I saw him."

A sigh. "You didn't, Em."

"I swear, I saw him, Grady."

Jace frowns, moving closer. *Saw who?*

"I ain't crazy. Or delusional."

"No one's sayin' that. I'm sayin' he hasn't been back in years and he ain't about to show up now."

Jace stands silent in the dim glow of the hallway. The voices in the room change to hushed whispers, almost as if they can feel him lurking. He moves closer to the door to hear better, hating himself for eavesdropping, but he can't stop it. The frightened tone in Emmy Lou's voice worries him.

"There was someone there. There was a man. I know it because I saw it." She sounds indignant now. Annoyed.

There's a long, loaded silence.

Footsteps. Grady pacing the old floorboards. "I don't know, Em. I just don't know."

A tendril of worry curls inside Jace's gut. He thinks of the black sedan he saw earlier today, passing slow through the arena alleyway. He thinks of McCade coming to his Nashville farm, threatening his wife. He tries to talk himself down. There's no good reason the guy would come back for him. Would he? He paid McCade off. They're done. Even. Over.

Jace closes his eyes. Worry frays his edges.

But still . . .

"Next time" could be anyone. Be careful.

His hands curl into fists. What if it isn't over? What if McCade doesn't plan to leave him alone? Worse—what if he wants to hurt Emmy Lou?

Fuck. *Fuck.*

Sick to his stomach, Jace moves to the window, trying to shake off the building dread. Paranoia runs through him like a knife, twisting, staking in the doubt. The guilt.

You protect the ones you love, Jace. You do anything to keep them safe.

Jace stares down the twisted line of road. The gated entrance. The seclusion of the farm promises peace. Safety. If McCade followed him here, if Jace led the guy straight to Emmy Lou, he'll never forgive himself.

If something happens to her . . .

He can't breathe. Closing his eyes, he rubs at the ache in his chest.

"Hey, man." A voice at his back. "You're pacin' a hole in the floor."

Jace turns. Grady's stepping out into the hall, his jaw tight.

"Everything okay?" Jace asks, keeping his voice even.

Grady joins Jace at the window. "It's cool. She's cool."

Jace blows out a breath and stares Grady down. "Do I need to be worried?" It's the closest he'll come to asking Grady to betray his sister.

Grady's eyes flicker. "I don't know."

A muscle flexes in Jace's jaw. "You got a pistol or somethin' I can borrow while I'm here?"

Grady blinks. Then his features reset. "Yeah. I'll bring it by tomorrow." He tilts his head, his expression wary. "Do *I* need to be worried?"

"Not yet."

Jace pushes off the wall and heads for Emmy Lou's door.

He needs to see her. Now.

Steeling a breath, Jace gives a quick knuckle rap on the door and enters. Emmy Lou's at her vanity, scrubbing furiously at the mascara beneath her eyes. "Hey, Em." He sets the water on the nightstand. "How you doin', honey?"

He waits for it. For a snarl, a scream, for his wife to throw his ass out of their bedroom.

She blinks like she's a thousand miles away, and then her face resets itself into a kind of stoic composure. "Oh, my word," she says, standing. "This sure has been a day, hasn't it? Straight up causin' a fuss all over the place and now I got Grady worryin' and Wyatt's goin' to be here tomorrow harassin' me all about blowin' up Mama's big event . . . not to mention, today's the worst possible day for mascara."

Jace frowns, watching as she breezes around the room, fussing with the windows, with knickknacks on her dresser. She's talking fast like she does when she's nervous, trying to play off her jumpiness under endless amounts of babbling.

He grabs her elbow as she tries to pass him. "Em, Em," he says in a calm voice. She stills, locking gazes with him. "You don't gotta do that. Pretend. Not with me."

She opens her mouth to argue, then snaps it shut. Relief shines bright in her eyes. They know each other. They ain't gotta hide. She lets out a little sigh that shakes her body. "I'm embarrassed."

"I know it, but you shouldn't be. C'mon now." Taking her hand, he guides her to the edge of the bed and sits her down.

As he perches next to her, he takes a minute to glance around the bedroom.

Their bedroom.

An image of Emmy surfaces in his mind. Her hair wild and tangled, laughing, jumping off the bed into his arms. Seven years ago, and the Brothers Kincaid had just been nominated for vocal group of the year at the CMAs.

Jace glances over at Emmy Lou, frowning at his wife's appearance. Her eyes are wistful, haunted, and she looks fragile and delicate in the thin slip dress she wears.

"Are you sure this is a good idea?" He touches her forehead, checking her temperature. "You ridin' again?"

Her brown eyes flash in indignation. Jace smiles faintly, seeing some of that fire he loves coming back to her. "Of course it is. Besides, I promised Mama. I can't back out. I'm Wildheart's rodeo queen."

"No one's askin' you to do that. It's just . . . I've never seen you that nervous," Jace hedges. "At least not in the ring."

He wants to ask why. Why she's nervous in that ring. But he doesn't want to press. He has this moment, he's in her bedroom and she's talking to him. He'll take what he can get.

She only nods and lowers her eyes, her gaze on her hands, which sit limply in her lap.

"You were far away today, honey."

"I know I was."

A long silence.

Jace sits and waits, resolved to stick it out, to put together the pieces of the puzzle that don't yet click. He sees it, washing across Emmy Lou's face, fear, the desperate urge to tell him the truth. The longing to confide in him. But he also sees her clamming up. Because she doesn't trust him. Because he's not that person for her. Not anymore.

The truth hurts, but Jace sits with it. Lets it batter him black and blue.

Finally, Emmy Lou looks up. She licks her lips, swallows, gathering the words. "I haven't been to the arena since . . ." Her pretty face clouds, her face losing all color. "Since my last show."

Her announcement stalls his breath. Makes perfect god-damn sense.

"Shit," he says, feeling like an asshole for not making the connection. He knows all about Emmy Lou getting locked in the horse trailer for hours after she took home the title of rodeo queen. It's the reason for her claustrophobia, why she doesn't go on the tour bus with him and the Brothers Kincaid.

He reaches over to take her hand and though her eyes widen, she lets him. The way her small hand fits into his has him struggling to breathe.

One step.

Just one step closer and Jace can barely allow himself to hope.

He sighs, rubbing his thumb over her knuckles. "Honey, you should have told me."

Pride and worry war inside of him. He's so damn proud of Emmy Lou for facing her fears, yet he hates that she took it on alone. He wishes she would have told him, if nothing else so that he could have made sure she was okay.

Emmy Lou flushes at the admonishment, bright orbs of color darkening her cheeks. "It ain't exactly like we've been friendly lately."

"Is that all it was?" The conversation he overheard between her and Grady plays in his head. He's got the what. But it sounded like there was a who.

Emmy Lou's eyes go blank, worry crossing her face. Jace's heart twists, and it takes all he has not to grip her hand and pull her into his arms. But before he can say anything, Emmy Lou shifts and retracts her hand. "Speakin' of friendly, I'm sorry for the way Mama treated you today."

Jace sighs inwardly, knowing a subject change when he sees it. "It's okay."

"No, it's not." She huffs. "For all Mama's advice on etiquette, she sure can't seem to follow her own."

"Well, that's your mama. Sour in the sugar." They share a laugh and then Jace says, "I'm used to it by now."

"I know. But I'm sorry you're used to it."

Her words hang in the air between them. Emmy Lou shifts awkwardly on the edge of the bed and then, like they've shared too much, crosses her arms in front of her chest. The universal signal for back the fuck off.

Reluctantly, Jace stands, slapping his hands on the knees of his jeans.

"I'm gonna go," he says, even though that's the last thing he wants to do. He should be staying. In his bedroom with his wife, helping her through whatever it is she's going through. "You rest. Drink that water, you hear me?"

Emmy Lou only nods, her haunted gaze watching him as he crosses the room.

Jace hesitates. A war rages within him. It's dangerous territory to say what he wants to say, to actually acknowledge that this summer could end any other way than bringing Emmy Lou home to Nashville, but he has to say it. He wants her to know that he's still here. She has to know he means it, what she means to him.

That he is here for her and he's not going anywhere. Never again will he let her down.

"Look," he says, and she stiffens. "Whether we're together or not..." His voice breaks. "I have your back no matter what."

Her eyes widen in surprise, a faint pink flush spreading across her cheeks.

He starts for the door, only to stop when Emmy Lou says his name.

"Em?" He turns around, facing her, willing everything in him not to hope, when inside his chest his heart pumps out a frantic beat.

Her full lips part. There's an ache in her beautiful face, a vulnerability that Jace hasn't seen in a long time.

Stay, he thinks. *Ask me to stay.*

Her mouth opens, closes. Then she says, "Good night."

chapter
SIXTEEN

EMMY LOU SITS UP IN BED, WARMED BY THE BRIGHT sunlight cascading through the open window. She's also drenched in sweat. Last night's sleep was restless. Dreams that bordered on nightmares, all mingling together like a too-strong cocktail, leaving her with a bad memory hangover.

With a great huff that could rival Mama Belle's theatrics, she flops back against the mattress, her eyes on the dark ceiling beams, her mind on last night. The way Jace carried her offstage after she nearly fainted, like some burly bodyguard who'd take a bullet for her. She thinks back to what Jace said yesterday.

Whether we're together or not . . . I have your back no matter what.

The most beautiful words she's ever heard. Like some primal vow telling her he would always be around. They lit a fire inside of her. She almost called him back to stay with her. Because while her brain screamed no, her body remembered just how Jace could make her feel. Safe. Comforted. She ached for that.

For him.

Instead, she went to bed alone. Giving in would have been torture for both of them.

She growls at the ceiling. She keeps wanting to touch him. Like it's habit. Like he's still hers. What she needs to do is duct-tape her damn hands behind her back. All she's doing is giving him false impressions. False hope.

Rolling over in bed, Emmy Lou checks the time on her phone and groans. It's nearly ten. Wyatt will be here soon, no doubt ready to ride her ass about yesterday.

With that, Emmy Lou grabs fresh clothes and enters the bathroom. She washes her face and applies light makeup, running her fingers through her icy platinum-blond hair. Straightening up, she blinks at her reflection in the mirror, seeing a watermark of her seventeen-year-old self. A fragment of that scared girl who ran all the way to Nashville.

She closes her eyes, her fingers gripping the counter, and breathes steadily. She's never been afraid of coming back to Wildheart. Ever. It's her home. Slayton's been gone thirteen years; there's no reason for this messy madness of her mind.

It was that damn horse trailer busting up her nerves, spooking her like she was one of her own horses.

That's her story, at least, and she's sticking to it.

Last night, she was close to telling Jace about Slayton. He knew something was wrong, could always read her better than herself at times. But nerves got the better of her. Besides, what good would it do? Talking about the past won't fix it. It won't erase what happened.

A hot rush of shame fills her at the thought of Jace knowing her deepest, darkest secret.

Secrets.

It's why she didn't tell her parents, her brothers, isn't it? Appearances meant everything to Mama Belle. Their families thought she and Slayton were perfect for each other. It was her word against his. What if they didn't believe her? What if they *blamed* her?

The sick part is she blamed herself. Looking back, she should have seen Slayton wasn't the boy he pretended to be. She missed all the red flags. Moodiness when she didn't spend time with him. Always having to check in with him with they were apart. Not hearing the menace in his voice when he jokingly told her she loved the rodeo more than him.

Because she loved him. She stayed with him because their parents were friends. Because they had been brought up practically betrothed. Because there hadn't been anyone to tell her, a thirteen-year-old-girl, that maybe, just maybe, he didn't treat her like he should.

There was no one to show her the right way to love.

Until she met Jace, and she came to understand everything a good man should be.

If she told Jace about Slayton, he'd understand, she knows he would. But telling him after all this time . . .

She shakes her head. It doesn't matter.

The past needs to stay in the past. Right now, she needs to ride.

Emmy Lou exits the bedroom and descends the stairs. She checks the living room, the kitchen. No Jace.

She stands there, her heart pumping hard in her chest. A flood of annoyance fills her as she realizes she's disappointed he's not there.

To tell him thank you.

That's the only reason she's disappointed. She owes him that if nothing else. For being there, for taking care of her after her near-swoon on the stage.

Damn her, and damn her stupid feelings.

She's out of the house lickety-split. Standing in the front yard next to his pickup truck is Wyatt, a smirk on his boyish face.

"Well, if it ain't the talk of the town."

With a flip of her hair, she breezes past him, bound for the pasture. "You're one to talk. You remember Phantom? You farted, spooked him and he broke your toe in front of the entire country club, so I wouldn't be sassin' me, Wyatt Montgomery."

She makes her way to the pasture, where Outlaw stands, saddled and ready for the day, his inky-black tail flicking away flies. She takes in the barrels arranged for her first cloverleaf pattern. She pauses and scours the field, shielding her eyes against the sun.

"Lookin' for Jace?" Wyatt says in her ear.

She jumps, whirling around. She swats at her brother. "No, I ain't lookin' for Jace."

"Heard he scooped you up like Sleeping Beauty."

She prickles at being called out, at being so damn obvious.

She thinks of last night, of Jace, his fierce arms around her protecting her, and her body fills with heat.

Propping her hands on her waist, she glares at Wyatt. "Are we gonna ride or are you gonna nag me all mornin'?"

"He's at Daddy's," Wyatt says, watching as Emmy Lou eases her way into the pasture, one hand held out to Outlaw.

Emmy Lou turns his way, blinking in surprise.

"The house got thrashed in the storm." At the mention of the storm, she flushes, thinking about what else got thrashed that night. "Jace and Grady are up there helpin' him clean up that field of fallen trees."

"They are?"

"Yeah." Wyatt exhales a long, slow breath. "It's good Daddy's sellin' the farm. He's old, Em," Wyatt says when she frowns. "All he needs is a buyer."

She harrumphs. "The *right* buyer."

He laughs at the unhappy look on her face. "Don't bite my head off about it. I'm just tellin' you what I think."

"You sure you and Charlie don't want it?" She inches close to Outlaw, not wanting to spook him, to ruin the fragile trust they've been building. Though the horse's nostrils flare, he stands still, his dark eyes on her.

"We got the ranch in Montana, you know that. Besides, we both know Charlie ain't livin' here." His throat works. "Not after Maggie . . ."

He trails off. Emmy Lou's eyes water at the mention of Charlie's feisty fiancée who died in the rodeo ring. The reason he left Georgia and moved to Montana. The reason all his brothers followed. Maggie's death is like a rain cloud that still follows Charlie around. He hasn't set foot in Wildheart's arena in years.

Charlie ran.

She ran.

Montgomerys don't cry, but they sure got runnin' down pat.

There's a gentle bump on her arm. Emmy Lou glances over. Outlaw's nudging her arm with his nose as if sensing her sadness and wanting to offer comfort. She stares into Outlaw's eyes; his calming gaze seems to call her to ride. After the night in the storm, her saving him, not giving up on him over these last two weeks, he trusts her. She can feel it.

"Alright, sugar," she drawls, taking the reins in her left hand while simultaneously gripping the saddle horn. "You're gonna let me do this, ain't you? We gotta show off for my dumb big brother."

Their eyes lock. Then, almost as if he's personally given her his approval, Outlaw stands still and calm, and with an ease she never imagined, Emmy Lou swings herself up onto the horse's back.

Wyatt exhales, his grin proud. "I'll be goddamned."

Outlaw paws the ground, willing and ready to go, to follow Emmy Lou's lead.

She smiles. "C'mon. Let's ride."

They begin.

Emmy Lou approaches the designated starting point. The barrels shine in the sun. Wyatt, on his horse, trots beside her. "Let's mark the pattern first."

She nods, her stomach in knots. Excitement or nerves, she can't tell.

Emmy Lou walks the pattern. It's slow, tedious work, when all she wants to do is go fast, but it lets her and the horse know what they'll be doing.

Finally, once she and Outlaw are comfortable, they're back at the starting point. Ready to take the pattern at a trot.

Wyatt shouts, "Heels down, shoulders back, Em! Keep it controlled, not fast!"

She inhales a steadying breath, then—

Emmy Lou leans forward and gives Outlaw a good kick. "Ha!" she yells to spur the horse. The world races by her. Standing in the stirrups, she leans forward, going with Outlaw's momentum. The wind whips her hair. It feels like flying. Like freedom.

When she gets to the first barrel, she sits, righting herself on the saddle and pulling the reins slightly to slow Outlaw down. He turns when she tells him to, leading him with the reins.

Then Outlaw slows down. Too slow. She jerks in the saddle and comes to a stop.

"Lean in," Wyatt barks. "You ain't leanin', Em!" He shakes his head, his face creased in frustration. "Again. Do it again."

Emmy Lou tries again, tries to concentrate, to focus on Wyatt's sharp snap of instruction, but every time she tries to take the second barrel, a harsh one-eighty-degree turn, she can't.

She can't keep to the pattern. Can't get her grip on herself, the ride, the horse. It's like some sick, foreboding feeling has overtaken her body. Like yesterday knocked her off-balance. Knocked her confidence out of the ring.

Wyatt whips his horse over to her. "You ain't takin' this seriously."

Her lower lip juts out. "I am, Wyatt."

"No. You ain't. You're slowin' Outlaw down." Worry, annoyance flickers in his eyes. "You're better than this. You're both better than this. You got to listen to what I tell you, or I'm just wastin' my time. The horse can't do it alone; you got to work as a team."

"I hear you."

He gives her a doubtful look. "Are you sure?"

No. She isn't sure at all. The only thing she hears is Slayton. His voice in her ears, hissing, *You can't say no. You're mine.*

Slayton's here with her. On her farm, in her arena, worming his way into her brain. To Emmy Lou, it feels like the minute she rides Outlaw into the arena, everyone will know what happened to her. Everyone will see her pain on a pedestal. They'll see her secret.

"Let's go again," Wyatt says in a low voice, backing his horse up a few feet.

Emmy Lou releases a breath and picks up the reins.

Again and again and again.

"No!" Wyatt shouts, arms up toward the sky. The sun now dips below the pasture.

Again.

"You're chokin', Em."

Emmy Lou swears, hot tears of frustration beading her eyes.

Everything Wyatt's been trying to teach her feels like it's gone in one ear and out the other.

She's wanted to do this for so damn long, and even now, Slayton's taking away her joy.

And she wants it back.

Finally, fed up and frustrated, she digs her heels into Outlaw's side. "Ha!"

Outlaw lunges forward. She wants to go fast, to be reckless and wild like she can outrun Slayton's ghost. Faster and faster. She takes the first barrel. The second. Coming up on the third, the wind roaring in her ears, Outlaw's muscled body moving beneath her, the finish line in front of her, she realizes it's too fast.

Shit.

She tries to stop, but she doesn't lean back. She forgets to put her feet forward.

She sees Wyatt's mouth moving around a warning, a warning she should know, but it's too late.

She's thrown forward over Outlaw's head.

As she sails through the air, Emmy Lou keeps her head tucked and her chin down. She hits the ground with a hard thud, taking the brunt of the impact with her shoulder. Coughing as the breath's pummeled from her body, she rolls out of the way of Outlaw's legs. A pebble's lodged in her shoulder. Dazed, she slowly sits up, blinking away dust and tears.

"Goddamnit, Emmy Lou." Wyatt's stomping over to her, cowboy hat in his hands. His light brown hair stands on end. "I told you so many goddamn times to lean back, and what do you go and do?" He drops beside her, assessing her for injury. His anger, his worry boils the air between them. "You go and get yourself thrown."

A shaky breath and then Wyatt's squeezing her arms, her wrists. "You okay? Anything broken?" he asks in a serious big-brother voice.

She turns her face away from him. "I'm fine, Wyatt."

"Bullshit."

"Let's go again," she says and tries to get up, but Wyatt shakes his head and grabs her arm to steady her on her feet.

"I don't want you hurt, Em."

She huffs. "I can do it."

"You can't." His narrowed eyes take her in. Both Emmy Lou and her horse are slick with sweat. "The horse needs a rest. And you need, hell, you—you need an exorcism or somethin'."

Emmy Lou scowls and dismounts. "I ain't in the mood, Wyatt." She knows she rode like shit. She doesn't need her older brother reminding her how awful she was. But Wyatt won't take the hint.

"What's wrong with you?" His voice is confused, his eyes earnest. "You ain't never rode like this in your life. Like a beginner. Like—"

Emmy Lou's shaking her head. She puts her hand on Outlaw's thick mane, willing the sensation to calm her. To ground her. "Don't you say it."

"Like you got the yips," he finishes, bulldozing over her warning. He looks past her to Outlaw. "You turned him into a kitten and you still can't even nail the move."

"I know what I got and it ain't the yips," Emmy Lou snaps.

"Well, you got somethin'," Wyatt mutters.

Anger flares in her. Anger that Wyatt's right. Anger that the past won't let her loose. Anger that she can't do a move that should be second nature. Anger at feeling that sharp sting of love for Jace and still wanting to throttle him at the same time.

She stabs Wyatt with a glare. "Since you're so damn impatient, excuse me for wastin' your damn time, just like I'm wastin' my damn life."

He draws back, eyes widening in surprise at her outburst. "Em. I didn't mean . . ."

She puts her hands out and backs up. The space around them is suddenly too small. Her chest squeezes tight with anxiety. She inhales a shaky breath, gulping air.

Wyatt's dark blue eyes soften, but he keeps his distance. "If you want, let's go again. You'll get it right. Let's—"

"No." She blinks, resurfacing from the darkness. "I'm done."

Her cheeks burn with embarrassment and shame.

Some rodeo queen she is.

Wyatt examines her for a long second, then whisks his dusty hands together. Plumes of dust billow in the air. "Go on inside and get some water. I'll round up the horses."

Whirling around, Emmy Lou starts for the house, her heart a drumbeat in her chest.

Her throat tightens as the unbidden thought hits her.

Suddenly wishing for, wanting, what she can't have.

The one person in the world who can make her feel alright.

Jace.

Jace groans as he hops out of his truck. He's dusty, hot and dead tired. Every body part he owns is screaming for a shower, a glass of whiskey and a bed. Together with Grady, he spent the entire day helping Boone clear out a shitload of fallen trees from the woods. He didn't realize how much work the farm was, how much Boone and Mama Belle would be on their own once Grady, Wyatt and Charlie returned to their respective lives.

Jace steps inside the front door of the Happy Hideaway and instantly, the smell of summer disappears. In its place: hot dough, cinnamon stick, flour-dusted air.

His stomach growls. He's fucking famished. These last two weeks he's been living off gas station meals and beer. Emmy Lou and her torture tactics are working.

Jace stops at the threshold of the kitchen and stares.

Shit.

It's an explosion of goodness. The counters are covered in every baked good imaginable. Chocolate chip cookies. Brownies.

A three-layer German chocolate cake. Casseroles. Cornbread. Peach cobbler.

Emmy Lou's on a food tear. It'd be adorable if he didn't know what it meant. Something's bothering her.

Emmy Lou drops the oven mitts from her hands when she sees him. "How was Daddy's?"

He grins. Removes his cowboy hat to mop his brow. "Got the trees cleared out. How was your ride?"

The sides of her bright smile droop, apprehension in her gaze. "Fine," she drawls.

He lifts a brow, his eyes roving the assortment of baked goods. "Did some damage in the kitchen."

"I did." She peers at him. "You look beat."

"Yup." He stretches, groaning in exaggeration. "Boone put me through the wringer. For an old man, your daddy sure runs a tight ship."

She nods, then huffs. "At least you were out there. My own lazy brothers can't even be bothered."

He laughs. "Grady held his own."

"Grady's the only one with common sense and good manners."

Jace's chest squeezes tight when she smiles at him. A spark so good it should be illegal crackles up his spine.

Then, replacing his hat on his head, he gives a nod to the doorway. "Gonna head down and shower, get out of your hair."

"Wait. Jace."

Emmy Lou's biting her lip. She gestures awkwardly at the stove, where a stock pot simmers. "If you're hungry . . ."

At the offer, every part inside of him ignites. Still, he keeps cool, calm. He inclines his head. "You askin' me to have dinner with you, Emmy Lou?"

She gives him a wry look. "You gonna argue with me, Jace Taylor, or come fill your belly?"

He chuckles, loving the almost-shy blush that's darkened Emmy Lou's cheeks. "Think I got time for a shower?"

She flicks a dishrag in his direction, a playful smile on her lips. "Go on and git and I'll set the table."

Fifteen minutes later, Jace is back in the kitchen after taking a shower, and a cold one at that. Hell, he damn near tripped over his own feet in his hasty rush to get back to Emmy Lou. He doesn't know what this means; all he knows is this offer is some kind of gift from the universe and he ain't passing it up. He's got a long way to go to get back in her good graces, but this is still one step forward.

"That smells fuckin' amazin'," he says, leaning across the island. Emmy Lou is ladling out crater-sized dumplings into bowls. She looks up as he enters.

She grins at him. "Just wait till you taste it."

"Can I help with anything?"

"Drinks?" She hefts the two bowls in her hands. "I got the rest."

He goes to the fridge, his gaze on the whiteboard. Memories swallow him up. This feels like old times. *Their* old times. Nashville. Late-night talks on their porch, listening to the horses nicker in the field, sharing glasses of whiskey and sleeping in late the next morning. Emmy Lou lighting up the kitchen with amazing smells, with her happy laugh and bubbly bounce.

All of this—he misses it. Misses her.

He grabs two beers from the fridge, trying to shake loose the bittersweet memories.

They settle into chairs at the table. The bowls in front of them are heaping and piping hot. Emmy Lou fiddles nervously with her napkin, all kinds of prim and proper.

"Thanks," Jace says, picking up a spoon. "For askin' me to dinner. Otherwise, I'd be at the diner right now lettin' Miss Desiree scrape together whatever she's got on the grill."

Emmy Lou feigns mock horror. "Talkin' like that about Miss Desiree? You should be ashamed." She lowers her voice conspiratorially. "Even though we both know she hasn't cleaned that grill since seventy-nine."

They both laugh, the tension broken.

"Well, anyway, you're welcome," she says almost indignantly, like the thought of asking him to dinner is like asking a serial killer to join her. She lifts a dumpling, letting it steam. Then her eyes, her voice soften. "I really appreciate you helpin' out my daddy." A little line of worry appears between her brow. "It sounds like he needs it."

Jace sips his beer, letting the soup cool down, considering how to tell her that she's right. That Boone's getting up there in age. He saw it today, the old man trying to haul loads of lumber by hand, only to be intercepted by Jace or Grady, the look of relief creasing his dusty face when help arrived.

"He does," Jace says, carefully choosing his words.

"How do you think he's doin'?" She puts a hand on his arm and Jace's heart flares at the simple contact. "Tell me real, Jace."

Tell me real. Emmy Lou's phrase for wanting the truth.

"I think... I think it's a lot for him to take on. He's been doin' it for so long he doesn't know how to quit."

Forgetting about her soup, Emmy Lou props her chin in her palm. Her pretty face crinkles up. "I know Daddy's sellin' the farm because he needs to but... I love it so much. Maybe more than Nashville." She gives him an abashed look. "I know it's a sin, but—"

"But it's your home." He holds her gaze. Her eyes are so wistful, so beautiful, he can't look away. "I get it, Em. I've always loved the farm too."

"My daddy and I—we always had the best days on the farm. When I was little, seven or eight, I had this pony, Pinkie. I'd ride him down into the ridge. And one day he was spooked by a rabbit and he threw me." She smiles soft. "Pinkie took off, and I—well, I didn't know how to get back to the house on my own. But I remember I wasn't afraid. I found this beautiful spot under a tree, a spot I never knew how to find again. Some days, I think I just imagined it. The tree was gold and was like some gigantic gnarled hand liftin' from this earth to the heavens. Otherworldly. But I was fine. I was happy. I was just waitin' on Daddy to come and find me. And he did."

Jace grins, picturing his wild farm girl, big brown eyes, tangled hair. "Boone sounded the alarms, I'm sure."

She laughs, her eyes bright. "I remember now. The whole lot of 'em—Daddy, Davis, Ford, Charlie, and Wyatt—all came trompin' down."

A silence falls over them. The perfect silence. Comfortable, easy as they dig into their food.

"What about you?" Jace asks, tapping his spoon against the side of the bowl. "The food, Em. You cooked all the food in the damn house."

She flushes, lowers her eyes. At her embarrassment, Jace laughs. "I know you, honey."

"You do," she admits softly, tracing an invisible line across her napkin with her fingernail.

"So. Tell me what's wrong."

She hesitates, then says, "Outlaw threw me today." She holds a hand up as he starts. "But it was my fault. I wasn't listenin'." She sighs. "I can't take the second barrel. I trained all day with Wyatt and I just kept drillin' it with my thigh. Lord knows I'm bruised as hell." She makes a face. "He thinks I have the yips."

He chuckles. "Do you?"

"Yips are for cowards, Jace, and I ain't no coward."

"I know you ain't." That's the last thing his wife is. It's one of the best reasons he loves her. Because she's fearless and fun. She taught Jace that you don't give up, and you definitely don't give in.

"I can't give the speech, and now I can't ride in the ring?" Frustration is etched across her pretty features. "And just when I got that damn horse to like me too." Her mouth flatlines. "Lord, what am I gonna tell Mama Belle?"

An idea lights in his mind. A place where Emmy's always felt calm. Centered.

"Hell, if you're nervous onstage, give the speech on Outlaw."

"What?"

"The horses," Jace ventures. "They calm you; you calm them. Get a mic and give your speech there. Then it's just you and that horse. You ain't boxed in. And you sure as hell won't have Mama Belle breathin' down your neck."

She blinks, a broad smile overtaking her face. "That's a great idea." Then her face falls. "But that still doesn't solve for the move."

He leans forward. "What if . . ." He hesitates, unsure if his suggestion will get him booted from the dinner table. "What if we do it together?"

She flushes at the words.

"Ride Outlaw," he amends quickly. "I know you, Em. I know how you ride. The way your body moves. Wyatt doesn't. He's so dead set on makin' you a cowboy, he forgets all about *you*."

His own words have him lost in the past, lost in his wife. The way he knows so much about Emmy Lou. The way her mouth puckers up when he tells her they have to leave in five minutes, the way her body responds when he touches her, the way she likes three ice cubes in her white wine, a hot bath after a hard ride.

All of the little ways he knows her, and none of them he wants to give up.

She's nodding, slowly, chewing on the idea. "Okay," she agrees. She wets her lips. "We'll train together. There's only one thing."

"Name it."

"You can't go easy on me. I have to nail this."

"Deal. But only if you do one thing for me." She cocks her head curiously. He continues. "Tell me why you're doin' this. Barrel racin.'"

Her eyes widen in surprise. She thinks on it for a long second and then grins. "Deal."

Reaching out, he takes her small hand in his. A faint blush stains Emmy Lou's cheeks as her fingers curl into his palm. They shake on it. But she doesn't pull away; she lets Jace hold her hand, set on the table between them like some kind of truce.

A miracle is what Jace would call it.

"Jace," she says, fiddling with the edge of her napkin. "I need to say somethin' to you. I need to apologize."

"For what?"

Emmy Lou takes a breath. "That fight we had." She meets his gaze, shame on her face. "I never should have said what I did about not wanting to have a baby with you. That was rude and mean. My manners, Jace, they were awful. I'm sorry."

Jace stares.

Her apology means so damn much. Not that he needed one from her—he's the one who owes her an apology a hundred of times over—but it's a step. A step to fixing the shaky foundation that is their marriage.

"Don't be," Jace says over the stone in his throat. He's still holding on to her hand like it's an anchor. "I broke your trust. It's my fault."

"It's both of our faults, then." Tears glisten in her eyes. "I should have told you I started takin' birth control again."

"I can't blame you for not wantin' a baby." He hangs his head. "I know I ain't without my faults. I was a complacent asshole, a fool. I didn't work hard to fix us, Em. I was so busy, I forgot about you. And I'm so damn sorry, honey. I hate myself for it."

"Jace . . ."

"I come home too late. I go to bed too early. I've never even wrote you a song. Hell, I'm borin.'"

Emmy Lou squeezes his hand, silencing his doubts. "You're not borin', Jace. You're so steady. You are kind. You keep me grounded. Otherwise, I'd just fly away on the breeze." She laughs. "And if you are borin', well, I love that about you."

At the word *love*—not *loved*—her face flushes.

Jace tightens his grip on her hand. Heat arcs between them. He wets his lips, wanting nothing more than to kiss her. To strip her naked, bend her over the counter and slip inside her. To make her gasp his name and come over and over again. His dick jumps in his jeans, craving more, craving her body against his, but he fights the heady feeling, fights what he doesn't deserve.

At least not until Emmy Lou makes the first move.

"Jace." Emmy Lou's voice comes breathless. She stares at him through lowered lashes, longing etched all over her face.

First move? He's gonna say hell yes.

Slowly, Jace slides his hand up her bare arm. A small whimper comes from Emmy Lou, her body trembling at his touch.

For a moment, he closes his eyes, torn between keeping his distance or hauling her onto his lap.

Then he leans in, closing the space between them. His hand cups her warm cheek. Emmy Lou angles her face. He pulls her closer, feeling just the barest sweep of her sweet lips on his, when—

"Emmaline, sugar, you home?"

Mama Belle's voice rings out from the screen door, and Jace cringes.

"Oh, Lord, it's Mama." Emmy Lou rockets out of her seat, her voice extra high-pitched and shaky.

Jace groans, shifting uncomfortably in his chair as heat combusts through his lower regions. He thanks Christ for the protection of the table. The last thing he needs is for Mama Belle to walk in and see him sporting a raging erection.

Hastily straightening her clothes, Emmy Lou glances down at him. Apologies shine bright in her eyes. "Stay here. I'll get her out of here in two shakes."

He watches her go, his heart pounding in his chest. The feel of Emmy Lou's hand in his burns like the best kind of brand.

Has him feeling something he hasn't felt in a long damn time.

Hope.

"Mama, hey." Emmy Lou ushers her mother straight into the living room in the hopes she doesn't see Jace. "What're you doin' here? It's dinnertime."

But Mama Belle and her eagle eyes miss nothing. "Don't you *hey, Mama* me," she drawls, her tone heavy with disdain as they both settle onto the leather couch. "What on earth is he doin' up here?"

"Mama, he ain't the Phantom of the Opera," Emmy Lou says, keeping her voice low. "He don't gotta stay in the basement."

It's a heroic act to sit still in front of her mother, to resist the urge to fan her face, to replay that near-kiss over and over again. She's overheated. Mentally. Physically.

Lord, that conversation. Jace's hand on hers, his lips—

"I ain't doin' this, Emmy Lou." Mama Belle huffs and flaps a hand. "Not now. Not when I have plans."

Emmy Lou frowns. "Plans? What're you—"

"The anniversary party, darlin'. The rodeo. That means end of summer. That means Jace leaves." Mama Belle pats the side of her large bag. "That means you sign these papers."

Emmy Lou gapes at her, horrified. "Oh, Mama, you brought 'em with you?"

The reminder, the divorce papers practically burning a hole in Mama Belle's bag have acrid bile rising in her throat. If she knew her mama'd been carting the papers all over town like some sadistic courier, she would have lit them up in one of Luke's bonfires.

Emmy Lou can't ignore the truth anymore. That her head *and* her heart are still stuck back in the kitchen with Jace. There's something soft and reassuring about someone knowing you as long as they have. Tonight, Jace knew what she needed and offered it. He was patient, willing to talk to her and figure out her problem without an interrogation. Who else would do that for her? Who else knows her inside and out? Knows how she rides a horse, knows that she bakes when she's bothered, knows to give her space in tight places so she isn't boxed in.

No one.

Suddenly, throwing it all away, their past, their memories, their future, seems like a piss-poor idea.

"Mama—"

She's cut off by a raised hand. "Don't think I don't see it. He's tryin' to worm his way back into your life. He'll lie again, Emmy Lou. You can't trust that man."

"Mama, hush. He's right in there," Emmy Lou hisses through gritted teeth. Even though she is pissed at Jace for doing what he did, she's the one who gets to be angry and talk shit about her husband, not her mama. She glances toward the kitchen, but Jace is still at the table, scribbling words onto his old notepad.

"I think it's about time you make some proper declarations and important decisions." Mama Belle's tone is firm. "You've made some bad choices in life, Emmaline. Starting with your husband. But now—now we can fix 'em, sugar."

Emmy Lou nods, even as her chest constricts and her eyes burn. She hears Mama Belle's harsh words and knows what she wants. But this isn't what she wants at all. Jace was never a bad choice. He was the best choice.

He still is.

Her stomach rolls. "I don't know yet, Mama. It's a damn hard decision."

"That's a potty mouth, Emmaline, and I won't have it." Mama Belle pats her hand, effectively silencing Emmy Lou's objections.

"Yes, Mama."

"You gotta get Jace to sign these papers and you gotta get him to sign them soon." Mama Belle jostles her bag, pointing a finger at Emmy Lou. "I got a judge waitin' on a favor, Emmy Lou, how's it gonna look on the Montgomery name if I don't cash it in?"

Emmy Lou sits back on the couch, her head spinning. Her heart warring between telling her mother the truth and keeping up appearances. Keeping the peace. It's the southern way. Respect your mama, your elders, and don't talk back.

Suddenly, coming back to Wildheart to get clarity on her and Jace suddenly seems like the very worst idea. Not with her mother waiting in the wings to cast doubt on their relationship like some kind of gigantic energy suck.

Her own damn fault.

She always said yes to Mama Belle. To Slayton. To the rodeo.

It wasn't until she ran to Nashville and met and married Jace and started doing her life on her terms that her and her mother's relationship became strained.

Mama Belle stands before she can reply. "I don't want to get you worked up about this now," she says. "I want you to keep your spirits high, darlin'. I want you beautiful for the rodeo. Pretty as a princess."

A small smile curls Mama Belle's lips. "I think you'll see this is gonna be a summer of surprises."

THE EARLY-MORNING SUN CASTS THE PASTURE IN A ROSE-gold glow of gorgeousness. Emmy Lou grabs a bucket of feed and makes her way across the dirt drive. "Hello, you big ol' hungry babies," she drawls, greeting the horses. They flick their tails, making happy little neighs of greeting, and meet her at the fence.

She feeds and brushes them, relishing the quiet time, the bond between her and her horses, the slow build of heat in the summer air.

By the time she's halfway through her daily routine, all kinds of thoughts are running wild in her head. One most important: Jace. Last night, having dinner with him, their easy, unguarded conversation, was like old times. They had talked—actually talked and apologized and listened. It felt so damn good. Like they were dating again, like they could get back to them.

Maybe they could make it after all.

Maybe she could change her mind about Jace.

Instead of breaking up, they could be making up. Use this silly old summer to come together instead of fall apart. But can they? And should they?

She knows Mama Belle's answer: a cold, hard no.

Mama Belle's appearance last night was like being doused with bucket of ice water. The kiss between her and Jace forgotten. When she returned to the kitchen, they ate their dinner, cleaned up and went their separate ways.

Separate. Just what Mama Belle wants.

Emmy Lou sighs. She hates herself, hates that whenever she feels good about her and Jace, she lets Mama Belle cast doubt on their relationship. She doesn't know why she gives Mama Belle that kind of power, but she does. Because she's the perfect southern daughter. Because it ain't nothing new. Because she's a fool.

As she walks around the side of the house, she frowns when she sees a soggy cigarette. Muddy boot prints.

"What in the world . . . ," she murmurs, following the tracks. They travel from the front porch to the back of the barn.

Emmy Lou drops into a crouch. She traces the outline of the shoes, narrowing her eyes to get a better look.

That's when she hears footsteps.

The soft crunch of gravel.

Her senses, on alert, prickle. She stands and jumps back. When she sees who it is, she presses a relieved hand to her heart.

"Oh Lord, Jace, you tryin' to give me a heart attack?"

He's come from around the side of the barn. He puts a hand out to steady her, his gaze tracing over her face. "You okay, Em?" The cup of coffee he's carrying bobs in his hand.

Her nose scrunches up. "Someone's been comin' on the farm."

Jace stiffens. "You sure?"

She nods at the ground. "Big boots and cigarettes."

He chuckles. "Sounds like a country song." But even his lighthearted humor can't erase the storm cloud that's darkened his handsome face.

She tilts her head. "Who on earth would be comin' 'round here?"

"I ain't sure. But I'll handle it." His gaze holds on the boot print a minute longer, then lifts to her face. "Thought I'd get a head start on the day. You get the horses fed?"

She nods, letting out a breath she didn't know she was holding. "All done."

His hazel eyes flash bright in the sunlight. Brown-and-green sparkling pools that have her forgetting those muddy boot prints on the ground. His voice falls to a low rasp. "I can muck the stalls if you haven't already."

Her heart dips, flipping over in her chest. No matter what, he's always got her number, always has her back. This summer, he's shown her that.

It hits her like a bullet. Sudden and hot. She wants him out of the basement. She doesn't like not knowing where he is. It seems like a shame, bypassing each other, missing out on the daily routine of Jace. The way he hums like no one can hear. His soft shuffle, his intense concentration on everyday tasks.

She tries to nod, but she feels like a bobblehead doll, her head barely on and buzzing. "I'd sure appreciate that."

He lopes off, a lazy swagger in his step as he heads in the direction of the stables, then calls out over his shoulder, "Then we ride."

She blinks at him. "Today?"

"No time like the present, right?"

She tucks the feed bucket against her hip. "You're savage. I haven't even had coffee yet."

"Here," he says, reversing his direction to hand over the mug. "Have mine." The scent of black coffee steams her nostrils.

She laughs. "You're a cruel and unfair man."

"What can I say? You want me to ride you hard, I will."

Oh Lord. She bites back a retort, her face overheating at his words. She glances at the huge barrel full of rainwater, her body itching to climb itself in and cool off.

Jace grins and gives her a knowing look. "Drink your coffee, honey. Then giddyup."

She smiles, a sun of her very own rising up inside of her. "Let's do this, Taylor."

Emmy Lou lets out a wild whoop as the ground thunders under her. Every muscle in her body quivers. Her core tight, her legs limber. She leans down, leans into Outlaw, resting her body against his, letting his vibrations roll through her, fill her up, shake her own body like they're a connection of souls. Finally, he trusts her. Like her, he's slow to warm up, but when he does, he's fast to be friendly.

"Keep your momentum, Em," Jace shouts.

She looks over at him, a blur of tan skin and a flash of white teeth. Jace grins and then he's gone, disappearing on Gentleman in her periphery.

Emmy Lou stares after him, her gut tightening. Watching Jace being sweet and tender with the horses turns her on like nothing else. It's why she fell in love with him in the first place. It's a good measure of a man—the way he treats animals.

As she watches Jace, she thinks back to this morning. Together, she and Jace worked alongside each other, finishing up long-postponed farm chores like patching a front step and cleaning out the gutters. Then, they warmed up Outlaw, taking him out to the pasture, letting him walk for a bit, feeling his freeness before bringing him into a trot.

Now, the afternoon sun burning bright in the sky, Outlaw's in a full-throttle gallop. Sweat drips down Emmy Lou's back, beads her temples.

Hot.

It's damn hot.

Something Jace is feeling too.

His face red in the Georgia sun, Jace lifts his shirt to wipe the sweat from his eyes. Emmy Lou can't help but glimpse a catch of hard, tan stomach. That rusty trail of hair, leading down toward—

Emmy Lou huffs a growl of outraged frustration. She's wearing her heart on her sleeve, in her eyes, and it's unacceptable. He looks too damn good in those Wranglers. And those boots. The cowboy hat.

"What?" she asks when Outlaw nickers. Her eyes are still locked on Jace. "Ain't no law against lookin.'"

So she does.

She stares.

There's something about Jace sitting on a horse, arms corded with muscle, sweating like a hard worker, barking orders like some kind of countrified boss. Like a man. Like the man she fell in love with. All she can think about are his big hands squeezing her thighs. Moving up, moving high, moving for her—

A whistle from Jace takes her out of her daydream.

With a short jerk of the reins, she steers Outlaw back to Jace, who's watching them from his spot in the field.

He lifts his cowboy hat, wiping sweat from his eyes. "You ready to race?"

She glances over at the barrels, set up in the familiar cloverleaf pattern.

"Remember," Jace says, "mimic your horse's posture. Lean forward when the horse does. Sit back when you want him to stop." Jace's eyes pin hers, worry there. "If takin' the barrel don't feel right, don't do it. Because he's big and you're small, and damn, Emmy Lou, I don't wanna worry today."

"So don't," she says with a sweet smile, reaching down to pet Outlaw. She's finally built up enough trust that she feels confident in her horse.

Herself, that's another problem.

"Now you ain't gettin' timed at the rodeo, but . . ." Out of Jace's pocket comes a stopwatch. His eyes shine with mischief. "I'm timin' you here."

She gasps, a thrill going through her. "Sneaky."

He laughs. "Keep you on your toes. Ain't no slackin' on my watch."

Her stomach is jittery with nerves. With exhilaration. She cannot wait to run Outlaw wild into the arena and show the crowd just what Wildheart's rodeo queen can really do.

"You ready?" Jace readies the stopwatch. The way he looks at her has her breath catching. There's awe in his hazel-eyed gaze. Respect. "You got this, Em."

She nods. His confident gaze sends bravery soaring up inside of her.

Emmy Lou primes Outlaw, moving him into position at the chalked starting line.

Wind whipping through her hair, she snaps the reins.

She's not running, she's racing. Tuning out everything except the sound of the wild earth around her. Her Georgia home, her horse, her heartbeat.

She takes the first barrel. All she feels is the thud of the earth, the body of her horse, as he and she run the cloverleaf pattern.

She takes the second barrel. Her nemesis.

A whoop from Jace sounds.

As Outlaw approaches the third barrel, Emmy Lou sees the fall coming. He takes the sharp curve too fast, too tight.

Her grip slips on the reins.

Uselessly, she tries to grab on to something, anything, but finds only empty space.

She falls, tucking and rolling as she hits the hard ground. Her vision blurs. Her body trembles from the vibration as Outlaw thunders around her.

A soft voice. "Em, honey, you alright?"

Slowly, Emmy Lou uncurls, blinking away spots, to find Jace hovering over her, evaluating, his eyes as serious as she's ever seen.

She lies there for a long second, savoring her fall. The dirt in her hair. The sun on her face. She's the happiest she's been. She completed the run. No thoughts of Slayton. Her nerves were as steady as her horse.

She stares up into Jace's serious eyes. "No yips."

"No yips," he echoes. A small smile of relief tugs at his lips.

"How long?" she asks.

He checks the stopwatch. "Ninety seconds."

She groans. "Pitiful." Then she sticks out a hand. "Help me up?"

With an exhale, he stands, gently pulling her up with him. She gives Outlaw wry side-eye. The horse stands in the pasture munching on clover like he's completely oblivious to Emmy Lou's tuck and tumble.

Jace steps close. She can tell he wants to touch her, to pat her down, feeling for injury. "Can I . . . ?" he asks, the careful man in him coming out. She understands. At their farm, they've seen their share of accidents. After a seemingly harmless fall, the rider's fine, then later, they discover a bone's broken, a joint's out of place, a head's hit too hard.

Emmy Lou's body goes very, very still as Jace kneels. He runs a broad hand over each of her limbs. His warm palms curve to her calves. He squeezes her ankles, her knees, then her wrists, her shoulders. His fingertips fan out across her bare flesh. His hands travel over to cup her jaw and check her pupils. She shivers when he cradles the cap of her skull in his big hand, his burning eyes taking her in, like he can see every part of her.

Emmy Lou closes her eyes. She can smell Jace's shampoo and farm—grass, hay, leather. The scent of him like a lit fuse. Every part of her, including the lower ones, igniting.

Hands all over her. Next, she'd like to add Jace's mouth.

She's got absolutely no sense right now. Lord, if she gets next to him, she'll kiss him and then they'll be in bed, the sheets covered in sweat, their clothes in tatters, and it would be wrong. Wrong and great. So damn great.

"All good." Jace exhales and steps back. His orbit leaving hers is the saddest thing in the whole damn world. He grins. "You ride like you got extra lives, Em."

She laughs at that. "Maybe I do." She gives him a cheeky smile and sidles away. "You never know. I might go out for the circus next."

Jace blinks. He looks stunned.

And she knows why. They haven't flirted like this in forever and a day. Is that what she's doing? What she wants to do? How does flirting even work anymore?

She leans back against the barrel of rainwater. Trying to catch her breath, trying to rein in her heart. Hell, she should just take a dip in it to cool herself off.

"Oh, my word. My knees are Jell-O," she says, trying to steer the conversation to a neutral direction.

Jace frowns, glances up at the sun. He whistles. "We've been at this for damn near two hours." He takes off his cowboy hat and wipes his brow. "Hot as hell, that's for sure."

She grins at him. "Bet I could cool you off." With a quick swipe of her hand, she splashes a tidal wave of rainwater at Jace, soaking the front of his shirt.

He curses and sidesteps the stream. Then, his eyes light as he breaks for her.

She squeals and leaps away from the barrel.

He grabs her around the waist and lifts her off her feet. She's in a fireman carry, slung across his back. His body, his muscles shake as he laughs. "Think that pond's callin' your name, Emmy Lou."

"Don't you dare!" She slaps his back, but Jace only hoists her higher. She feels the rush of wind in her hair as he races across the front lawn. "Jace!" She hits his shoulders, solid muscle, and her toes curl. "If you think you're gettin' me in that nasty ol' pond, you got another thing comin' . . ."

Jace stops at the edge of the pond and slowly sets her down on the ground. He's grinning, his hands on her waist. She grips his broad shoulders to stay upright.

Now her legs really are Jell-O.

"Treatin' Wildheart's rodeo queen like this," she teases, lifting her chin regally to meet his eyes. "The nerve."

"You're right," he says with mock seriousness. "I apologize, Your Majesty."

She laughs.

Jace shifts in his boots, grave and serious once again, and clears his throat. "So, uh, what's on your agenda today?" His hands are still wrapped tight around her waist.

What *is* on her agenda? A nap? Seeing her parents? Her lazy brothers? No. She wants none of that. What she wants is . . .

Jace.

Shit.

She's holding her breath. His question is like a bomb, like some delicious dish she wants to eat. She hasn't felt like this in forever. Her heart has butterflies. Nervous, like she's about to go on a first date all over again.

She goes for a casual shrug. "No plans."

"Guess we could go our own way," Jace says, and Emmy Lou's body deflates. "Unless . . ."

She licks her lips. "Unless what . . ."

His throat works around the words. "If you're plannin' to hang 'round here today, I could toss some burgers and dogs on the grill for dinner."

"Why not." She lets out a deep breath. "Might as well make a night of it."

"Great." He looks so happy, her heart twists. Then he says, "You go on and get the feed and I'll cool off the horses." His hands drop from her waist.

"Sounds good."

He watches her for a long second, then turns and heads for Outlaw.

"Jace?"

He turns back. "Em?"

"Thank you. For . . . for this." She wets her lips, feeling all kinds of awkward but wanting to get it out. "I really appreciate you bein' here to help me."

He grins, his expression softening. Pride flickers in his eyes. "I'm glad I get to see you in your element. Hell, I've heard about it for so long. Watchin' you do this, it's pretty damn amazin.'"

With that, Jace lopes off in the direction of Outlaw, whistling a happy tune.

Emmy Lou watches him go. A familiar feeling, a slow curl of fire in her belly.

A feeling she's felt before. A feeling she's never denied when it came to Jace.

Love.

EIGHTEEN

JACE SNAPS THE TONGS TOGETHER, GETTING A GRIP ON A juicy chicken drumstick drenched in barbeque sauce. "Watch out," he says to Emmy Lou as he prepares to flip it. "You're in the splash zone."

She makes a big show of stepping back as the grill sizzles and the chicken finds its rightful place to be roasted.

Emmy Lou peers over his shoulder, her curious expression lit up in the glow of the sunset. "I'm surprised you got this down. I haven't seen you man a grill in way too long now."

Jace affects mock insult and flips a hamburger patty. "I may have been MIA from the grill scene, but be assured, my burger-flipping skills are still on point." He turns the heat down on the grill, transfers the burgers to the warmer, and shuts the lid. It'll be at least an hour before they eat.

He cocks an eyebrow. "And you're one to talk, Miss I'll Just Whip Up a Strawberry Shortcake."

Emmy Lou presses a hand against her heart. "What can I say? I am the queen of the rodeo and the queen of the kitchen."

He chuckles. "Honey, if that ain't the goddamn truth."

She breaks into a laugh, the jubilant sound drifting over the farm. As she takes a sip of her wine, Jace watches her. She's fresh from the shower, her blond hair towel-dried into loose waves. A pale violet sundress shows off her tan skin, unfair amounts of cleavage, pert breasts, tight ass, curves for days. So damn beautiful.

He tears his gaze from Emmy Lou before he can get lost in her face. Tonight, his best behavior beckons. As much as he wants to kiss his wife senseless, as much as today has given him boatloads of hope they might be on the right path back to each other, he can't push it. He won't. Hell, Emmy Lou having dinner with him for the second night in a row is more time than they've spent together in the last three years. The thought fucking guts him, but it also fills him with a determination to do more of this, and to do it right, all the time.

Starting with tonight.

All the pain he's brought her, he can't erase it, or make up for it, but maybe he can help her understand it. The longer he's been at the farm, the more he realizes she needs to know why he did what he did.

He has to tell her about his past, about Luke.

Emmy Lou's chirp of a twang float up between then. "I think the last time we grilled out was what? At Sal and Luke's?"

Jace thinks on it and sips his beer. "Yeah, it was . . . shit, last summer."

He doesn't miss the wince on Emmy Lou's face, both of them noting how long ago it was they did something fun. Something happy. Something together.

Jace, not wanting the sad moment to overcome, looks toward the pond. He's had a goddamn great day today and doesn't want it to stop. "How do you feel about a walk?"

She nods.

Together, both of them come down off the deck. The smell of barbeque chicken and hamburgers follows them as they make their way around the pond. Emmy Lou, barefoot, takes his elbow to steady herself on the muddy bank.

A surge of protectiveness shoots through his chest. He tightens his grip, keeping her close. As close as he can. Part of the reason he suggested staying in tonight was because of damn paranoia. A raw, unhinged ache to watch out for Emmy Lou.

He still isn't over seeing those footprints earlier today. He doesn't know what they mean, only that they unsettled him completely. If someone's coming on the farm, lurking, watching Emmy Lou . . .

His fist clenches.

God fucking help them.

"Oh!" she exclaims, a playful light in her eyes. "There!" She points at a shape off in the distance—the tan body of a deer darting through the trees.

Jace says nothing, trying to keep his body loose and even-keeled, but the feel of Emmy Lou's arm linked through his has every atom in his body on red-hot alert. Nerves have him sweating like he's on a first date. She has him feeling like the man she loved, a man who didn't need permission to pull her into his arms and kiss her. He could just do it, and she would answer, gladly.

"So," Jace says, looking at her, "I think it's time I cash in on a promise."

"Oh, you do, do you?"

"Our deal. You never told me why you want to barrel race."

She sips her wine and shrugs. "Because Mama told me I can't." She cuts him a sideways smile. "I know it's petty, I shouldn't care what my mama thinks, but this is the first time I can ride like my brothers. All my life I've been told what to do here in Wildheart. I was Mama and Daddy's only daughter. A Montgomery. I was never really given a choice to say no or do what I wanted. I suppose . . . I want to show 'em I'm more than a pretty face or a damn gossip."

"I never thought that's what you were." Jace evaluates her, loving this slice of insight into his wife. Pained that she's always felt this way. "You're the strongest woman I know."

"I don't feel strong. Not here." Her eyes, suddenly dimmed, drop to the pond. "Not always. Not even on my horse."

"Nah." He clinches his bicep to pull her closer. "You got this, Em."

"I guess this is my way of rebellin'. Or somethin' like that."

"Pretty big way to rebel. Doin' dangerous stunts that scare the shit out of me, that's your solution?"

"Didn't you hear?" She nudges him with her shoulder, a gleam of mischief in her deep brown eyes. "I've got a new trainer."

Jace grunts. The best part of training Emmy Lou is finally getting that girl on solid ground. He knows it's second nature to her, but watching his wife prep for the rodeo is just Jace muttering *be careful* every twenty seconds. Because that woman's gonna give him a damn heart attack the way she rides.

His jaw flexes. "Now I don't know how good I made out with that deal. Watchin' you defy death ain't my idea of a good time."

"No fear, Taylor," she teases, laughing at his expression. "That's what this summer is about."

The second the words are out of her mouth, Jace bristles. The realization that summer is ending bleeds into his skin like a wound.

As if she's read his thoughts, Emmy Lou makes a small noise of consternation. She looks away from him.

In silence, the two of them fall alongside each other. Jace guides Emmy Lou to the lip of the pond, which is when he sees it.

Releasing Emmy Lou, he crouches down. A bright purple daisy on a thin stem of green quivers in the humid evening air. It's second nature to pick it, to give it to his wife. A calling card of his love for her.

He stands, offering the wildflower to Emmy Lou. "For you, honey," he says quietly.

Startled, she stares at him for a long minute, then flushes pink. "Thank you," she says, taking it between her slender fingers. She tucks it behind her ear and gives him a soft smile.

Christ. That smile. It seeps into him like warm sunlight. To Jace, it feels like a break in the clouds. A light, a ray of hope. A way forward with his wife. With this beautiful woman he loves more than anything.

They walk in silence, a slow loop around the house, when Emmy Lou clears her throat.

"And after the summer," she begins, picking up the lapsed conversation, "y'all go to Vegas?"

"Yeah. In January."

The rock in his throat makes it hard to talk. It hits him then that Emmy Lou doesn't know anything about the Brothers Kincaid's new contract. He got his ass beat that night, and then the next day Emmy Lou beat it out of Nashville.

"It ain't announced yet, but the residency goes for eight weeks," he says. "Ain't too long. But Luke's psyched as hell."

"I would be too." Her eyes flit to him. "Y'all done good, Jace. Vegas ain't gonna know what hit 'em." There's a wistful tone in her voice that socks him in the gut.

She thinks she won't be there.

The thought of Emmy Lou not being there for the Brothers Kincaid's biggest break is a kick in the balls. Emmy Lou supported him, loved him when he was a poor country boy, packed his lunches when they were still busking on Broadway, baked them cookies when they went out on the road. Sure, the press saw her as some prim housewife, but she was so much more than that. She was his rock, his shining light, the woman who made him laugh, who picked him up when he was down and always supported him.

He stops, halting Emmy Lou. Gripping her arms gently, he turns her into him. He knows divorce is still an option and it might be too soon, too foolhardy, but he has to step up and make sure she knows what she means to him. That was his mistake the first time—not fighting for Emmy Lou. He'll never forgive himself if he lets this moment slip away.

"I want you to come on the tour, Em. It won't mean a damn thing if you ain't right there with me."

Her eyes widen, worry and uncertainty marring her pretty face. "Oh, Jace. I don't know."

His gaze holds hers. "You don't gotta take a bus. We'll fly. It won't be the same without you."

She puts a palm on his chest. Her head tilts at a sad little angle. "Jace . . ."

"I know the summer isn't over. I know you haven't made a decision. I know it—"

"Stinks."

He blinks.

She flushes. Points at the sky. "The chicken, it's burning."

Jace turns to see the grill belching a black plume of smoke. "Shit," he says. He gives Emmy Lou a look and takes off to save dinner, the conversation with his wife left unfinished.

Emmy Lou's on her second glass of white wine, the stars are extra bright above, and that moon—it's just begging for her to be kissed under it.

By Jace.

She sneaks a furtive glance at her husband. By now, they've finished dinner. They ate the barbeque chicken and burgers at the porch table. There were no angry barbs, no bringing up past mistakes. Just easy conversation. Whether or not Lacey and Seth will end up eloping in Vegas. Grady's stint in Nashville. When Wyatt will settle down; Jace predicts never, Emmy Lou in two years. They've talked about everything except themselves.

Now the two of them sit in a pair of Adirondack chairs in the front yard. George Strait plays on Jace's phone, the voice tinny from the speakers. The glittering Milky Way speckles the sky above.

Emmy Lou's still reeling from earlier. Jace boldly asking her to come to Vegas with him. It surprised and thrilled her all at once. Him coming out point-blank about what he wanted sent sparks through every inch of her. It made her feel desired, important, like she mattered to him.

She closes her eyes.

Every day on the farm, she's getting closer to Jace. Every day she's seeing the man she married, the real Jace Taylor. The man she fell in love with. Confident. Steady and calm. Fun. Which makes divorce seem like a very, very bad idea.

This entire summer, Jace has shown her he's willing to put the work in. He's not letting go. He's fighting. It's sexy as hell.

But is it too late to go back? To have that second chance?

Far off, an owl hoots in the distance.

"Barn," Jace says, his husky drawl taking her out of her night-time musings.

"Mmm," Emmy Lou says, tilting her head toward the sky. "Great horned?" She glances over and smiles.

Humidity has crumpled Jace's shirt. With the top two buttons undone, he looks all kinds of rugged and handsome. Very, very handsome. She bites her lip and holds on to her wineglass like it's an anchor because all she wants to do is crawl across and into Jace's lap.

Holy Lord, this man. He's gonna combust her and he don't even know it.

A gentle ping interrupts the still of the evening.

Emmy Lou glances down at the phone in her lap, groaning when she sees a text. Jace looks at her in the moonlight. "Perfect timin'. It's Mama Belle remindin' me of my daughterly duties. The anniversary party in two weeks," she explains when Jace arches a brow.

"Been married forty years," Jace muses. "That's something to celebrate."

The talk of marriage sobers her. She sinks lower into the Adirondack chair, suddenly hit by a melancholy mood. By the bravery to make a decision here and now. She doesn't want the yips. With her horses or with her marriage.

Staring into her wine, Emmy Lou says, "We've been married ten years."

Throat bobbing, Jace meets her gaze. "We have."

She shifts in her chair and forces herself to speak the hard truth. "Everyone around us is gettin' married, or celebratin' somethin' happy, or havin' babies and we're . . . what are we, Jace?"

He looks down at his hands for a long minute, then says, "I ain't sure, honey. But I know what I want."

"And what's that?"

His eyes spark. "I wanna be married a whole hell of a lot longer to you."

She closes her eyes for a brief moment, her heart pumping chaotically, but she wills her voice to stay steady. To go on before she can lose her nerve. "Why did we fail?"

He cringes. "We didn't fail, Em."

"It feels like it." Her gaze tracks across the yard to the empty spot where the old oak used to live. "Our tree came down." Her voice is a whisper.

"But we don't have to."

She looks at him. "You don't talk to me."

"I know." Jace, his expression etched with anguish, says, "You don't touch me anymore."

She flinches at that. The hard, angry truth.

Then—

"You're right." She chokes on the words, pressing fingertips to her lips to keep a sob in. "I was so hurt I wanted to punish you." Tears bead Emmy Lou's eyes. "I drove you away."

"No." Jace is shaking his head. He gives her a bereft look. "I forgot about you, Em. I forgot to grow with you. I forgot to talk to you. To listen. I stopped doin' things around the farm, asking you to come on tour with us. I wasn't the man you deserved. I wasn't the husband you needed." Regret stains his voice. "I should have talked to you instead of trying to solve everything on my damn own."

"It's not your fault." Emmy Lou sweeps away a tear. "Why would you wanna talk to me when all I did instead of forgive was be so hateful and mean?" She lets out a little growl and drives her small fist into her palm. "That's right. All I was was a mean old nag of a wife."

He chuckles. "You ain't a nag, honey."

"Oh, Jace," she says tearfully. "I'm so sorry."

He shakes his head—no, no, no—and then scoots his chair closer.

They turn toward each other like flowers toward the sun. Jace slowly reaches over to take her hand. When he brings it to his lips, he exhales a tremulous breath, laying a trail of kisses over her palm and fingertips.

Emmy Lou closes her eyes, her stomach a tumbleweed of relief. Of love.

She never in a million years thought she'd be here with Jace, calmly discussing their marriage. She was so sure they were done.

But talking.

It's so simple, and so stupid. This is what they needed to do. Not fight or avoid or blame.

Talk.

Suddenly, she has so much hope.

She has so much love, her heart feels like a sunrise inside her chest.

Suddenly, there's so much at stake.

"Listen, Em." Jace's soft voice has her eyes popping open. "You ain't gotta be sorry for a damn thing, you hear me, honey? Because you never understood, but that's on me because I never told you."

She pulls his hand closer. She can't get enough of touching him. "Told me what?"

If this is it, an explanation . . .

Jace meets her gaze, his eyes glassy in the firelight. He rubs his thumbs over her knuckles. "I never told you so much."

Emmy Lou inhales a sharp breath.

He looks so serious. More serious than he's ever been. His jaw, his shoulders tense with something she can't quite place. Anger? Pain? Guilt?

Releasing her hand, Jace dips down and drags a hand through his hair. "I don't even know where to fuckin' start."

"Oh, Lord." She sits up straight, steadying herself. "Just please, Jace, tell me you ain't in witness protection or have another family somewhere."

"That ain't it, honey." He takes a long minute to control

himself, the look in his eyes matching the night's blackness. When he speaks next, the air feels almost electric with solemn tension.

"You know my mom died, and my dad and I never had a good relationship, right?" His voice is mechanical. He's had this bottled up inside of him for years and only just now is letting it free.

She nods. She does. Jace did his damnedest to keep her away from his father. In fact, the only time she got within ten feet of the man was at his funeral. Jace had gone, had tried to keep her away, but she had won that battle, stubbornly insisting he wasn't going through it alone.

Jace inhales, then, keeping his eyes straight ahead, says, "My dad hit her. All the time."

His words make her ache, and she stares at him, pain rolling over her as he pauses to gather his next thoughts.

"He was a drunk." Jace looks at the ground. "When he wasn't drinkin' he was hittin' her and when he wasn't hittin' her he was passed out on the couch."

Emmy Lou licks her lips, her heart squeezing painfully in her chest. She's barely able to ask it. "And you? Did he hurt you?" Her voice shakes. Lord, if he touched Jace she's gonna find that man's grave and dig him up herself just to kill him all over again.

Jace's face hardens. "My mama wouldn't let him. It was how he kept her with him. He wouldn't touch me as long as she stayed." He shakes his head. "I went to Luke's when I needed to. I wanted to take her with me. I tried so hard to make her leave, but she wouldn't go. Because she thought she was protecting me."

Emmy Lou slides to the edge of her chair, reaching over to take his hand and cradle it in her lap.

"One night, I snuck out. It was late and the old man had been raggin' on my ma all night. I was thirteen and all I wanted to do was go down to the pool hall with Luke. Maybe see if we could get onstage and play. When he realized I was gone, they got into it. Started fightin'. Bad." A tremulous exhale. "The sheriff picked me up from the pool hall, but we didn't go home. We went to the hospital. He hit my ma so hard he knocked her into the coffee table." Bitterness wells in his voice. "He paralyzed her. He put her in a fuckin' wheelchair."

She covers her mouth.

Jace goes on, like if he stops talking, he'll never get it out. "She waited until I left for Nashville. It was like she had planned it, like she knew what she was going to do because I was gone and I'd be okay, I'd be with the boys and then she . . . she put a gun to her head and she pulled the trigger."

Emmy gasps. "Jace. No." Her heart's breaking, splitting into a million pieces. The pain, the secret he's kept inside all these years. It guts her.

"My mama was the best. She was always steppin' in and I—I let her down. If I hadn't left that night, she never would have been in that wheelchair." He puts a palm over his face, clears his throat. "I fucked up. I left her. I broke the rules. It should have been me he hit, not my ma."

She squeezes his hand. "I wish you would have told me." Her heart feels like it holds a bomb. For Jace to sit on a hard, hurtful part of his past all these years . . . she feels shell-shocked, blindsided.

But she also feels even more of a connection to Jace.

He's not the only one who kept secrets. She did the exact same thing with Slayton, with her past, because she didn't want it to touch her present. She wanted to forget. And so did Jace.

Almost to herself, softly, she murmurs, "You hid it."

"No. Em, no."

"I understand, Jace, I—"

"That ain't it," he growls. "Listen to me, honey. When I met you, you were this girl, this goddamn gorgeous woman, who had me forgetting everything bad I came from." His face twists up in disgust. "My shit life touchin' you—I didn't want you around that. I thought if you knew how I grew up, what I saw . . ." A ragged exhale. "I didn't want you to think less of me, or Christ, what if you thought I was like him?"

Embarrassment, tears, rage darken his eyes.

She tangles her fingers with his. He grips her tight, desperate. "You'd never hurt me, Jace. I know that."

He raises his head, his face a mess of pain and shame. "But I have. Not telling you about my gamblin' put you in danger, Emmy Lou. You could have been hurt, and I wasn't around to protect you."

It all makes sense. Jace's careful ways, ways she loves, her husband always playing by the rules because of his guilt, because he slipped up once, because he's still torturing himself because of the past, because of something he had no control over.

"My father beat my mother. I saw that. And I did nothing to stop it." He won't look at her. He shakes his head slowly. "What kind of man am I?"

"Jace, you were thirteen," Emmy Lou says sharply, her heart breaking for his anguish. "You were a kid. You weren't supposed to play hero. You were just tryin' to survive."

The thought of Jace—her sweet, kind Jace—having such an awful childhood, when she has parents who love her, brothers who'd kill for her, a daddy who'd give her the moon, has her heart shattering.

"Thank God you had Luke," Emmy Lou whispers, like the night can hear her secrets. She thinks of her own brothers, of Jace often saying Luke and Seth were his only family, his true blood, and knowing he meant it. They were his life preservers in a sea of sadness and pain.

"That's why," Jace says, but he breaks off.

She strains to hear. "Why what? Jace?"

"Why this all happened in the first place." He swallows, lets go of her hand, and sits up straight. Rallying. "Luke. After Sal. He tried . . . he tried to . . ."

Jace's sentences are abrupt, staccato, but Emmy Lou gets the meaning plain and clear. She gasps, hot tears filling her eyes.

"No," she whispers, her hands covering her mouth. "Oh no."

She knew Luke was lost after Sal went missing, but she never knew how deep he sank. How much Jace pulled him back. She cooked casseroles while Jace was trying to save his best friend's life. She remembers him during that time, going back and forth between their house and Luke's at all hours, worn thin, yet still ticking for his best friend. To keep him together.

To keep him alive.

"I was fuckin' there," Jace says, squeezing his eyes shut, lost in horrifying memories. "He had a fuckin' shotgun and Seth wrestled it away from him. We stayed with him for two nights. The day he was steady, I left. Instead of goin' home, I went straight to Broadway. I needed a drink. But all I got was fuckin' trouble."

He looks at her, tears swimming in his eyes.

"It ain't an excuse, but it's a reason. I didn't want to talk about it. It was too close to my ma—almost losin' my goddamn best friend . . ." He swallows. "I kept goin' back and gamblin' because it let me forget."

Emmy Lou sits silently, processing the news, a string of forgiveness unraveling deep within her. Like she's hooked up to an IV of relief. Answers she's so desperately wanted the last three years. Why Jace stepped out of line. It makes sense. Everything makes sense.

It was because of grief. Out of grief, Jace made a mistake. Not being reckless or deceiving her. He wanted to protect her. He wanted to bury the past. A choice she made when she left Wildheart and ran to Nashville.

She's needed his explanation for so long and now that she finally has it, it's simple.

She understands.

Jace smears his face in his hands. "I didn't tell you back then because it was Luke's business. But now—I can't lose you because of that, Em. I won't."

Emmy drops fingers from her lips. "Luke . . ."

"He knows I'm tellin' you. He told me to."

A surge of pride hits Emmy Lou for the man her husband is. Loyal. True. A damn good friend. He's been sitting on his truth for years, not wanting to betray his best friend's confidence.

Jace, taking her silence for disgust, slips out of his chair. He falls to his knees in front of her, sliding his arms around the curve of her thighs to brace the small of her back. She shivers at his touch.

His eyes are haunted as he looks up at her.

"I'd go back if I could. Remake all my bad decisions. My fuck-ups. Treatin' you better. Puttin' you first. Askin' you to come to more shows. I should have done all that, but I didn't." His voice breaks as she rests a trembling hand on his shoulder. Bracing herself. "I tried to protect Luke, protect you by hidin' it, by tryin' to handle it the first time, the second time. But I didn't protect you. I pushed you away by not tellin' you. I ruined us. I lost you."

"Jace," she whispers, her heart straining.

"I don't want us to end things," he whispers back.

She dips her head, a sob wrenching from her lungs.

"I can't be five fuckin' miles away from you, let alone a lifetime." His hands grip her waist like he'll never let go. "I love you, Emmy Lou. I can't let you go. When you walked away, my world meant nothin'. Not one damn thing without you. I'm beggin' you to take me back. To give me one more chance." He closes his eyes, his voice throaty with emotion. "To love me again. Because I can't go on—not if I ain't got you."

His words, his primal vow, cycle through her like sunlight. Like a miracle. Like love. She stares at Jace, at this man she married years ago, a handsome, caring, kind man who treats her like a queen. A man who made a mistake and paid the price because of his past, because of grief, because time sure as hell does not heal everything.

Then and there, she makes a decision. Her heart is telling her she has what she's needed.

And Emmy Lou lets go. All of her anger, her pain, her blame, she lets it uncoil from deep within her chest, like a heart up in the sky.

She and Jace—they could grow apart or grow together. Their marriage is going up in flames, but they're the ones holding the matches. They get to choose if they watch it burn. And she knows what to choose.

She chooses forgiveness.

She chooses Jace.

"We can't go back, Jace."

They can't go back, but they can start again.

Jace dips his head, wincing, a hard breath shaking out of him.

"But you haven't lost me."

Slowly, so slowly, he raises his face. His hazel eyes darken. His throat works the words out. "I haven't?"

The way he's looking at her—so hopeful, so lost—melts her. "No." She palms his scruffy cheek. "I have to tell you something too." She locks her eyes to his, an inherent fierceness flooding her veins. "I forgive you, Jace."

A sob wrenches from his lips.

Then she does the only thing she can think of to show him she's still his, that she loves him.

Because she does.

Lord have mercy, she loves Jace Taylor.

With aching fingers, she grabs the front of his shirt and yanks his mouth to hers.

Long-buried sparks jump between them. Electrifying and lit. Jace, making a hungry sound in the back of his throat, wraps an arm around her waist and hauls her closer, into his body, like he's trying to pull her through him, into flesh, bone, heart.

Jace takes her face in his hands, breathing her in, frantically swiping at her tear-stained cheeks. *I love you, I love you*, he whispers through fevered kisses. Kisses so deep and hard their teeth knock. He runs big hands over her body, trembling like he's feeling each curve for the first time.

This is love, she thinks.

This is her and Jace in love.

Only not falling back in love. Finding it again.

Emmy Lou drags her fingers through Jace's hair, down his face, feeling the sexy curve of his jaw, the stubble beneath her palm. A needy moan erupts deep in her belly. She cries out, lost, desperate, gone, relishing the way she fits perfectly in his arms. So tiny to his big. The way Jace's sturdy body pressed against hers, skin to skin, heart to heart, damn near crushing her, but she wants that. No, *needs* it. To feel reassurance that they've come to life.

That they've come together.

She grabs his hair and pulls him closer, letting out a desperate cry of frustration. She's a foolish woman thinking she could give Jace up. Give up their memories, more good than bad, give up her heart.

To walk away from Jace, unthinkable.

Never.

Finally, they rip away from each other, leaving Jace dazed and panting. "Fuck." His voice is strangled as his hands slide down her waist, then up again to cup her cheek. "Fuck, Emmy Lou. I love you."

She captures his mouth again. "Make love to me, Jace," she whispers against his lips. His words are a match burning down the walls between them. "I can't wait."

In answer, he picks her up in his arms with easy strength, a strength that thrills her, that has her clenching warm down below.

Jace stares at her, his eyes so solemn, so fierce, she shivers. In them, she sees that anything she wants is hers.

She sees they are not over.

They are just beginning.

NINETEEN

IT'S A DREAM. IT IS.

Jace would almost believe he was on cloud nine if it weren't for the mad pump of Emmy Lou's heart against his, her words, *make love to me*, echoing in his ears, and her breath of a promise he doesn't quite believe he deserves.

He picks up and carries Emmy Lou into the house, trying not to break into an embarrassingly fast run. He told himself he'd go slow, he wouldn't push, but here he is kissing down Emmy Lou's throat, her legs wrapped around his waist, his hands tangled in her hair. To hell with planning, with waiting.

Tonight, he plans to kiss her until his heart stops, until he's barely capable of breathing.

He has everything he's been wanting since he came back to Wildheart to bring Emmy Lou home.

That kiss.

Her words. *I forgive you, Jace.*

They combusted his goddamn brain.

Emmy Lou was telling him what she wanted and it was him. That it isn't over. Not yet. Not now.

Never, if he has anything to do with it.

Upstairs in their bedroom, Jace sets Emmy Lou on her feet, but he doesn't let her go. He runs his hands down the curve of her back, beneath the silk of her sundress, where he cups the gorgeous peach that is her ass. She shivers against him, pressing up on her tiptoes to gently nip at the hollow of his throat. Soft, tender bites that have him hardening.

Jace buries his face in her wavy blond hair. He inhales her fragrant scent—honey, clover—and trembles as memories sweep over him. "God," he whispers. "I missed you. I missed you so goddamn much, Em."

"I missed you too." She wriggles against him, unbuttoning his shirt to shuck it off. Jace groans, heady with anticipation. A hard-on the size of Texas tents the front of his jeans.

Sex with Emmy Lou was always their time. After he returned from a long tour or a stint on the road, it was how they reconnected. Spending all day in bed, between the sheets, her name on his lips, his mouth on hers.

Now, her hands drift low, slipping beneath his waistline. His eyes close. Her hands, wrapped around his cock, are like velvet. She strokes smoothly, letting him lengthen in her palm. Jace groans, falling away at her touch, but before he loses himself completely, he grabs her wrists, pinning her hands to her side.

Emmy Lou gasps at the rough contact. Her eyes glitter. She likes it.

He grins. "Oh, hell no." Cupping her cheek, he traces her plump bottom lip with his calloused thumb. "We're goin' slow. Tonight, this is all about you. I want to make you feel good, Em."

He'll never replace the last three years, but he can start tonight by showing his wife she's the most important thing in his orbit. There's only Emmy Lou and what she means to him.

She arches in his arms. Her body opening to him, blooming. "You always make me feel good."

Emmy Lou inclines her head almost delicately. And then she responds to his coaxing touch, her pink lips opening as she swallows his thumb into her mouth. The contact—hot, wet—has Jace gritting his teeth. The pant of her breath against his fingertip, the feel of her lips on him, has him going molten.

Jace groans, tortured.

Hell, if they're gonna go back to the good old days, then they're gonna fuck like they never ended.

He walks Emmy Lou backwards to the bed, laying her down on the mattress.

He undresses her slowly, his eyes trained on her as he peels the thin dress from her body.

"Christ," he croaks.

Damn.

Goddamn.

He's stunned. Still stunned by the beauty of his wife after all these years.

She's a fucking vision.

The sight of Emmy Lou lying there, naked, staring up at him like some angel he don't deserve, nearly knocks him off-balance. His eyes eat her up. Hourglass curves. Blond hair fanned out across the mattress, her skin sun-kissed, her dark brown eyes intent, her breasts flush with red, the nipples rose-colored and hard.

"You're fuckin' beautiful."

It's all he can say. He's a soundtrack stuck on repeat. "It's fuckin' insane how gorgeous you are," he says, and Emmy Lou's eyelids go heavy.

He reaches out and cups her bare breast in his hand, feeling its heavy weight. Her eyes flutter as he pinches her nipple, rolling it gently between his fingers. Emmy Lou makes a little sound of disbelief, of pleasure. Her hips arch, and she moans.

In that moment, Jace thanks Christ she's still his.

That he's got this second chance.

This isn't just one last fuck between them. This is a reclaiming, a release, a recommitment. He's going to make love to his wife with intention and he's going to make her remember what she thought they had lost. Because Jace ain't letting her go again.

Because she is everything he has ever loved.

The first song he ever played on his bass, a cold beer on Broadway, the stage lights of the Opry, the smooth drop of a needle on his favorite record.

Everything.

She is his everything.

Jace kneels in front of Emmy Lou, spreads her thighs and smoothly removes her panties. Emmy Lou whimpers, the needy sound sending a jolt of fire straight through him. He takes his time, dragging a finger through her blond curls. He digs his fingers into her thighs, appreciating the gorgeous little dimples that appear in her creamy flesh.

Slowly, so slowly, he dips a finger inside her. Achingly slow. He feels her shiver, clench around him. Her wetness slips over his fingers as he finds her clit, rubbing it in small circles.

Emmy Lou shudders violently, her entire body lifting up and off the bed. An arch so gorgeous, it's torture to watch, to wait for his turn.

Smooth circles, slow, skilled. He feels her pulse against him, a wave of pleasure sweeping her away. "Jace," she begs, and her eyes fall shut. A mewl slips out of her as Jace palms her stomach, pinning her to the bed.

His fingers circle and stroke. Emmy Lou's breath comes in small gasps of air as she's pushed further and further toward the edge. Then, minutes later, she throws her head back and cries out. "Oh God. Oh yes. Jace. *Jace.*"

Finally, her body deflates, trembling on the bed as her orgasm overtakes her.

Jace waits while she gathers herself, and then she pushes herself up on her elbows to look at him. Her icy blond hair spills around her shoulders, her eyes heavy-lidded and dark with lust. "Inside. Now."

When he hears the sharp, breathless edge of need in her voice, when he sees how open and wet she is, how much she wants him, his dick clenches.

He's never been more turned on in his life.

He's on her whip-quick, slipping an arm behind Emmy Lou's back to pull her further up on the bed. It's a race to unbuckle his jeans. Laughing, Emmy Lou's legs come up to help him out, to frantically kick at the denim until it's off Jace and on the ground.

Breathing hard, heart racing, he braces his forearms on each side of Emmy Lou, caging her. She curls her hands over his shoulders, drawing him down to her. And then Jace spreads her legs and slips inside her.

At the skin-to-skin contact, they both shudder.

"It's too much," Emmy Lou tells him, her voice reverent. Her entire body shivers, and he feels her break out in goose bumps. "It's too much."

"It's everything," he whispers, kissing her slow. He burrows himself deeper into his tiny wife and just like that their bodies adjust to what they used to know. What they're good at. Emmy Lou hooks her legs around his waist, while Jace gathers his wife in his arms.

"Em, Em, my gem," he breathes into her mouth.

Emmy Lou's pink lips form an O as Jace rocks against her. He gets down, low and close, their breaths hot and heavy in the space between them as he pumps. Emmy reaches down and grasps his balls, fondling, stroking a finger down the sensitive area.

Jace grits his teeth and tries to slow his rhythm. Else, he's going to go off like a gunshot.

"Jace," Emmy Lou whispers, lifting her hips. Her nails dig into his shoulder. Her eyes roll back in her head as she arches on the bed. Hip bones, stomach, breasts all rising as one. "Don't stop. Please. Harder. Harder."

He can't think anymore. His brain sizzles as he loses himself. Love overtakes him. Emmy Lou. His gem. The only woman he's loved since forever. His wife. He'll love her, protect her, always.

Reaching back, Jace slides his hands beneath her peach of an ass and lifts her up, levitating, pulling her closer against him as he buries himself to the hilt inside of her.

Then Jace pulls back and slams into her. Rocking. Rhythmic. Over and over.

Emmy Lou cries out. She trembles as she clenches tight around him.

His wife satisfied, it's his turn.

Jace lets himself go, lets himself boil over. Lets the last three years of pent-up pleasure pulse out of his cock and into Emmy Lou. He throws his head back and comes, a strangled, savage moan erupting from deep in his core.

When the world stops spinning, Jace comes back to the present. Comes back to Emmy Lou lying slack beneath him, her eyes closed, her expression content, her hair looking like a cloud of fluff.

Chest heaving, Jace gently eases off her. He pulls out, kissing down her chest, her breasts, her stomach, hip bones. When he presses a kiss against her sex, she shudders. Her fingertips graze his hair, his jaw, his chin, his wife beckoning him back to her.

"You can't leave me after that," comes Emmy Lou's sleepy, satisfied drawl. "Leave me and I'll die."

"Ain't goin' nowhere," he says, grabbing a quilt from the end of the bed. Crawling back into bed, he gathers her in his arms, tucking the quilt tight around her small frame. "Ain't ever goin' anywhere, honey, not unless you make me."

She's quiet, snuggling deep into his arms.

Jace closes his eyes, letting himself feel the weight of this moment. Lying next to Emmy Lou, sweet heat radiating from her naked form.

How damn much he missed this.

How damn lucky he is.

How? By Emmy Lou's good grace, that's how. Because God knows he didn't deserve it. Now, they start fresh. No secrets, no lies.

That's when he hears it. Soft sniffles. Emmy Lou burrowed up in pillows, her shoulders silently wracking.

"Hey," he says, shifting his weight to ease out from under her. He props himself up on his elbows and sweeps hair from her eyes. "What's wrong, Em?"

Slowly, she rolls toward him. The look on her face has his stomach clenching. Her brown eyes are glazed with tears, her expression wary.

He sweeps a finger across her cheek, catching a tear. "Talk to me, honey. What is it?"

There's a hitch in his heart, a worry, that maybe this moment was nothing. Even though to him it was everything.

"Oh, Jace." She smiles even as a tear falls from her eye. "I'm so happy. I've been happy here with you. Is that stupid?"

"Nah," he says, tracing a finger over her collarbone. "That ain't stupid. I'm pretty goddamn happy myself."

"I want to start over," she says, and he closes his eyes. The love, the hope in her voice has him unraveling. "I want to be in it with you." She presses a palm to his chest, staring up at him. "I want to trust you. I *do* trust you."

Fuck.

Her words spread through him like a ray of sunlight. Warming all the dark, shameful parts of him he kept locked up for so long. Tonight, he told her everything. She forgave and she understood. It's more than he deserves, but he'll take it if it means he's got Emmy Lou.

She's given him a second chance. They survived all his shit to make it back here. To a place that's tender and kind and theirs. But that doesn't mean he's relaxing. Hell no. This summer isn't over yet. Divorce not yet off the table. He's putting in the work for the rest of his life. Never taking Emmy Lou for granted again. Because he sees that even with the truth, she's wary. She's still guarding herself against getting hurt.

"Honey, the only thing between us now is this damn pillow." He grabs it, rips it from the bed and tosses it across the room. A laugh tumbles from her mouth. "I love you so damn much, Emmy Lou. I don't tell you enough. That I love you. That I can't live, can't fuckin' breathe without you."

Her eyes glisten as she stares at him. Jace gathers her hand in his. "I ain't losin' you. I came damn close and I won't do it again. I'm goddamn thankful you don't hate me."

"I could never hate you." Mischief sparkles in her eyes. "Even if I did throw a brick of cheese at you."

He laughs. He laughs and he laughs and the sound sets off Emmy Lou and together they lie in bed, shoulders wracking, barely able to breathe.

With a happy sigh, Emmy Lou rests her head on his shoulder. "We don't do enough of that," she murmurs.

"What?"

"Laugh."

"We will." He strokes fingertips down her arm. "We'll do so damn much, Em. I promise."

Her eyes sparkle. "Like Vegas?"

He sits up. "You'll come?"

She takes a bracing breath. "Only if you come with me."

He cocks a brow. "Where?"

"To my folks' anniversary party." She snuggles deeper into his arms. "If you're not doin' anything . . . I could use a handsome country singer as a date."

He grins, honored that she's asked. Mama Belle's a pain in his ass, but it don't matter a lick to him. He'll be on her arm and there ain't a damn thing Mama Belle can do about it.

"Honey, you always got a date. You always got me."

She drags her thin fingers through his chest hair. "Mama's gonna be so disappointed."

"I don't give a damn what your mama wants, honey." He cups the top of her blond head protectively and leans down to kiss her temple. "It's what you want. It's always what you want."

With a sweet sigh, she opens her mouth for him. Jace captures it in one achingly slow kiss.

He's the luckiest man alive.

He's got Emmy Lou. This fresh start. A second chance.

No secrets between them, nothing and no one standing in their way back to each other.

"THERE! THERE YOU GO, EM! GET ON UP!"

Wyatt's joyous shout rings out across the field as Emmy Lou swings herself up onto Outlaw's back. Whip-quick, the reins are in her hands and she digs her heels into the horse's side, spurring him faster.

Fast as fire fly she and Outlaw. She laughs, her cry whipped on the wind as they wind around the barrels in the typical cloverleaf pattern. This style of riding is totally different from what she's used to. Wild and freeing. The way she's been this summer. A new woman ready to conquer the world and her marriage. To show her mama and Wildheart she is not the same girl who left so long ago.

Over and over again they practice.

Finally, when the sun's high in the sky, both Emmy Lou and Outlaw are drenched in sweat.

"Hell yeah!" Wyatt exclaims as she brings Outlaw to a stop. He checks the stopwatch. "You got your fastest time yet. Fifty-five fuckin' seconds. You nailed that, Em!" As she dismounts, Wyatt grabs her in a hug, kisses her on her cheek, swings her around and sets her back on her feet.

"That how you treat all your cowboys?" she teases.

He laughs, big and boisterous, then gives her an adoring grin. "Only my little sister."

She smiles, her heart a bright moonbeam in her chest. She feels like she could conquer the world. And Outlaw helped her. She kept control on her horse, kept her feet in the stirrups, and stayed on. Finally, *finally*, after over three weeks of butting heads, she and Outlaw are in sync.

Just like her and Jace.

Today's the first day they've been apart in a week. Ever since they made love, they haven't been able to tear themselves away from each other.

Emmy Lou walks Outlaw over to the water barrel. "Take a break," she says, patting his inky-black coat. "You've earned it."

"How you feel?" Wyatt asks, perching on the fence. "You feel ready?"

She nods. "I do. Now all I gotta do is put on a crown and make Mama smile."

"And then knock her goddamn boots off."

"You're damn right."

Lines appear around Wyatt's mouth. "And what about Jace?"

"What about Jace?" She grabs a rubber currycomb from the fence post and busies herself in brushing Outlaw's snarled locks. "He's down at the arena with Grady—"

"Nah, nah, nah. Not that. I'm talkin' about *you* and what you're doin' with Jace."

"What I'm doin' with Jace is my business. We're tryin' to work it out." Her gaze narrows. "Lord, you'd think shackin' up with your own damn husband was a good thing."

"I do. I just—" He tugs a hand through his thick brown hair. "You were ready to leave him a month ago and now you're ready to get back together?"

At the doubtful look Wyatt's giving her, Emmy Lou cringes. "Have y'all been talkin' about this?"

Her brothers worrying about her has her stomach curdling. She knows they have her best interests at heart. All her brothers are as loyal as a dog, but they're also ready to tear Jace apart like one too.

"You can't blame us, Em." Wyatt's lips thin out. "Y'all are

playin' house here, but what happens when you go back to Nashville? You'll be on the farm; he'll be on the road . . ."

Anxiety pits her stomach. Except for Vegas, she and Jace haven't discussed next steps. In fact, they haven't discussed much of anything. She hasn't even said those three little words yet.

She wanted to. She was so close the night they made love. But giving in felt like jinxing it.

She has two weeks. She has to be sure.

"We want you to be sure," Wyatt says, as if picking up on her train of thought. "We want Jace to treat you right."

"I am. And he does."

Wyatt gives a shrug and hops off the fence. "As long as you trust him . . ."

Trust.

A feeling of cold unease creeps along her spine.

Emmy Lou chuckles, despite her worry. "Good Lord, Wyatt," she says, dusting off her blue jeans. "You're the naysayer of the century."

Wyatt groans, his hands held out in appeasement. "Look, this is all Davis's idea, but the son of a bitch ain't here, so we drew straws. Someone had to talk to you about all this love shit." He shakes off a shudder.

She cocks her head, smirking at Wyatt's obvious discomfort. "Why, Wyatt Montgomery. Ain't you ever been in love before?"

Wyatt grins ruefully. "Nope. Never."

"Never? What about Kat McKinney?"

A lascivious brow. "Lust."

"Chrissy Thorne?"

"Like."

"Wendy Wythe?"

Wyatt thinks on it. Flashes a devil-may-care grin. "Very, very strong frenemies with benefits vibe."

Emmy Lou props a hand on her hip and lifts her brows. "Wyatt, you really never been in love?"

Wyatt barks out a laugh as he walks away to remove Outlaw's saddle and bridle. "I'm leavin' that to you and Jace. So don't screw it up."

Emmy Lou stares after her brother, a cloak of doom draping itself over her sunburned shoulders. Her good mood popped like a balloon.

Don't screw it up.

What if they do?

What if it's only a honeymoon of a summer? Enchanted, glorious, but it won't last. Sure, Jace is here now, all his attention on her, but eventually, they'll have to go back to their real lives. What if back in Nashville they'll be their bickering, butting-heads selves again?

What if nothing's changed?

No.

Emmy Lou inhales a hard breath. Chin up, she strides for the house, her entire body craving a hot shower. She has a fitting today for her parents' anniversary party. An afternoon filled with champagne and fancy dresses sent personally from one of her favorite Nashville designers. A slice of her old life here in Wildheart. She's missed it. No way will she let Wyatt's words kill her happy mood.

Unlike Mama Belle, her brothers just want the best for her. Davis, the oldest, nosiest of them all, worries and it spreads through them all like wildfire.

She and Jace—they'll get to where they need to be. Because she's in it with Jace Taylor.

No matter what anyone in her meddling family wants to think.

Jace pulls onto the shoulder of the dusty dirt road. The song won't let him go. It's been running through his mind all after-noon as he and Grady toured the arena, offering input on stage setup, FaceTiming Luke about the set list they plan to play.

Now, notepad in his hand, he begins to write.

> We used to kiss in those old stables
> July nights, young kids, wild and free
> Picking wildflowers from the riverbank
> Wasn't very long before I started to think
> About weddin' bands and puttin' one on your left hand
> Now I'm standing here watching you light out of town,
> wonderin' where things went wrong
> Guess sometimes it seems we're one key, one line off
> the melody in our song

A buzz has his attention jumping. He grabs his phone, ex-pecting a call from Luke to discuss the Wildheart show in more detail. Instead, it's a text message notification. An unknown number.

His thumb calls up the text.

Jace goes cold.

It's a picture of the Happy Hideaway. The front door wide open. No accompanying message, not a word, but Jace gets the message clear as day.

It's a threat.

To Emmy Lou.

"Fuck," he blasts.

The world closes in around him.

Heart pounding, Jace puts the truck in gear and punches the gas, fishtailing as he swerves erratically back onto the road.

Emmy Lou. Emmy Lou. Emmy Lou.

Her name's a chant in his head. Rage and worry pool in his guts as he fumbles for his phone and punches in a number.

He let his fucking guard down.

He forgot about McCade and trouble found him.

"Grady," he says when the line's picked up. "Emmy Lou's in trouble. You gotta get to the house, now."

Seconds later, he's barreling down the thin road, driving like his life depends on it. The ten-minute drive feels like two hours. Every awful scenario replaying in Jace's brain. His mother's words scattering inside him like shrapnel.

You protect the ones you love, Jace. You do anything.

Finally, he's back at the farm.

He rips his truck into the drive and cuts the engine. He clocks his surroundings. Emmy Lou's car. Horses in the pasture.

Then he's out of the truck and running, running until the air in his lungs is shredded, nearly stumbling as he comes upon the open front door.

"Emmy!" he hollers. He bursts into the kitchen. "Emmy Lou, honey, where are you?"

Silence.

Dead, awful silence.

He checks all the rooms on the lower floor. The back door is locked.

Bile stirs in his stomach as he takes the stairs two at a time. He sprints down the hallway to the bedroom. "Emmy! Emmy Lou—"

"Jace, what on earth?"

He freezes at the soft drawl, grabbing the side of the wall to hold himself up.

Emmy Lou's stepping out of the large walk-in closet, staring at him like he's off his rocker.

It takes him a minute to fully understand.

She's okay.

She's fine.

She's fresh from the shower. A white towel wrapped around her curves. Her skin shimmers pink. Her wet hair curls around her neck.

He stares at her.

Vulnerable, breathtaking beauty.

In one swift movement, Jace crosses the room and pulls her small frame into his embrace. His eyes slam shut, absorbing the feel of her. Trying to calm the wild beating of his heart. She's here. Safe. His.

A soft laugh from Emmy Lou. She untangles herself to look up at him, her brown eyes wide with confusion. "You're shakin' like a leaf, Jace. What's wrong?"

He swallows the thickness in his throat. Takes her face in his hands. "I was worried," he says hoarsely. The words stick. "I couldn't find you."

Her face softens. "Well, ain't you frettin' so sweet." Her smile's amused. "I'm right here. Where else would I be?"

He kisses her. Hard. Desperate. It's all he can do.

When they pull back, Emmy Lou's heavy-lidded. Her sigh, her voice like fine china.

Beautiful. Breakable.

She tilts her head, concern in her deep brown eyes. "Are you sure you're okay?" Small hands palm his face, sweeping over the stubble he's been letting grow since he came to the farm.

He tightens his hold on her. "Fine." The word's dry as a lie.

"Oh, shoot," she mutters, ripping herself back from him. The front of his shirt is drenched. "Look at me, I'm gettin' water all over you."

Emmy Lou scampers off to the bathroom. Jace follows her movement, catching a glimpse of her naked form in the reflection of the steamy mirror, all curves as she tosses the towel onto the hamper.

Her soft chirp of a drawl floats. "I was a mess after ridin' with Wyatt. I gotta run to get my dress fitted. I'm late as it is. Mama's gonna have my hide . . ." There's a clattering of makeup tubes and compacts. A flash of black as she pulls out a hairdryer.

But Jace barely hears her bubbly chattering. His eyes scour the room, his panic damn near overtaking him. The open window. The confined space. The turned-up radio drowning out the outside world. If he hadn't made it in time. If someone had come today. Cornered her.

Fuck.

The thought terrifies him.

He steps to the nightstand and rips open the drawer.

Jace's stomach plummets.

The pistol Grady loaned him is still in its drawer.

But it's been moved. It's out of its case, staring up at him like some kind of macabre taunt.

Jace doubles over, bracing hands on the knees of his jeans, breathing hard.

Someone was here today. With Emmy Lou.

All the strange things happening on the farm, the cigarettes, the footprints, ain't a coincidence. Danger is at his doorstep. By his wife's side. His beautiful, innocent wife, who doesn't know a damn thing about the kind of trouble that just showed up. But what? And who?

Guilt lashes his spine.

Fuck. He's fucked up again.

All he does is let Emmy Lou down and put her in danger.

Emmy Lou reappears, clad in silk panties and a bra. "I gotta get," she says, adjusting a gold hoop earring.

"I'll drive you," he says. "I'll take you to the house." He doesn't want her alone. He ain't letting anyone touch her.

"It's a dress fittin', Jace. I ain't gonna be quick." She frowns. "And it's at Mama's."

"I'll wait in the car." His palms spread over his shoulders like he can anchor her to him. Like he can hold her forever.

"In the car? Are you sure?"

"Sure I'm sure." He tries for a smile. "Got nothin' better to do."

Emmy Lou beams. She stands on tiptoes to kiss him, the fullness of her breasts pressing against his shirt. Then she's off again, a flurry of prim curses as she flies around the room in her haste to get ready.

Jace jolts at the sound of a sputtering engine. Fists curling at his side, he goes to the window.

Grady.

Jace catches Grady by the shoulders right as he's barreling through the screen door. "Outside," he says, moving the wild-eyed kid to the porch.

Grady, breathing hard, slicks a hand through his hair. "What's goin' on, Jace? I get a phone call from you sayin' Emmy's in trouble." His worried eyes flit to the house. "Where's my sister? Is she okay?"

"She's fine." Jace hands over his phone. "I got this text earlier."

Grady drops his eyes to the photo. A muscle tics in his clean-shaven jaw as he reads. "This ain't cool, Jace."

Jace shoves the phone into his back pocket. "Yeah, no shit."

"What's goin' on?"

"Fuck if I know."

"Is it them? Those guys you got mixed up with?"

"I don't know."

"Well, what do you know?" Grady demands. His eyes flash with fury. He paces around the porch, a deep scowl on his usually cheerful face. "Because right now all I know is you're mixed up in some shit and my sister's caught up in your mess. Again."

"Someone's been comin' on the farm," Jace admits. "It could be McCade, but I ain't sure."

Grady swallows. "What if it is him? What if she gets hurt?"

"She ain't gonna get hurt," Jace promises in a low voice. Fury grips him hard. "I won't let anything happen to her."

For a brief second, Grady closes his eyes. "Man, I love you, but I don't know if you're fuckin' worth it."

Anger ripples through Jace. Grady telling him he's not worth it ain't fucking helpful. He already feels like shit. He already knows that for the rest of his life, even though Emmy Lou's forgiven him, he'll never forgive himself.

"Save it," he tells Grady. "I know I fucked up. But I fuckin' paid for it."

"Walk away." Grady's eyes blaze. "Leave. Go back to Nashville. Let her go if she's in trouble."

"I can't," Jace grits out, his heart feeling as if it's dying. Grady's plea like a knife to his chest. "I love her."

Grady shakes his head. "You don't fuckin' deserve her."

His words twist something in Jace.

Snap him in half.

Send him over the edge.

"Fuck you," Jace says and swings a right hook. His fist connects sharply with Grady's nose, sending him back against the porch railing.

Grady swears and lunges for Jace, wrapping arms around his waist and driving him back against the house. The screen door clatters.

With a shove, Jace tears away from him and swears. He takes a huge step backward, staring at Grady. They both breathe heavily, bodies tense, fists balled. A beckoning of round two. A breaking of tempers. Then he drops his hands.

He doesn't want to do this. Fight with the one person who's on his damn team.

Finally, the tense silence is broken by Grady. "Christ," he exclaims, wiping blood off his upper lip. "You punched me in the fuckin' nose, man."

Jace grunts, tiredly running a hand down his bruised jaw. "Yeah, well . . . you deserved it. Asshole."

They stare at each other for a long second. Then Grady busts out into a great laugh. Jace follows with a slow chuckle.

A sound behind them has Grady going rigid.

"Shit," he swears, looking for all the world like a three-year-old who's been caught lying. He inspects his face in the window, adjusting his wild mop of hair. "Emmy Lou catches us fightin' we're dead."

Jace moves close to the kid. "No one's gonna hurt Emmy Lou," he says in a quiet voice. "I swear it to you. I'll protect her. Whatever this is, whoever it is, I'll figure it out."

Fix it. He's got to.

A muscle jerks in Grady's jaw. "Emmy Lou's been through enough. I just want her to be happy."

Jace nods, unease curdling his stomach. The kid's face is haunted. Tormented, even.

With that, Grady turns and stalks off down the steps.

Jace watches Grady lope off. He stares out toward the wild country, the thin dirt road.

Wondering, worrying what's coming.

chapter
TWENTY-ONE

EMMY LOU HUMS A TUNE AND RUNS A BRUSH THROUGH her bouncy curls. Day thirty-three of being at the farm and she's high. High on life. High on the last week of living with Jace. It's like they're newlyweds fogging up the windows all over again. Skinny-dipping in the pond late at night. Sharing wine and whiskey on the front porch. Midday naps that end with long romps in the bed.

She can feel her life resetting itself, intertwining with Jace, and even though they've been married for years, her feelings are growing roots. Growing hope.

For the first time in a long time, she's starting to think about the future. They can go back to Nashville, happy. To friends and family, to the music, to shared lives, not separate. Sunday suppers. Vegas. And maybe . . . God, does she even hope? Down the line, babies. A whole bunch of babies with Jace Taylor.

This summer, she's seen so many sides to her husband. Sides that always existed, sides she loved about him but forgot about over the years. The caring man who would always have her back. The son-in-law who stepped up for his family. The loyal friend who tried to protect his best friend.

Jace came to make things right and he's doing it.

He stormed his way back into her heart and he's been burning her up ever since.

Divorce isn't what she wants anymore.

She knows that now.

It's her worst mistake. Signing those papers.

She was running on rage that day, ready to get that fool man out of her mind, to appease her mama and let the topic of Slayton die.

God, the thought of Jace seeing those papers—it sickens her. She thanks the good Lord above Mama Belle took them away that day. Jace finding them—it'd kill him.

Still, at times, nights, when she lies awake next to Jace, she can't stop the desolate doubt creeping through the cracks of her mind. Wyatt's words from a week ago. She trusts Jace, she does. But there's a part of her holding herself back. If this summer is just a fantasy, a flash-in-the-pan moment like last Christmas in the Smokies, if she's hurt again . . .

She couldn't take that.

It would end them.

Exhaling, Emmy Lou glances at herself in the mirror. After fastening her hair with a magnolia flower clip, she smooths a hand over her corset-style bodice and fluffs out her gauzy skirt. The layers and layers of lavender tulle are extra puffy thanks to the petticoat layered beneath.

Tonight is her parents' anniversary party, and she's bringing Jace.

Emmy Lou's eyes rove around the bedroom they've been sharing. He's moved his stuff upstairs. A simple action—her husband finally back in her bed—that has a hot rush of tears filling her eyes.

She's still ashamed about how she fled Nashville. She was so damn angry with Jace for more lies, for breaking her trust. But now she knows. The truth. His truth.

The little voice inside of her pipes up. *What about your truth. Huh? What about the lies you've kept?*

She flinches.

They're not lies. They're scars.

Emmy Lou pats her hair, pretending not to see the way her hands tremble.

The past is in the past. She never lied to Jace, she withheld. Besides, she's fine. It's over. It doesn't matter.

A sharp intake of air has her glancing over her shoulder.

She turns, folding her shaky hands together, trying to rope her emotions back into the pasture of placid.

Jace stands in the doorway, his eyes eating her up. Emmy Lou's entire body flushes with heat. She's still not used to the way he's looking at her. Ever since they made love, he's been staring her down like she's his undoing.

Before she can say a word, she's in his arms. Jace runs his big hands down her shoulders, his gaze lasered on her. He looks like he's been punched in the stomach. "Damn," he says faintly. "You look beautiful, honey."

Emmy Lou eyes him with appreciation. His rusty-brown hair is mussed, his face dusted with the perfect amount of scruff. "Well, don't you look handsome all done up fancy-like in your tux."

He gives her a twirl, the hem of her dress lifting, then pulls her against his chest.

Desire wings through her, puckering her nipples, warming her down below. She reaches out. Grips his black tie and pulls him in for a breathless kiss. With a groan, Jace drags her into him, his hands in her hair, his tongue parting her lips.

When his hands slide slower, to the small bow around her waist that could undo the whole damn dress, Emmy Lou rips away.

"No." She wags a finger, recognizing that wolfish look in his eyes. "I know you. Holster your hands, Taylor."

Jace grins, his hazel eyes heavy-lidded. "What can I say? You're damn hard to resist, Em." Adjusting himself, his cuffs, he asks, "What time do we have to be at this shindig?"

"Seven o'clock sharp." She gasps, seeing the time. They're late. "Oh, you know Mama is gonna make some big production out of it. Canapés, cake, god-awful speeches."

Jace tilts his head. "What do you think it is?"

Emmy Lou laughs. "Somethin' she can show off. Like Daddy's takin' her on a cruise or buyin' her a Waffle House."

Jace laughs, then he sobers. He lowers his voice. "Does she know I'm comin'?"

Dropping her eyes from his, she turns to the mirror to adjust an earring. "No. I haven't had a chance to tell her."

No, because she's been acting a coward avoiding Mama Belle for the last three days.

Her mother will be less than pleased to hear that she and Jace are back together. Showing up together unannounced is the best way to do it. Mama Belle won't make a scene in front of everyone. At least, that's her plan.

Uncertainty clouds Jace's face. His eyes drop to her hand, to her bare ring finger. "Do you wanna tell her, Em?"

Her heart aches at the pained look on his face. She's hurt him by not telling her mama, by once again not taking his side.

"Oh, Jace, I do."

She moves close, lacing her hands with his.

She knows he's wondering where they stand. That he's afraid she's going to wake up and say she wants out. And why shouldn't he? She isn't wearing her ring. She hasn't said *I love you* back. Emmy Lou doesn't know how to tell him that she's still afraid. Like if she gives in to her happiness and voices all her heart's desires aloud, it will jinx the good thing they have going. Something so damn beautiful she barely believes it.

And she doesn't want to break their bubble of happy.

Not now.

Not yet.

"Em?"

She shakes off her dark thoughts. Forces a smile. "You know me. Avoidin' dustups because my family thrives on drama."

Jace chuckles. "I'm used to it."

"You're still my husband, Jace," she says, cupping the scruff on his jaw. "Mama Belle takin' shots at you ain't happenin.'"

Jace grins, love in his eyes. "Let her." He leans in, sweeping a kiss against her lips. "I got you. Only thing I care about."

"Maybe I should usurp Mama's big announcement. Tell everyone that we're back together."

"I won't argue with that." Sliding the strap of her dress off her shoulder, Jace dips to kiss her bare skin. "Save me a dance."

She looks at him in astonishment. Jace has a phobia of dance floors and two left feet. "You don't dance."

His lips curve. "I do now."

Warmth flashes over her, a bright burst of joy. "Who is this man and what have you done to my husband?"

She leans in, her teeth snagging Jace's lower lip in a light bite. He moves closer against her, hand on the small of her back, and she feels the male shudder working its way through him. He's pressed against her, hard, wanting. He smells like coffee and hay and her heart thunders.

The smell of Jace, of the memories he conjures, there's nothing better.

Finally, they have to come up for air. Both pull back, panting, flushed.

Fanning herself, Emmy Lou grabs his hand and squeezes. "Lord, let's get out of here before I overheat."

"Hey." He stops her at the door. Grins. "It's gonna be a good night."

She smiles. Hope, joy and love rush through her. And then she whispers, "A great night."

Emmy Lou takes a glass of champagne from a tray, her second of the night, and glances around the parlor. Her parents' southern mansion is done up in glam and glitz. No muted colors, everything is draped in glittering gold and ruby-jeweled tones. A decadent white frosted cake sits in the center of the room. Waiters balance petits fours on oversized trays. Bartenders pour whiskey and a jazz band hammers out "Cheek to Cheek" on a raised stage.

Every well-to-do family from Georgia is in attendance,

including rodeo stars, Thoroughbred horse breeders, and old Wildheart friends. The air is hot and honeyed, the French doors thrown open to the backyard, letting in a spectacular view of the fountain and gardens.

She and Jace have been here for over an hour. So far there's been no sign of her daddy and Mama Belle. No doubt her parents are schmoozing with Georgia's finest. Which suits Emmy Lou just fine. The longer she can delay talking to Mama Belle about Jace, the better.

As they wander throughout the ballroom, the sea of people, Jace, a highball of whiskey in his hand, leans into her. "You know all these folks?"

Emmy Lou shakes her head. "I have no idea who on earth half these people are. I've never seen so many bolo ties in my life."

Jace chuckles, the pitch of his laugh bright and happy. Emmy Lou's heart hums. It feels so natural, so right to be here with him.

"Is it bad if all I wanna do is go back home?" She tugs on his tie, thinking of their bedroom. Comfortable. Quiet. Beckoning.

His hazel eyes flash. "Honey, you just say the word . . ." He wraps an arm around her waist, adjusting her against him. She turns, feeling like fire in his arms. Quickly, she glances around, trying to remember where the closest bathroom is because all she wants to do is take Jace into one and—

Behind them, a very deep, very male voice rumbles, "Mama see him yet?"

Emmy Lou pulls out of Jace's arms to see Charlie peering at them. Her big brother's giving her a serious look.

Emmy Lou huffs, props hands on her hips. "Charlie, it is bad enough I'm gonna have to deal with an interrogation from Mama Belle, now I gotta deal with you?" She waves away his bossy scowl and scans the crowd. "Where's Grady and Wyatt? My other favorite brothers?"

"They're runnin' a train on the hors d'oeuvres," he replies, nodding at the food station, where Grady and Wyatt hover like Hoovers.

A hand on her shoulder. "C'mon, honey."

Charlie reaches out and stops her before she can follow Jace.

"About the rodeo. I know you've been practicin' for your show. Barrel racin.'" Her mouth snaps open and he holds up a hand before she can plead her case. "Wyatt told me. I won't tell Mama. But I wanted to tell you that . . ." He swallows. "I ain't comin', Em."

"Oh, Charlie, I understand." She puts a hand on his arm and he looks away. The hard bob of his throat tells her he's struggling. "It's okay. No one expects you to."

"I just . . . after Maggie . . ." A crack in his words. Then he sighs, clearing the brokenness from his gruff voice. "You be careful."

She smiles up at him. "I will." She hooks her arm through his. "C'mon, let's git before they hog all the food."

Grady looks up from his deviled egg as Emmy Lou and Charlie approach. "Hey, y'all," he crows. "Welcome to the party!"

Wyatt smirks and pulls out a flask. "I got the real party right here." He sticks the flask in Emmy Lou's face. Never one to back down, she takes a pull and passes it to Jace.

A disgruntled mutter. "Christ."

Emmy Lou grins at the disgusted look on Charlie's face, her older brother fighting hard to be the responsible one. Then she grimaces. Her turn to be responsible. Tutting, Emmy Lou fixes a stern gaze on Wyatt. "You couldn't dress up one night?"

"I look good," Wyatt boasts. He turns back to his chicken wing.

"You look about as sexy as a dog turd," Emmy Lou retorts, tugging on her brother's torn T-shirt hem. "Jesus take the wheel, Wyatt, because if he doesn't, I will throttle you myself."

Grady slings an arm around Emmy Lou's shoulder. "So what are we bettin' on? Mama Belle descendin' on a white cloud while Daddy tap-dances and sings 'Dixieland Delight'?"

A giggle rises up in her as she pictures the lavish scenario.

Jace lifts the flask. "You know, I wouldn't put it past Mama Belle."

"You and me both." Wyatt smirks. He grabs a flute of

champagne and hands it to Emmy Lou. "What do y'all think this big announcement is?"

"Where is she anyway?" Grady asks.

"Probably preenin' her feathers," Emmy Lou says.

Jace and Charlie double over, snickering.

"You know Mama. She's gotta show off her—"

"Emmaline Louise, you mind tellin' me what is the meanin' of this?"

The voice drenches them all like a cold bucket of water.

Wyatt chokes on his whiskey. Charlie, Grady and Jace all wince in unison.

Emmy Lou spins around, her full skirt sweeping the floor. Mama Belle stands there, mouth pursed. She wears a dazzling champagne-colored sequined gown with a dramatic cape. Beside her is Boone.

"Hey, Mama," Grady drawls, trying to lighten the mood. "Fancy party you got here."

Emmy Lou grabs Jace's hand and pulls him to her side, a move that promptly has Mama Belle's right eyebrow shooting off into space. She refuses to be scared off. She's got a gorgeous dress on her body, a sexy man on her arm. Not even Mama Belle's sour face can get her down.

At least her daddy's smile is genuine. "Well, this is a sight," Boone booms. His eyes sweep over his sons, then he nods at Jace. "Jace. Glad you could make it."

Jace nods back, respect in his eyes. "Thank you, Sir."

"Congratulations, Mama. Daddy." Wyatt's eyes tick between Emmy Lou and Mama Belle, eager for fireworks. "With the exception of Davis and Ford, we got the whole damn family here."

Mama Belle ignores Wyatt's curse as she lasers her gaze on Emmy Lou. "Emmy Lou, may I speak with you in the parlor?"

Grady flinches, biting his bottom lip.

Charlie and Wyatt automatically all take one step backward. Cowards.

Her chest tightens, and she tries valiantly to control the flush of dread creeping up her neck. "Of course, Mama."

Jace gives her hand a squeeze as she steps away. He holds her gaze, solidarity and worry softening his face. His reach protective, his stance aching to go with her, to take whatever scolding Mama Belle plans to dish out.

She follows her mother down the hall, stopping in the secluded cove of the foyer.

"What on earth is Jace doin' here, Emmy Lou?" Mama Belle's voice is a hiss, barely heard above the background din of the party.

She inhales a breath, steeling herself. "He's my date."

"Your date." The word drips from her lips like poison. "You're supposed to be divorcin' him, not datin' him."

"Mama—"

"I don't believe this." Mama Belle wrings her hands and looks up at the ceiling as if she can work a miracle. Her body is stiff, full of an anger, a strange distress Emmy Lou can't place. "I had plans tonight, Emmaline, plans that are now all messed up."

"Plans? Mama, I don't understand." She peers at Mama Belle, confused. "I'm tellin' you Jace and I are gonna work it out. Most people would say that's a good thing."

"Well, I most certainly do not. I don't understand you and that man. He lied to you and you're takin' him back? He has never been to your standin'. A man like Jace."

Her temper flaring, Emmy Lou props her hands on her hips. "What exactly is my standin', Mama?" she hisses, her southern drawl coming out at full throttle. "Do enlighten me."

"Your standin' is not embarassin' your family."

"Embarrassin'? Just how am I doin' that?"

Mama Belle's nostrils flare. She fixes Emmy Lou with a look so fierce it's a wonder she doesn't spontaneously combust. "It's embarassin' you changin' your mind. Especially now when I told everyone you were a free woman."

Emmy Lou groans. "Oh, Mama."

"I hope you're happy," Mama Belle snaps. "I was tryin' to look out for my only daughter, fixin' things where you went wrong. How is this gonna look now? What will I tell—"

"Good evenin', everyone," a booming voice says over the speakers, interrupting Mama Belle's tirade.

Boone stands on the curved stairwell, a microphone in his hand. "I'm fixin' to get this party started, as my son Wyatt would say." He pretends to scour the crowd. "Now if I could find my lovely wife . . ."

Mama Belle goes rigid. "What in the almighty heaven is that man doin'?" Her hands fly to her hair, adjusting the sparkling tiara nestled in her beehive. "He's startin' without me."

Savin' me, Emmy Lou thinks, giving her daddy a grateful smile.

Mama Belle grabs her skirts and rushes as ladylike as she can to Boone's side.

Emmy Lou drifts back to her brothers and Jace, feeling bulldozed and confused as hell.

"You okay?" Jace asks, reaching out to draw her into him. He holds her tight, his steadiness like a balm. She leans into him, resting her head against the curve of his neck.

"Fine," she says in a hushed whisper, then tunes in to her father's speech.

"We appreciate all of our friends and family bein' here to celebrate our fortieth weddin' anniversary. It's a big one. Belle and I met when we were just kids and since then we've done a lot of darn good things together. Like our beautiful children, for starters. I'm a blessed man, havin' almost all my boys and my baby girl by my side. Raisin' them on the farm Belle and I made together has been everything I could want." Boone wraps an arm around Belle. "Which brings me to the big announcement we've been teasin' y'all with."

Emmy Lou shoots Grady a confused glance, and he gives a beats-me shrug. All her brothers look equally confused.

That's when she notices Dean and Cora, Slayton's parents, standing in the crowd of party guests. Though her stomach twists at the sight of them, she tries to shake off her unease. Of course they'd be here. They live in Wildheart. They're still close friends with the Montgomerys.

Boone continues. "We love this farm, but let's not kid ourselves, Belle's not gettin' any younger"—a round of chuckles float through the crowd—"and my children got lives of their own to sort. As you know, our farm's been up for sale for a while now, but I'm pleased to tell y'all we finally found a buyer for our farm."

Charlie's eyes shoot open.

"Oh no," Emmy Lou breathes out. Beside her, Jace's body goes as tense as a wall.

"But not just any buyer. As many of y'all know, our farm has been me and Mama's heart and soul for the last forty years. In fact, when an offer came in weeks ago from someone who's like family to us, it seemed too good to be true. But it isn't. In a few short months, after proper business decisions are done, there will be a new owner of Montgomery Farm and Stables."

Boone extends an arm.

Before Emmy Lou can even pick out what's happening, the parlor doors open and in walks Slayton Holt.

GHOST.

She's seeing a ghost.

Emmy Lou nearly drops her glass of champagne when Slayton joins her parents on the stairwell. As always, he's tall, dark and handsome. Dressed smoothly in a dark blue tux with a pocket square. The perfect southern gentleman.

Emmy Lou closes her eyes.

The perfect nightmare.

She wants to faint. To run. To scream. But she can't. She forces herself to stand tall and listen as Slayton makes his smarmy speech thanking the Montgomerys, proclaiming himself excited to be the new owner, to move back to Wildheart, to take over a farm he loves as much as his parents'.

As Slayton ends the speech, his steel-gray gaze scours the room. She watches as his eyes travel from Jace's hand in Emmy Lou's to her hips, breasts, lips. A grin spreads across his face and Emmy Lou fights a shiver.

Ghosts.

It was Slayton, she thinks, her breath catching in her throat. *At the arena.* She wasn't crazy or seeing things. He was there. Living and breathing and watching her.

"Em? Emmy Lou?"

Emmy Lou jumps at the husky voice in her ear.

"Em?" Jace peers at her, running a broad hand down her arm. She blinks, trying to focus. Her head's still spinning from what just happened. "I've been sayin' your name for the last minute, honey." He nods towards the stairs where Mama Belle, Boone and Slayton are swallowed up by well-wishers. "That was a lot your daddy dropped on you. You okay?"

She inhales a steadying breath. The kindness in his eyes has her wanting to fall apart right then and there. A reminder that Jace is on her side at the party. He's here and she's safe. She's steady.

"I'm fine. I . . ." Her mouth works the words over, while she shakes away her daze. "I don't believe this." She looks up at her brothers who form a loose semicircle around them. "Did y'all know about this?"

Their faces mirror hers. Confusion. Sadness. Shock. Though Wyatt looks more amused than pissed, Charlie's face is set in a grim frown.

"Nothin'," Charlie says in a tight voice. His cell phone's in his hand. "I'm gettin' Davis and Ford on the line right the hell now."

"I'm actually impressed Daddy went through with it." Wyatt nudges Grady. "Now you ain't gotta feel so bad for takin' off to Nashville."

Only Grady's silent. He stares down at Emmy Lou, his expression twisted. She reaches out and grips his forearm. His rage radiates. So much passes between them—that night, her running to Grady, Grady taking off to kill Slayton, the cops bringing Grady home.

"You can't," is all she says.

Grady squeezes his eyes shut. Her youngest brother's ready to explode. He wants to fight. To finish what he couldn't do that night.

"Here." Wyatt shoves a glass of champagne at Emmy Lou. "Drink this."

Jace sighs, unhappy. "Wyatt, man, ease up . . ."

Despite Jace's objections, she slugs down the bubbly liquid. Then she balls her fists, gathering courage. As much as she wants to run, she has to figure out what in the hell has possessed her Daddy to sell to Slayton Holt.

Gathering her skirt in her hands, Emmy Lou draws herself up

with a huff and faces her brothers. "I'm goin' to see what Mama and Daddy are thinkin'."

Grady shoots her a look of worry, but before anyone can object, before Jace can ask her why her hands are shaking, because he's seen it—she didn't miss the concern in his hazel eyes—Emmy Lou's off, bound for her parents.

She finds them on the stairs. "Mama, Daddy, how can you do this?" It takes all of her effort not to break protocol, to keep prim and pleasant, when really, her nerves are snapping all over the place like a downed power line.

Boone sighs, long and tired. "Em Bug, I'm sorry. I know it was a surprise. But when Slayton heard the farm was on the market—"

"I couldn't resist," a dry drawl intones. Slayton appears beside Mama Belle, his dark, wolfish gaze on Emmy Lou, a bottle of Stella in his hands. "How you been, Emmy Lou?"

She bristles at the nearness of him but ignores Slayton, keeping her eyes on her daddy. She owes that man nothing, not one single word.

"Answer the man, Emmaline," Mama prods, her smile bright. "Slayton came all this way for you." She presses a palm to her heart. "Oh, would you look at this, Boone? What a sight for sore eyes. Wildheart's king and queen back together again."

At the comment, Emmy Lou jerks her head back so fast she nearly gets whiplash. Realization hits her, stark and awful. Slayton doesn't look shocked to see her. In fact, he looks like he expected this.

Suddenly, it all makes sense.

Why Mama Belle was so upset she had brought Jace tonight. She was planning to play matchmaker, hoping she and Slayton would pick up the past. And what about the farm? Did she arrange that too? The very thought has her feeling faint, has hot swirls of nausea rolling throughout her body in a slow wave. She reaches out, gripping the staircase railing so her legs don't give out.

She turns to her mother. "Oh, Mama, tell me you didn't." She can feel the blood dripping out of her face.

Boone rushes to reassure, propping a gnarled hand on Emmy Lou's shoulder. "We ain't sellin' it all, Em Bug. We're keepin' the main house. This is your home. All Slayton is managin' is the stables, the property down over on the left side of the ridge."

She swallows, sickened by the knowledge that Slayton will be on their farm. Close to her home, close to her.

"It won't be the same, Daddy. It won't be kept in the family." She tries again, pleading with her father. "Slayton don't know a thing about runnin' a farm. He ain't a farmer. He'll turn it into a McStables."

Mama's perfect smile slips. "You're bein' dramatic," she snipes. "Slayton will take great care of the farm."

"I really will, Em. You have nothing to worry about."

Emmy Lou scoffs.

"Go fix your makeup, Emmy Lou." Mama Belle nudges her backwards toward Slayton. "Then you and Slayton can reconnect."

He nods. "I'd like nothing better."

"Well, I wouldn't," she snaps.

"Emmy Lou," Mama Belle breathes, mild horror on her face. "You're bein' rude."

"No, Mama, you are."

With that, Emmy Lou whirls around and climbs the stairs. She snatches two glasses of champagne from a nearby server and downs each one in quick succession. Then she beelines in the direction of her childhood bedroom. All she wants to do is hide out and have the mother of all breakdowns.

Her heart pounds hard in her chest, hot tears in her eyes. How could her mother do this? Play matchmaker with the farm, with Emmy Lou like she's some kind of prize. She's so damn sick of everyone pretending that she and golden boy Slayton were a match made in heaven.

Every time she sees her parents, she wants to scream, *Do you know what he tried to do to me?*

She's in the hall when there's a hand on her arm. She turns, hoping it's Jace, but it's not.

"I'm sorry," Slayton says, hands out, eyes apologetic. "I'm sure this is a shock."

"Stay away from me," she hisses, but he steps closer.

Finally, she gets a good look at him. He looks like a rat standing on two feet. Greasy slicked-back black hair. Expensive Wall Street–looking clothes. Not a cowboy, not like Jace or her brothers. Her eyes narrow on the scar she gave him. The thin lash across the corner of his left eye, down his cheek. It's faint. Barely noticeable thanks to the work of a plastic surgeon. Emmy Lou's hit with a surge of anger. It's not fair he gets to wipe it away, like that night never happened, when she carries it with her every day of her life.

She hates him. His laugh, his smug smile, his attitude that he can get whatever he wants, get away with anything because he's Wildheart's golden boy.

"What do you want, Slayton?" She draws her arms around herself. "You're not just here for the farm."

His eyes fall to her bare ring finger. "Why, I'm here for you, Em."

Her heart slams into her high heels.

"I miss you. I've missed you for years. When your parents told mine the farm was for sale, and I heard you were back in town, I figured it was the perfect chance to reconnect."

Emmy Lou gapes at him.

He tilts his head, like he's amused she doesn't get it. Then, so casually, he says, "You're still mine. You know that, right?"

Slayton smiles and her legs nearly give out.

You can't say no. You're mine.

She squeezes her eyes shut. Everything comes rushing back. That night. His words. His hands on her wrist. Pinning her in that small space.

All the letters he sent her for years. Reminders that she'd never truly escape him. That one day he'd be back.

A slithery and slimy feeling churns her stomach as Slayton reaches out to stroke a finger over the curve of her cheek. The scent of his cigarettes drifts between them. "I loved you for a long time, Emmy Lou. I've watched you this summer. At the farm. The arena. You look so good on a horse, Em. You'd look good on my arm."

Nausea clenches down tight on Emmy Lou, the world swirling around her. She wants to be in Nashville. She wants Jace. But most of all she wants to scream at Slayton that he took a piece of her that night, a piece she'll never get back, a girl that went missing.

"Don't touch me." She grabs the wall, pushing herself backwards, her heart pounding hard. All she wants to do is get away from him. "Don't you dare think for one second I owe you anything."

He takes another step toward her. So close. Too close. Then he drops his hand and grabs her wrist. In horror, Emmy Lou watches as his face slowly monsters into the boy she remembers.

"You owe me everything," Slayton rasps.

Tears sting her eyes. Helpless rage and terror sweep over her like a hot wind.

"Fuck you," she bites out.

With that, she tears her wrist from his hard grasp, turns and runs.

She hates herself for running, but she has to get away. Her entire body is a cringe, is desperately failing her.

Inside her bedroom, she slams the door shut and wrenches back against it, her chest heaving. Her trophies and her rodeo crowns stare back at her like mocking memories from the past. The walls close in around her. Everything inside of her is spontaneously combusting. Tears slip silently down her face and she presses fingertips to the corners of her eyes like she can keep them in. But they can't. They just keep coming.

"Oh Lord," she whispers. "Help me."

And then there it is.

Get away, get out, run.

That little voice from years ago finds her again.

Jace steps through the French doors and into the Montgomerys' back gardens, where Emmy Lou's brothers have gathered after Grady grumbled something about needing fresh air.

Sipping his whiskey, Jace stares out over the backyard. The garden hangs heavy with fragrant scents, magnolia and jasmine. It also hangs heavy with memories. Jace's wedding reception—Luke and Seth pulling him away for cigars. Barbeques and Christmases with Emmy Lou's family. Thanksgiving football games with her brothers. His eyes move to the ivy-covered side of the mansion, where an ancient trellis hangs beneath a window. Emmy Lou's bedroom. He chuckles. Twelve years ago, he climbed that exact trellis to get into Emmy Lou's room when they first dated and her parents made him sleep in the guest house in the name of proper southern decency.

His thoughts drift to his wife and he turns back toward the house, frowning at her absence. He hasn't forgotten about the threatening text he got the day of Emmy Lou's dress fitting. Letting her out of his sight for even a minute has him on edge.

He hopes she's okay. He knows the announcement about selling the farm hit Emmy Lou hard. She had gone rigid beside him, her face white as a sheet. Hell, Jace had been about to get whiplash trying to decipher the looks on Emmy Lou and Grady's faces.

The farm is her home, and for Boone to sell it has got to sting. And even though she had plastered an *everything's okay, nothing to see here* smile on her face as she bustled away, Jace saw something else in her deep brown eyes.

Fear.

Why, Jace doesn't know, but he damn sure plans to find out.

A barrage of laughter takes him from his thoughts. Charlie and Wyatt in the shadows, drinking from flasks. Only Grady sits silently on a small stone bench. Attentive to the scene in the house.

Alert, Jace thinks.

As he glances back at the house, his eyes narrow at the man talking to Mama Belle and Boone. Thin, dark-haired, the guy's greasy-looking. Like some sort of Wall Street stockbroker-looking dude Seth would rail on for days.

Jace lifts his whiskey, pointing at the man with a tilt of his glass. "So who is that guy?"

The conversation falls silent, hushed. Then—

"Slayton," Wyatt offers. "Emmy Lou's old squeeze." A lazy chuckle. "Mama Belle thinks he shits gold."

Jace bristles. His fingers curl into tight fists as a pathetic primal jealousy overtakes him. "Like an old boyfriend?"

Charlie snorts dryly. "Hell, more than that. Boyfriend of the century. He and Emmy Lou were practically married in high school. Mama was plannin' their wedding when they were babies. She was a wreck when they broke up." He shakes his head. Gives Jace the most sympathetic look he's ever gotten from the guy. "Mama's got some balls of steel to try and play matchmaker tonight."

Jace's jaw goes tight. Pissed off. So damn pissed off. Hell, he and Emmy Lou ain't divorced yet, goddamnit.

He thinks back to the past. If Emmy Lou ever told him about old flings or serious boyfriends. Lord knows he had his share of girls on the road before he and the Brothers Kincaid got famous, before he met Emmy Lou, but of all the girls he chased, none of them could hold a candle to his wife. She was the gem he had found out of all the bullshit he had mined.

"Why'd they break up?" Jace asks, sipping his drink.

A hard voice breaks the silence. "Because he's an asshole."

Jace turns to see Grady glowering. He looks like Seth in his younger days, his entire face a disgusted scowl.

"Somethin' tells me you don't like him," Jace says evenly, gauging his reaction.

"I hate that guy."

Wyatt chuckles, looks to Jace. "Ol' Grady and Slayton had words once upon a time."

Jace lifts an eyebrow at the information.

"Fuck you, man," Grady snaps.

Wyatt and Charlie glance at each other, their brows furrowed by their youngest brother's outburst. "What's up your ass?" Wyatt asks, staring at Grady.

"Nothin'," Grady grumbles and shoves himself up off the bench. He grips his beer bottle like a baseball bat. Paces around the courtyard. "I don't even know what he's doin' buyin a farm. He's some city slicker from Chicago. Never comes home. He don't know the first thing about animals anymore."

Watching his brother closely, Charlie says slowly, "Grady's right. Slayton wouldn't know hard work if it bit him on the dick." He looks at Jace. "Davis thinks Daddy got desperate. The Holts are the closest he can get to keeping the farm in the family." Charlie's face turns contrite. "No one thought Daddy would actually sell it."

Wyatt claps Jace on the back, rocking him forward. "Don't worry about Slayton. Emmy Lou invited you tonight. You're livin' with her." He wiggles a suggestive brow. "You're golden, man."

Jace doesn't know about that. Sure, things are good—are perfect, even—but he's not pushing his luck or assuming things are fine between them. Not ever again. Even in his dreams.

Emmy Lou ain't yet wearing her wedding ring. There's been no talk of her moving back to Nashville. No *I love you* from her sweet lips. But he doesn't blame her. He knows she's wary. Her heart's tender. And he won't push. Until the six weeks are up, he's working harder than he ever has. He's going to prove to Emmy Lou that he deserves her, that he won't take her for granted again, that he won't fuck with her trust.

Jace eyes the house warily. He can hear the jazz band starting back up, and he can see Slayton. The guy's staring up at the staircase where his wife rounded a corner and disappeared a good fifteen minutes ago.

A fierce flare of possessiveness wings through him. The way Slayton's looking after Emmy Lou, practically drooling on the Montgomery stairs, has Jace seeing what life could be like if he lost Emmy Lou. Watching from the wings while she moves on with her life.

Not to mention some sleazebag sniffing around his wife doesn't have Jace too happy.

It has him fucking furious.

Charlie leans in. "You might be golden, but I wouldn't trust Slayton as far as I could throw him. He's been hung up on Em ever since she left town. Thinkin' he might ask her on a date. God knows Mama Belle told him she's single."

Jace stiffens, an electric anger rolling up his spine. He can't tell if Emmy Lou's brothers are putting him through the shit, trying to rile him up, but he don't like it. Not one goddamn bit.

Some alpha growl rolls out of him. "You're tellin' me that rat-faced fuck is back here for my wife?"

Charlie and Wyatt both cackle.

"Now *that's* the Jace I know," Charlie says with a grin that softens his stern face. "Relax, man. Emmy Lou's just—"

"Climbin' out the goddamn window."

"What?" At the sound of Grady's strangled announcement, Jace and Charlie both turn and look up. Wyatt swears.

Sure as shit, Emmy Lou's climbing out her second-story bedroom window. In her big puff of petticoats and tulle, all Jace can see is the dangle of her high heels.

"Emmy Lou, what in the hell are you doin'?" Jace calls up, positioning himself beneath her. Charlie edges on the other side of him.

"Christ, Em, you goin' for a midnight stroll?" Wyatt says, his arms out like he's going to climb up.

Emmy Lou freezes, the lower half of her body draped across the windowsill. Her feet kick out as they try to find their footing on the trellis. "Oh Lord, y'all are out here?" A groan of embarrassment goes up and Jace can see her contemplate whether to drag herself back in or continue with her escape route.

Grady appears to Jace's right. His expression is grave. "That trellis is old as shit."

Jace rips a hand through his hair.

It's a twenty-foot drop to the ground. She won't kill herself, but the fall's far enough that she'd break something or knock herself out cold.

What the hell is she thinking? The answer is—she isn't. She's drunk as a goddamn skunk.

"She did this in high school, you know," Wyatt says with a grin.

"This ain't fuckin' funny," Charlie growls, punching a finger in Wyatt's chest.

"Shut the hell *up*," Grady barks at Wyatt.

Slowly, Emmy Lou begins her descent. She climbs one rung at a time. One foot after the other fits into each square groove like a ladder. "I need some fresh air," she slurs, swaying like a reed. "Y'all just mind your own business."

"Careful," Jace says, running a hand over the back of his neck, where a small sweat has begun to build.

"Mama's gonna kill her," Wyatt cackles, only to get a sharp elbow in the ribs from Grady.

The trellis creaks.

Everyone swears when, in a sudden swift movement, Emmy Lou's shoe slips on a wooden strip. She shrieks as she momentarily loses grip with one hand, dangling in the air for a long moment before she manages to pull herself up. Her right shoe slips off and hits the ground with a thud.

No longer laughing, Wyatt rips a hand through his hair, twisting it in agitation. "Goddamn."

"Go upstairs and pull her through the window," Jace orders Charlie in a low voice. "She's gonna hurt herself."

Charlie takes a few steps toward the French doors.

Another creak.

Everyone freezes.

Then her grip slips.

Emmy Lou lets out a sharp scream as she falls through the air.

"No!" Jace lunges forward, barely catching her in his arms. He and Emmy Lou both hit hard earth, Jace rolling her beneath him to cover her with his body as the remnants of the trellis fall and scatter around them.

Silence.

Jace pushes himself up on his palms, his stomach twisting in terror. His pulse kicks up its beat. Emmy Lou lies on the ground, her dress floating up around her like some cotton candy–colored dream. Frantic, Jace peels the layers of her full skirt down to find his wife.

She lies on the ground, her eyes closed, her face pale.

"Fuck," Wyatt whispers.

With a shaking hand, Jace cups the back of her neck, her head lolling in his palm. "Emmy Lou? Em, honey?" Panic has him seized.

And then she laughs. Big, giggly perfect laughs that shake her entire body. Jace closes his eyes for a brief moment, so damn relieved, drinking in her laughter and trying like hell to pull it together.

Exhaling, Grady kneels beside his sister. "You okay, Em?"

Emmy Lou sways as Jace helps her sit up. He clocks her pupils, runs a hand over the back of her head in case she hit it on the way down. Despite her pale face, the bright orbs of color on her cheeks are the telltale sign she's had too much to drink.

Giggling, Emmy Lou reaches for Jace. "Lord, I'm as dizzy as a goose," she slurs.

"Next time get your own damn selves drunk," Jace snaps, pissed as hell at her brothers for urging Emmy Lou to this state. He pulls her closer, bracing her body against his. She practically slumps in his arms, the slow flutter of her eyes telling him she's fighting to stay conscious.

"Shit." Wyatt stares at his sister, his expression contrite. Then he looks apologetically at Jace. "I'm sorry, man. I wasn't thinkin'."

"You gotta get her out of here," Charlie says in a tight voice. "People are startin' to look."

Fury boils through him. "That's all you fuckin' people care about." Jace throws Charlie a disgusted look that tells him to go to hell.

Charlie grimaces. "Damn it, you know that ain't what I mean," he says, kneeling beside his sister to pick a paint chip out of her blond hair. "It's Em. Anyone in there could snap a picture and sell it to the *Star*."

Jace softens, getting it. They're all trying to protect her. In Wildheart, gossip reigns and getting a picture of their rodeo queen obliterated on bubbly would be the cherry on top.

At that, Jace gives Charlie a nod of understanding before turning back to his wife. "C'mon, Em, lean on me." He scoots close, pulling her into his chest.

"Shit," Wyatt blasts. "Mama's comin.'" He finishes the remains of his flask and tosses it into the bushes.

Over his shoulder, Jace sees the beehive swimming among the crowd like a hungry great white out for blood.

"I'll head her off," Grady says, standing. He gives his sister a long, worried look of concern, then lopes for the back door.

Emmy Lou smiles up at him, her brown eyes wide. "You carryin' me out of here, Jace Taylor?"

"Sure am." He kisses her brow. "Damsel it up for me, will you, honey?"

Jace gets her up in a wobbly standing position. Giggling, she loops her arms around his neck, melting into him as Jace picks her up in his arms. An amused expression on his face, Charlie removes her other shoe and tosses it next to Wyatt's flask. Then he gives Jace a look of thanks as Jace moves in the direction of the house.

Emmy Lou laughs, then hiccups. "It must be a thousand miles back to the farm."

"I got you," Jace says, securing his hold on her. He kisses her brow and she lets out a soft sigh. "I got you for a thousand miles, Em, and then some."

Back at the house, Jace gets Emmy Lou upstairs and on the bed. As he helps her rinse her mouth out and spit into the trash can with gusto, Jace can't help but think, how many times have they done this? Trusting each other to take care of one another, after shows, on the road. Sneaking out of awards show afterparties, sneaking into back seats, sneaking home to the farm they loved because at the end of the night they were homebodies. He and Emmy Lou didn't party much, but when they did, especially with Sal and Luke and Seth, they earned some raging hangovers more nights than not.

"C'mere," Jace says, propping her up against the pillows. He grins at her. "Let's get you naked."

Emmy Lou cackles. "Filthy—you are filthy, Jace Taylor." She goes to swat at him and misses. A fact that tells him she's even drunker than he pegged. Damn. She does look cute, though. With her rumpled dress and dirt-smudged face, Emmy Lou looks like some downhome country girl. Straight up gorgeous.

Carefully, Jace gets her out of her mushroom cloud of a dress, shimmying the gauzy fabric from her breasts to her waist to her ankles. After draping her dress over a chair, he grabs one of his T-shirts from the floor and slips it over her curves.

He chuckles as Emmy Lou flops back on the cool sheets, covering her eyes dramatically. "I'm so tired," she murmurs, her Georgia drawl one long blend of consonants.

Leaning over her, he sweeps a finger across her cheekbone. "Don't go to sleep, Em."

A growl. "Why on earth not?"

She pushes herself up on her elbows, her blond hair haloed across her head. Her bottom lip stuck out in a sulky pout as she stares at him, waiting on an answer.

His wife's tiny. She doesn't drink a lot. He ain't putting her to bed until she sobers up some. The last thing he wants her to do is get the spins or get sick.

But instead of telling her that—she's just feisty enough she'd scold him for fussing—he says, "You still owe me a dance."

She blinks, wide-eyed. "You wanna dance? Now?"

"Yep. Right now."

She bounces on the bed, her bare feet kicking out a rhythm. "We need music."

Jace puts Chris Stapleton on his phone, the singer's throaty croon filling the bedroom.

Eager for a dance, Emmy Lou scoots forward, too fast, and sways on the edge of the bed.

Jace moves quick, reaching out to catch her. He hooks an arm around her waist and gently lifts her onto her feet. Emmy Lou's knees start to buckle as Jace maneuvers her closer to him. She starts to slide downward, but Jace holds her tight, holds her up. Her body is pressed against him, so close not even sunlight could get through. She's all curves, warm and soft, leaning into Jace like he's her rock.

Which he is. Until the end of goddamn time.

Slowly, they sway, letting the music take them away.

Emmy Lou stares up at Jace, cradling his jaw in her palm. Her eyes are loved-dazed and drunk. "You look so handsome tonight."

He squeezes her tight. "You look beautiful. I swear, you're the most beautiful woman I've ever seen." He leans close, resting his forehead against hers. "Em. Em, my gem. I loved you the moment I saw you, you know that?"

A happy murmur comes from Emmy Lou. Jace kisses the top of her blond head. She smells like champagne, like bubbles and sweetness. He inhales it. Christ. His chest is tight, damn near close to bursting. He loves her so goddamn much. He can't live without her. It's not new knowledge, but it is a new start. This summer, it's been a lifeline to his wife.

"Jace," Emmy Lou murmurs, tilting her mouth to his.

Then they kiss. And they don't stop. They kiss like teenage sweethearts, like overheated newlyweds. Emmy Lou's hands tug at his tie, his hands slip over the curves of her waist, both of them mesmerized, tangled up in each other.

When they pull back, gasping for air, Emmy Lou laughs. "Drunken kissing. We should do that more often."

Jace smiles. "Plan to."

With a sigh, she collapses against his chest, burying her face against his shoulder. He and Emmy Lou sway, slow and steady. Her heartbeat pumps against his.

When they're about halfway through the album, Jace says, "What happened tonight, Em?"

Her voice is muffled. "What happened with what?"

"You climbin' out the bedroom window." He traces a finger over the line of her back, feeling her shiver. "You scared the shit out of me. Fallin' like that, you could've hurt yourself."

He feels her smile against his shirt. "Yeah, but you caught me."

"I'll always catch you."

"I know you will," she breathes.

More silence.

Jace frowns and glances down. His wife's face is still buried against his chest. She's tense and trembling in his arms.

Tonight's been hard on her. Why, Jace doesn't know.

"I had to get out of there," she whispers, her voice distressed. Her fingers curl into Jace's shirt, pulling him closer. "I had to. I always run away, don't I? From you. From the rodeo. From—" She stops herself, quiets.

Her cryptic words chill him. He's not sure what to make of them. Only that something has his wife on edge. Something that would have her crawling out her bedroom window at night while drunk during her parents' anniversary party.

"From what?" he asks, cupping the back of her blond head.

She looks up at him. The cross of her eyes, the slow flutter of her eyelids, tell Jace she's fighting to stay conscious. "I've been so awful to you, Jace. And you were there tonight when I needed you. That counts. So much."

Her head bobbles against his chest, and then she goes limp against him.

He glances down, confused, frustrated, wishing he knew what was going on inside his wife's mind.

"Em? Honey, will you talk to me?"

No response.

"Em?" Gently, Jace adjusts his grip on her arms, maneuvering her gently to get a better look at her face.

Jace groans at what he sees.

Emmy Lou's passed out cold in his arms. Her head falls back over the crook of Jace's elbow, exposing a long white throat. Her eyes half-shut, long lashes dark against her cheek. Her rosy-pink mouth parted in sleep.

Jace blows out a breath and curls his arms underneath her. He carries her to the bed and pulls the covers over her body. He sits beside her, his gaze tracing over his wife. The slow rise and fall of her chest, her shallow breaths, her face pretty yet pale with exhaustion.

He's worried. Emmy Lou wasn't herself tonight. Drunk as a skunk and trying to run away from something.

Maybe not something but *someone.*

Jace's jaw goes tight. An electrical storm rages in his head. Pieces of the puzzle clicking into place.

Slayton.

His fingers curl to fists as he remembers the panicked looks passing between Emmy Lou and Grady. The kid was on edge as much as his wife was. And Emmy Lou, she looked like—

No. God, no.

The familiar thought hits him like a sledgehammer.

Emmy Lou looks like his mother.

Tonight, when she saw Slayton up on those stairs, she had that look on her face, the one his mother used to wear when his father would get home from the steel mill.

She knew what was coming.

Terror.

And that's when Jace knows it without a doubt. Knows it with every inch of his thumping heart.

Slayton hurt Emmy Lou.

EMMY LOU OPENS HER EYES TO A BEDROOM BATHED IN sunlight. She sits up, swaying slightly, taking in the glass of water on the nightstand, a bottle of aspirin, the tightly drawn blinds. Her puffball of a dress is draped over a chair. She glances down and blinks. She's been changed into a ratty Brothers Kincaid T-shirt.

She frowns, sitting very still as the night, the cold sweat of a hangover, washes over her. Then she groans. It's all back. At least most of it. Every awful thing she remembers from last night. Daddy's announcement. Mama playing matchmaker. Slayton stroking a finger down the curve of her cheek. Chugging champagne in her childhood bedroom. And after that . . .

She tilts her head. After that it's a black blur.

She smears her face in her hands. Her head pounds, a god-awful headache courtesy of last night's champagne binge. A hot wave of embarrassment and shame curdle her stomach. She already knows what Mama Belle will say.

Montgomerys don't act like that. They save face. They behave.

Well, last night any semblance of proper etiquette went out the damn window. It was too much. Seeing Slayton in her space, swaggering around her family home without any worry or care about what he did to her, pushed her over the edge. He's a nightmare of a man and she wants nothing more than to scrape his eyeballs out with her fingernails.

Thank God for Jace.

Jace.

Her mind turns, a flash of last night bursting in her mind. Jace carrying her . . .

She frowns at the memory.

Down a hill?

She doesn't even want to know.

Scooting toward the nightstand, she takes a swig of water, swishing it around her mouth, willing the nasty taste to go away. Wishing she could remember. Which is bad.

Which means she definitely caused a scene.

She closes her eyes. Another vague memory of her and Jace slow-dancing. All she knows is Jace took care of her. Like he always did.

Like he always will.

Slipping out of bed, Emmy Lou stumbles to the bathroom. She drinks straight from the tap, then rubs furiously at her smeared mascara. Her face is puffy and peaked. Her hair wild and rock star–like, a pale halo swirled around her head. A bedraggled hot mess Mama Belle would gasp at.

Just then there's a knock on the door.

Emmy Lou hurries out of the bathroom to see Jace cautiously entering the room. He's already dressed for the day in blue jeans and a pearl-snap shirt. He peers her way, a cup of coffee in his hands. "Up and at 'em, huh?"

"Barely." Emmy Lou drops onto the edge of the bed, wrinkling her nose. "What time is it?"

"Noon."

She groans. "I slept the day away."

"You needed to." Jace sets the coffee on the nightstand, staring down at her with concerned hazel eyes. "How are you feelin'?" he asks, his face solemn. Her stomach tightens as he presses the back of his hand against her brow.

"I'm okay." She inhales a deep breath and locks her eyes to his. "Tell me, Jace. How bad was I last night?"

He chuckles and sits beside her. "Ain't gonna lie, you were bad. But you were also adorable."

She huffs and crosses her arms, wanting the truth to fill the gaps in her memories. "Tell me real, Jace, I can take it."

His grin widens. "Real, huh? Well, let's see, after you drank a bottle of champagne, you climbed out your bedroom window."

She gasps in indignation. "I did no such thing."

"Sure did. Straight up crawled down the trellis. Then you fell into a hedge." His hazel eyes sparkle with laughter. "You left your heels somewhere between the farm and our house."

Her hands fly to her mouth. "Holy shit."

It's worse than she thought. She ghosted her parents' anniversary party. Mama sure as hell noticed that. She'll never let her live it down. She'll make her grovel for forgiveness until the end of time.

"We came back here and danced. And then, well, sorry to say it, honey, you kissed me." He laughs. "Can't say I'm complainin' about that," he adds, and she feels her cheeks heat.

"Oh, I acted a fool, Jace." Emmy Lou stands and starts pacing. "Mama's gonna kill me."

"Take it easy, alright?" He arches a brow, extending a broad hand. "There ain't nothin' to be embarrassed or worried about."

Worried about.

Right.

She squeezes her eyes shut. How about Slayton in her hometown buying up her family farm? Slayton grabbing her wrist last night like he owned her?

All of a sudden, she feels so damn tired. Tired of running, of pretending, of always letting Mama win even when she's wrong.

The bed squeaks and Jace is standing. There's a worried line on his brow that wasn't there last night. He reaches out to touch her cheek, to take her in his arms. "What's goin' on with you, honey? You're scarin' me, Em."

Her heart blazes at the concern in his husky voice. Still, she doesn't want to talk about it. It's too close. The room suddenly too suffocating. Her heartbeat too loud, thumping maniacally against her breastbone. Squeezing her eyes shut, she takes a step backward, out of Jace's arms. He doesn't follow her. Instead, he lifts his hands. There's understanding on his face. He wants to hold her, but he won't because he knows her.

Too well.

He knows she's freaking out. Knows how she feels without feeling it himself. The cramped room. The space that shrinks and doesn't stop. Only he doesn't know why. He doesn't know why at all.

Her fault, her fault, it's all her fault.

Jace.

Or Slayton?

She has to tell him. Soon. Because Jace told her his secret and that's what this summer is for, isn't it? Healing. Secrets. Especially now that hers is so close. For so long she's kept her secret entombed in bombproof steel, but now it's all over her. Suffocating. Terrifying.

She's scared of Slayton. She is. Because she never dealt with it, because she buried it, because she ran away. Because, last night, she got a glimpse of the boy who cornered her in that horse stall. Cruel. Trying to take what he wanted without asking. Her farm. Her sanity. Her body.

Slayton was never the boy she thought she knew.

But Jace was always the man she could trust.

"Honey?" Jace's soft voice breaks through the hazy darkness of her mind.

When she opens her eyes, Jace is peering at her close, worry etched across his handsome face.

She blinks back tears and swallows hard.

"Let's go for a ride," he says slowly, his voice gentle. He meets her surprised eyes. "You feel up for that?"

Her legs are shaky and she has one hell of a headache, but the thought of a ride, of her horses, of being with Jace in wide-open spaces steadies her. Just like that, just like always, he knows what she needs.

"Yes," she says, loving him.

He leaves her, and Emmy Lou stands there, staring at the shut door.

Regret fills her.

Regret for not making Jace stay, for not telling him thank you, for walking out on him five weeks ago in Nashville.

She has to tell him.

To get back to them, she has to tell him the truth about her past.

She won't run. Not anymore.

Jace slows his horse to a walk as he and Emmy Lou turn on the old dirt path that leads up into the meadow on top of the ridge-line. The air's humid and smells of pine and sun. Bald cypress and tall Belle of Georgia peach trees line the narrow curve of woods. A chipmunk skitters across the path.

Beside him, Emmy Lou sits silent on Gentleman, the reins held loose in her left hand. Though Jace is focused on the ride, he's also paying attention to his wife. She's lost in her own little world, a troubled expression on her pretty face. She's barely said a handful of words to him since they started out on the ride an hour ago. Which kicks up a storm of worry within him.

Damn it, he wants to help her. But he also knows he won't get answers if she doesn't want to give them.

The one thing he can do is fix this farm situation for Emmy Lou. After last night he got to thinking, and this morning he called Luke. He has a plan he doesn't know if she'll be receptive to, but he'll put it out there. His wife comes first and she has to know that.

Emmy Lou's soft drawl floats. "Where are we goin', Jace?"

Jace points at a clearing high on the ridge. "There. That meadow."

She looks at him, a glimmer of mischief in her eyes. "Race you," she says and slaps her reins. Her hair, golden in the bright sun, dances around her as she takes off.

Jace lets out a hoot and brings his horse into a gallop. They rush down the hill, their horses neck and neck when they come to a stop in the center of the meadow.

Emmy Lou laughs, halting her horse and sliding off him in one graceful move. "Beat you," she says.

Jace dismounts. "Ain't so sure about that. Think someone got a head start."

She shrugs and pats Gentleman on his rump. As Emmy Lou takes care of the horses, wrapping their reins around a branch to keep them from straying, Jace spreads out a blanket on the ground beneath a peach tree. Earlier today, he haphazardly tossed together a picnic while Emmy Lou got ready. Bottled water, a few cans of beer, cookies, pickles, ham and cheese sandwiches on rustic seeded bread. For a long second, he pauses to watch as Emmy Lou stands on tiptoes to pick fresh peaches, the silk of her dress hugging her curves.

Emmy Lou's eyes widen when she walks back to him. She looks down at the ground, at the spread of food, and then her gaze moves to his. "Jace, you did this?"

He clears his throat. Her shock socks him in the gut, a reminder of how long it's been since he's done something like this. "Yeah."

She gives him a kiss. "Thank you."

They sit, settling on top of the blanket. Stalks of gold rustle around them in the light breeze, the tree giving them just enough shade to keep cool. Slowly, almost tentatively, they dig into the food.

"I don't remember the last time we did this," Emmy Lou says, opening a sandwich wrapped in cellophane. "Maybe the stables back in the day."

Jace looks her way, his brows lifting. "Those were some days."

"Mmm," she agrees. "The best days."

"Sharin' a beer and a sandwich, ain't nothin' like it."

"No," she says softly. "There isn't."

They devour the food, cracking beers, tearing off hunks of crusty bread. Emmy Lou unearths the peaches she's picked from the trees. Trails of juice run down the inside of her wrist as she bites into one.

Jace shifts on the old blanket, pushing up on his knees to move closer to his wife. "There," he says, pointing. "What I wanted to show you."

She follows the line of his finger, then presses a hand to her heart. "Oh, Jace."

He smiles.

In the light of the late-afternoon sun, the earth's lit up. They can see everything. The Montgomery Mansion, the emerald green of the farm, the yellow of the fields, the glitter of the pond by their house, the severed trunk of the old oak tree they were married under. Beautiful and broken, but somehow still standing.

That's when Emmy Lou gasps. "This is the place," she breathes. She stares as if in a daze. "The spot where my horse threw me and I got lost." She turns to him, her brown eyes wide. "How'd you find this spot? I never thought I'd see it again." Her voice is amazed. "It's beautiful."

"It is," Jace says, still staring at Emmy Lou. The thin dress she's in, pink with wildflowers, and her barely-there makeup have her looking otherworldly. She wants to talk about beautiful, he's got all damn day.

With a sigh, she sinks back into a seated position, her pretty face pained. "I can't believe Daddy's sellin' the farm." A shaky sigh. "I lived here all my life. We got married here."

"I know." He scoots close and she curls up beside him. "Em, listen. Boone doesn't have to sell it to Slayton."

"What're you talkin' about?"

"What if we bought the farm?"

Her jaw drops. But before she can say anything, he goes on. "I won't have a part of it. It'll be yours and yours alone."

Tears fill her eyes. "What about the Brothers Kincaid? Livin' by the boys—that's your band, Jace."

He takes a breath. He's a planner. He's thought things through so he can give Emmy Lou what she needs. "I already talked to Luke. And I wouldn't be leavin' the band. Wildheart's only three hours away. It'd be long distance. We could keep the Nashville house. Split our time together between places. Hire who we need to take care of the farm here when we're back in Nashville."

She stares at him, yearning and doubt warring in her eyes. "You make it sound so simple."

"It is simple, honey."

"What about . . ." She shakes her head, her blond curls bobbing. "The money?"

"We got the money, Em. I've been savin' it in the account you hate, and damn, I'm sorry about that, but now we can use it." He takes her hand and gives it a squeeze. "Vegas is comin' up. We make more than enough."

For so long he's been doing his thing. He wants Emmy Lou to have hers. He'd give it all up and then some, but he doesn't have to give it up. He can compromise. He can give his wife what she needs. He can have his band, his friends and family, and make his marriage work.

"I don't know." Her voice is wistful. "It all sounds so wonderful, it really does. I just . . . you'd have to talk to Daddy. Who knows if Slayton signed somethin' yet?"

He doesn't miss her wince when she says the name Slayton.

"I will. And he didn't."

"How do you know?"

"I don't," Jace says, meeting her stare. "But I'm bettin' on it."

Literally. He'll bet the farm.

"Do you want it, Em?"

"I do. Oh, but Jace . . . will we be okay if we do it?"

"We will. Except we won't have any money for retirement."

Her lips thin. "Jace Taylor."

"I'm kiddin'," he says, sobering. He crooks a finger beneath her chin, tilting her face up to meet his eyes. "We are fine, Em. I promise. I'll never let you down again, honey. I swear it."

A breathy sigh, the slow flutter of her eyelids as she considers his words. "I believe you, Jace. I do. It's just . . . all so complicated."

"Is it Slayton? Is that why it's complicated?"

Emmy Lou goes white, her big brown eyes dark orbs in her pale face. The raw fear in her expression hits him hard.

"Your brothers told me he was your boyfriend," Jace says

gently. He dips his head, his gaze on hers, his heart breaking at what he sees.

Emmy Lou—his bright, bubbly Emmy Lou—she's like a piece of a star that's fallen. Like the light's gone out.

Eyes dull, she looks away. "It ended bad. I broke it off." Her voice is flat. She draws her hands into her lap, picking at the silk hem of her dress.

"If you don't wanna talk about it, you ain't got to," he says, watching her flinch. "All I know is that somethin' was hurtin' you last night, Em. Burnin' you up inside. I'm here, honey. You can tell me."

Trust me.

He can't tell if he's doing the right thing. Hunting around for answers. He always let Emmy Lou hold whatever secrets she had in her past, but he won't do it anymore, especially not after last night.

Especially since he knows firsthand what keeping it in does. This summer—telling Emmy Lou about his mother, about Luke— was like a weight lifted. He wants that weight gone for his wife. He wants her to know he's here, he'll take it with her. Because if not, whatever is haunting her will eat herself up on the inside.

She starts to nod, slowly, battling tears. Wanting to tell him, but her body is rigid, her secrets locked.

Jace stares at her, neither of them speaking. His heart feels like it's on its last beat.

Christ, don't let him be right. Don't let it be what he thinks, make it something else. Anything else.

For a long second, Emmy Lou closes her eyes, and when she reopens them, he sees fear. But he also sees a determined strength, a helpless resignation. "You're right," she says. "You need to know."

Then, physically, literally, Jace sees her defenses drop. Like an unlocking, her shoulders slump, her hands fall open in her lap, her eyes turn glossy with tears as she finally lets him in.

"Slayton—he and I were together throughout high school. All four years. Prom king and queen. Our parents were best friends. We were practically brought up with rings on our fingers." She looks at Jace almost guiltily. "I loved him so much. But I wanted to wait until we were married. And Slayton agreed. At least I thought he did." She chuckles bitterly. "Grand illusions, right? Silly Emmy Lou."

"That's your mama talkin'," Jace cuts in softly. "That ain't you."

"I guess so," she says in a helpless, hollow voice.

Jace sits, watching Emmy Lou gather her emotions, her eyes downcast. He can tell she's revving up for something big, something he's dreading, something he needs to know.

"The night of the rodeo, I was crowned queen. Slayton and I, we were on a cloud nine high. Packin' up, laughin', kissin'. But then . . . it started goin' too fast. I told him no. I told him to stop. And then he . . . he—" A broken look crosses her face.

Jace's stomach flips over.

Fuck. Please, God, no.

She lifts her fingertips to her mouth and whispers, "He tried to rape me."

The way she says it—in wonder, in horror—tells Jace it's the first time she's said the words aloud.

Rage. A rage so insane the world ceases to exist washes over Jace. His fingers dig into the knees of his jeans. He wants to punch something, to kill someone, to track Slayton down like a hound and rip the bastard's throat out, but he shoves his feelings aside. He forces himself to stay silent. None of what he's feeling matters. Not when Emmy Lou's in pain, reliving a memory that's haunted her for years.

Emmy Lou stares off into the distance, her voice soft, her expression tense. "He cornered me in the horse trailer. I couldn't breathe in there." Tears shimmer in her eyes. "I couldn't move. The space, it was so small and he was so big. I just froze. I could feel everything. The horses outside, his breath in my ear, his hands on my body. It was like slow motion, like being underwater. You can't say no. You're mine. He just kept sayin' it."

Her voice breaks and she swipes at her eyes.

"Gentleman—he saved me. I heard his whinny and he called me back before he . . ." She shakes her head. "I went wild like

Outlaw. I bucked and I got him off me and I grabbed the reins and lashed him across the face. That scar, I gave him that."

Jace aches to have reins in his hands. To whip Slayton until the man's halfway dead, and then bring him back and do it all over again. But it'd still be too kind.

"Grady tried to kill him," Emmy Lou chokes out. "He went crazy when he found out and tracked Slayton down at his house. He broke Slayton's nose. He got himself in trouble with the cops, with Daddy. I never should have told him."

Good, Jace thinks. He wants to give that kid a goddamn high five for beating the fuck out of Slayton.

She's talking fast, her voice a rolling ramble of nerves and tears, but Jace stays silent, letting her talk. Letting her have space. She stares off into the distance as if she's watching the past come alive in front of her.

"Grady's the only one who knows. Not my parents. Not my other brothers. I couldn't tell them. I was too ashamed. I mean, Lord, Jace, he was my boyfriend. What if no one believed me? What if no one cared? The only thing I could think to do was leave Wildheart." Her eyes dart to his, almost as if she's waiting for him to recoil from her, then drop to the blanket. "I didn't tell you either. I wanted to start fresh with you. I didn't want you to know. Or think I was messed up. Or broken."

Jace closes his eyes. "Em—"

"I loved him," she blurts. She breaks off, wipes her eyes as a shaky shudder rocks her small frame. "I never imagined he would do that to me. I trusted him."

"And that ain't your fault," Jace says, tenderly reaching out to cup her face. "He's the one who broke your trust. You did nothin' wrong. You never did anything wrong."

She nods, numbly, a single tear slipping over the apple of her cheek. Jace whisks it away with his thumb.

"Sometimes it doesn't feel like it, though."

Jace frowns. "What do you mean?"

Her face crumples. "I ran away. I always thought over the

years I should have said something. What if he did it to someone else in Chicago? To his wife. To some other girl. And I never said anything. I let him get away with it."

The pain, the guilt in her voice breaks Jace. Her pain palpable. Her pain his.

Emmy Lou hugs herself with her arms, bricking herself up. Jace eases himself close, as close as she'll let him get, and takes her hand in his. She whimpers at his touch and then leans into him.

"Listen to me," he says fiercely, gripping her closer, pulling her small frame into his body like he can shield her. "You didn't do this. He did. He hurt you. Do you hear me? He hurt *you*."

Something cracks inside of her. Jace hears it. It sounds like the snap of something welded tightly together splitting at the seams.

A violent gasp wrenches out of Emmy Lou and then she bursts into tears.

Jace gathers her in his arms, sweeping his lips across her golden crown as she buries her face into his chest and weeps. He lets her cry, rubbing her wracking shoulders as his spinning mind pieces everything together.

He understands secrets, but this. Christ. How Emmy Lou's kept something this heavy bottled up for so long, he doesn't know. Never grieving or working out her anger and pain. Instead, she came to Nashville battling a storm inside of her, while only portraying smiles and sunshine.

Strong. So goddamn strong is his Emmy Lou.

Everything makes so much sense now. Her fear of enclosed spaces. Her almost fervent love for horses. Her fierce demand of honesty and trust. Because she loved a man who betrayed her in the worst way, who shattered her trust completely. It's why she's tough, why she's strong, why she survived. Why Jace's lie mattered so damn much to her.

He understands something else too.

Rage. Real, honest-to-God rage.

You can't teach the kind of anger Jace is feeling.

A rage his best friend would be familiar with. He never fathomed how Luke dealt with Sal, with the man who had hurt her, but now he knows. Violence. It ain't the answer, but he wants it to be. Goddamn does he want it to be.

He can't imagine what kind of a traumatic shock that was for his wife last night, seeing her attacker out of the blue after thirteen years. He fucking hates himself that he didn't know. That he wasn't there.

"I'm sorry I never told you." Emmy Lou's voice comes muffled against his shirt. "I'm an awful person for keepin' it from you. I'm awful for leavin' Nashville and walkin' out on you the way I did. I'm a yellowbelly coward of a woman."

"Don't," he says, rubbing her back in slow circles. "You ain't any of those things."

"I am."

"No, you ain't."

Sniffling, she raises her face, her small hands curving around his shoulders like she needs the grip to stay upright. She stares at him, her face a mixture of relief and weariness.

Jace reaches out to cup her cheek. "You're beautiful. Strong as hell. And I'm so damn sorry that happened to you, Emmy Lou. I'd give anything to change it if I could."

Her smile is wobbly. "I know you would."

"No more apologies, you hear?" Jace says, tucking her into his arm. "You're gonna be okay. We're gonna be okay. We'll get the farm."

And send Slayton on his merry fucking way.

"What if Slayton comes to the house again?" she asks in a low voice.

Jace stiffens, his blood turning to ice. "Again?" When she hesitates, he gives her a look. "Emmy Lou."

A brief flash of fear crosses her face. "He's been in town the entire summer. It was him at the arena. He let the horses out the night of the storm. He's been watchin' me."

Jace swears through his teeth. "*Motherfucker.*"

All this time he'd thought it was McCade. Paranoid that his

past was planning to come back and bite him in the ass, but all along it was Emmy Lou's. It was Slayton. Sniffing around his wife.

"Last night he said I owed him." Her voice trembles. "He's trying to mess with me. To punish me for leaving him."

If Jace thought he couldn't have any more rage left inside him, he was wrong. "Whoa. Hold up. He said something to you?"

She bites her lip.

Anger boils in him. Rage curls his hands to fists, trying to keep it together even as he consciously tells his jaw to unclench. Why wasn't he there? Why wasn't he paying attention to what was going on right in front of his fucking face? Emmy Lou damn near got pushed to the edge last night and he wasn't there to protect her.

Just like fucking always.

Reading his expression, Emmy Lou tightens her grip. Like Jace is planning to take off and murder Slayton. "Jace, you didn't know."

Jace barely hears her reassurance. Vengeance pounds through his veins. He wants to burn the world down and Slayton with it. That unhinged piece of shit has some goddamn nerve being in the same room as Emmy Lou.

But he can feel Emmy Lou. Holding him so tight, she shakes against him, and that brings him back down to earth. Jace's gut knots. Emmy Lou reassuring him isn't what she needs to be doing right now. It's his job to reassure her. To protect her.

Keeping it together, he looks his wife in the eyes. "He won't touch you," he says, pulling her even closer into his body. She clings to him, burrowing her face into his chest. Jace presses his mouth to the top of her golden head. "I have you, Emmy Lou, you hear me? I have you."

A promise of protection.

Because God help Slayton if he comes near his wife again.

chapter
TWENTY-FOUR

THE NEXT MORNING, EMMY LOU STARES OUT THE window, watching Jace's pickup drive up the hill to the Montgomery Mansion. She fights the urge to grab on to a dust trail and rope Jace back to her. Her nerves are in knots. Jace plans to ask her daddy about buying the farm. She hopes it's enough to get the farm and chase that scumbag Slayton out of town.

She closes her eyes. Emotions wash over her. She feels stripped bare but in the best way.

Relief, such grateful relief for Jace. She was stunned by his offer to buy the farm. Potentially giving up the Brothers Kincaid for her. If they get the farm, it won't be easy—she knows Jace has a job, and they have Nashville but . . . if they can work it out somehow and keep Montgomery Farm and Stables in the family, it would mean everything.

And then there was telling Jace about Slayton.

The way he listened to her, held her and reassured her. No pity or judgment in his eyes, just understanding. Talking to Jace—it made her feel like she wasn't alone. Like someone else knows her story now, understands it, and she doesn't have to hide.

Not only did she connect with Jace, but it feels like she shed something. Not the past, because what Slayton did will never leave her, but she shed the guilt, the shame, the secrets and stepped into a new future, one where she can cope, where she can really feel what she experienced and learn to live with it. Not just run.

Not anymore.

Not ever again.

At the sight of a long black Mercedes pulling into the drive-way, she swears under her breath and rushes to the kitchen. There, she steadies her shaky hands to arrange a tray of pastries.

She's faced Jace.

She's faced Slayton.

Now she needs to face Mama Belle and apologize for her atrocious behavior at the anniversary party. She may have been knocked for a loop, but that doesn't excuse a lack of proper southern etiquette.

Without a knock, Mama Belle enters the house. The sharp stride of boots on the tile and then she's in the kitchen, placing a pair of heels on the counter. "These were in my begonia bush, Emmaline."

Emmy Lou flushes, but she looks her mother in the eye and says, "I'm sorry, Mama. I don't know what came over me."

A minute of quiet.

Mama Belle's mouth purses as if she's considering accepting Emmy Lou's apology, then she nods, satisfied. "Well, let's let the past lie. I'm sure you were put off by your father's announcement." A raise of a thin mischievous brow. "Not to mention the arrival of Slayton."

A curdle of disgust rolls through Emmy Lou. She stacks a cheese Danish next to a cinnamon roll. "I'm not talkin' about Slayton, Mama."

"You're right. It's time to talk about what comes next, darlin'. After the rodeo, I was thinkin' you need to join the country club. Somethin' sociable. A community to lean on. If you need money, Daddy and I will open up your trust. Not a word to your brothers. Those lazy boys need to work for a livin.'"

Mama Belle sidles across the kitchen, plucking a grape and popping it into her mouth. A sly smile spreads across her face. "And of course, eventually, there'll be the matter of Slayton."

Emmy Lou's neck goes hot. She shakes her head, trying to fend off the frustration hitting her like a gale force wind. "Mama, you ain't listenin' to me. Slayton and I, we ain't anything. I'm goin' back to Nashville at the end of the summer. With Jace." She inhales sharply. "Jace and I are gonna buy the farm, Mama."

It's like a bomb's gone off.

Mama Belle stares.

Then she slams her bag on the countertop. With vitriol, Mama Belle yanks out the divorce papers. Emmy Lou flinches. Flinches at her signature in bright blue ink scrawled across the bottom line. It seems like a thousand lifetimes ago that she signed it, like some other Emmy Lou had possessed her body, ready to wreak havoc with her signature, wreak havoc on Jace's heart.

"You signed these, Emmaline." Mama Belle slides the papers across the glossy marble countertop. "Beginnin' of summer. Now I've bided my time while you make up your mind, but now, dar-lin' it's time to shit or get off the pot."

Emmy Lou blinks, so startled by Mama Belle's off-color curse, she can't do anything other than gape at her. When she regains her bearings, lets her hands drop to her side and says, "I still love Jace, Mama."

Mama jerks back like she's taken a shot of fire water. "Does he know that?"

She tilts her chin up. "No. But he will."

"He'll lie again. You can't trust that man."

"I can. And I do. I ain't holdin' Jace to the sword. Not anymore."

Mama Belle crosses her arms, her face ruddy with anger. "I'll never understand you, Emmy Lou. Running from this to that. It's only a matter of time before you'll be back here. Askin' for help." She rolls her eyes to the ceiling. "Lord, I pray your daddy has the good sense not to sell that man our farm. You were ready to leave him and now you're ready to buy a farm together?"

Emmy Lou stares at Mama Belle, a pit of doom forming in her stomach.

Still, she tries. Tries to open herself up and make herself

vulnerable. "Mama, I was wrong to leave Jace. This summer, it's been so perfect. It's been—"

"Of course he's been perfect," Mama Belle needles. "He's tryin' to win you over with his good graces. And then what happens when the summer's over and he gets you back in Nashville? He's got his music and you? Nothin'." Belle tuts. "I swear, Emmy Lou, next time you're in trouble don't come cryin' to me."

Emmy Lou's eyes swim with tears, angry at never being heard, angry that one negative word from Mama Belle has her conjuring up every awful doubt in the marriage playbook.

But her doubts are just doubts. Because deep down, she knows her marriage has changed.

She's felt it.

This summer she fell in love with Jace all over again.

In the truest way possible.

They went back to themselves and the love that made them. Just like their tree, they were broken, but their roots remain. She's seen the green sprouts growing in the muddy earth. Something new and beautiful blooming from pain and destruction.

She knows how much Jace loves her. Seen how hard he's worked these last five weeks. Yes, this summer at the farm won't fix everything, but it doesn't need to. They're planning for the future. Therapy. Vegas. They're going to work on themselves and their marriage.

And nothing, especially Mama Belle, can stop them.

A flare of anger.

A righting of her strength. Her heart.

Emmy Lou draws herself up and places a steady palm on top of the divorce papers. "I'm not givin' these to Jace and I never will." Her voice rises in the quiet house. Mama Belle's face sours. "Take 'em back with you. Burn 'em for all I care. And you need to start treatin' Jace better. He ain't out of this family and if that's what you're fightin' so damn hard for, then you can just show yourself out."

She gives her mother one last look and then turns to face the window.

"Fine, darlin." Mama Belle's voice is brusque at her back. "I won't say another word about it."

Emmy Lou listens. The soft shuffle of boot strides across the old hardwood floor, the slam of the front door.

When she turns around, the divorce papers, and Mama Belle, are gone.

Jace sits in the hallway outside of Boone's office. He should be pacing right now; instead he's writing love songs. One hell of a way to work out his nerves. He's finally finishing up his first song for Emmy Lou. She'll probably laugh him out of Wildheart, but he wants to give it to her. She needs a song. Needs to know what she means to him. What this summer has meant.

These last few weeks have been a kick in the balls, but they've forced Jace to take a hard look at himself as a man, at his marriage, and it's all been worth it.

He glances down, his eyes sweeping across the notepad.

> Ain't gonna let you run, ain't gonna let you go
> Honey, I'm comin' to bring you home
> Because I've loved you down in Georgia, and up in Tennessee
> And all I can do I'll do it to bring you back to me . . .

"Sir?"

Jace blinks, breaking from his song. Standing in front of him is Eve, the Montgomerys' housekeeper. "Mr. Montgomery will see you now."

Exhaling a steadying breath, Jace shoves up from his chair and tucks the tattered notepad in his back pocket.

Here goes nothing.

He's going to do it. Buy Emmy Lou her farm.

Fuck, but it does scare him.

He's a planner and he's planned nothing besides withdrawing the funds. He's talked to Luke, got the blessing of his best friend, the frontman of his band, but he doesn't have much more beyond that. Doesn't know how they'll live, split their time, but this is one gamble he's got to take.

If he can do one good thing with the money he hid from Emmy Lou, this is it.

This is everything.

He enters Boone's office, freezing when he sees Charlie, Wyatt and Grady sitting solemn-faced on the long leather couch beneath the window. Jace wonders what he just walked into—an interrogation or an execution.

Boone, behind his desk, documents and coffee mugs spread out in front of him, extends a hand.

"Jace," he booms, his sun-weathered face crinkling into a broad smile as he rises to shake Jace's hand. "Have a seat, son." As Jace settles across from him in a chair, Boone says, "I hope you don't mind I asked the boys to sit in on all this farm business."

A crackle from the phone. "Yo. We're here too."

Charlie snorts.

"Not at all," Jace says. He leans into the speaker. "Hey, Ford. Davis. How goes the ranch?"

"Oh, it's goin'," comes Ford's jovial drawl. "Same shit, different day."

Boone chuckles. Then he turns his gaze to Jace. "So what can I do you for? Somethin' about the farm?"

"It is about the farm. Emmy and I want to make an offer on it."

Boone's bushy brows lift. "What about your farm back in Nashville?"

"We plan to keep it. I haven't got that far yet, but we'd—"

"Pivot," Grady speaks up. "Ain't that right, Jace?"

Jace gives him a grin. "Damn right, Grady."

"We're plannin' to divide our time. We'd make it work. Get help here or there. This farm is Emmy Lou's home. She loves it. To see you sell it to—" Jace's heart twists as he meets Grady's eyes. He amends his words. "To someone else, someone not in the family, would kill her."

"I've always liked you, Jace. You're a good man for my daughter."

Jace decides to be blunt. "You don't want to sell to Slayton, sir." In his periphery, he sees Wyatt and Charlie exchange a pointed look.

Boone's curious eyes stare back at him. "Care to tell me why?"

"I would, but it ain't my place. Just trust me when I say that."

"I see." Boone steeples his fingers together, considering this information. "Well, the good news is we haven't signed anything yet. But I hate to disappoint longtime friends."

"But friends ain't family," Davis interjects, his deep voice crackled with static. "And Jace is."

Wyatt nods. "Handshake deals don't mean shit."

Charlie grunts. "Says you."

Boone's face turns serious. His solemn eyes pin Jace down. "I'm gonna treat this like you're askin' for my daughter's hand all over again. Only right now, my daughter ain't wearin' her weddin' band. What're your intentions with her? With my farm if worse comes to worse?"

The words tear him up inside, but Jace hears the message clear. His heart twists thinking about divorce. Emmy Lou promised him she'd hold off until the end of the summer. And he hopes like hell these last six weeks have been enough to prove to her that he's ready to do the work and fight for their marriage.

Jace nods. "Whatever happens between us, it's hers. The farm. I'll pay for it, sign all the papers you want, support her no matter what." He meets Boone's eyes and exhales. Bares his naked truth. "I want my wife to have everything, even if it's not me."

A glimmer of a smile appears on the old man's face. "You love her?"

"Rest of my life, I'll love your daughter, sir."

Boone inclines his head toward his sons. "Boys, what do you think?"

A crackle from Davis on the speakerphone. "Do it, Daddy."

"Emmy Lou deserves it," Ford says, adding a hoot to emphasize his point.

Charlie, his arms crossed, narrows his eyes at Jace. "As long as it's Emmy Lou's, I have no problem with it."

"Keepin' it in the family is the way to go," Wyatt agrees.

"Give it to Emmy Lou, Daddy," Grady says. "Not Slayton. He don't belong in Wildheart."

Jace's chest squeezes tight. Damn near choked up by the show of support. He's still got his family. On his side and backing him.

Boone nods. And then he stands. "Son, you got yourself a deal."

Jace stands to meet him and the two of them shake hands.

"We'll draw up the papers and get 'em signed today." Boone exhales. "I imagine Slayton won't be too happy."

"If it's a problem, I'll explain to Slayton." Jace itches for the chance to put a fist through that son of a bitch's face.

As if seeing Jace's rage, Boone frowns. "No, son. That's my job."

Grady stands. "I'll walk you out."

Outside in the hall, Grady chucks Jace on the shoulder. "Holy fuckin' shit," he drawls. "You're really gonna go for it."

Jace grins, feeling like some dopey lovesick fool. "It's my wife, man."

"Yeah." Wyatt grins back. Then he lowers his voice. "You know about Slayton?"

The smile drops off Jace's face. "Yeah. Emmy Lou told me."

"Good." Grady's throat works, his face stone. "You know he's been here all summer?"

Jace nods. "Emmy Lou put it together pretty damn quick."

"At least this'll get him gone."

"That's all I want. Get him away from Emmy Lou."

A hard breath shakes out of Grady. Like he's been carrying it around with him for the last thirteen years and is only now letting it lose.

Jace posts a hand on the wall. "We still playin' the tavern tomorrow?"

Grady's eyes lighten. "Hell yeah. Nine o'clock." He laughs. "Don't be late. You need the practice."

Jace lifts a middle finger.

Jace slows his truck as it snakes down the narrow dirt road to the house. Coming from the opposite direction is a black Mercedes-Benz. Jace stops. The Benz pulls up alongside him.

Not even the sight of Mama Belle is enough to chase the smile away from Jace's face.

"Ma'am," Jace drawls.

Mama Belle holds him in her narrowed gaze. "Let me guess, Boone sold you the farm."

A nod. "He did."

"I suppose you're goin' home to gloat."

"I suppose I am."

"Let me tell you something, Jace. Once Emmy Lou gets what she needs from you, she'll run. Emmy Lou's always been finicky."

"That ain't my wife," Jace says evenly. "And that ain't your daughter."

"I reckon you know her better than me."

"I love your daughter, ma'am, and I'll do whatever it takes to make things right between us."

Mama Belle turns her stare to the sunset. "I sure hope she knows that."

"She does."

Then Jace shifts the truck into gear and makes his way back to the house. He's done talking to Mama Belle. Nothing she can say is enough to have him doubting Emmy Lou. Nothing can kill this mood he's in. What he's got at home.

Home.

When he pulls into the gravel drive, his heart skips. The most perfect sight in the goddamn world.

Waiting on the front porch, sitting in the rocking chair, a glass of tea in her hand, bare feet dangling in the breeze, is Emmy Lou. Waiting on word. Waiting on him.

His farm.

His wife.

His entire world.

He wants this every damn day for the rest of his life.

Seeing him, Emmy Lou steps off the porch and they come together. He takes her face in his hands, his fingers tangling in her wavy strands as he stares her in the eyes.

"Well?" she asks.

"We got the farm," he tells her. "Honey, we got it."

A sharp squeal and then Emmy Lou is leaping into his arms, legs looped around his thighs, arms around his neck. Sweet warm kisses pepper his face, the feel of Emmy Lou in his arms like an anchor. He spins her around and around. "You got champagne in the house?" he asks.

"Yes," she says breathlessly. "Why?"

"So we can celebrate." He grins. "Naked."

"Naked." She gives him an eager kiss, sweeping her tongue over his. "We celebrate naked."

TWENTY-FIVE

"**Y**OU STILL REMEMBER HOW TO PLAY A GUITAR?" Grady asks from the back stock room of Tiny's Tavern.

Jace grits his teeth and ignores the kid as he tunes the Gibson. His big upright bass is leaned precariously against the wall and a sack of potatoes. He plans to play the guitar with Grady for the first set, then his bass for the last few songs. While he's skilled in a variety of strings, the bass is his true love. It's always been his compass rose onstage, content in the background, plucking out baritones as deep as Seth's voice.

Everything in the cramped, smoky tavern smells like grease and alcohol, but it's about damn near perfect.

What would be perfect is playing with his band. He misses the Brothers Kincaid. He's ready to get back to his boys, their music, their tours. Most importantly, he's ready to do it all with Emmy Lou.

"I really appreciate you doin' this," Grady says.

Jace side-eyes him. Tonight is the kid's way of saying goodbye to Wildheart, showing his town and his family what he can do before he takes off for Nashville. It's a brave way to go out.

"Yeah, well, when you get to Nashville, you listen to Luke and focus on the music." The best advice he can give the kid. He's seen so many musicians give into the limelight, fuck up and then sink as low as they can go. The poster child for that is Beau Dallas. He nearly killed Lacey last Christmas after knocking her into a lake. Seth's never forgiven the guy and all but got him exiled from Nashville after that.

Grady's got a good head on his shoulders, but Emmy Lou will knock it off if her little brother screws it up or gets in trouble.

"Oh, hell, I'm gonna," Grady drawls. "Never gonna get another chance like this again."

At a bright boom of a laugh, Jace peers out the door of the stock room. Emmy Lou's entire family is taking their seats at a long high-top. Boone, Charlie, Wyatt, and Mama Belle. But, as his eyes scan the room, Jace only needs to see one person: Emmy Lou.

"I wrote her a song, you know."

"Who?" Grady sticks his head out the door, following Jace's gaze. "Mama Belle?"

Jace chuckles. "Emmy Lou."

"You gonna play it tonight?"

"Fuck no." He's starting to sweat. "Not now. I'm gonna ask Luke about playin' it at the rodeo."

"Whooo, man." Grady whistles, his eyes laughing. "Nothin says true love like a public display of embarrassin' your own damn self."

"Who's embarassin' who?"

Jace turns when he hears the bubbly voice. Emmy Lou, looking like a goddamn queen, is sneaking through the back door. She grins up at him, her face bright. She looks beautiful, and Jace's stomach tumbles. In tight jeans, a pair of boots and a plaid print short sleeve western snap shirt, Emmy Lou looks just as gorgeous in ranch clothes as she does dolled up in a ball gown.

"Your brother," Jace says quickly, moving to intercept her.

"Ah, the hotshot is gracin' us with his presence before he takes off and leaves us for Nashville," Emmy Lou teases, looping her arms around Jace's neck.

Grady wiggles his brows. "Get used to it seein' as how we're gonna be neighbors in Nashville."

Jace watches Emmy Lou, waits for a word about them going back home together, but her eyes drop, moving to the door.

Jace swallows past the dryness in his throat. Shakes off his nerves. His doubt. He tells himself it's the stage. He ain't played in nearly three damn months. It's not Mama Belle's voice in his head. *Once Emmy Lou gets what she needs from you, she'll run.* It's not Emmy Lou, or her keeping mum on the subject of going back to Nashville. Of three little words he hasn't heard yet.

"It's nice," Jace says, taking Emmy in his arms. He drops a kiss to her lips. "Havin' you here for a show."

"It is." She opens her mouth, a pink flush misting her cheeks. "Jace, I—"

"C'mon." Grady claps him on the shoulder as he passes. "Kiss your wife, get your shit, and let's go."

Jace barks a laugh. But he does just that. He takes one last kiss from Emmy Lou, grabs his Gibson and exits the stock room.

As he climbs onstage, everything falls away. His hand comes up to shield his eyes from the glare of the stage lights and his heart drops into his boots.

His wife, her eyes glued on him, staring at him from the front row is the best damn sight he's ever seen.

Emmy Lou clutches her heart as she stares up at Jace. He's got a happy half-smile on his face as he saws his bass. His husky voice melds with Grady's sharp, reedy drawl. He wears that calm demeanor that Emmy Lou loves. So damn sexy. Strong. While Luke and Seth whoop and holler around onstage, Jace listens and plays passionately.

That's Jace.

The big bass beat of her heart.

Emmy Lou stifles a yawn. After today's grueling practice with Wyatt, she's beat, but there's no place she'd rather be than in this tavern, listening to her husband's husky croon. Tomorrow, she has a list of to-dos in front of her. Not to mention a surprise for Jace. She smiles, a content, giddy feeling overtaking her.

This summer has been better than a fairy tale, better than anything she could have dreamed up.

She had been close tonight. So close to telling Jace she loved him, but it wasn't the time or place. Not with Grady lurking in the wings.

Soon.

She'll tell him soon.

A voice rumbles in her ear. "Look at you standin' up here like a horny groupie."

Emmy Lou scoffs and slaps Wyatt in the stomach. "Hush. I'm tryin' to listen to Jace."

"They're kinda good." Wyatt nudges her. "Don't tell Grady that or he'll get a big head." Affection stains his voice as he watches their little brother sing into the mic.

"How do ya feel?" Wyatt asks, leaning in close. "You ready to roll next week?"

She is.

Earlier today, she and Jace were called to the Montgomery arena. Their last run-through before the kick-off event on Friday. She did her daughterly duty—her speech and her wave—conveniently leaving out the part where she barrel races. She's saving that up for her grand finale. One last love letter to Wildheart, and one hell of a shocker for Mama Belle.

Not like Mama Belle showed up. After their big blowup at the house, she conveniently stayed home.

Home.

Which is where she should be right now. At home with her husband, in bed, naked, Jace's lips on hers.

Charlie edges in on her other side. "Mama and Daddy just left."

Emmy Lou sighs, an instant tension settling into her muscles. It figures. Mama Belle's stuck around to support Grady, but the minute Jace takes the spotlight she's sneaking away like a possum in the night.

"That woman will never learn," Emmy Lou huffs. "Now y'all hush and let me listen to my husband."

Soon, the night ticks away to neon and song. Jace and Grady end their set, the room erupting into applause.

Bodies shift behind her, pushing to the front of the stage. Townspeople who have come to gawk and snap their photos of the big shot country superstar and bid Grady farewell.

Emmy Lou squeezes her eyes shut as that old familiar feeling overtakes her.

The crowd's too thick.

The room shrinking.

Thankfully, there's a clear path to the back door. She makes her way through the crowd, easing it open to slip outside. She doesn't want Jace to worry. Wants him to enjoy the spotlight for once in his life.

Outside, Emmy Lou inhales deep, letting the fresh country air clear the tightness from her lungs. The full moon lights up the space in front of her. The stars wink above. The tavern sits in the center of town on Main Street. In the distance, set against the inky midnight of the sky, she can see Montgomery Farm and Stables high up on the hill.

Just the sight is enough to calm her pounding heart.

Hers.

Hers and Jace's.

She touches fingertips to her lips and smiles.

And then, from behind, there's the soft crunch of gravel. A voice, rough and ragged, saying, "Hello, Emmy Lou."

TWENTY-SIX

E MMY LOU GASPS AND WHEELS AROUND.
Every breath in her body leaves her. Her scream falls silent in her throat.

It's Slayton. Coming around the side of the tavern, a cigarette dangling from the corner of his sneering mouth. Waiting for her, God knows how long.

The malicious look on his face makes her blood run cold.

He's here to confront her about the farm. She knows it. Slayton never took no for an answer.

He would try. He would always try something.

Drawing herself up, she levels a cool stare his way. It takes all she has not to shrink into herself. "What're you doin' here, Slayton? I told you at Mama's party, I don't want to see you."

"Well, your actions seem to say otherwise." He chuckles, a greasy sound that curls her spine. "Taking my farm right out from under my nose, that's some devious shit, Emmy Lou."

Power. It was always about power with Slayton. Telling her to quit the rodeo, sending her those terrible letters when she ran to Nashville, and now trying to buy up her farm like he can buy her.

"That's *my* farm," she fires back, strength overriding fear, "and it'll be a cold day in hell before you get your hands on it."

His nostrils flare. "I don't like losing and I don't like waiting." His fingers, wrapped around a cigarette, trace the outline of her form. "You should know all about that."

She stiffens. That smug son of a bitch.

He steps closer. She feels the blood drain from her face, but still, she stays put. Never again will she run away. The air crackles with tension.

"I thought we could play nice this summer," Slayton drawls. "I thought we could reconnect. I loved you for a long time, Emmy Lou. But this . . ." His face changes like it did that night in the horse trailer. Man to monster. "You fucked me," he snaps. "You and your husband and your brothers fucked me."

"Good," Emmy Lou hisses. She clamps her teeth together. "Now you can take your bad suit and your money and mosey on back to Chicago."

She turns to leave, but his hand snaps out and grabs her wrist. She cries out in pain as he twists it. Violently, he yanks her forward into him, then shoves her back, nearly knocking her off-balance, until she slams against the wood siding of the tavern. Cold terror envelops her as Slayton presses his heavy body close to hers. He leans down and says in her ear, "Mine. You were always mine."

She opens her mouth to scream, but his hand is there. Smothering.

Twisting her face, she clamps down and bites.

Skin. Bone.

Slayton swears and she tastes hot blood in her mouth.

Fight.

Gritting her teeth, Emmy Lou wrenches her body, driving a knee up into Slayton's crotch. He screams. Then she blasts forward, falling to her hands and knees in the dirt and the gravel.

Heavy footsteps as he advances. "You fuck with me, I'll fuck with you."

With trembling hands, she grabs a handful of dirt and rock. Whirling around, she flings it at Slayton.

Curses fill the air. "Goddamn you, bitch," he growls, shielding his eyes.

"I said no, Slayton," Emmy Lou says, her voice like a whip. "Did you hear me? Well, hear me now. I said no, and I'm still sayin' no." On shaky legs, she stands. Her heart thumps fiercely in her chest. She hurls dirt and rock. Wildheart earth. Her home. It will protect her and she will protect herself.

With each step, she drives Slayton back. Her body vibrates with rage. Damn if she backs down now. She channels the girl, the woman she's turned into since she left Wildheart. A woman who knows it's not her fault, a woman who doesn't back down, who has trust like a fountain in her heart. For her friends, her family. Those who deserve it.

Wiping his face, Slayton steps closer.

Emmy Lou balls her fists.

And then there's a voice, hard as a hammer, that says, "Take one more goddamn step toward my wife and I break your fuckin' jaw."

Emmy Lou gasps. She twists around to follow where Slayton's gaze has flickered.

Her eyes close in relief.

Jace.

Jace and Grady break into a sprint when they see Emmy Lou.

Across from her, Slayton.

Emmy Lou, her eyes wild and fierce with fury, turns her gaze toward Jace, and he almost falls over at the relief filling her face.

He was almost too late.

Almost.

Jace stalks toward Slayton, feeling dangerous and deadly. He's gonna kill him. Straight up murder the guy in cold blood if he so much as touched a hair on Emmy Lou's head.

"What the fuck are you doin' here?" Grady asks, incredulous, as he advances on Slayton.

Slayton smirks at Grady. "Kid. You haven't changed a bit."

"Step the fuck back from my wife," Jace demands, placing himself in front of Emmy Lou to shield her with his own body. His fists curl. "Now."

Quickly, Jace runs his eyes over Emmy Lou. She's covered in dust, her face pale, her gaze still wary and locked on Slayton, but her eyes have a fire lit in them. Not that she didn't have it handled—she did. Emmy Lou's never weak. But she is important to him, she is his wife, and he'll be damned if he doesn't protect her.

"Are you okay?" he asks in a low voice and she gives a small nod.

"Just discussing business," Slayton says, his beady eyes lasered on Emmy Lou.

"There ain't no business," Jace says coolly. "The farm's Emmy Lou's. We signed papers. The deal's done."

"You lost, asshole," Grady shoots back. "Deal with it."

Behind them, a small crowd has formed. Charlie and Wyatt stand with arms crossed. Spectators with hands pressed to their mouths, eager for a small-town fistfight.

"This ain't over," Slayton warns.

Jace takes a step forward. "Yes, it is."

"Jace." Emmy Lou palms the front of his chest, a glimmer of fear in her eyes. "Let's go. Let's just go."

He looks down to tell her everything's okay.

And that's when he sees the red, raw ring around her wrist.

He lifts her hand. "What's this from?"

She trembles against him, her eyes glistening. "Jace . . ."

It breaks something in him—the wary fear on Emmy Lou's face. She doesn't have to answer for him to see she's hurt.

Fury igniting all over again, he looks over the top of her head at Slayton. "You touched my wife?"

"Wasn't the first time," Slayton sneers.

Jace's frame locks.

Motherfucker.

That's all he needs. But Grady has the same thought.

"You piece of shit." Grady launches himself forward.

A gasp goes up in the crowd. Charlie and Wyatt tense.

"No!" Emmy cries, scrambling to her brother. She puts herself between him and Slayton. "You can't fight." Gripping his bicep, her gaze moves to the crowd that's gathered, the raised phones at the ready. "Your contract. They're filmin' it."

Grady freezes, his lean body straining against his sister's grasp. The angle of his body itching for a fight. To finish what he started years ago.

The smug chuckle that rolls out of Slayton boils Jace's blood.

Fury courses through him.

Maybe it's his mother's voice in his head. Maybe it's McCade's.

Either way it's his wife, and sure as shit, Jace is gonna protect her tonight.

"He can't fight." Jace steps forward, hands curling to fists. "But I can."

Lightning fast, Jace strides toward Slayton and punches him in the face. He knocks the guy off-balance and lunges forward.

He's never started a fight before, never been the one to throw that first punch, but tonight, he damn sure is. Tonight, he ends this.

Slayton tries to take a swing at him, but Jace ducks and lands a sharp punch in the gut that brings Slayton down to his knees.

"Oh, Lord, Jace, *stop*!" Emmy Lou shouts, but Jace barely hears her.

He barely hears the shouting voices, barely feels the swing in his fist, barely sees the red and blue lights flashing in his periphery. It feels damn good to pummel Slayton. He knows it ain't the right thing to do, and the old Jace would stop it, he ain't some hothead, but this is what Slayton deserves. For hurting Emmy Lou. For taking that bright, beautiful sparkle from his wife.

One last punch has Jace knocking Slayton flat on his back.

Jace leans forward, grabbing Slayton by the collar of shirt. His voice lethal. "If you ever come near my wife again, if you look cross-eyed at Emmy Lou, I'll fuckin' kill you. I'll bury your body on our farm, you worthless piece of shit." Jace gives him a shake. "You hear me? You fuckin' got that?"

Slayton gulps, blood streaming down his face. Fear in his eyes.

Then Wyatt and Charlie are there hauling Jace away.

The slam of a car door. Jace turns. Two small-town cops are heading right for him.

"Aw, hell," Wyatt gripes. "Who called the cops?"

"Let me handle this," Charlie says to Jace. "It's Randy Hodges, he's a buddy of ours."

Charlie looks at Wyatt, a silent conversation passing between the brothers. A dangerous one. Charlie's steely blue eyes drift to Slayton, who sits in the dirt, head bowed. "Then I'll handle Slayton."

Jace just grins and puts his hands up.

Emmy Lou paces the waiting room of the police station, the late-night quiet swelling around her. Grady sits in a bright orange chair to her left. She's fuming. Some piddly podunk kid she grew up with arresting Jace, cuffing him like he's a serial killer, when it's Slayton that should be behind bars.

Frustration fills her. But also love.

She's never seen her husband like that before. All fury and fists. Ready to fight, to protect. For *her*. It shouldn't turn her on, but it did. Not to mention he stepped in for Grady. If her brother had swung just one punch, if this had gotten out, it would have wrecked his chances in Nashville before he ever had them.

"Em?"

She wheels on Wyatt. "Stay away from me."

"Jesus." Wyatt freezes, a Snickers bar held out in front of him. "I just wanted to see if you wanted a candy bar."

"Well, I don't," she snaps. "I want Jace out of there."

Whirling around, she stalks to the front desk. She slams her palms down on the counter and levels a scalding glare at Randy through the plastic partition. "You better sing for your supper at Sunday mass, Randy Hodges, arrestin' my husband the way you did. That is straight up shameful. You oughta—"

"Easy, tiger," Wyatt says, steering her away from Randy. "They haven't arrested him. They're just holdin' him."

"Well, they're gonna be holdin' my boot in their ass, they don't let him out." Her eyes fill with tears. "Oh, Wyatt. What if they rough him up in there?"

Grady snorts. "Only thing Randy can rough up is a donut."

The station door slams opens and Charlie strides in. He moves deeper into the waiting room, coming to a stop at her side. He's covered head-to-toe in dust and red dirt. The skin over the knuckles of his right hand is broken and bloodied. His jaw pulses. He glances at Wyatt, a look of confirmation passing between them.

Emmy Lou props her hands on her hips. She narrows her eyes. "Where've you been? What'd you do to Slayton?"

Lord, if that man's dead in a ditch right now . . .

"Don't worry about it."

Heart thundering, she pulls her hands to her heart. "Charlie—"

His hard gaze softens. Fierce protectiveness radiates in his steel-blue eyes as he stares at her. "You're our little sister, Em. Nothin' and no one touches you. Not while we're around."

"Damn straight," Wyatt drawls, eyes locked on the candy machine as he works the knot out of his throat.

Determined not to cry, Emmy Lou wipes at her eyes and then launches herself into Charlie's arms. Her protective older brothers are blowing up her entire heart these days.

"Thank you," she whispers, her words muffled against Charlie's broad chest.

His voice is soft. "I'm sorry we weren't there before."

Nodding, she just squeezes him tighter. Charlie and Wyatt know what happened. But they won't press. They'll let her tell them in her own time. And she will. One day.

After a beat, Charlie releases her from his embrace. Keeping an arm around her shoulder, he looks at Wyatt. "Jace out yet?"

Wyatt, a hunk of candy bar in his mouth, says, "Nah." He jerks his chin at Emmy Lou. "Been wranglin' this one."

Grady grunts at Charlie. An unhappy scowl fogs his face. "Shoulda let me get a goddamn punch in."

"You're lucky you're not in there," Charlie snaps.

Grady rolls his eyes.

"Fuck, what a night," Wyatt groans. "Come for the music, stay for the sucker punches in the parking lot."

A door creaks somewhere in the small station. Seconds later, Jace emerges from the hallway, amusement on his face.

Emmy gasps. She flings herself at her husband, pulling him to her. His body, steady, strong, is like sun-warmed ground.

"Jace, are you okay? Did they hurt you?"

Jace laughs as she frantically pats him down. "Em. Em, I'm fine," he says in that quiet, serious way that makes her makes her melt. He looks her in the eyes, love in his face. "Are you?"

"I'm fine." She slides her palm over the sandpaper grit on his jaw. "Protectin' my brother, me. You're somethin' else, Jace Taylor."

"He won't ever come near you again." His voice goes husky. "I promise you that, Em."

"I know," she breathes.

She knows so much after tonight.

Her brothers, each looking at Jace like he's the man of the hour. Because he is. He saved her. He's always saved her.

Her heart—a bloom of love, rolling out like a red carpet to her forever love story with Jace.

Her husband.

She's finally ready to say them. Words she's been holding back. Words that were hard to say for so damn long. But not anymore.

"Jace, I have to tell you somethin'."

"What is it?" he asks, seeing the expression on her face.

"This." She cups his face in her hands, looks him in the eyes and says, "I love you, Jace. You are steady and you are true. But I've got bad news for you. I don't love you like I used to. I love you more than I did. This summer, I saw the man I married. The man I fell in love with, and all I wanna do is hang on to him forever and ever."

The words slay him.

Jace exhales, a broken tremble of a breath shaking out of him, quickly followed by a smile of joy. He wraps her up tight in his arms. Tears shine in his eyes. "Well, you've got me, honey. Forever and ever."

And then he kisses her. Hungry and tender. His big hands tangle in her hair, his mouth whispering against her throat, her neck, every free inch of skin, *I love you, Em. Em, Em, my gem, I love you.*

"I don't believe this. Kissin' in the damn police station," Wyatt grouses from somewhere far off, but Emmy Lou tunes him out. She tightens her grip on Jace and presses their lips back together, letting her heart bloom open, so that all those years of not living and not loving are the past, and the past can stay in the past, and just like that, she and Jace begin again.

J ACE STEPS OUT ON THE FRONT PORCH TO A NEW DAY. THE bright sparkle of sunlight cascades over the green hills. Beige bodies of deer dart through the ridge of trees. They're in the home stretch of summer. Five days until the rodeo, until the Brothers Kincaid come rolling into town to save the day.

He looks down, making a fist. Tossing that right hook at Slayton felt so damn good. He feels like a new man. But he ain't. And he's glad of that. He's still Jace. Still the man Emmy Lou fell in love with, but a better man because of his wife. Because of this summer.

A summer that changed everything.

He closes his eyes. The memory of last night sends his blood racing. Him and Emmy Lou kissing senseless at the station. Going home, coming together, and falling into bed like teenagers. Waking this morning, tangled in sheets, his wife curled up by his side.

And then there was her *I love you*. Soft words that took his breath away. That absolutely slayed him. All summer he was holding out for those three little words, and now that he has them back, he ain't ever letting them go again.

Quiet movement behind him. The clatter of the screen door.

Jace turns to see Emmy Lou stepping out onto the front porch. His heart swells. She's wrapped in a robe, her feet bare, her wavy blond hair tousled. Her doe-brown eyes sparkle in the sun.

Beautiful. Too goddamn beautiful.

A tight feeling swells in his chest as she approaches. Jace marvels at how damn lucky he is. To love her. To know her. This strong, fierce woman who challenges him daily, who he's loved his entire life, who he plans to love for the rest of it.

"How's the sunrise?" she drawls, coming to his side.

"Goddamn perfect," he says, tucking her against him. He ducks his head to look at her. "I was tryin' to let you sleep."

Emmy Lou smiles. "Sleep's overrated. Besides..." She stands up on her tiptoes to steal a kiss. Looks at him with such helpless devotion it nearly undoes him. "We got things to do today."

His cock flexes inside his pants, telling him last night wasn't enough. Never enough.

Tempting. To carry her back inside and strip her bare.

He drops his lips to hers. "What kind of things?"

"You'll see," she murmurs against his mouth.

They relax into each other, Jace holding Emmy Lou close as they stare out at the golden sun, the wheat fields swaying soft in the sun-sweet breeze. The glitter of the pond, the soft whinny of their horses, the broken stump of the old oak tree.

Theirs.

This view, the stables, the future, is all theirs.

To be here with the woman he loves beside him is paradise. It can't get any better.

As if to prove him wrong, the rumble of a pickup truck has Jace blinking himself out of his daze.

Beside him, Emmy Lou claps her hands together in delight, a bright beam of a smile tugging at her lips. "The cavalry is here."

Eyes widening, he pulls out of her arms. He takes a step forward, watching the caravan of vehicles cruising down the snaky road to the house.

"No shit." For a moment, he doesn't believe it. "When'd you do this?" he asks, turning to Emmy Lou.

She gives a coy shrug. "Called 'em a few weeks ago." She runs her palms up his chest. "I know you missed the boys. I thought they could come a few days early before y'all kick off the rodeo.

Like old times." Her brows wiggle. "You know, barbeques, beers and bonfires."

Jace looks at the road. The bouncing Bronco, Luke's shiny pickup truck hauling a trailer full of instruments, Griff's jacked-up GMC. His throat bobs. Emotion has him in a stranglehold. He doesn't know what he's done to deserve his friends. The mere fact that they're here for him in a heartbeat when all he's done is fuck up tells him he's forgiven.

Tells him he's a damn lucky man.

"I love it," he says, clearing the rock from his throat. He gently tugs her against his chest. "Thank you."

Then he dips his lips to hers, a slow tangle of tongues. Heat builds between them, as hot as the August sun above.

A heartbeat later, car doors are opening, slamming shut. A wild whoop has them pulling away from each other, both of them breathless, chuckling.

Seth's deep lazy drawl rolls out of the Bronco. "Never thought I'd see the damn day. Jace Taylor sprung from the clink." With gusto, he shakes out a physical copy of the *Nashville Star*.

"Oh Lord, Jace," Emmy Lou murmurs, hiding her eyes. "They got a picture."

Two pictures, in fact. Jace snapped mid-punch. The other of him strolling out of the police station, Emmy Lou on his arm.

"It's not your best angle, Jace," Lacey says, waltzing out of the Bronco, trying to lug an enormous suitcase out of the back seat.

"Best kind of press if you ask me," Griff crows. "Punchin' out assholes who talk shit about your wife."

Alabama, rolling her eyes at Griff's comment, floats a wave to Emmy Lou. "Hope you don't mind us invadin'."

"Invadin's what we do best," Seth cackles.

"Hell." Jace takes Emmy Lou's hand and together they step off the porch. "Y'all gonna bust my balls all day or get your asses up here and say hello?"

"Thought we'd come a few days early," Luke calls as he helps Sal out of the cab of the truck. "Keep your ass out of trouble."

Breaking from Jace, Emmy Lou goes straight to Sal, sweeping her up in a big hug. "Where's Cash, sugar?"

"With Luke's mom," Sal says, her eyes bright with tears.

"Grandma's got it handled, Sal," Seth says, yanking Lacey's third bag out of the back of the Bronco. He sets it down, then makes his way to pull Emmy Lou into a hug.

Jace whisks his hands together as he approaches Sal. It's the first time he's seen her since everything went down. He doesn't know how to tell her how sorry he is for putting her in danger. How he regrets everything that happened.

Luke hangs back. Tenderness overtakes his face as he watches Jace and Sal have their reunion.

Jace swallows as he comes to stand in front of her. Then he drags a hand through his hair. "Listen, Sal, I'm—"

"I'm glad to see you, Jace." Sal's pretty face pulls into a smile as she opens her arms to him.

Jace's throat constricts. He hugs her back, relief, thankfulness flooding him.

The simple gesture says everything. He's forgiven.

Jace lets Sal go, watching as the women reunite. Laughter and happy squeals fill the air.

Luke crosses the distance and gives Jace a tight embrace. "Goddamn, it's good to see you."

Jace looks his best friend in the face. His chest tightening, he says, "Damn straight, man." He shakes his head. "How'd you manage this?"

"Rescheduled a few gigs, is all," Luke says with an easy shrug.

Jace arches a brow. "Oh, that's all? Bobby's gotta love us."

Blue eyes glinting in the sun, Seth lopes over, followed by Griff. He claps Jace on the shoulder, a wicked smile spreading across his face. "We gonna get this party started or what?"

Jace grins.

Just like old times.

The small farmhouse buzzes like neon. Happiness in the air. Loud chatter and laughter. A piece of heaven right in her Happy Hideaway.

Her scene. Her people.

Emmy Lou's chest tightens. To think she almost let it go.

"You did good surprisin', Jace, Emmy Lou," Alabama drawls. The women are gathered on barstools around the kitchen island, bottles of pink champagne and platters of dips and chips spread out in front of them.

"Oh, I know." Emmy Lou smiles. She pulls a tray of preformed burgers from the fridge. "He looked like a little kid on Christmas Day."

"I think they all look like little kids," Lacey adds, nodding at the guys who are in the living room boisterously bantering. Clearly happy to be reunited. "Now that they've got the band back together—"

"Can't tear 'em apart," Sal says, grinning in adoration.

The clatter of the back door has Emmy Lou looking over.

Wyatt and Grady hover on the threshold of the kitchen.

"Engaged, married, married." Emmy Lou points at Lacey, Sal and Alabama when she spots Wyatt's wolfish eyebrow arch. "Don't even think about it."

Instantly, Wyatt makes a beeline for the living room.

Grady strides in, pulling Sal into a hug. "Hey, Sal. How's the baby?"

Sal beams. "He's amazing."

Emmy Lou makes introductions. "This is Sal's sister, Lacey, and, as I'm sure you know, Alabama Forester."

Grady goes red, starstruck. "Nice to meet you two." He shakes their hands, then loops an arm around Emmy Lou. "Y'all ready to see my big sister in the ring?"

"Lord, it's been the highlight of my life for the last month," Alabama says.

Lacey claps her hands together. "I've never been to a rodeo before."

A pink flush warms Emmy Lou's cheeks. She's floored by her friends' support. It means so much that everyone came to see her ride.

Grady wiggles his brows. "Well, you're in for a treat because my sister's the star of the show."

"Oh, get outta here with that charmin' tongue of yours," Emmy Lou says, shooing Grady out of the kitchen.

Barking a laugh, he swaggers into the living room.

"Refills?" Emmy Lou asks, picking up the bottle of champagne.

"Yes," Sal and Lacey say in unison.

"This farm is beautiful," Lacey says, her eyes on the window, on the acres of rolling green hills and horse pasture.

Emmy Lou offers a smile. "Jace and I were married here."

Lacey, braided blond hair curling around her shoulder, lifts a brow. "You were?"

"We were." Emmy Lou gestures at the window. "Right out front there."

Sal laughs. "Don't give her any ideas." She wags a finger at her sister. "You just picked a venue. You can't change."

"Princess, don't make me hog-tie you and carry you to the altar," Seth calls out from the living room.

Lacey blushes and lowers her voice. "Seth thinks I'm taking too long to plan it."

Emmy Lou pours champagne into fluted glasses. "Ooo, I'm gonna need all the juicy details about this weddin'. Where's it at and when?"

"We're having it at the Old School." Lacey's eyes light up. "It's a renovated schoolhouse with modern vibes."

"That's gonna be amazin', Lacey," Alabama says.

"We're planning it for after the residency." Lacey makes a face. "Seth doesn't want to wait that long, but . . ."

"You want a real weddin'," Emmy finishes.

Lacey fiddles with the pink engagement ring sparkling on her finger. A sheepish smile. "I do. I don't want to rush."

"Then you should have it, sugar," Emmy Lou says, leaning on the counter. "If it's gonna be your only one, make it count."

The women fall silent at the subject of weddings and marriage. Emmy Lou sees the sisters lock eyes. Lacey grips the stem of her glass and takes a big swallow.

It's Alabama who steps up. "Speakin' of weddings . . ."

"How are things with you and Jace?" Sal asks.

Emmy Lou glances at the whiteboard on the fridge, the question stirring fluttery feelings in her stomach. What to tell them? How much? And then she realizes, she doesn't have to hide or pretend. It's okay to be vulnerable, to be honest with her friends. These women who care, who always have her back, who listen with their quiet strength, and are a fierce force of friendship.

She smiles, her heart a mirror of the champagne. Pink. Bubbly.

"This summer was so good for us," she breathes. "Fightin'. Makin' up." She blushes and dares a glance at the living room, where Jace and Seth are bickering about God knows what. "At first, I wasn't sure we'd make it, but . . . we did. We ain't perfect, but we're workin' on it." She sweeps a lock of hair from her eyes. "We're gonna go to therapy when we get back to Nashville. Give it everything we got." She inhales a breath. "And—I'm goin' to Vegas."

Sal gasps. "On tour? Emmy Lou. That's wonderful."

Emmy Lou's face pinkens. It's brave agreeing to go to Vegas. But she wants to. She wants to be part of the group, to be with Jace.

Sal reaches out to squeeze her hand. "We couldn't get along without you two. I mean it, Em. You and Jace—we need you around."

"We missed you," Lacey adds.

Alabama, smiling, echoes their sentiment with a raised champagne flute.

Emmy Lou's eyes fill with tears at the conviction in Sal's voice. "Thank you, sugar. You don't know how much I appreciate that."

As the women grab their drinks to take into the living room

and join the men, Emmy Lou stands very still in the kitchen, letting this magical, emotional day wash over her.

This moment, with her friends and her family, it feels like a way back in.

A way back to herself.

Then, from across the room, she meets Jace's warm gaze. And they grin at each other like they're right where they're supposed to be.

"One hell of a party."

Jace turns from the porch that overlooks the front yard, the humid night air dewy around him. "Cold beer and good ol' country music. Can't ask for much more."

Luke's coming out of the front door, two glasses of whiskey in his hand. His expression relaxed and content. Jace is feeling the same way. After a huge dinner courtesy of Emmy Lou, the night's turned rowdy. Everyone's hammered after Griff mixed up a drink called pink panty-droppers, and now the group's outside, setting up for the picking party. The bonfire rages next to the lake. An infectious energy in the air. Flames dance in the dark, seeming to lick the sky. Lawn chairs are set up in a half-circle. Griff strums his guitar, Grady hanging on his every word like the kid doesn't know what to do with the appearance of all the famous country singers.

Jace cocks a brow as Luke joins him on the porch. "Think you built a big enough bonfire?"

Luke laughs. Hands Jace a glass of whiskey. "It's a celebration." A pause. "Ain't it?"

"Yeah." His eyes fall on Emmy Lou, lit up in firelight, laughing with the girls. "It is."

"Y'all comin' back to Nashville? After the rodeo?"

"We are. We're gonna get things in order here, hire some help, then head back."

Luke exhales. "Those are some big plans, Jace."

He grins. "Yeah, but they're for Emmy Lou. Besides, it ain't an option. We'll just be back and forth for a while. But I ain't missin' any gigs or the residency, and I sure as shit ain't leavin' the band."

"I get it. You have to put your wife first. That's one damn thing I ain't gonna argue with you about."

"It's about time I did," Jace says over the sounds of the guitar and fiddle.

Luke looks him in the eyes. "You're always gonna be part of our band, Jace. You're our brother. Ain't nothin' gonna change that. Not blood, not where you live. Not one damn thing."

Jace swallows the rock in his throat, giving a solemn nod of thanks.

Luke's words mean the world. So much of his life would be nothing without Luke and Seth. His boys. His brothers.

For a long second, he and Luke stare out into the dark, watching their girls, listening to the sound of strings and laughter.

The silence is broken by Seth, beer bottle in hand, loping up to the front porch. His deep drawl a rumble in the night. "Y'all gonna join the party or let Greyson steal the show?"

Jace chuckles. "In a minute." He studies the scene by the pond, then turns his eyes to Luke. He drags a hand through his hair and exhales. "So listen. I wrote Emmy Lou a song."

Seth's eyes gleam, no doubt glad he showed up when he did.

The edge of Luke's mouth turns up. "No shit."

"I was thinkin' I could play it at the rodeo."

Seth howls with laughter, leaning up against the porch railing to clutch his stomach and catch his breath. "What a time to be alive. Jace Taylor writin' a girl a song."

Jace rolls his eyes. "Alright, jackass."

"Sounds good, Jace." Luke claps him on the shoulder, giving it a firm squeeze. "You've had a hell of a year."

"And it's only gettin' started." Jace lifts his whiskey, nostalgia washing over him. "Seems damn strange we're here, don't it? Thinkin' we'd never make it . . . and now. Now we got—"

"Everything," Luke finishes, his eyes on Sal.

"Shit, man," Seth swaggers, a boyish grin on his face. "We're the Brothers Kincaid. Can't nothin' or no one keep us down."

It's true. These last few years, each of them has fought their own hard battles and won. But without each other, without family, they never would have made it.

Luke chuckles, his voice, his eyes proud as he looks between Seth and Jace. "You're goddamn right." His face cracks into a broad smile. "We got shit to do when we get home and we ain't stoppin'."

Seth's eyes land on Lacey. "Gotta get hitched."

Jace raises his scotch. "We got the album."

"Hell." Luke lets out a whoop. "We're goin' to fuckin' Vegas!"

"To Vegas," Jace and Seth echo, clinking beer bottles and whiskey glasses together.

"I'll be there," Jace says hoarsely. His heart swells. "Emmy Lou and I will both be there."

"Hell fuckin' yes," Seth crows.

"Hey, uh, Seth . . ." Luke points across the lawn, choking down the rest of his whiskey and a laugh. "You might wanna check on Lacey."

"Shit." Seth swigs down his beer and tosses the empty bottle in the grass. Then he shoves off from the porch, his eyes following the glow of the bonfire. "Looks like I gotta go save the princess."

Lacey, tipsy, dancing with Sal on the bank of the pond, looks like she's about five seconds away from tumbling into the fire.

Jace barks a laugh. "Go get your girl, Seth."

As Seth and Luke stride toward the group, Jace stands for a long second on the front porch, taking it all in.

This moment. The backyard packed with friends and family who care about him, who've come through for Jace when he didn't deserve it. Who are here celebrating his and Emmy Lou's reunion.

This, he thinks as he stares out over the flickering bonfire illuminating the faces of his friends and family. This is his life.

It feels like he's sitting on top of the goddamn world.

TWENTY-EIGHT

T WO DAYS LATER, JACE PUSHES THROUGH THE BACK door, a bright blast of morning sunlight following him inside. He stops in the doorway, watching as Emmy Lou whips up a bowl of batter. She's in full cooking-concentration mode, stirring with intensity, her tongue quirked out the side of her mouth.

Jace raises a brow. "Pancakes, biscuits *and* waffles? Think you're makin' enough for an army."

She glances up. There's a streak of flour across her cheekbone. "Well, that's what y'all are. A small army of country singers who eat me out of house and home."

Chuckling, he drops a handful of wildflowers he's picked in a vase. Evaluates the empty kitchen. "Where is everyone?" he asks, coming up behind Emmy Lou to wrap her in his arms.

The past two days have been a dizzying blur of Wildheart for both Emmy Lou and Jace. Showing their friends around the small town during the day. Antique stores and diners and country drives. Late-night bonfires and song and wine and whiskey. Jace and Emmy Lou tumbling into bed, keeping their promise about their plans to continue their drunken kissing habit.

"Lacey and Seth are still sleepin'," she says with a laugh, reaching back to cup his stubbled cheek. One-handed, she measures out a teaspoon of cinnamon. "And the rest are up at the main house. Daddy corralled 'em for a ride."

"Think we got time to go upstairs?"

She gasps at the hand he slips down her waistband. "Jace

Taylor, you dog. I got breakfast to make." Pushing away, she gives him a wicked grin. "Maybe if you help me finish fast . . ."

His eyes prowl after her as she sashays across the floor to the fridge.

"Honey, you just tell me what you need and I'll get you there."

She laughs, a delicate trill filling the kitchen. "I need MeeMaw's gravy recipe."

"Where is it?" Jace moves into the living room. "The cookbook cabinet?"

"No," Emmy Lou returns. "The desk."

In the living room, Jace flips on the desk's tableside lamp and opens the cluttered pencil drawer. He digs around, finding nothing, then moves to an adjacent drawer. Buried deep inside is a thick stack of white papers. Emmy Lou's swirly signature catching his eye.

Carefully, curious, after a glance at the kitchen, at Emmy Lou, who's humming a sweet tune and slapping biscuits together, he picks up the thick stack of papers. He frowns. Legal jargon. Notarized.

Jace reads them once. Reads them twice. Three times.

His heart stops. A wrecking ball of shock socks him in the gut.

The words blur and spin, but he makes them out clear as day.

Divorce papers.

All they need is his signature.

Emmy Lou had signed and hadn't told him.

The deal from this summer blasts through his brain.

If she's serious, she'll sign.

If she signs, he'll walk.

The room begins to tilt beneath his boots. Jace feels destroyed. Betrayed. Like all the progress they've made this summer—gone. She could have talked to him. He gave her so many chances to talk to him. Why did she hide it?

Mama Belle's words rise in his head, mockingly.

Once she gets what she wants . . .

The farm. That's why Emmy Lou's been acting like she was

in love with him all over again. He signed the house, the farm over to her. He told her she could have it all. And she wanted it all. Just not him.

Because she wants to be gone. He didn't do enough to keep her.

He failed. He fucking failed.

He closes his eyes. He can't face the papers anymore. They're like a fist to the face.

He broke all the fucking rules to get his wife back. And it didn't work. He can't hold on to her.

"Jace?" Emmy's soft voice floats as she enters the living room. "Did you find—"

She trails off. Seeing him with the papers, she gasps. A hand flies to her mouth.

"Oh, I found somethin' alright." With shaking hands, Jace thrusts the papers at Emmy Lou. "You mind tellin' me what these are?"

She steps further into the living room, her face pale. Her brown eyes wide and stunned. She shakes her head. "Jace, I—"

"You signed, Em. You're callin' it quits."

"No. That's not it at all." She steps forward, shaking her head and reaches for him. "I know it looks bad, but you were never supposed to—"

"Find them?" He takes a step back and Emmy Lou drops her hands.

"Mama, she—"

"What?" Jace cuts in. His hazel eyes blaze. "You're tellin' me she signed 'em? That's her signature?"

"No. It's . . ." Emmy Lou falters, her mouth opening, then closing. There's no denying it.

"It's yours." He stares at her and she drops her gaze to the ground. "They're notarized, Em. They're ready to go. When were you thinkin' of asking me to sign 'em? After the rodeo? Now that you've got the farm?"

Her head whips up, hurt in her eyes. "That ain't it, Jace. I signed 'em at the beginning of summer because Mama—"

He laughs bitterly. "Don't blame Mama Belle. I'm so goddamn sick of you never standin' up to her. All this time you've been givin' me shit about trust when you've been lyin' to me from the beginning. I asked you straight up if you signed somethin'."

Her lower lip trembles. "I know."

"You never had any intention of makin' up."

"No, Jace. No!" Her face is pale. Her look is bereft, hurt. "You're thinkin' everything wrong. I don't want a divorce, I want you," she says again, but he doesn't hear her. "This whole summer's been amazin'. We were makin' plans—"

"You mean you were makin' plans," he flings back. "Now that you got the farm, the Brothers Kincaid are bailin' your family out, you're out."

She shakes her head, tears filling her eyes at the accusation. "That ain't true and you know it."

"I don't know what's true anymore."

While he was doing everything he could to win Emmy Lou back, thinking she was working as hard as he was, she had signed divorce papers and was sitting on them for the right time.

"You have to believe me, Jace. I want our marriage."

The pit in his stomach grows larger.

Their marriage. If she really wanted it, why did she sign papers in the first place? Why didn't she come to him before he found them in a fucking drawer?

Jaw clenching, he rips a hand through his hair. "Fuck."

He's spiraling. He can't stop the awful thoughts running wild in his head. He thought he'd just gotten her back . . . losing Emmy Lou again . . . seeing everything he fought so damn hard for slipping away . . . he can't take it.

"You have to let me explain." She props her hands on her hips, frustration on her face. "You're shuttin' down like always."

"It's always my fault, ain't it?" He's angry, boiling over, unable to stop the flood of words. A deluge of pain. "You keep talkin' to me about trust, when you ain't been honest with me." He lifts the papers in the air. "This is just like the birth control. You hide it until it works out for you, don't you? Just stringin' me along until you found the right time."

She flinches like he's slapped her. "If you think that, Jace Taylor, then you can go to hell." Her voice cracks with pain.

"Maybe I will. Maybe I should have done that in the first place," he says, completely defeated. Words he uttered mere days ago tumble through his mind.

I want my wife to have everything, even if it's not me.

Swiping a pen from the desk, Jace shifts his gaze to Emmy Lou's. "I promised I'd sign, so I will. I ain't gonna rope you no more, Em."

Before she can respond, he leans over and signs the papers with a violent scrawl.

Emmy Lou presses hands to her heart. Tears stream down her cheeks. "Jace, please."

"I need to go," he says through numb lips.

He can't be here in this house with Emmy Lou thinking the worst. He needs time to cool off. To pull himself the fuck together.

He has to step away before he does anything else he regrets.

Like he's being shoved forward, like his heart isn't breaking in his chest, he turns away from her, walking out the front door to his pickup truck. Refusing to look in his rearview mirror at the plumes of dust and dirt following him down the snaky trail of road. When he reaches the gate, he guns it, letting the sound of his engine drown out the doubts in his head.

Maybe he was wrong. Maybe they can't go back.

Maybe they never could.

G RIEF PIE.

Sad cookies.

Desperation brownies.

Tomorrow's the rodeo. She should be out practicing with Wyatt; instead, Emmy Lou can't stop cooking. She won't. It's all she can do to get her mind off Jace, to fend off the waves of despair threatening to crash over her. She concentrates on her hands, kneading pie dough instead of punching the door. Measuring sugar instead of the slow beat of her heart. Stopping the weep of meringue, not her own salty, streaming tears.

The party, the warmth that filled up the house only days ago is gone.

This entire summer, and Jace, it's all just gone.

By now the fact that Jace stormed out yesterday is the talk of the town in Wildheart. Worse, it's in the *Nashville Star*. The headline this morning screamed *Brothers Kincaid Bassist Jace Taylor Calls His Marriage Quits!*

No doubt Mama Belle's doing. All her doing. She left the papers where, sooner or later, Jace would find them. She notified the *Star*. Ready to wreak havoc, to put the final stamp in the coffin that is their marriage, ready to have her own way, all because Emmy Lou said no for once in her life.

The front door cracks. Footsteps in the hall. Creaking floorboards. Emmy Lou holds her breath. Hoping against hope that Jace came back. That he forgives her.

Emmy Lou looks up to see Sal, Alabama, and Lacey in the

hallway. They all peer into the kitchen, matching expressions of sympathy on their faces.

"I'm so sorry y'all have to deal with this," she says glumly, not even bothering to hide her emotions. She doesn't have the energy to put up a prim and proper facade. All she wants to do is break down into a puddle of tears. "This is supposed to be a vacation and instead you're stuck with some sad sack of southern woman."

The joke doesn't land and Alabama shakes her head. "We don't care about that, Em."

"We care about you," Lacey sniffs, following Sal and Alabama inside the kitchen. "And your stupid husband."

"Luke's out looking for Jace," Sal says softly.

Emmy Lou huffs, hard. "I don't care if he finds him at all. Find him in the bottom of a lake, for all I care."

"Em." Sal cups her shoulder. "You don't mean that."

"What happened?" Lacey asks, setting a tray of coffees on the table.

Emmy Lou glances down at her dough-covered hands and stares. Guilt and sadness weaving through her like a needle. "I had divorce papers and he found 'em."

Alabama winces.

"They were signed?" Sal asks.

She nods.

"I signed 'em at the beginnin' of summer because Mama wanted me to. Because I'm a fool woman who can never, ever stand up to her." She blinks back tears as she looks at the women in front of her. "At first, I did, I wanted a divorce. But I still loved Jace. I was just so damn angry with him for lyin'. Then, as the summer went on, we worked it out. Only Mama kept bringin' over the papers, hopin' I'd change my mind, and finally I told her to get rid of 'em, but she didn't. Jace found 'em and got the wrong idea and, and—" Emmy Lou can't keep the sob in. "It's all my fault. Mama's been meddlin' since the beginnin' and I never put my foot down. I let all this in. I never should have come back here."

She's ugly-crying now, her tears made worse by the fact that she can't wipe them away because of her dough-covered hands.

"Oh, Em," Sal says, and then the women are moving as one, Sal grabbing a towel to wipe dough from her hands, Lacey taking her shoulders to steer her toward a kitchen chair and Alabama helping her sit. Her friends surround her, dabbing her tears with a tea towel, their voices soft and comforting as they sweep her tangled hair from her face, bringing her a glass of water and getting her settled.

"Tell us what happened," Sal says as they all sit around her.

When her tears have stopped, she starts from the beginning, telling them about the deal she and Jace made this summer. Six weeks for Jace to prove himself. And if she signed the papers, he'd take it as a sign they were done. He'd go.

"And he did," Emmy Lou says mournfully.

Her husband's a literal man. He saw those papers and took them as her endgame. They devastated him. Defeated him.

She slams her eyes shut against the memory of Jace storming out. There was so much pain and sorrow in his eyes. But it's what she deserves. He left her like she left him.

"We said awful things to each other." Emmy Lou presses her trembling lips together. She stares down at the wedding ring on her hand. Back in its proper place. But does it matter anymore?

"Maybe we never fixed anything," Emmy Lou moans. "Maybe this summer was just a band-aid."

Alabama shakes her head. "I don't believe that."

"We didn't learn anything. We were both so mean."

"You fixed so much." Sal covers her hand and squeezes. "See? You're recognizing it. You know what went wrong."

Her whispered words are wet with tears. "I don't know. I don't know anything anymore."

"Jace loves you," Sal continues. "He was hurt when he found them and said some awful things. I remember when I saw the article about—" Her eyes rise apologetically to Alabama. "Luke and

Alabama. I was caught so off guard. I took off down Broadway and—"

"And nearly gave everyone a heart attack," Lacey mutters, crossing her slim ankles. Her frosty face softens. "But Sal is right. Sometimes when we're hurt, we're idiots."

Sal's eyes, her voice, turn gentle. "Jace is walking away because he thinks you want that. But it's not what you need."

"No," Emmy Lou agrees. "I need Jace."

She understands Jace's overreaction. Because he loved her. Because he finally fought for her, only to think she was pushing him away. She saw the grief-stricken look on his face as he left the house. Losing her all over again was too much. It was easier for him to sign, to give her what he thought she wanted.

But it's not what she wants.

This summer she learned that there's no one else for her. The farm, the horses, this is theirs. She doesn't want to do her life with anyone else.

She can't.

Her eyes well when she sees the whiteboard on the fridge. *Em, Em, my precious gem.* The vase of fresh wildflowers on the counter that Jace had picked a day earlier. A day when everything was different.

"Ugh," she moans, swiping at her eyes. "How could Mama Belle leave those papers for Jace?"

Alabama squeezes her shoulder. "It's awful what your mama did, Emmy Lou. Sometimes the people who want the best for us, screw it up completely."

Emmy Lou sniffles. She knew Mama Belle was like a bulldog with its fangs on the issue of divorce, but she never imagined she'd stoop so low as to leave the papers for Jace to find. All to get her way.

"What're you going to do now?" Lacey asks softly.

"I can't ride in the rodeo." Emmy dips her head and covers her eyes. Fresh tears stream down her face. "Facin' Wildheart, seein' Jace up there playin'. I can't. Not after that awful article in the *Star*. Not after what Mama did."

"You damn well can." Alabama's gray eyes are fierce. "Don't you dare let Jace or your mama take your shine, Emmy Lou. Whatever happens between y'all ain't the rodeo. *You're* the rodeo."

"You're a queen," Lacey says. "And we'll be there to cheer you on. You know, rah-rah." She lifts her hands, mimics pom-poms.

Emmy Lou sob-laughs and dabs at her eyes.

"We sure as hell will," Sal says, giving Emmy Lou a determined smile. "You're not alone, Emmy Lou. And whether you're with Jace or not, you're still our friend, and you always will be."

Emmy Lou sniffles, gratitude filling her as she looks around the table. These women, these friends, chosen family who always have her back. No matter what happens between her and Jace, she'll always have them in her life. She knows that now.

Another thing she knows is that she can do this.

She promised herself she was done running and she is.

She knows where she belongs and what she wants, and it'll be a cold day in hell before she lets go of the life she worked so hard for.

She'll ride in the rodeo.

And when she's done, she'll go to Jace.

She'll bring him back. Just like he did to her.

Jace sits back on the motel bed, the comforter beneath him a grubby, dull yellow. Woodgrain walls like some bad '80s basement. The neon light from the sign flickers outside, casting a hot-pink glow through the window. Jace grips his glass, tilts his head back against the headboard and drains his whiskey.

He closes his eyes and needles his brow.

All he wants to do is forget. Forget the fact that he fucked up. That he walked away. That he left her.

The first thing he did when he stormed out of the house was

get in his truck and hightail it back to Nashville. He got as far as the Tennessee state line when he realized he was an idiot.

He thought of McCade, his words, that hot summer night six weeks ago.

Fire. Fight. It's what you've been missing.

Walking out on his wife wasn't any of those things.

But most importantly, he thought about Emmy Lou, alone in the house, her face a mess of hurt and tears. He thought about his friends and family. The promises he had made, the rodeo, the concert, and he wasn't about to fail them again.

So, he turned back.

But he didn't go to Emmy Lou—he came here.

Giving her space or wallowing in his own damn pity, he doesn't know.

All he knows is that when he saw those papers, it hurt so goddamn bad, he immediately blew up. He thought the worst. He saw his world slipping away. His wife leaving him all over again even though he damn well deserved it.

He's got no one to blame but himself for this mess.

He's a shameful asshole who blew it by walking out on Emmy Lou. He never should have walked away. He should have stood his ground and stayed. Heard her side of the story, because Christ knows, she was trying to tell him what had happened.

Worst of all, he threw her trust back in her face. He brought up the birth control, the baby, the past. He let Mama Belle spook him, when really, all this summer, Emmy Lou's shown him nothing but complete and honest love. She opened up to him, told him the painful secrets from her past, and he took a shit all over that. He signed those goddamn papers like it meant nothing.

He spent an entire summer working on his marriage to his wife . . . and to throw it away . . .

To fuck it up this quick like he did . . .

How could he have doubted her? How he could walk out on the one person he loves the most in this world?

She'll never trust him now.

She needed that—trust. And he didn't give that to her. Trusting people means getting hurt, and sure as shit, he proved that yesterday when he walked out on her.

For better or worse and he's the worst.

Jace swigs down the last of the whiskey, wishing it stung worse than it did. Wishing it could drown the memories until there's nothing left.

A hard knock on the door has him groaning. With a sigh, he drags himself up and swings it open. Maybe it's Emmy Lou's brothers finally coming to beat the shit out of him like he deserves.

Luke, Seth, Grady and Griff stand there.

"We gave you a day to mope." Seth lifts a bottle of Jim Beam. "Now, we brought booze."

Grady lifts a bottle of Tito's. "And more booze."

Luke rolls his eyes and then locks them on Jace. "You gonna let us in?"

Jace smears a hand down his face and moves to let them inside. "How'd you find me?"

"Ain't hard." Seth claps him on the shoulder. "Only motel in town."

Jace sits on the edge of the bed. Griff, his rugged face uncharacteristically solemn, glances around the room and whistles. "Bachelor pad don't look good on you, Taylor."

Jace waves a hand but doesn't look up. "You guys don't gotta be here. All I do is drag y'all into my bullshit business."

"It's our business," Luke says, sinking into a chair across from him as Seth and Griff uncork the whiskey. "How many times I gotta tell you, you fuckin' owned your shit, Jace. It's over. You paid your dues."

Jace shakes his head, wishing he could believe it.

"The last few days, the bonfire, you two together," Luke says. "That was the Jace and Emmy Lou I knew. Whatever you lost—y'all had it back."

"I know," Jace grits out, swallowing the whiskey Seth passes him. "I walked out on her. I didn't trust her and I should have. I got it fuckin' wrong. Again."

"Yeah, but you didn't give up," Grady says from his perch on the windowsill. "You came back."

Jace tugs a hand through his hair. "She ain't answerin' her phone, though."

"Because she's too busy cryin' her damn eyes out," Seth grumbles.

He swears, disgusted with himself. He's the one who's got her hurting right now.

Who messed up the best damn thing that ever happened to him.

"You went to jail for your wife, Taylor," Griff says with a grin. "If that ain't true love, I don't know what the hell is."

Grady leans forward, elbows on the knees of his jeans. "She did sign those papers. At the beginnin' of summer, man, when she was pissed as hell at you. When she was gettin' shit tons of pressure from Mama Belle. But she didn't want a divorce. And she sure as hell wouldn't do you dirty like that." He gives Jace a nod. "She told Mama Belle to trash 'em. And I think you know the rest."

"Fuck." Jace closes his eyes.

The assumption he made was wrong.

Seth sits beside him. "Lace is sayin' she don't want to do the rodeo no more."

Jace's head snaps up.

The thought of his wife—fierce as hell Emmy Lou Taylor, his rodeo queen, his fucking life force—giving up something she loves because of him . . .

Fuck him and fuck that.

With a growl, he shoves up from the bed and paces. "She can't do that. She has to ride." He looks at his friends. Pride and love spiraling inside of him. "She's so goddamn amazin'. Y'all gotta see her. She's got these moves—and this crown. She's gonna blow your fuckin' mind."

He stops, looking around the suddenly silent room, at the faces of his friends.

They're grinning at him.

"Shit, you're still sunk," Grady quips.

Luke laughs. Then he stands and crosses the distance between them, his soft southern drawl filling the room. "You worked damn hard this summer, Jace. And you can still fix it." He lifts a brow. "We gotta play tomorrow. And play right."

Jace hears what Luke is saying.

His throat tightens as he stares into the dark eyes of his best friend. A friend who's never given up on him, who always offered him a safe space with music and family and friends. A friend who's forgiven him, who's telling him it's never too late.

Jace straightens up, determination spiking inside of him.

It's never too late to fight.

This entire summer he's been fighting. His family demons. Emmy Lou's. Fighting for their marriage. To get that ring back on her hand. Hell if he gives up now. Gives it all away because he's the sorry son of a bitch who let go of the woman he loves.

"Luke?"

"Yeah, man?"

Jace hands Seth his whiskey and straightens up. "Tomorrow," he says, meeting his best friend's eyes. "We fuckin' sing. Emmy Lou's song."

chapter THIRTY

S HE WANTS TO RUN.

And she promised herself she was done running.

Face glittery with shimmer powder, Emmy Lou smooths a trembling hand down the thighs of her blue jeans, her heart a frenetic pump in her chest. Through the thin partition separating the corral from the arena, she takes in the space. It's set up how she remembers it. Billboards and broncs. Her friends and family in the stands. The Brothers Kincaid onstage, ready to play their first song. Dust and dirt and grit.

"Five minutes," Erica whispers, popping her head in. She taps the clipboard in her hands before darting away.

Emmy Lou's guts churn.

She doesn't want to do this. She *can't* do this.

The rodeo emcee and announcer—world-famous Ty Weir—introduces Emmy Lou with gusto, proclaiming her Wildheart's rodeo queen, but she barely hears it. Her attention drifts to the stage, where the Brothers Kincaid are setting up.

No sign of Jace.

She gets the message loud and clear. They're done. He's beat it back to Nashville. Without her.

Tears fill her eyes. Needing comfort, she rests a palm on Outlaw's velvety neck. "Oh, sugar, how am I gonna do this?"

Outlaw's big black eyes rise up.

Her horse trusts her. At least someone does.

How can she ride? Her nerves are lit and on fire. Not to mention, her head and her heart aren't in it. And if they're not—how can she ask her horse to give it all he's got?

She had thought after her conversation with her friends, she had rallied. But here, in her arena, her husband MIA, it all feels so damn hopeless.

She's hopeless.

She's not a quitter. Montgomerys don't quit. But she doesn't feel steady or ready enough to do this. Her confidence in everything—her marriage, her riding—is shaken.

As if to dig the knife in further, Mama Belle's chipper voice floats over the grandstands. Her mama's big speech about how proud she is of her only daughter feels like one big fat lie. If she was so proud of her, if she loved her, how could she do this?

Emmy Lou closes her eyes. The chattering crowd, the bleat of the announcer, the voices in her head—she wants it all to go quiet. To just stop.

Behind her, the sound of boot steps.

She turns.

Wyatt.

"Hey," he says, his eyes dark and scrutinizing beneath his dusty cowboy hat.

"Hey yourself." Her voice warbles.

He folds his arms across his chest. "We're waitin' for Mama to finish up her big to-do, then the barrels go up and you ride." He grins devilishly. "I can't wait to see her face."

She swallows. "I can't do it, Wyatt."

"Sure you can."

The confidence on his face is ending her. She inches closer to her big brother. "What if I take the reins and ride out of here? Go back to Montana with you?"

He snorts. "Real mature."

"Like you're one to talk with that Roadrunner T-shirt you're wearin.'"

Wyatt sighs. "Em . . ." His soft gaze flicks over her outfit:

riding boots, blinged-out blue jeans, a gold pearl-snap shirt with fringe and rhinestones. Then he frowns. "Where's your crown?"

She shakes her head, tears pooling in her eyes. "It's too much," she whispers helplessly. "It's too heavy."

"Nah," he says, plucking her crown from a large wooden crate. He peers at her, a sentimental grin softening his face. "It ain't. In fact, I'd say it fits pretty fuckin' perfect to me."

With steady hands, Wyatt rests the crown on her head. Gently, he adjusts it, bobby pinning it in her strands of loose hair so it doesn't fall off during her ride.

"Wyatt . . . ," she whispers, her breath shaking out of her like a rattle.

"Listen to me," he says, gripping her by the shoulders. "You've been through a lot this summer. With Jace. With Mama. With Slayton." His throat bobs, emotion crossing his handsome face. "But you didn't do everything you did this summer to end it like this. You're Wildheart's rodeo queen and they came to see you ride. This is your town, Em, and you're their girl."

She lets out a laugh, or maybe it's a sob. She doesn't know.

Wyatt continues. "Jace is an idiot, but he's gonna come back. And even if he don't—" He shuts his eyes for a second as if his next words pain him. "I'm only sayin' this once, so pay attention." He looks her square in the eye. "Jace matters, but he don't make *you* matter."

Emmy Lou smiles at her brother, at his sweet words of wisdom, because it's all she can do. Anything else and she'll be a puddle of tears.

She inhales a determined breath.

Then closes her eyes and conjures up the last six weeks. Every small, beautiful thing from this summer—purple and pink wildflowers in jelly jars, licking the sticky juice of a peach off her wrist, *Em, Em, my gem* scrawled on a whiteboard, and Jace's big, broad hands, clutching her waist like he'd never let her go.

She reminds herself it's not over.

Everything is possible. Everything can be fixed.

With love. With hope. With time.

Like herself.

She didn't just survive this summer, she lived it.

Finally facing Slayton. Forgiving her husband. Healing her heart and her past.

She is not just Wildheart's rodeo queen. A pretty face. A wife. She is all of that and then some. A fighter. Fearless. She is this summer. Her and Jace's oak tree—a little broken, but alive. Growing roots, sprouts. Not the end, like she thought, but the beginning of another life.

Their life.

Wyatt's right.

She can exist without Jace, but she doesn't want to.

She opens her eyes and lifts her face. "I love you," she tells Wyatt.

He raises his hands. "Now let's not get sappy."

Erica scrambles into the corral. The arena's fallen silent. "It's time!"

"Go," Wyatt says, nudging her in the direction of the alley. "Ride safe."

Emmy Lou straightens herself tall, every fiber of her body loosening, relaxing.

Outlaw comes to her. Her hands grip the saddle horn as she mounts her horse and directs him to the starting point a few feet away from the entrance to the arena.

She breathes, waiting for the signal. One steady breath and then another.

She can do this.

She *is* this.

Then the signal sounds, and she explodes into the arena.

Showstopper.

Heart dropper.

Jace's breath catches as Emmy Lou, hot as a pistol, enters the arena at top speed. She's a force. Beautiful, confident, blond hair flowing behind her like sunshine, tangled up and wild around that sparkling crown.

A gasp goes up in the crowd.

Leaning forward, Emmy Lou guides Outlaw through and around the first barrel turn. Jace stares, mesmerized as Emmy Lou commands Outlaw with ease. The trust she built with her horse over the summer is breathtaking.

She's breathtaking.

A queen in denim and diamonds. Not just a queen, but his wife. His southern belle, badass and brave, sweet and soft. This is her spotlight and he's fucking ecstatic people finally get to see who Emmy Lou is beneath the bubbly exterior, the runaway mouth. Someone fierce and wild and brave. A woman he is endlessly proud of. A woman he loves more than life itself.

In fact, everyone is staring, mouths agape as Emmy Lou and Outlaw hug the barrels with perfect precision.

Her routine has the crowd charmed, in awe. Even Mama Belle sits stunned, a prim hand to her mouth. He glances over at Luke and Seth. They watch Emmy Lou in wonder and Jace can't help but grin. That's his wife.

His.

Emmy Lou readies to take the second barrel. But the turn's sharp, and on Outlaw's second stride, she slips.

The crowd gasps as Emmy Lou falls forward onto Outlaw's neck.

"No!" Jace lunges forward like he can teleport down there and save her, but there's no need.

She recovers, holding on to the reins and quickly righting herself in the saddle.

"Fuck," Seth mutters beside him, white-knuckling his fiddle.

For a brief second, Jace closes his eyes, steadying himself. Relief mixed with ebbing fear. Christ, she nearly went down.

She's got his heart racing. His nerves electrified, frayed.

As excited as he is to play Emmy Lou her song, all he wants is for this to be over. Her ride, his song. He needs her back in his arms. Needs to tell her he loves her and apologize like hell for walking out.

Outlaw takes the third barrel and he and Emmy Lou race down the last stretch.

The arena erupts into wild applause.

Seth whoops, shouts, "She fuckin' killed it!"

Fast as fire, Emmy Lou rides out of the arena, giving her horse a chance to slow down. Seconds later, she's back, coming to a stop in the center of the arena, where she waits for the thunderous applause to fade. She's breathing hard, coming down off her adrenaline rush, but as she's passed a mic, she gives her speech on the back of Outlaw.

With a bright beam of a smile on her face, she thanks Wildheart, introduces her parents and the annual Labor Day rodeo.

Jace doesn't break his gaze from Emmy Lou.

This is his wife. The woman he fell in love with all those long years ago.

His girl. His queen. His gem.

And it's time she knows that.

Tears shimmering in her eyes, Emmy Lou turns to the stage.

To the Brothers Kincaid.

"You're in for a real treat," she drawls, extending a delicate hand to the stage, "because they're my absolute favorite band in this whole damn world."

Jace's heart pumps fast in his chest.

His wife introducing him is about as good as it gets.

Luke, coming up beside him, gives him a knowing grin. "You ready?"

Jace nods, excitement gripping him. "Let's light it up."

Emmy Lou's turning Outlaw around to exit the arena when a mellow guitar riff catches her attention. She frowns at the stage, the tune unfamiliar, and then instead of Luke's smooth voice, a husky croon.

At first her brain doesn't place the voice. She shakes her head, sure she's imagining it. But she isn't.

Her breath catches in her throat.

Jace.

He's still here.

He stayed.

And then the stage lights dim and he begins to sing.

> We used to kiss in those old stables
> July nights, young kids, wild and free
> Picking wildflowers from the riverbank
> Wasn't very long before I started to think
> About weddin' bands and puttin' one on your left hand
> Now I'm standing here watching you light out of town, wonderin' where things went wrong
> Guess sometimes it seems we're one key, one line off the melody in our song

For a second, she's frozen. She stares, her lips parted in awe. Then her breath catches.

Oh Lord.

She can barely believe it. It's a song. Jace is singing a song.

For her.

He's not at his bass. He stands at the front of the stage, smiling that confident smile she loves. Behind him, Seth saws his fiddle. Luke's on his guitar, strumming, harmonizing with Jace.

She's never heard him sound like this. So confident, so damn sexy, every word from the heart. His voice a slow twang like dripping molasses.

> Ain't gonna let you run, ain't gonna let you go
> Emmy Lou, I'm comin' to bring you home
> Because I've loved you down in Georgia, and up in Tennessee
> And all I can do, I'll do it to bring you back to me

She sits on Outlaw, listening. Her breath quickening. She's

falling in love, over and over to the beat of Jace's song. His sweet husky timber sends shivers down her spine.

Hot tears fill her eyes. She's never heard anything more beautiful. More from the heart.

And she knows—this is her song. This is Jace's way of saying he's still in this. He never left.

Her trembling heart is no longer in her chest. It's with Jace, dancing across the arena, ready to be swept away in his song. In one of the truest loves she's ever known.

> Yeah, and now I'm comin' to get you, headed south in this old truck
> Lovesick like some sad cowboy song
> Because I've been goin' crazy since you've been gone
> Thinkin' of all my rights, but especially my wrongs
> I know I've left you lonely, I haven't been all you need
> Too many nights of not playin' it straight, cold shoulders, not apologies
> We used to burn like we were made of fire, so let's hold on one heartbeat more
> Tearin' down the walls between us, including this damn door
> Hey now, Emmy, come on, Emmy
> Let's do this thing again
> This little thing called love, Emmy, and let me be your man
> Because I've loved you down in Georgia, and up in Tennessee
> And all I can do, I'll do it to bring you back to me
> Hell, I'll show up on your doorstep, get down on bended knee
> Because the cold hard truth is we ain't gonna get to where we need to be
> Not unless you slide up on this old bench seat, climb on in and let's go

I'll tell your mama we ain't coming back, forget about
my next show
Fire and fight is gonna fix us, no more empty beds, some
good ol' loving fits us just fine
Just one kiss and let's see
All I can do, I'll do it to bring you back to me . . .

As the song trails off into soft guitar pulls, Emmy Lou meets Jace's eyes.

He's grinning.

The house lights come on. The wall of people in the grandstands break into a wild cheer.

"Ha!" With a slap of the reins, Emmy Lou whips Outlaw to the alleyway.

They race down the long length of corridor to the backstage area that joins the arena. At that minute, a door slams open. Hard boot steps. Her name shouted out like some heaven-sent plea.

She dismounts Outlaw right when Jace turns the corner. He stops, stares. And then she's running, on legs made of wobbly noodles, right for Jace.

They crash into each other.

Emmy Lou throws her arms around his neck. The kisses rain down, one after the other. On every free inch of bare skin. Hands everywhere, like some frantic need to touch every part of each other as a reminder they're here. They're really here.

Emmy Lou whimpers as Jace's big hands fill with her hair, skim over her throat, cinch her waist. "Don't let me go," she whispers into his mouth.

"Never," he chokes out. Pain stains his voice.

She melts into him, closing her eyes as he holds her, as he devours her mouth. It feels like it's been ages, years without Jace. She never wants to be apart from him, never again.

At the same time, they both pull back, gripping each other furiously.

"Your song," Emmy Lou whispers. Tears stream down her face. "It was beautiful."

"*Your* song." His lips linger against hers. "I wrote it this summer. It's about damn time too."

"I loved it, Jace." She curls into him, curls fingers around his shirt collar.

"You and Outlaw—" He lets out a shaky breath, shakes his head. "I'm so damn proud of you, Em. You were amazin' out there." Jace tugs her tighter against him. "You owned the ring." A shaky laugh rumbles out of him. "Hell, you had me shakin', honey."

"As you should be." Her face sobers, realizing the real reason they're standing here clinging to each other. Her voice breaks. "Oh, Jace. I'm so—"

"No, Em. I'm—"

"Jace—"

"Listen to me." He swears, regret etched across his handsome face. "I acted like an asshole. I flipped out when I saw those papers. Seein' 'em was like a knife to my chest. I thought I was losin' you and I lost my damn mind." He cradles her face in his hands. "I'm sorry, honey. There ain't no excuse for it."

"I understand, I do, Jace." Her chest fills with a hot rush of love. "I never meant for you to ever see them. I never meant to hurt you."

"I know that. I do."

Their protests turn to pleas.

"I'm fightin' for you, honey," Jace says, staring her in the eyes. "If we need to talk, we'll talk. If we need to argue it out, we'll do that too. But I ain't walkin' away. Not anymore."

She smiles, hot tears streaming down her cheeks. "Me either. You're stuck with me, Jace Taylor."

He wipes at her damp cheek with a calloused thumb. "Honey, I wouldn't have it any other way."

A teary laugh of relief bubbles up in her. "I love you."

He kisses her. "I love you."

"Will you come back home with me? You tell me, Em. You decide."

She nods, choking on a sob. "Home," she says, flinging her arms around his neck. "With you."

Closing her eyes, she lays her head against Jace's broad chest, absorbing his sturdiness, his warmth. Jace smooths a steady hand over the crown of her hand, sifting through her curls. Her ears fill with the sound of his heartbeat. Steady and true and perfect.

Everything feels perfect.

It's the most honest, most alive she's felt in years.

They're talking now. Apologizing instead of letting it fester. Yes, they'll always make mistakes. They'll still fight, retreat to old habits. But they recognize them now. They can fix them. Their marriage is one to fight for and damn if Emmy Lou won't keep doing it over and over again.

A soft clearing of the throat has Emmy Lou looking up.

Stiffening, Jace draws her closer.

Mama Belle stands there, arms crossed, her face full of scorn. "Well, it's a good thing we have Luke Kincaid out there to save the day," she says, her tone sharp. "Not singin' some silly love song."

"Mama," Emmy Lou says. "That song was for me."

A scoff. "Another way he thinks he'll win you back."

Jace tenses like a whip.

Mama Belle extends a hand. "Come, Emmaline. I saved you a seat."

Emmy Lou stands taller. She links her hand with Jace's. "Mama, no."

Mama Belle's eyes narrow. She looks at Jace with disgust. "You couldn't let her go, could you?"

"And you couldn't tell your daughter you're proud of her one damn time, instead of comin' here to ruin her day," Jace says through clenched teeth.

Mama Belle points a finger at Jace. "You could have ruined her life."

"I know." Jace's tone is thick. "But I love your daughter. I know I don't deserve her, but I ain't walkin' away." His voice breaks. "I can't."

"At least you know your worth." Mama Belle rolls her eyes. "You've never been good enough for my Emmy Lou. Some poor country bum, losin' my daughter's money, wreckin' her future. Slayton would have been a better man for her."

A sharp intake of breath.

Emmy Lou glances over at Jace. Pain in his eyes. Hurt.

Emmy Lou's vision swims with red. With rage.

Her temper snaps.

Enough.

She is a southern woman with manners, but Lord if she ain't gonna lay into her mama here and now.

Fists clenched, Emmy Lou steps forward. "Jace is too polite to tell you you're bein' rude, so I will."

Mama Belle's jaw drops. "Manners, Emma—"

"I'll mind mine when you mind yours and listen to me. And listen good. I will not tolerate another word about Slayton Holt. Not one more, Mama, ever. Because let me tell you somethin'— Slayton was mean. It might not matter much to you, but it does to me. It matters who you treat nice in this life, and Slayton wasn't nice." Emmy Lou lifts her chin and locks eyes with her mother. "And he didn't treat me nice either."

To her astonishment, Mama Belle's expression cracks. A sudden realization hitting her like a storm. The woman swallows, a misty sheen in her eyes. "Emmy Lou—"

"Now Jace is the best person I have ever known," Emmy Lou says emphatically, her voice carrying loud over the faint strains of guitar and fiddle. "He's worked hard all his life, put up with shit you never even dreamed of, and he's a country star. He did all this himself. He's not an accessory or backup, he is important and he is my husband. And he is the reason the Brothers Kincaid are here right now, savin' your precious rodeo."

Her mother opens her mouth in a rebuttal, but Emmy Lou steps forward and cuts her off with a raised hand.

It's out. Her anger, her pain. Her voice carries like a torrential downfall. Finally, finally, standing up for Jace in a way she never has before.

In the way she always should have.

"Yes, Jace has made mistakes. We've all made mistakes. Especially me. I never should have come back here when there was a problem in my marriage. I shoulda manned up and talked to my husband. I never should have signed those papers.

"But if you wanna talk mistakes, Mama, let's talk about you." Her sharp tone snaps like a raging fire. "I gave them to you to take away, but you put them where Jace would find them, didn't you?"

Jace sucks in a breath.

Her mother turns a bright shade of red. "I love you, Emmaline. I want what's best for you. I wanted—"

"You wanted your way, Mama. Well, no more. I want Jace. I love Jace. And most days, I love you too, but I will not let him take any more of your shit, do you understand me?"

Reaching back, Emmy Lou threads her fingers with Jace's. She needs something steady to stop her own hands from trembling.

"No more trash talkin' Jace now or until the end of time. If you wanna know your grandbabies, Mama Belle, because believe me, we're gonna have a whole house full of 'em, if you want me at the house for Christmas or holidays or rodeos, then you *be nice.*"

Emmy Lou exhales a long breath, the knot in her chest loosening, unraveling.

Jace stares at her, his mouth agape.

Mama Belle can only blink back the tears shining in her eyes.

That's when Emmy Lou sees her daddy standing there, having heard everything.

As he approaches, Boone gives them a nod, puts a hand on Mama Belle's shoulder. "I think you said it best, Em Bug." He glances down. "Didn't she, dear?"

Mama Belle stands mute. Shell-shocked.

Her spine stiff, eyes narrowed to tunnel vision, Emmy Lou grabs Jace's hand. Together they walk fast toward the exit and when they slam outside, Jace busts out laughing.

"Holy shit. I ain't never seen Mama Belle speechless before."

"It's been a long time comin'," she says, pulling him toward her.

"Thank you," he says, sobering. He kisses her, warm and sweet. "That meant so damn much, honey."

Her stoic face scrunches up. She presses hands to her mouth to keep in a squeal. "Oh Lord, I can't believe I told off Mama like that. I'm goin' to hell."

"Nah," he says, sweeping her up in his arms. "You're comin' back to Nashville."

"And then Vegas."

His entire face lights up. "And then?"

She smiles. "And then whatever we want."

Jace lets out a whoop, sliding his hand over the curve of her hip. His grin is roguish. "Does that include drunken kissing?"

"Oh yes." She grips his shirt collar, dragging him closer. Whispers against his mouth. "Inappropriate amounts of drunken kissing."

Jace groans in happiness, his lips sweeping over her throat. "Goddamn, I love you."

Closing her eyes, Emmy Lou melts into Jace, hearts syncing, and together they sway slow and steady. From the arena sounds wild, raucous applause, the bullhorn of an announcer, the tremble of the dirt, but Emmy Lou barely hears any of it. It's all white noise to her.

Because her soundtrack, her forever fairy tale, starts now.

Five Months Later

J ACE HOPS OUT OF THE PICKUP TRUCK, SLAMS THE DOOR and makes for his house. Snow crunches beneath his boots as he passes the old wooden barn. The horses graze hay in the pasture. As his eyes sweep across his Nashville farm, he lifts a hand to wave at George, the farmhand hired to take care of the horses and rehab center when he and Emmy Lou can't.

His gaze turns to the January sunset, a medley of pink, purple and orange. He swears at the late hour. He's been running since sunrise, wrapping up tour rehearsals before they hit the road for Vegas next week.

Once upon a time, he'd have doubt, being this busy. Worrying about Emmy Lou, making her happy, but now, turns out, life is right where it should be.

Emmy Lou is his focus every day. Never again will his wife question his love for her.

Though their schedules are eventful and demanding, they still see each other more than they ever did. Because they make time for their marriage, and they always make that time count.

All because of last summer. His clusterfuck of a mistake. Emmy Lou walking out on him. He never imagined life would shake out like this. He never thought he'd give credit to a man named McCade and words Jace still carries with him.

Fire. Fight. It's what you've been missing.

Fighting for Emmy Lou was the best gamble he ever made.

And the last five months have been some of the best times he's ever had.

After the rodeo, Jace and Emmy Lou had spent another month in Wildheart tying up loose ends at their farm there before they returned to Nashville. They hired an amazing team of people to help manage Montgomery Farm and Stables when Boone finally stepped down three months ago. Now, both of the farms are thriving. Emmy Lou goes back to Georgia every two weeks to coordinate and supervise, pay bills and make sure everything is running smoothly and get in time with the horses.

It wasn't an easy transition, splitting time between the farms, Jace traveling back and forth while playing with the Brothers Kincaid, but they made it work. Eventually, it became just another smoothly running piece of their life.

Hell, he's a sentimental son of a bitch when it comes to Montgomery Farm and Stables. The summer he spent there, rekindling his marriage to his wife, slaying his demons, he'd never dream of parting with it now.

His gaze drops to a bucket of feed left behind on the front porch. He chuckles and shakes his head. Without a doubt, Emmy Lou's been outside all day puttering around, taking care of the farm even though they have help. His wife works damn hard, has thrown herself into running both farms, and while he's glad for it, he also wants her to slow the hell down.

At least for the next nine months.

The second Jace enters the house, he freezes. Food. He smells food. An assault of delicious smells. Garlic. Hot bread. Melted butter. A slight flare of panic goes through him.

Emmy Lou doesn't bake like this. Not unless—

Shit.

Something's wrong.

They go on tour in seven days, so for her to be filling the house with food don't make a lick of sense.

"Em?" he calls out, stalking into the kitchen. "Emmy Lou?"

His wife stands at the stove, barefoot, stacking loaves of bread in a furious fashion. She looks sexy as hell in her tight farm jeans and a long-sleeved tee, dirt streaked across one cheekbone. Her hair's tied up in a bandanna, loose blond waves framing her face. Which means she came straight here without washing up and started cooking. A frown mars her brow.

His heart lurches. "Em, honey, what is it?" His gaze sweeps to her pretty face, then her stomach. "Is everything okay?"

She glances up, props a hand on her hip. "I am so mad at Mama, I could scream."

He chuckles at her grumblings, relieved that's all it is.

Though relations between Emmy Lou and her mother have improved over the last five months, they're still on shaky ground. His wife has forgiven, but not forgotten. They see Mama Belle when they go back to Wildheart, but they know when to exit the chat, choosing to prioritize their marriage instead of Mama Belle's drama.

"What'd she do now?" he asks, bringing her in for a kiss.

Her dark brown eyes flash as she stares back at him.

"It ain't what she's done. It's what she did." She gestures at a thin envelope on the counter. She bites her lip, stubborn, impatient, worried. "Go on. Open it."

Jace does.

His eyes scan the official-looking documents. When he gets to the end, he shakes his head and chuckles. "Well, I'll be damned."

They're divorced.

He glances up, his mouth opening to ask the question when Emmy Lou jumps in. "Mama must've mailed 'em after you signed. I looked everywhere for those papers after the rodeo and they were long gone." Her beautiful face reddens as she fumes. "I really cannot believe that woman. Sneakin' in *my* house and grabbin' em up like a thief in the night." She punches a small hand into her palm. Fire in her eyes. "Oh, I'm gonna wring her fool neck. I'm gonna call her up right now and—"

"You ain't gonna do no such thing," Jace says, stepping in to intercept before she can grab her phone. He tugs her into his arms and sweeps a kiss across her brow. She smells wild, like flowers and warm honey. Happiness all wrapped up in his arms. "I want you to relax. You hear me?"

"How can I?" Emmy Lou moans. "Oh Lord, Jace, what will we tell our baby?"

He smiles, his hand drifting to palm Emmy Lou's stomach. It's early. Only eight weeks, but it's got him lit up inside. Getting pregnant so soon wasn't on their agenda, but after one wild night on Broadway, they figured it was a meant-to-be mistake.

A second chance.

And Jace is damn sure gonna take all of those he can get.

It's what he's always wanted. Putting down roots. Making a family.

He always had a family with Emmy Lou, just the two of them, but being a father, being a better father than the one he had, is just one more step away from his past. Toward his future. Because his wife and that baby are gonna be his whole damn world.

Emmy Lou drops her voice to a hiss. "Jace, we've been livin' in sin."

He grins, brushing his lips over hers. "Sin I'm fine with."

Her gaze turns sly. "Fine then. Maybe we stay divorced. Shock some sense into Mama Belle." Wiggling out of his arms, she shimmies across the kitchen. Her eyes shine with mischief. "You hear that? You ain't my husband no more. You're just some random guy I like to sleep with."

Jace growls and pulls her back into his arms. "I ain't no random guy. I'm your damn husband."

She giggles, looping her arms around his neck. "Not anymore."

He blinks at that, then laughs long and loud. Bright gut-busting laughs that fill the warm kitchen and rattle both their bones.

"You know what we gotta do, don't ya?" Jace says.

"What?"

"Get married."

She laughs, tilting her head. "Jace."

"Hell, I'll call up Luke. He's gotta be my best man. We'll all meet at the courthouse tomorrow." He squeezes her tight. Excitement like a big bright sun burns inside him. Filled with the need to plan, to fix. "A celebration." Taking her hand, he gives her a little twirl, then tugs her back into his arms. "Lacey can plan it."

Emmy Lou grins up at him. "This quick?"

"Fuck yes, this quick." He kisses her. "Ain't no way I'm takin' you on tour without you bein' anything but my wife."

Emmy Lou flushes in joy.

For the first time in ten years, she'll be on the bus with him. Four months of exposure therapy has helped Emmy Lou learn coping techniques to deal with her fear of small spaces. She started out gradually, looking at photos, talking about her experience with Slayton. But two months ago, she mucked her first stable. Soon, she'll be on the bus. She's conquered so much in the past year.

He's never been prouder of his wife.

"We'll have to tell everyone." Emmy Lou's voice thickens. She holds her stomach. "No way they won't notice if I ain't drinkin.'" Her bottom lip pushes out into an adorable pink pout. "Grady's already lookin' at me funny."

"First of all, Grady don't know shit. Second of all, let's tell 'em." Jace stares into her eyes. "They're family. Why wait?"

She smiles up at him. "Yeah," she breathes. "Let's tell 'em."

Marveling, Jace leans back to take Emmy Lou in.

The love of his life, his gem, the woman he's gotten a second chance with. Who showed him a new song, forgiveness, grace, and now is giving him a baby.

Turns out, almost losing everything got him everything he ever wanted.

Fighting for his marriage wasn't just a life lesson, it was a gift.

He had to work for it, but he got it back in spades.

He and Emmy Lou have a new chapter. No more falling apart. Now, there's only falling together.

Jace brushes his lips against hers. Then with a wild whoop of joy, he picks her up in his arms and gives her a spin. Emmy Lou laughs, as golden as sunshine. Jace sets her on her feet and steps back. "Well, what the hell are we waitin' for? We got a weddin' to plan!" He holds out a hand to her. "Marry me all over again, Em?"

She nods, tears sparkling bright in her eyes. "Always. Over and over and over again."

Then he takes the woman he loves in his arms and kisses her breathless.

Starting over never felt so damn good.

resources

If you are a victim of domestic or dating violence or
know someone who is, please visit thehotline.org or call
1.800.799.SAFE (7233).

For a list of resources for sexual assault, please visit rainn.org or
call 1.800.656.HOPE (4673).

acknowledgments

Thank you for reading *Bring You Back*! This was a hard as heck story to write. Before I wrote this book, I felt like Jace and Emmy Lou flew under the radar. So, I was so happy to sit down and really explore their characters and dig into what made them tick. In writing *Bring You Back,* I feel like I understood Jace and Emmy Lou better. I appreciated them. I empathized with two broken people with bad pasts who kept secrets. I wanted them to fight for themselves and their marriage. And I think they did.

I hope you loved them as much as I do.

Now here come the thank you's.

Thank you to my beta readers for making this a better story. Your feedback is everything.

Thank you to Angela Taylor for her wonderful expertise on everything horse and rodeo/riding related.

Thank you to Jenny Bunting and Anna P. for their keen eyes and sharp skills when it comes to working blurb magic. I appreciate you!

Thank you to my editor Eliza Dee for the edits. Thank you to Sarah Hansen for the gorgeous cover.

Thank you to my fellow indie writers, bookstagrammers, readers and reviewers who are passionate about all things reading and writing. Thank you for making this indie writing thing so memorable and special. I couldn't do it without you.

Thank you to my family for always supporting my writing and never once scoffing at all my weird ideas.

Thank you to the Nashville Star series! You made me a published author. I love you. And this is not good-bye, it's I'll-see-you-later. Because who knows what will happen down the line.

about the AUTHOR

Ava Hunter is a strong believer in black coffee, red wine, and the there's-only-one-bed trope. She writes contemporary romance with healthy amounts of angst, where the damsels are never quite damsels, but the men they love (good, bad and rugged) are always there for them. Her first series, Nashville Star, centers on sexy country singers and their honky-tonk drama-filled lives. When Ava isn't parked in front of the computer writing, she is mom-ing, reading, traveling, drinking wine, baking and watching good TV. She writes from her home in Arizona, where she lives with her husband, daughter, and a very chonky cat.

Don't miss out on Ava Hunter's upcoming books!
Subscribe to her newsletter:
www.authoravahunter.com